GOLDEN HOUR

Stephanie Blackburn

For the girls who sing to an audience of one in their bedroom mirror.

For the guys who understand the benefits of therapy.

But most of all, for Wyoming.

May she stay wild.

INTRO.

January, 2022

George wasn't the type to claim she'd made it to this moment on her own, because that wasn't even half the truth. It wasn't like she opened her eyes one morning, pulled on her favorite jeans and thought, *I'm going to be a country music star today*, and then did it. Not even close.

A lot of people had given her a leg up to help her along. She'd been really lucky—being offered the chance to step onstage that first night, for starters.

The rest of it though. The digging, the pushing, the tireless work that often felt like her wheels were spinning and she wasn't gaining any ground, that was all her. She'd lost parts of herself along the way, pieces that still ached like phantom limbs. But that pain had gotten her here. To this moment. With the lights dimming, the crowd calling her name, and the band waiting for their cue.

It was wonderful, the way the mic felt both precious and heavy as it warmed in her hand. Sometimes it felt like she'd blinked and gone from ranch hand to sold-out tour in the span of a moment. But inside she was still that girl back in Jackson who didn't think anyone would care whether she joined them for a song.

That was the thing about that night so many years ago. People asked her about it like it was lore. They wanted to know everything about her first time onstage so they could plant themselves in the memory. But truth be told, that first time in front of the mic was fuzzy for George. Her focus, adjusted in hindsight for clarity, was on a guy who'd been seated at the bar.

Walking onstage that night had changed the course of her life. It was the foundation of her origin story, the first step on her journey to now.

But *him*.

He'd changed the person she was and who she became. After all, if you looked at where she was standing now, just out of reach of the lights, letting the crowd's anticipation build, he'd had a hand in creating *this* George, the one people paid good money to see. All because he'd believed in her.

She closed her eyes, breathed the moment in, and prayed she always remembered to be thankful. God, she was so thankful for this life. For all of it. For everything she'd gained and everything she'd lost.

She opened her eyes, already smiling as she held the mic to her lips and stepped onto the stage. She nodded to the band and turned to face the crowd, their energy washing over her like a rising tide.

"How y'all doin' tonight?"

VERSE I.

August 2016

1. CALEB

Flying into Jackson Hole in August, you might be surprised to spot snow on the highest peaks of the Grand Tetons. Caleb sure was, it being his first time in Wyoming. He was so surprised that he turned to the person beside him, but his father was either asleep or pretending to be. And anyway, Caleb reminded himself, his excitement dying quickly, his father wouldn't care because nothing excited him. A good golf game was deserved. A stellar market closeout was expected. Everything else received pinched brows and pursed lips.

Across the aisle, Caleb's mother's mouth hung open, the rest of her sharp features hidden behind a face mask. That wine she'd requested just after takeoff had clearly done its job.

Next to his mother, Caleb's sister's nose was so deep in a book he worried it would come out smudged. *Phil*, he whispered, leaning forward to try and get her attention without disturbing the parentals, but she was oblivious. The plane banked and the moment passed as they began their descent.

But what did snow in August matter when Caleb couldn't shake the feeling that something was off about this vacation. His family didn't fly first class, not if they could help it. And they didn't do layovers. Ten hours and two flights later, here they were.

Caleb knew how gross it sounded, doused in a migraine-inducing spray of eau de privilege, which was why he hadn't voiced it aloud. He didn't think there was anything wrong with flying commercial. It was better for the planet than the alternative. It's just that the Browning Richards family didn't usually partake in what Phil referred to as *plebeian activities*.

If Phil was worried, she'd state her concern because she was the brave twin. But she'd spent both flights indifferent, alternating between sleep and reading. So maybe there was nothing to worry about. Maybe their family was turning a corner, becoming more economically and environmentally conscious.

Caleb scrolled through filtered lives on his phone as they taxied to the gate. He thought about turning to his father and asking *Why no private jet?* as they slipped out of their seats and down the ramp, the warm mountain air rushing up to greet them. But the thing about Caleb's relationship with his father was that the moment he opened his mouth he'd regret it. Twenty-two years as his father's son had worn him down to silence.

One moment, the haute bougie concern was an ear worm settling between the creases of his brain, and the next it had evaporated, his head empty of all cohesive thought, as the view across the runway flooded his senses and sucked the air out of his lungs. The Tetons stood majestic and feral, spotlit by clear, blue sky. There wasn't a single cloud.

Holy shit, Caleb thought, as a weird feeling settled in his chest. It was hard to name, like standing in front of a wild beast, the hairs on his body rising to attention at the danger, while simultaneously feeling the weighted-blanket warmth of coming home. He absentmindedly rubbed his chest and sucked in a lungful of the warm, dry air. Was this place real?

He tried to catch Phil's eye as they made their way under the antler arch and into the charming Jackson Hole airport, collected their luggage, and climbed into their rental car. But she was busy facetiming her girlfriend. Caleb made the obligatory two-second appearance in the corner of the screen and kept quiet.

Maybe it was a simple explanation, a non-issue. There hadn't been a plane available. All the planes were in the plane shop for maintenance. Or, maybe he needed to stop thinking like an asshole one-percenter and come back down to earth.

As they drove out of the airport and headed towards town, Caleb couldn't get over the view out the open window. It made him think back to college, where guys had Ansel Adams posters tacked above their beds. It had seemed so obviously pretentious at the time, a way to lure in sexual partners under the guise of being serious and mature. *Focus on this imposing black and white landscape over my twin bed and ignore my crusty, unwashed sheets.* Now though, driving through one of those pictures, Caleb found himself looking at Mr. Adams with newfound respect, because *shit,* this was really something to behold.

"Caleb, please roll up your window. It hurts my ears," his mother said from the passenger seat.

Her piercing grey eyes were hidden behind monstrous sunglasses, but Caleb knew the look she must be giving him. He wanted to argue, because it was eighty-one degrees and sunny, but he wanted to survive this vacation.

The silence stretched down the road, occasionally broken by the GPS. His mother scrolled her phone and his father followed the directions out of Teton National Park. Phil had earbuds in, her eyes glued to her phone.

Look out the fucking window! Caleb wanted to scream at them.

His attention pinballed between each family member and the view. Why were they here if not to see and experience *that* out the window? A view unlike any he'd ever seen.

Caleb wasn't an outdoorsman by any stretch. He drove a SUV, had a boating license, could tie a Half-Windsor with elite precision. Growing up he'd played pirates not cowboys. He had no interest in trading his battered Red Sox hat for a Stetson. But there was something wistful about the land here that he'd never experienced before. He felt it deep in his chest, a heavy warmth that rooted him to this moment. *Is this a core memory?* He wondered as the GPS pierced the silence.

"The destination is on your right."

They turned into the driveway and drove along a copse of trees before the ranch finally emerged. But what made it a ranch? There were no fenced pastures. No horses grazing over yonder. There wasn't even a barn. Just a house that was made from an entire forest, loads of windows, and a quarry's worth of stone.

While some families crowded four to a room on vacation, Caleb's family needed at least four thousand square feet to cohabitate for five days. His mother had inflexible standards whether at home or on vacation. And the house looked great, but a tiny part of Caleb wished he were staying in a cabin. Something small, one room maybe, where he'd roll out of bed in his boxers, cross to the tiny kitchen sink, and stare out the window at the trees while stretching sleep out of his muscles. A dream for another vacation, perhaps.

A man in jeans, cowboy boots, and a white button-down was waiting for them as they pulled around to the front door and climbed out of the car.

"Richards family! Welcome to Golden Hour Ranch! I'm William Carpenter. So pleased to have you staying with us." He extended his hand to Caleb's mother as she was closest.

"Dara Browning," She accepted the extended hand with the tips of her fingers, as if William touching her was taxing or gross, and Caleb wondered for the thousandth time why she hadn't taken his father's last name. Or both last names like he and Phil had been forced to do.

"My apologies." Flustered, William patted his body as if looking for something in his pockets. "I could have sworn the reservation said—"

Caleb's father made his way around the car and stuck out his hand in greeting. "John Richards. You had it right."

"Welcome." William recovered his smile as they shook. It was the kind of smile bought with many zeros, the kind that let just about anything slide. "Let me show you around and we'll get your things brought inside."

Caleb swung his backpack over one shoulder and trailed his family through the double front doors. They paused in the foyer and William started in on a well-practiced monologue about the property.

"This home was built in 2005 by an architect out of Bozeman who's known for luxury log cabins. With this property he was tasked with keeping the classic aspects of a mountain home—wood beams, stone fireplace, focus on bringing the outdoors in, rustic color palettes—and elevating it to a new level of luxury, starting with the—"

"William, was it? Would you be so kind as to point me in the direction of the primary suite. It's been a long day and I need a moment to freshen up."

Phil and Caleb shared a look when their mother predictably interrupted.

"Yes, of course. Let me show you."

William gestured towards a hallway on one side of the foyer and off Dara went without waiting, John close behind, neither acknowledging nor apologizing.

"And then there were two," Caleb said.

William turned back to his remaining audience and forced a smile.

"There are three guest suites down that way," he explained, gesturing to a hallway in the opposite direction of where their mother had disappeared. "I'll have your things brought in and the chef will be preparing dinner early tonight since you're on East Coast time. Cocktails at five on the patio off the dining room."

"Don't take it personally," Phil apologized. "They don't get out much."

William looked like he wanted to say something, but ultimately decided against it. He nodded once and headed back out the front door.

"Shall we?" Phil swung an arm wide to let Caleb lead the way, and off they went in search of their rooms.

The first door they came to was a linen closet, if a room the size of a college dorm room could be considered a closet. Next was an office adorned with oversized, overstuffed leather everything.

"I bet the owners know Paul Bunyon," Phil said, closing the door.

"Who?" Caleb wracked his brain for that name, but came up empty.

Phil scoffed.

"I sometimes wonder how you managed to graduate, but then I remember that donated wing and I think, oh, *right*."

"No one is close enough to hear you scream, Philippa." Caleb puffed himself up to his full six-foot two-inches, not that his sister had ever found him menacing.

Phil looked bored, like this whole display was beneath her. And just as Caleb started to relax, his spine softening, she faked a punch directed at his crotch, cackling wickedly. Caleb crumpled in protection mode. Some things never changed, no matter their age.

She smirked as he straightened, having won this round without even touching him.

"Hey, so, not to sound like the epitome of privilege," Caleb took a step out of Phil's range in case she decided to get an actual punch in for funsies.

"By all means, straight white man, please continue this train of thought," Phil adopted a pinched-mouth accent and steepled her fingers.

Annoyed that she wasn't taking him seriously, Caleb went in for a headlock. But Phil wiggled out of his grasp by distracting him with an elbow to the gut. She bounced on her feet, fists held in front of her face.

"Come at me, bro," she taunted, but Caleb was over it, the jetlag catching up to him so quickly it made him sigh.

"Are you not even a little concerned that we just flew commercial? With a *layover*?"

"When did you become an elitist snob?" Phil scoffed, and continued down the hall.

She opened the door to a room with a sprawling four-poster bed draped with a pale blue comforter. Beyond the bed, simple, flowered curtains were pulled wide to reveal a picturesque wooded landscape, blue and white plaid wallpaper wrapping the room like a present.

"Oooooooh, this one's mine."

Caleb didn't care about the bedrooms. In a house like this you were guaranteed memory foam and the highest possible thread count, so what did it matter which room he ended up sleeping in?

"I'm talking about traveling as a family. When have we ever not flown private?"

Phil plopped down on her new bed, punched a pillow into submission, and leaned back appreciatively. She clasped her hands behind her head and crossed her legs at the ankle, the poster child for unbothered princesses everywhere.

"I mean you're right, but I don't know that it's worrying, per se. Maybe Mamá and Papá have finally had a come-to-Jesus moment about climate change. Wouldn't be the worst thing in the world."

The bag on Caleb's shoulder grew heavy. Maybe it was the weight of realizing how grossly privileged you were. It had only taken him twenty-two years, but better late than never.

"Mom flew private to Paris in April." Caleb remembered.

Phil's face went slack. "Huh. Right."

"Please accept your nomination for VP on the Council of Confusion."

"You sexist ass. I should be President." Phil sat up, tucking her legs under her. "Okay, well, Mom's never going to run out of money so we aren't broke. And we're still on vacation, so. Dad probably just waited too long to book the plane and nothing was available. It wouldn't be the first time he goofed, and also it's summer so that's highly plausible. But I mean, they don't seem to be fighting, so it's not divorce. Honestly, I don't think there's any reason to worry."

"How are you so sure?"

Phil sat up a little straighter, the elder sibling in her element of always knowing more.

"When Soph's parents divorced there was a lot of yelling leading up to and during divorce proceedings. Remember she slept over a lot back then? Couldn't get any studying done with all the fighting going on at home."

Caleb scrolled back in his memories of high school to remember this time.

"Are you sure it was because of her parents' divorce and not because you two were finger banging?" How he managed to keep a straight face was nothing short of a miracle.

Phil threw a pillow at him. "Grrrr! You're embarrassingly uncouth. It *was* because of the divorce that she slept over so much!"

Caleb knew that even if he jumped on her and tickled her until she cried, Phil would never admit to being wrong. That was the unfortunate trait she'd inherited from their father. That, and the ability to hyper-focus on a topic for an unhealthy amount of time. Caleb knew that by entering his concern into Phil's consciousness, she'd be unable to let it go until it was solved. Which was why he'd mentioned it in the first place.

"It's purely coincidental that it also happened to coincide with discovering our feelings for each other."

"That's a lot of coincidensing." Caleb said, his straight face slipping as Phil's clambered off the bed like an angry cub.

The knock at the door interrupted Phil's attack and William entered with Phil's bags in hand.

"Thank you, William." She turned back to her brother. "Let me unpack in peace, you childish nitwit."

Real mature, Caleb mouthed, allowing her to push him out of the room. The door closed with a resounding click.

"How about this room for you?" William opened the door at the end of the hall and rolled Caleb's suitcase to the edge of the bed before continuing to the wall of glass sliders. "In my opinion, this room has the best view." He pulled the slider open and motioned for Caleb to step out, then quietly left.

Caleb walked out onto the stone patio and the warm, dry air soothed his fraying nerves.

Two loungers faced a stone firepit and beyond it, hovering behind the trees like a goddess loomed the Tetons. Caleb couldn't blink, couldn't tear his eyes from the view. It made him feel things, things he couldn't quite name. But he'd unpack those feelings later. Because right now he was succumbing to the exhaustion of the day, both traveling and being conscious of every thing he said and did in his parents' presence.

He walked back inside, drew the heavy curtains closed, and flopped down on the bed. Whatever was or wasn't going on with his parents, it was Phil's problem now.

2. GEORGE

George glanced at the Tetons over her shoulder, turned back to the path lined with purple wildflowers, and sat deeper in the saddle. This view never got old and getting paid to ride horses was a privilege she'd never tire of. Some days it felt like she was on vacation, if she ignored the sunrise wakeup, the dirt in the creases of her skin, the lingering hint of leather that followed her everywhere.

They were nearing the end of the ride, the fences where they'd started from coming back into view. The trail of people behind George got quiet, taking in their surroundings one last time before they hopped off and returned to their itinerary.

A couple from New Jersey was at the back of this group. The wife had boasted that she was an experienced rider. *But I usually ride with an English saddle.* Tucker, George's boss, had lifted his brows just enough so George noticed, as the woman accepted the leg up and held the reins like they were dainty teacups.

They'd both mastered their poker face, because you never wanted the customer to know what you were thinking about them. But George and Tucker had their tells. Tucker's eyebrows were a dead giveaway.

After three summers of working on the ranch, George had learned there were three types of customers. The newbies, who'd never ridden or maybe only once before, and were open about their inexperience because they needed reassurance that they'd be okay. George loved these people for their honesty and wanting to try something that maybe scared them a little. She understood that and could easily support them.

There were the old hatters, who either casually mentioned having ridden before or maybe didn't mention it at all, but you saw how their entire body exhaled the moment their spine connected with the saddle, and you knew there was history. They'd be fine no matter what they ambled across on the trail.

And then there were the over-sharers, like the woman at the back of this group, who'd acted like this was all mundane, and yet the moment Sugar shifted a leg she got squirrelly, her voice rising in pitch, knuckles going white around the reigns.

George didn't fancy herself an actress, but she managed to keep her thoughts off her face when this happened. Because the ranch relied on customers to stay afloat. Appeasing the customer was the second most important part of her job, right behind safety.

There was a lot of time to think while leading trail rides. Sure, people asked questions about the animals, about the history of the ranch, about Jackson Hole and the Tetons. But for the most part, the people talked to their companions. So, George did an awful lot of thinking. About the imagined lives of the people in her care. About the monstrous homes in the distance. About what she would have for her next meal.

Now back at the ranch, her charges slowly trickled in, their horses knowing the drill and heading straight to the post. George hopped off her own horse so she could help each member of her group dismount.

This was when she could potentially make more money. It was one of the reasons she came back to this job year after year. Because yes, she loved Wyoming and riding horses, but she didn't make all that much per ride. But the tips, they made it worthwhile. Sometimes a twenty-dollar bill, which George appreciated, because it wasn't nothing. But often, usually by older men donning wide-brimmed hats they'd recently purchased just off the town square, she was handed a hundred-dollar bill.

The first time it happened, her first summer here, George had tried to return it. She'd imagined the panic the man would feel when he looked for the bill later and realized he'd accidentally handed her a hundred instead of a twenty.

But the man had laughed at her. Her insistence that he'd made a mistake amused him. Her face was hot enough to melt as he chuckled to his companion as they walked bow-legged back to their rental truck.

Tucker had pulled her aside at the end of that day and George just knew she was getting fired. The customer was always right and she'd assumed differently. How foolish of her to question him. But Tucker hadn't admonished her.

"The people who come through here, money to them isn't like money to you and me. That guy who tipped you today, he'll probably toss that hat out before getting on his private plane home. Just thank them and move on," Tucker said, not unkindly.

And then there were the people who didn't tip at all. They showed up in their squeaky, new cowboy boots and designer jeans, pretended to be someone *rustic* for an afternoon, and left without looking back. George would see them later at the bar ordering top shelf tequila, hundreds of dollars disappearing in a single night, and have to stop herself from shaking her head.

She had decided early on that those people would not take up space in her head. She focused on the grateful faces that shook her hand, even on occasion asking for a picture with her after their ride. The ones who went on with their lives but would return to those memories because the place, the moment, all of it had meant something to them.

George watched the last of her group walk away and pocketed the bills she'd been handed. She could feel the long day settling in her bones. She deserved an iced coffee on the way home—*needed it*—if she was going to get through tonight without looking as tired as she felt.

"You're doing round up tomorrow morning?" Tucker asked as he led two horses into the barn for their meal before evening turnout.

"I said I would." George followed behind with two more.

The air changed the moment they stepped into the barn. It condensed into thicker, heavier smells. She loved it—horsehair, sweat, hay, leather—but she also couldn't wait to wash it off at the end of the day.

She and Tucker moved among the horses like a well-practiced routine, removing saddles, blankets, bridles, picking hooves, and wiping them down before returning everything to its rightful place.

"Just giving you the option to come later. I know you've got a long night ahead of you." Tucker nudged his horses towards their buckets. Neither needed much of a shove, but it was habit for him.

"Are you coming tonight?" George wiped down her bridles and hung them on their designated hooks.

"You know how I feel about paying for drinks when there's free stuff at home."

"You don't actually have to drink at the bar, Tuck."

They headed back outside to get the last of the horses. George knew this was a privilege, having a boss like Tucker who was kind, who didn't bullshit or mistreat those around him. At some point during the previous summer, she'd started to think of him like an uncle. He had that way about him, always looking out for her while not being overbearing about it.

"I'll come for a drink at the end of the summer, when it's not so tourist-crazy."

"My treat." George knew that would get him. Sometimes she missed living on the ranch in the quarters above the barn. But the drive from the bar back to the ranch late at night was long and potentially treacherous. That, and she liked not having to share a room with the other ranch hands.

"I'll hold you to it." Tucker shooed her off. "See you in the morning."

If she timed this right, she could stop on the way home for her coffee *and* take a quick nap. But first, she desperately needed a shower.

3. CALEB

Caleb awoke in a dark room having no idea where he was. Then, the quiet brought it all back, the weight of the silence as serious as those jagged peaks on the other side of the curtains.

Wyoming.

He'd never heard quiet like this. You grow up in a city and the contempt of traffic becomes its own sort of white noise that settles in your skin. But this was the absence of noise. No angry horns, no rumbling trucks hitting potholes with a bang, just his steady heartbeat *tha-thump*ing in the ear pressed to the pillow.

Caleb dragged himself off the bed and pulled back the curtains. The sun was setting, the sky turning sherbet orange and pink. He pulled the slider open and wild noises rushed in—crickets, the trumpet of a frog. The hair at the back of his neck stood and he rubbed at it reassuringly. He didn't hear nature back in Boston, aside from the occasional Canada goose on the banks of the Charles.

As Caleb made his way to the kitchen, he noticed that someone had turned on all the lights. He couldn't remember what William had said about dinner. Was Caleb early or had he slept through it?

His answer was in the absence of his family, and in the fridge— three perfectly portioned dinners wrapped in plastic amongst a myriad of grocery items. He'd missed dinner. But so had two other members of his family, so he wasn't necessarily in for a lecture.

The steak, haricot vert, and couscous with slivered almonds and some kind of berry looked decent, but he wasn't in the mood. He wasn't sure what he wanted, but it wasn't that. He found deli meat and cheese in a drawer and rolled them together for quick and easy consumption. When he turned around, he nearly choked.

"Jesus, Philippa."

"You missed dinner." She leaned a hip against the island, her features schooling into lecture mode.

Caleb pulled a bottled water from the fridge and drank the entire thing in one go. He could feel a headache coming on, probably from the altitude and travel.

"I'm guessing I wasn't the only one?" Caleb thought about the time and effort put into preparing those plates and felt bad for missing it. He pictured Phil showing up alone to apologize to the chef and wished she'd woken him, but that wasn't on her. She wasn't his keeper.

"I knocked, but you sleep like the dead. And anyways, Chef Sven is a lovely conversationalist and even let me sous for most of it, so truly your missing dinner offends *me*. It was—" She kissed the tips of her pinched fingers, eyes closed in bliss.

"I'm sorry. Where are the parentals?"

"I haven't seen Dad since we arrived. Mom tried to convince me to join her at the gym, but I said absolutely not, Mommy Dearest."

Caleb's interest was piqued by the absence of their father, but not enough that he wanted to seek him out. Right now, he needed to get out of this house. The quiet was starting to get to him. It was like they were vacuum-sealed in here.

"Did Mom take the car to the gym?" Did Uber exist out in the middle of nowhere? The idea of being stuck in this house for the next five days made his skin crawl.

"Silly old bear, the gym's down that way just before you reach the garage." Phil pointed to the hallway their mother had disappeared down when they arrived.

Relief flooded into Caleb's veins. "The car's still here?"

Phil shrugged.

"You want to get out of here?"

"Does a bear shit in the woods?" Phil pulled the car keys from her back pocket. "Probably these woods, actually."

They turned towards the windows shrouded in deepening darkness and looked at their surroundings anew. Maybe sleeping with the slider open to enjoy the wild soundtrack wasn't such a good idea.

"What do you think the chances are of finding an ice cream place around here?" Caleb asked moments later, stepping cautiously out the front door. He held up a hand to make Phil stay inside as he looked around. Then, deeming the driveway safe from ferocious beasts, he led the way to the rental car.

"It's like you don't know me at all." Phil scoffed, sliding into the passenger seat and buckling her seatbelt. "I already Yelped it. It's called Jackson Drug, we're splitting the loaded tots, I'm leaning towards the huckleberry shake, and you're paying."

"Just because you're ten minutes older doesn't mean you have to be this bossy."

Caleb turned the key in the ignition and the headlights came on automatically. They lit up a pair of eyes staring at them from the tree line. Both he and Phil held their breath until the eyes blinked and were gone.

"So, rule number one is we don't go out alone after dark so we make it out of this trip alive, okay?" Phil said, her eyes wide.

"Wimp." Caleb put the car in drive.

Caleb was familiar with places being called one thing but actually being something else entirely. Back in Boston, a spa might sell massages and pampering, but it also had a fifty percent chance of selling subs and soda, so he wasn't that surprised when Jackson Drug turned out not to be a pharmacy.

It felt like stepping back into a simpler time. Burgers, fries, shakes, and a bar with round stools. This was the kind of place where nothing bad happened aside from expanding your waist.

Phil had already eaten dinner, but she had always been a fiend for potatoes. Caleb watched her inhale half the loaded tots, a grilled cheese, and a shake like she hadn't had dinner earlier. Meanwhile, Caleb was twice her size, hadn't had a real meal all day, unless you counted the half-baked attempt at food on either of their flights, and picked over his half of the tots. He chalked it up to jetlag and pretended being stuck on vacation with his parents wasn't at all decimating his appetite.

When Phil slurped the last of her shake with unnecessary gusto and patted her stomach, Caleb paid and let her lead him out of the packed restaurant. Out on the sidewalk he stopped.

Across the street on the corner of the town square, a couple stood taking selfies below an arch made of hundreds of antlers. Jackson was small, no question, but somehow felt packed with people. In that one block, there were restaurants, storefronts, a neon bucking bronco rotating above the rooftop. Cars drove slowly and people walked unhurried down the wood-plank sidewalks and Caleb had the odd sensation of being on the edge of something, his sense of self suddenly slightly off-balance.

Was he secretly meant to be a country boy when he'd only ever known boat shoes, blazers, and crusty, old-moneyed conversations? Nah, the cowboy attire didn't appeal to him. He'd always choose duck boots over cowboy boots. But still, it felt like there was the potential for something to happen on this vacation. It made his blood hum, the exhaustion from earlier leaving him in a rush.

Phil was already walking in the direction of where they'd parked the car.

"Do you want to get a drink before we head back?" Caleb called to her.

Phil stopped and let her head fall back with a dramatic grunt, her face flushed with annoyance.

"I didn't bring Lactaid. If I had known you wanted to go *out*-out I would have planned accordingly. I have twenty minutes until there's a really bad situation at hand, Caleb."

Part of him was disappointed, but there was also this thrill of getting to explore a new place alone.

"I just, I saw that—" He pointed to the neon lights of the Million Dollar Cowboy Bar, "and, you know, thought…" He wanted to check it out, even if it was just one drink and then home to bed.

"Can't we go tomorrow night?" There was a whiny undertone to Phil's voice that happened when she grew tired.

"Sure. But I might wander around for a while. You can take the car back and I'll get a ride when I'm ready."

Phil's face started to crumple in an overly-tired pout. Caleb took her by the shoulders and steered her towards their car.

"Go home, watch something on Netflix, and call Amelia." He opened the door and waited until she climbed in and adjusted the seat for her significantly shorter legs.

"Wake me up when you get home so I don't worry."

Caleb closed the door and waited as Phil turned the key and rolled down the window.

"Text me when you get inside the house so I know you didn't get eaten by a moose."

Phil shook her head but smiled.

"You're an idiot. Moose are vegetarian. I think." Lines appeared between her brows as she second-guessed herself.

Caleb watched Phil drive off and then headed back up the street toward the bar. Normally, a neon sign would deter him as he preferred small hole-in-the-wall dives, but he promised himself if there was a mechanical bull inside he could leave and find someplace quieter.

There was congestion at the door, but once he'd handed over his license and paid the cover charge, he realized he was excited to see inside. Maybe he'd needed noise to drown out his thoughts. Maybe he needed to drink his irrational worries away. If Phil wasn't worried, why should he be?

The air was heavy from too many bodies, zero windows, and a lack of air circulation. Pool balls clacked sharply in the middle of the room, and somewhere, a band was playing country music, but Caleb couldn't see a stage through the sea of cowboy hats and bachelorette tiaras. Bars lined both sides of the room and nearly all the seats were taken, but he spotted one saddle—*literally a saddle on top of a stool*—open at the bar on the right. He swung a leg over, thankful for being so tall that it eliminated most of the awkwardness, and sat.

As he looked down the length of the bar he spotted the band. They were dressed like cowboys at the far end of the room. There were tables packed with people, then a small dancefloor opened up, and beyond that was a small stage. Between the band and the volume of people around him, Caleb could hardly hear his own thoughts, never mind get the bartender's attention.

She had shoulder-length hair and the kind of face that looked like it might smile at you one second and bite your head off the next, like she had zero interest in bullshit. When he caught her eye, she nodded like he'd been added to the queue. Caleb pushed his sleeves up and leaned forward in the saddle to rest his forearms on the bar.

The band stopped playing and the bartender yelled down the bar to someone, "You better sing me a good one!"

The absence of the band was quickly swallowed by a wave of conversational noise. Caleb tried to see who she was yelling to, but there wasn't any point. They'd slipped out of view, the tail end of a braid there and gone.

The bartender worked her way down the bar until she was standing in front of him, but instead of taking his order, she handed him a glass of water, leaned against the bar top, and stared down at the stage, like he hardly mattered.

Caleb wasn't offended. He'd come to drink, not make small talk.

"What can I get you?"

Caleb was almost certain she was talking to him even though her focus was anchored to the stage. In his limited experience—three years with a fake ID and nearly two with a legal one—bartenders never seemed all that interested in him. They did their job with minimal interaction and moved on. He didn't take it personally. It was business.

"I'll have a whiskey, neat."

Why had he said that? Caleb had never ordered whiskey before. God, he hoped she couldn't tell how much he was regretting not thinking before speaking. He couldn't explain it, except that there was something about this place that felt stuck in the past, where confident, unbothered men sidled up to the bar and ordered a whiskey. For one night he wanted to embody that.

"Any brand in particular?"

"Something local?"

"Small batch, bourbon, or regular?"

What did any of that even mean?

"Regular," he guessed.

The bartender turned away and Caleb felt the heat of embarrassment crawl up his neck. He thought about getting up, pretending this never happened and returning tomorrow night with Phil to wipe the memory away. But as he stood, a woman's voice spoke into the microphone. Something like, *Please be kind to me*. Whatever she said, it sweetly tickled his ear and set his butt right back down in the saddle.

The room grew a shade less loud, like a cool breeze had blown in momentarily stunning everyone. He felt bodies around him shift and he wanted to see what they were seeing, but suddenly a drink was there in front of him.

His neat whiskey.

He took a big swallow and choked, the liquid fire burning his throat and settling like embers in his stomach. Why did people drink this stuff?

A bead of sweat dripped down Caleb's spine and his tongue tingled. But then, there was sweetness afterward. He took a smaller, more measured drink and it went down a little easier.

He looked up to thank the bartender, but her focus was turned towards the stage, her hands clasped under her chin, eyes glassy, lips pressed tight to suppress a smile. He turned, leaning forward on the bar, to see what was making her swoon.

Caleb swore there'd been a male singer leading the band, his voice deep and unpolished in that singing-round-the-campfire way. But his eyes snagged on a woman in jean shorts, a black tee, and cowboy boots, standing with her hands wrapped around the microphone stand.

Maybe it was the whiskey in his belly that colored the room as she began singing unaccompanied, notes falling like rain at the beginning of a storm. The room took on sunset's yellow-orange glow and Caleb's thoughts went hazy.

It had to be the whiskey. This must be why people drank it, to feel warm, life taking on a dreamy hue. Or maybe it was the woman onstage muddling his thoughts, her head tipped forward like the weight of the moment was too much to hold up. Her long braid twisted over one shoulder and the loose pieces that framed her face threw just enough shadow that Caleb couldn't tell if her eyes were open or closed in concentration.

Whether the rest of the bar was as enchanted, Caleb couldn't say. He couldn't tear his eyes away from her. What anyone else was doing didn't matter anyway. She was the only thing worth looking at.

Caleb had never heard this song before, but he rode the rollercoaster of notes in that opening with his stomach in his throat. He couldn't make out all the words, but he could understand the framework of remorse and wanted to step into the song with her and make the hurt go away.

There was a beat of silence, the singer looked out at the audience, and though everyone else seemed to be frozen in wait, Caleb want to get on his knees before her and beg for a moment of her time. *Another vice,* she sang, a smirk lifting the corner of her mouth, and the band crashed in around her.

A whistle pierced the air and Caleb tore his eyes away from the stage. He needed confirmation that this was real, that he wasn't hallucinating. The bartender paid him no attention as she whistled again, fingers pinched between her lips.

"She's so fucking good, right?" She yelled, now looking across the bar at him.

Caleb could only blink and nod. He felt like Prince Eric, flopped water-logged and disoriented in the sand, while onstage Ariel sang her siren song, filling his head with magical notes that tangled around his soul and messed him up in the best way.

She sang about crawling out of a bed and he couldn't swallow around the dryness in his throat. Was he even breathing? His skin was on fire, every nerve-ending standing at attention like this song was a declaration of war on his nervous system. Who was she and how could he get his hands on the rest of her music so he could relive this moment again and again?

Someone whistled across the room and Caleb startled out of his trance. He fumbled for his drink, gulped it down. It didn't burn this time. Was the whiskey the reason his heart was racing and his mouth so dry?

"Can I get another?" He couldn't tell if the bartender heard his request, but it didn't matter. He felt so warm and content, like being wrapped in a soft hug.

The band softened behind the singer, mere whispers of sound as she called out to Caleb about not knowing how she got there. He wanted to yell back to her that he felt the same, but managed to swallow the words down before making a fool of himself.

He'd been drawn to the bar, forsaking hydration and a good night's sleep for some pull he couldn't name. Maybe it was her he'd felt calling to him.

He was drunk. That was the only explanation. Definitely drunk. He needed Phil to come get him. But he couldn't turn away from the stage long enough to compose a text.

Wait. No. She wasn't Ariel at all. She was Ursula in disguise. Had to be.

What is happening? Caleb asked himself, tearing his eyes away from the stage to discover a new glass of whiskey in front of him. He looked for the bartender to say he hadn't ordered this, but she was further down the bar talking with customers. And actually, he *had* ordered another drink. Right?

The band's notes spun tighter around the singer while she looked back at them in awe, like she truly couldn't believe this moment was happening. She'd done it. She'd weaved her spell. Caleb was a goner.

The band hit their final notes and let the music peter out and the audience's applause took up the slack. The singer laughed like everyone was being ridiculous and Caleb watched her hug each band member before walking off the stage. When she disappeared from view, he finally felt the air return to his lungs. And then some guy in a Canadian tuxedo took her spot at the microphone and the spell was broken.

"Wasn't I right?" The guy asked the audience to more hollering and applause. "Hard to believe that she doesn't sing for a living with a voice like that. Let's give her another round of applause!"

Caleb turned back to the drink in his hand. If he sat forward and focused on one thing maybe he'd get a better handle on reality. If he could get some water that would certainly help too.

He took a sip of the whiskey as he waited for the bartender to come back down this end of the bar, and fumbled for his phone in the depths of his pocket. But the way he was sitting—*right, straddling a saddle*—made it nearly impossible to extricate.

"Can I have some water?" He stared at the polished wood beneath his hands, hoping a tall glass of ice water might magically appear. If beautiful women could weave spells through song, then maybe he could conjure water on a wish.

The band started up again, but it was that guy in head-to-toe denim singing. The absence of her on the stage, whoever she was, caused the trance Caleb had been in to burst.

He was definitely buzzed, thanks to the whiskey and an empty stomach. But he wasn't drunk. His heart rate returned to normal and he almost felt himself.

Sea witch for sure.

As he focused on the bar, his eyes tracing the wood grain, the water he'd wished for slid between his hands.

"Thank you," he spoke to the ice-cold glass.

"You're welcome. Can I get you anything else?"

He looked up and—

It was her.

Caleb felt his body betray him, his mouth breaking into a childlike grin that could not be called back once it was out in the open.

She nudged the glass of water into his fingers and smiled.

"You okay?"

She smiled encouragingly and all Caleb could do was nod. He felt like he was back in kindergarten, starstruck when his teacher Ms. Morris sat them down in a circle and read *Goodnight Moon*. She'd noticed Caleb mouthing the words, but the moment she paused to let him fill in the blanks he'd lost all ability to function. Instead, and Phil still brought this up at the worst times just because she could, he'd burst into tears because he was afraid of getting it wrong and disappointing her.

Why was he thinking about Ms. Morris right now? He was not allowed to cry in a crowded bar in front of this beautiful woman.

"Okay, well, drink some water and I'll be back to check on you in a bit."

She tapped the bar before moving down to attend to the next customer, and she might as well have chucked him on the chin. He could picture himself so clearly—googly-eyed and grinning like a fool, all control handed over to the glass of whiskey and his hormones.

He wrestled his phone out of his pocket and opened a text to his friend Toby.

I need a pep talk
I just met the most beautiful girl
Struggling to put 2 words together
HELP

33

Caleb waited, the noise around him drowning out every thought. The telltale ellipses started and his heart resumed beating. Support was on its way.

Caleb Ducking Browning Richards doesn't need a pep talk!
FUCKING
I meant fucking
You may not exude sex appeal

Fuck you

Hard truths my friend
Really though girls love u
You make them feel seen
And you don't dick around
UNTIL YOU DO DICK AROUND!

This was a bad idea. If Caleb had wanted a pep talk, he should have gone to Phil. But if he texted her, he'd have to tell her everything. And if he was honest about how it was going... it wasn't looking good for him and he didn't want to admit that.

I had two gummies.

I tried falling asleep and it didn't work so I took
them and now I'm all over the place.

You don't need a pep talk.
Just be yourself
She should be so lucky

Caleb tucked his phone in his pocket and chugged the water. If he couldn't figure out how to talk to this girl then he didn't deserve to take up her time. He didn't want to look back on this night ten years from now and reminisce about being twenty-two and an idiot. He had to at least try.

He took a couple deep breaths, adjusted his seat in the saddle, and looked down the bar to where she was chatting with a couple his parents' age. As if feeling his eyes on her, she looked over at him.

Caleb felt his mouth go dry under the heat of her questioning stare. He couldn't blink for fear this was another hallucination. And if so, he didn't want it to end. Even if he stuck out like a sore thumb, even if he was starstruck and acting like a fool, she didn't look away and that felt like a win.

His brain rebooted and he smiled. And not the goofy grin he'd given her moments before. But his real smile. By some miracle, she smiled back.

4. GEORGE

George was never surprised when a day turned on a dime. And then when it turned again.

She'd walked away from the ranch that afternoon with a hundred and twenty dollars in tips in her back pocket. It wasn't the most she'd ever made in a day, but it gave her comfort. She stopped for an iced coffee on the way home and that needed boost of fuel had her flying high. Until she listened to the voicemail from her grandmother saying she had to have hip surgery. George called back immediately, palms sweating. Grandma Jeane was all she had in the world.

Surgery was scheduled for October when George would be back in Texas and could help her get around after the fact. But George was worried about her level of pain until then. The idea of it, of her grandmother suffering, made her eyes burn. She offered to leave Wyoming early and head back south, but Grandma Jeane wouldn't hear of it. George made good money at her summer jobs and that came first. Her old hip wasn't going anywhere in the meantime.

George couldn't say she'd left the conversation relieved, but she felt reassured that her grandmother wasn't suffering in her absence. Unfortunately, the call had eaten up whatever time she'd intended for a nap.

The nap she could live without, but a shower after working on the ranch all day was non-negotiable. The problem was that her probably-not-legal, above-the-garage apartment bathroom was essentially a jazzed-up port-a-potty with a garden hose. And the air circulation in the apartment was piss-poor, so it was either freezing or sweltering. Hence why the apartment was affordable and only available May to October.

George could've stayed on the ranch like she did her first summer. But she liked the convenience of being in bed within ten minutes of punching out at the bar. The problem—and it was a horse-size problem—was that she desperately needed to wash off the day's grime and her "shower" wasn't going to cut it.

Kathleen, her closest friend and fellow bartender, was a godsend. She rented a place over the mountain in Idaho, so using her shower wasn't an option, but she carried a mom-purse with her at all times. The kind big enough to contain all manner of saving graces, like nail clippers, a tiny first-aid kit, a spare tri-pack of underwear, *because you just never know.* She had sample sizes of various perfumes, but even smelling faux-flowery, George still felt the dirt embedded in her pores. What she wanted more than anything was ten minutes with solid water pressure and a decent bar of soap.

A few hours into her shift, the day turned on that dime again. The Billings Boys were in town for two nights and just as they'd promised the previous summer, they called George up to sing a song. A whole year had passed since they'd offered in the early-morning hours, so she hadn't expected the offer to hold up.

They'd been sitting around the bar after closing the previous August, begging Kathleen and George to join them for a drink. Danny had been tuning his guitar while they told stories from the road, and George had marveled that after a night of performing he still couldn't seem to tear himself away from the instrument. He'd plucked at chords and without meaning to she'd begun to sing along.

She wasn't even aware of it until she looked up from wiping down the bar to see all eyes on her. Duncan, the drummer, had urged her to continue, but she couldn't. She'd overstepped, heat climbing her neck and cheeks. But after a bit of coaxing from Lane, the lead singer, she'd joined him in harmonizing. Because how could she possibly stay silent when "Little Green Apples" was played?

"Next summer, you're coming onstage with us. Whatever song you want," Lane had said.

George had agreed, deep down knowing an empty promise when she heard one.

But Lane had been true to his word.

She'd served them a round of drinks an hour before their set tonight and they'd brought it up. She'd shrugged them off. They didn't need to interrupt their set for her.

"You're honestly telling me you don't want to see what that feels like?" Lane had pointed at the stage, his eyes pinched in disbelief.

It felt like a trick. What would be expected in return, because nothing was free. She had nothing to offer them.

"It's one song, Georgia." She'd been too stunned to correct him.

She'd walked down the bar to where Kathleen was pulling a tray of glasses from the sanitizer.

"Please tell me he asked your permission for my hand in marriage?"

Kathleen had been nursing a crush for a year with no forward movement. She tossed George a wet rag and nudged the spray bottle in her direction.

"He said I can sing with the band tonight."

"God, I love him." Kathleen looked up from cutting orange slices. She was a perfectionist about the smallest details, but it was part of why she was so good at her job. "You said yes, right?"

George looked at the stage. Teenage George had sung in her bedroom mirror so many times. But why would a bar of strangers care about her?

"She'll sing a song!" Kathleen yelled to the band, making the decision for her.

And sing she had. Or at least, she thought she had. She'd kind of blacked out as she'd made her way toward the band. She had flashes of memory. The cool metal of the mic in her fingers. Her legs unsteady, every nerve ending on high alert. The way she'd felt breathless after the fact, like she'd given every ounce of air from her lungs and left it in a heap beyond the lip of the stage.

And even now, back behind the bar as if nothing had happened, she still felt tingly, the adrenaline swirling through her.

"Hey hon, you wanna get me a Jack and Coke?"

George moved down the bar to serve this man in a Stetson, suede suit jacket, and a shit-eating grin.

"That comes with a smile, right?" He turned to his friends and laughed.

That dime just kept on turning.

George poured his drink with her fake smile—nothing was going to ruin this night for her.

"I don't know if it's a rule of thumb," Kathleen said under her breath as she sidled up next to George and wiped aggressively at a clean spot on the bar. "But why does it always seem like assholes and money go hand in hand?"

George shook her head and swallowed down a laugh.

"By the way, you've got an adorable admirer."

Down at the other end of the bar a guy was watching George. His face was lean with sharp edges like he never ate his fill. George could relate.

The way his hair flopped over his brow gave him an air of being young. In a few years, when all his sharp edges finally filled out, he'd be the kind of handsome a girl would want to keep forever. George didn't mind if he stared.

"Want me to handle it?"

George looked down at the overflowing glass in her hand and quickly stopped the tap.

"Shit! No, I'm good. Pretty sure he's harmless."

"Suit yourself. But I'm here if you need me. You know I love a good game of interference."

Kathleen went to fill an order from one of the servers and George washed the sticky ale off her arm. Towel drying her hand, she chanced another peek at the guy down the end.

Still staring.

The thing was, George knew she was beautiful. Contrary to her current state of uncleanliness, she knew how to dress to accentuate her assets. Tonight, she was in a bar tee and jean shorts that her grandma would have *tsked* at. So, sure, that could have been what he was staring at. Except, any time she peeked a glance, he met her gaze and didn't stray south.

She walked over with another glass of water, his credit card, and the bill. Kathleen had served him three whiskeys, so she was cutting him off, and hydration couldn't hurt. Maybe he just kept staring because he was thirsty.

"You doing okay?"

When he only managed to blink at her after signing a generous tip, she wondered if it was his first time here, if the whiskey had too much, or if the altitude was getting to him.

"I'm George, by the way."

She watched him mouth her name and tried not to laugh. *Adorable* was the word that popped up, along with a fluttery feeling in her chest.

"What's your name?" She ventured, ready to call him a ride if things continued in this direction. He must be drunk.

"My name?"

This seemed to jolt him out of his trance, his eyes widening. He looked at her like she was something wonderful and George wanted to hold on to that feeling.

"Caleb." He stood, dwarfing his saddle seat, and held out his large hand.

As a rule, George didn't interact this way with customers. She never gave out her name unprompted, and even then made something up. But as she let Caleb's warm fingers wrap around hers, goosebumps galloped up her arm. She let him hold on longer than a person should hold a drunk stranger's hand across a crowded bar. But it felt really nice.

Someone coughed nearby and George finally shook herself loose.

"I have to, uh—" She hooked a thumb over her shoulder and spun off down the bar to deal with another customer.

Why had she given him her real name *and* let him touch her?

But she knew why. Because he had looked at her with those big eyes of his. He was like a golden retriever inside a man's body, full of goofy openness, not an ounce of pretense.

When she looked back down the bar, Caleb was lost in his water glass. There was only a hint of stubble across the lines of his jaw and she imagined him checking the mirror each morning, hoping for ten more hairs than the day before. As her eyes lingered, Caleb looked up and met her stare. He visibly exhaled and she imagined cartoon hearts ballooning in his eyes.

She broke eye contact and surveyed her customers. She needed to focus on work. The Stetson guy from earlier returned, ordering another smile, this time drunkenly knocking over his glass, which splashed down George's legs. He left without so much as an acknowledgement, never mind an apology.

George wanted a shower so badly she felt on the verge of tears. Hosing down behind the barn tomorrow was not going to cut it. She was sticky and stinky and just plain exhausted. She needed good soap, a few minutes with detangling conditioner, and if someone offered her a loofa she might cry. But she wasn't going to be able to accomplish this on her own.

A thought started to form. A devious, delicious thought.

She made her way down the bar to the man who looked all too eager to solve any problem she put before him.

"So Caleb," she leaned on her forearms, closing the distance between them. She'd have to lead this horse to water, but she was up for the challenge. "Where are you from?"

"Boston." He picked up his glass and tried to take a drink, fumbled with what to do when he realized it was empty. "I'm here on vacation."

Perfect.

George tucked her elbows into her ribs and he looked down briefly before his eyes shot back up to meet hers. The pinkest sunset crept up his neck as he adjusted in the saddle, like the gentleman in him was warring with drunk desire.

"Where are you staying?" She asked. Though it really didn't matter what his answer was because it was guaranteed to be better than her own accommodations.

Caleb sat up, his upper half tilting towards her. This might just work.

"Um, I think it's called Golden Hour Ranch."

He looked hopeful, so she nodded like she knew it. All the monstrous homes throughout the valley had names. That's how the management companies kept track of them. She didn't know this one, but they were all the same—rustic in the most ostentatious way, windows facing the Tetons, costing millions of dollars if you wanted to make one yours for more than just the week. Not that she'd ever been inside one, but she could imagine the dead carcasses mounted over the fireplace.

"I really liked your song, by the way." His voice came out a little breathless, which tugged a smile across George's lips.

"Sadly, it isn't mine. I borrowed it from Miranda Lambert."

"I don't know who that is," Caleb apologized.

George shrugged. None of this mattered. Come tomorrow, he probably wouldn't remember any of this.

"You have plans after this?" She asked, her head down, pretending to be busy behind the counter.

She could practically feel the stream of scalding water pouring over her, the dirt washing down the drain in a soapy puddle. She couldn't remember what truly clean felt like. Yesterday, she'd dunked her head under the hose while filling the water trough.

"Nope." Caleb responded, full of that eager-to-please good-dog energy. He really was adorable.

"Look at us two peas. I don't have plans after this either." She let her shoulders drop slightly, her mouth turned down at the ends under the false weight of disappointment, and she slowly walked away to serve another customer.

There was a chance—George didn't want to admit this possibility, but it was worth considering due to the amount of alcohol he'd had and his disarming lack of cockiness—that Caleb wouldn't understand what she'd just served him. But if he didn't, she'd outright ask. She was that desperate for a shower.

She gave Caleb ten minutes alone while she moved up and down the bar, occasionally stealing glances at him. She could see him working up the courage so she walked purposefully slow on her next pass.

"Um, hey," he started.

George wanted to lean across the bar, take his face in her hands, and kiss him in thanks. But she had to play it cool, so she turned doe eyes on him.

"Yeah?"

"If you're not doing anything after this, do you maybe want to come back with me to where I'm staying?"

He looked so hopeful that she wanted to muss his hair and tell him he was a good boy.

"I get off in thirty minutes." She tried to sound surprised and flattered by the offer that she'd just finagled.

"Great. That's—"

He honest to goodness jumped up and stumbled backwards over the saddle and she gasped as he right himself. Drunk for sure.

While he had been seated, George paid little attention to his appearance. She'd been kind of distracted by his eyes. But now she got a clear view of how his jeans hugged his hips, how perfectly his button-down shirt fit, even if it was completely wrinkled. *Adorable* erased itself from her vocabulary and *mouth-watering* slid into place.

He righted himself, his smile never faltering, and pointed at her. George bit her lip to keep from laughing at how embarrassingly unselfconscious he was. Were people watching? It felt like eyes were on them.

"You—um, I'll just—awesome." He pointed double finger guns at her, then practically skipped out of the bar.

Kathleen materialized at her side and George just knew she'd witnessed the entire exchange.

"I really enjoyed that, whatever it was. I feel like the word *besotted* comes to mind?" She chuckled and moved on to the next customer.

George stared at the door.

He'd left. Her chance at a shower, the first real shower in over a month, had finger-gunned her straight to the heart. And skipped out the door.

5. GEORGE

The last thirty minutes of George's shift were like someone had pricked her with a pin and the air slowly leaked out. To go from such a high to the disappointment of watching her shower skip out the door. She'd agreed to go home with Caleb and then he… left.

As she clocked out, grabbed her things, and headed out the door, she realized the answer to the problem. She would ask Tucker to let her shower at the ranch tomorrow after her last ride of the day. He'd probably ask her why she hadn't said something sooner. With that figured out, she paused on the sidewalk outside the bar and tried to remember where she'd parked.

"Hey!"

George hated walking alone this time of night. It felt equally terrifying that she could cross paths with an inebriated, entitled man or an ornery moose. Wyoming was wild. She clutched her keys and began walking away from the voice, keeping her pace normal and not allowing panic to show.

"Georgia! It's me, Caleb! Wait up!"

She stopped and watched him jog across the road, her insides loosening as the threat disappeared. He pulled up in front of her on the walkway, hands on hips as he took a steadying breath. He was tall. Taller now that they were standing only feet apart. And yet, even as he towered over her, George wasn't at all wary. She didn't trust easily, so this feeling of safety in his presence unnerved her. He was a stranger, after all. And yet, she found her shoulders loosening as he stepped closer.

"It's George, actually. Not Georgia."

She wasn't sure why she corrected him. Afterall, she owed him nothing and could have said her name was Cinderella, for all it mattered. After tonight, she'd never see him again. But something about the way she felt standing next to him made her want to be honest.

"George is a beautiful name."

In her twenty-four years, no one had ever said that to her. Usually, people told her she should change it. That George was a boy's name. Caleb's declaration, said quietly like an afterthought, lodged in her chest and made her short of breath.

"So, um."

Caleb stuffed his hands in his pockets and rocked back on his heels. She couldn't remember ever making a guy nervous before and it was kind of heady realizing the power she held. Usually, guys shot straight to acting cocky around her. This new feeling was refreshing and made her feel a little light-headed.

"Everything good?" She asked.

George tried to think how to make herself less intimidating, how she could set Caleb at ease. But all she could think was of her grandma's warning as she packed up her truck to drive north that first summer. *Don't you make yourself small just so some man can feel big, you hear me?* But certainly, Grandma Jeane had meant men with already inflated egos. Caleb, who seemed on the verge of tucking his tail and walking away, didn't fit that bill.

"Yeah. I just—" He looked down at the sidewalk, then sheepishly at her. "Do you still want to come with me? I wasn't sure if you really meant it, back in there. Or maybe you changed your mind. Which is fine, you're allowed to change your mind."

It occurred to George that for a man this attractive to be that unsure of himself someone had to have made him feel insignificant. How was that possible?

On some level she knew they were very different—he was vacationing here for starters, so he definitely had means. Not that money bought happiness. She shook her head of this train of thought before she got too involved. Whatever was going on with Caleb wasn't any of her business. She just needed to use his shower. Nothing more.

"Caleb?"

He took a step back, like he was bracing for the impact of her imminent rejection.

"Do you want me to come home with you?"

When he finally let the air out of his lungs it felt like a promise. "Yes."

"And you're not going to murder me, right?"

"In bed."

A beat of silence stretched between them swallowing up all other night sounds, and then laughter exploded out of George choking her. She coughed and tried to catch her breath, foregoing any attempt at being cool about this. Was he for real?

Caleb scrubbed a hand down his face and George was positive if they had been standing under direct light his neck would be beet-red. She almost felt bad for him.

"Fuck. I'm sorry—that wasn't funny at all. I would never murder you, in bed or otherwise. I had whiskey—you know. And I've never had it before so maybe I'm drunk, I don't know. Or, maybe it's the altitude or something? It's kicking my ass—and you sang that song! So really, it's your fault because you put me in a trance, like the sea witch—"

"What?" The smile slid off George's mouth like butter on grilled corn. First, he said he was going to murder her *in bed* and now he was calling her Ursula? Whatever George had expected, it wasn't this.

Caleb took a step back, and turned away, his hands in his hair. When he turned back to her, he looked miserable, like she'd already rejected him even though she had yet to figure out what she wanted to say. It was in the press of his lips, in the inward hunch of his shoulders, and it kind of broke her heart.

"I—this isn't my best me. I swear, I'm a nice guy. I think I might be a little bit drunk right now. I didn't have much to eat today—and you're beautiful and I'm a little nervous because I didn't think you'd actually say yes to coming home with me and you did and now I'm fucking it all up and probably should have stopped talking a long time ago and I…"

George watched him get smaller with each word. The moment she shifted onto her back leg putting more distance between them his voice turned to breath.

"I ruined it," he whispered.

It was like she'd been given a glimpse of the boy he'd been. It was there, mostly in his eyes, but also in the way he held himself, admitting his defeat before the verdict was even in.

Money wasn't everything. George knew that to be true even if she often felt like it was the sun, the earth, the air she breathed. That's how she'd always lived, on the razor's edge of having nothing. But even if Caleb came from money, and she had a sneaky suspicion he did, then what had it not provided him? Was it love? Because it seemed like he was far too familiar with disappointment if he was reacting this way and she hadn't even said a word.

She didn't know him and he didn't know her, but in just the few moments they'd shared she already felt a pull in her stomach when she was around him, a need to protect him, to wipe the deep creases from his brow. He was beautiful in a way she was unfamiliar to her, with sharp, clean lines like he'd never worked outside a day in his life, definitely not under the sweltering summer sun or the pinprick of icy rain. He was more like a painting of a man from yesteryear, all manners and posture, but the artist had neglected to draw him with confidence. Beautiful in too many shades of blue.

George crossed the distance between them. She pulled on Caleb's wrist until his hand came free of the pocket it had been shoved into. His skin was so hot it almost hurt to touch.

"Caleb, you didn't ruin anything."

She felt his surprise in the way he hesitated at her touch. Then, realizing this wasn't the rejection he'd expected, enveloping her hand with his. It grew around George's, like water and sunlight were pouring into him, giving him confidence and strength.

"What's the address of your rental? Or, I can follow you if you're parked around here somewhere?" George asked, her eyes on how safe her hand felt inside Caleb's warm hold.

It made George smile seeing him coming back into himself. This was the problem with one-night stands. You weren't supposed to get invested, but already she was wishing for a little more time to get to understand him better and maybe help him find his long-lost confidence.

"I got a ride into town, so can I go with you."

George could feel herself unspooling as she led him down the sidewalk to her truck, her hand still tucked snugly in his. She wanted a shower, she reminded herself. That was all. She didn't intend to let anything happen between them. She didn't do that when she barely had time to sleep between work and more work.

When the idea first came to her behind the bar, she'd imagined them having a drink, excusing herself to use the bathroom, locking it and jumping in the shower. And then when an awkwardly long time had passed and she finally came out, she'd thank him for the drink and walk her impeccably clean self out. But somewhere between the bar and this moment with her hand in his, she'd started to feel things. His warm, strong hand was one of those things, but there was something else taking shape that made her nervous.

It could just be the excitement of the long-awaited shower, she told herself.

But if she was being honest, she felt like she was walking toward something. Something that was huge and scary and would change her. Like a cliff out beyond the reach of her headlights, just waiting for her to fall into the abyss.

6. CALEB

Caleb let go of George's hand when she climbed into the driver's seat, but by the time he'd rounded to the passenger side, he'd lost the courage to take her hand back. Her truck was old with a bench seat from window to window. If he'd been braver Caleb might have just slid closer to her. But he wasn't brave and the truck smelled so strongly of animal and old leather that Caleb almost expected to see a horse behind them in the truck bed. It reminded him that he did not know a single thing about this person.

But he wanted to.

It was darker than dark out in the middle of nowhere as they drove. It was as though ink had been poured over the earth drowning out all light. He imagined that on a clear night the stars would be breathtaking in clarity.

When George cut the engine, Caleb climbed out first. He'd sobered up a bit on the drive and was questioning what he was doing bringing a girl back to the house. What if his parents were awake? How would he explain this? The last thing he needed was to give his parents a reason to be annoyed with him. But he didn't want to say goodnight to George. Not yet.

All the lights were on as Caleb started towards the front door, only to realize that George hadn't exited the truck yet. He walked back to open the door for her.

"This is where you're staying?" She climbed out of the truck, her eyes wide.

Caleb instinctively moved closer. Maybe it was just ingrained manners, or maybe it was that anything could be out there in the dark. In the absence of interior truck smells, Caleb caught the sour tang of spilled beer, sweat, and animal, and some ancient gene in him insisted on protecting George from anything out there beyond the light.

"Yeah."

George shook her head so minutely that Caleb almost missed it, and then a smirk settled across her face that he didn't understand.

"What?" He asked, hating the feeling that he was doing something wrong, that she might turn around and leave before they even got inside.

"Nothing," she said, shaking the smirk off her face. "It's a beautiful home. Should I leave my boots here?" She pointed to a shoehorn Caleb hadn't noticed beside the front door.

"You can take them off in my room."

"Are you sure?"

"Yeah, don't worry about it."

Caleb led her into the house. He hadn't seen his father since their arrival and this wasn't the kind of interaction he wanted to have. If they ran into his mother, he wouldn't be able to handle the look of disdain she'd give before walking away. And Phil, she'd insist on sitting down and interrogating George until she knew their Zodiac signs were compatible.

But by some miracle the foyer was empty. So was the kitchen and living room. Caleb watched George take everything in, her eyes wide as she took in each room. If only she knew the views hidden behind the curtain of darkness.

Caleb led her down the hall, pausing to quietly pass Phil's door. If George found this weird, she didn't let on.

Caleb held the door open so George could enter his bedroom first, that animal smell washing over him as she passed. She tugged off her boots and Caleb's eyes devoured every inch of her legs, because those jean shorts were almost indecent. She stepped further into the room as he closed the door behind them, sealing them in silence.

Caleb kicked off his shoes beside hers, but stayed by the door as she walked around, noticing the rumpled duvet, the curtains pulled wide, though it was too dark beyond to see anything out there. While her back was to him, he rushed to pull the duvet straight, wishing he'd cleaned up a little before he'd left. He really wasn't putting his best foot forward.

"I haven't unpacked yet," he apologized, as if that affected whatever was about to happen.

"No worries," she said, squinting as if she could see anything out the sliders.

Caleb's thoughts kicked into gear. Should he sit on the bed? Should he sit in the chair beside the fireplace and let her sit on the bed so she didn't feel any pressure? Should he make the first move or should he let her?

"This is going to sound weird," she said, interrupting Caleb's spiraling thoughts. Whatever she asked of him, however outlandish, he was going to say yes.

She bit her lip, looking away from him, and Caleb felt his body stir.

"Would it be okay if I cleaned up a bit?" She finally looked at him and Caleb's thoughts sputtered out. "It's just that I'm really gross from work and I'm pretty sure I smell like horses and beer, so I just thought if I could have a couple minutes to clean up?"

She was going to get naked. Without him asking. In his room. Well, in his bathroom. But he'd be here and she'd be just there, and even if nothing else happened afterward how could Caleb say no?

"Yeah, of course. There's probably towels—"

He hadn't been in the bathroom yet, but when he walked in, turned on the light, all of his toiletries were arranged in the shower and on the vanity. It had probably been Phil. She was type A to a fault. Or maybe it had been William. Either way, there were two towels already on the hooks by the walk-in shower.

"Use whatever you need."

He turned and she was right behind him, so close he could see an eyelash just there on her cheek. He could reach out and—

"This is a big ask, but do you have a clean shirt I can borrow? If I put this back on I'm still going to smell."

Caleb's brain went fuzzy. He couldn't remember a single item of clothing he'd packed. All he could think about was George's skin—which was probably so soft—wrapped in his clothes.

"It's no big deal. I can just wear these," she apologized, backing away from him, and it took everything for him not to reach out and hold her in place.

"I have something. Definitely. Just give me a minute to look."

He walked back into the bedroom and heard the door click behind him. His heart began pounding against his chest and he couldn't explain why. Nothing had happened.

The water turned on and Caleb kicked into action. All of his clothes had been hung up or folded with elite precision and shelved in the closet. It took him a few minutes to find a shirt—it would be ginormous on George, but it was his favorite and softened from wear—and a pair of plaid pants he'd planned to sleep in.

He knocked on the bathroom door.

"I have clothes for you. I'll leave them right outside the door."

"Thank you!"

He set the clothes on the floor and began pacing. Should he throw her clothes in the washing machine? Where was the laundry room? Should he turn on the fireplace for ambiance? What about music?

Hating how anxious he felt, he decided to head to the kitchen. If he stayed in the bedroom, he'd wear the rug bare.

But in the kitchen, he was no better. He stood in front of the fridge staring at the options. Too many options. His brain went blank from the overstimulation. Was the move to mix a drink? Should he also bring a snack? But what if George had dietary restrictions?

Contrary to his anxious behavior, it wasn't like Caleb had never slept with someone. He'd slept with multiple someones. And yet here he was, losing his shit because there was a beautiful, naked woman in his bathroom. He'd already stuffed his foot in his mouth multiple times and his cool was nowhere to be found. What was he doing wasting time in the kitchen!

He grabbed two bottles of water and raced back.

The shower was off, the bathroom door was still closed, but his clothes were gone. He set the water on the table by the bed and stood at the sliders wondering if it was more romantic to have a view of outside when they woke or if it was better to have no light so they'd sleep in. But that was fucking presumptuous of him. Who knew if she'd even want to stay. For all he knew this was a *hey, thanks for letting me shower, but I'm good now, k-bye.* And even if by some miracle something did happen between them, she might just head out after to avoid an awkward morning.

He slumped into the armchair facing the bed and prayed she'd stay.

When the bathroom door finally opened, Caleb startled and stood. George was in his pajama pants and white tee, towel drying her hair. He could see the faint outline of her nipples through the shirt and blinked up to her face, feeling like he'd been caught with his hand in the cooking jar.

The scent that wafted into the room was his body wash and deodorant, and there was something incredibly sexy about her smelling like him.

"I needed that. You have no idea," she drawled.

She disappeared back into the steam and returned without the towel, her damp hair leaving translucent streaks that slid precariously south, and it took momentous effort for Caleb to keep his eyes above board.

"I got water," he offered.

He'd never been thing tongue-tied before. Then again, everything about this felt different. Maybe it was that the girls he'd slept with were people he'd known from school or through friends. But Caleb knew nothing about George except that she had an enchanting voice and looked ridiculously hot in his clothes.

"Thanks." But she didn't move towards the water.

"I really want to kiss you." Caleb blurted. His heart was beating so fast and he was worried he might have a heart attack before anything had the chance to happen.

Of course, George had every right to rebuke him, but the least he could do was try. And if it didn't work out—if he'd ruined everything with his stupid mouth—then so be it.

"Okay," she said, and he felt the air rush back into his lungs.

He crossed the space between them, but stopped just shy of touching her. He was close enough that he could smell his toothpaste on her breath.

"You're sure?" He asked, not daring to move until she nodded. Then, permission granted, he brushed the damp hair off her shoulder and cupped the back of her head. Water tickled his wrist as it slipped down his forearm, but he hardly noticed.

If all he was allowed was one kiss, he'd still consider this the best night of his life. But when he brushed his lips over hers and she opened her mouth, beckoning his tongue inside, he knew this wouldn't be just one kiss. There was no way.

George reached up to his shoulders, hesitant at first, her hands feather-light. But as Caleb deepened the kiss and her tongue caressed his, she took bunches of his shirt in her hands, holding on like she was claiming him.

"You're sure this is okay?" He asked, coming up for air. Her eyes were impossibly big as he rested his forehead against hers. God, she was beautiful.

An hour ago, he'd sworn he was either drunk or under a spell. And now he had George pulling him towards the bed. He just wanted to make sure this was real and that he wasn't dreaming this while passed out in the back of an Uber.

"Very sure."

Her legs hit the bed and she scooted backward, pulling Caleb with her. The moment she was laid out, half pinned beneath him, her leg hooked over his hip, Caleb knew for sure this wasn't reality. It couldn't be, because she was perfect and Caleb wasn't that lucky.

"If at any point you want to stop—" Caleb tried, but her hands grazed the strip of skin between his shirt and jeans, and a heavy feeling pooled in his belly. But what did words matter anyway? He should just stop talking and let her go about her business unhindered.

He struggled out of the arms of the shirt and pulled his undershirt over his head, tossing both away. The absence of George's mouth on his brought an ache he didn't even know could exist. He was breathless but also desperate for more. More of her touch, more of her mouth. Just more.

He leaned back over her and she framed his head with her hands, her thumb brushing across his bottom lip. He feared he might come in his pants like a horny teenager.

"I very much do not want to stop." She said and nipped at his bottom lip.

Caleb's hands found her hips, his fingers pushing the shirt up so he could feel how soft her skin was. Of course it was impossibly soft. He wanted to touch her everywhere, taste her everywhere.

He trailed kisses along her jaw, down her neck, slipping along her beautiful body, until his mouth found the spot at her hip that he'd already touched with his fingers.

"Is this okay?" He paused only long enough for the nod of approval. He lifted the shirt so he could see her stomach and kiss his way across to the other hip. He made some plans, decided to map her body with his tongue, but before he could begin, she squirmed. And then his shirt was off her, disappearing over the edge of the bed leaving her so beautifully bare.

"Was I going too slow?" He could take constructive criticism. He would work so hard to make this night perfect if she only told him how.

"It was obstructing my view of you."

George licked her lips.

He crawled urgently back up her body, a growl building in his chest. Her perfect mouth had him under a spell. The moment she'd opened it and let music pour out, he'd been a goner. And now—

"Tell me what you want," he all but begged. He bent to her breast, his eyes locked on hers as he placed his mouth over it and sucked.

"I want you," she said, squirming to get her hands on the button of his pants.

Together, they got his pants undone and he kicked them off ungracefully. He desperately wanted to be suave and self-assured. But if she got her hands on him, he was going to be spent in under a minute.

"Can we just hold on a second," he breathed, realizing his body was too revved up to make this last. And *my god*, he wanted it to last.

George stilled beneath him, her pupils blowing wide on the bulge in his briefs.

"I just… if we could slow down. Otherwise, this is all going to happen way too fast." He couldn't look at her, afraid she'd be annoyed with him. So he focused on her breast, how it rose and fell, and he realized, like a sharp flick to his breastbone, that she was just as breathless as him. And that, not being alone in this feeling of anticipation, calmed his racing heart.

She traced his face with a gentle finger, drawing his eyes back to hers.

"Hi," she said, running her hand through his hair.

It was like warm waves rolling across his head. It was unbelievably good and he sent up a prayer to whoever might be listening that she never stopped. His breathing calmed and he felt himself starting to drift as her nails raked back and forth across his scalp.

Her other arm came around his back and held him to her like the warmest, most perfect hug. Caleb wanted to tell her she was the best body pillow he'd ever snuggled and he wanted to kiss her—he really did—but his lips were too tired to do a proper job, and he only wanted her to have the best.

His eyes closed and he buried his nose against her neck. God, she smelled like that moment before a thunderstorm hits, mixed with deep pine forest, and a sprinkle of spice. But under it he smelled the salt of her skin, and he inhaled, getting high off it.

His body grew heavy, the tide pulling him under, and he held on tight, wrapping his body around her because she was his life raft. She was, wasn't she? He'd been weary and numb and she'd shocked him back to life tonight. And most of all, he didn't feel like he had to be someone else with her. She'd accepted him at his most-bumbling and hadn't run.

"Caleb."

Her breath tickled his brow as she brushed hair off his forehead and everything felt so good. He wanted to live in this moment forever.

"I want you inside me."

"You're already inside me," he mumbled against her neck, and her laughter tickled his chest.

Wait, what had he said? Never mind. It didn't matter. All that mattered was that she was warm and soft, smelled like heaven, and fit perfectly against him. Could they just stay like this forever? Maybe he could buy this bedroom and they'd never have to leave.

He could no longer tell where his body ended and hers began, because he'd melted into her and they were now a warm puddle coalescing on the duvet.

"Caleb," he heard, but the voice was carried away with the tide.

He wanted to call out to it to come back, to stay longer, but his lips were too heavy to form the words.

7. CALEB

There was someone chasing him. Caleb heard their shoes slapping the pavement behind him.

No—it was the sound of his own shoes. He was late for something important.

He crested the hill and the marina came into view—boats of all sizes. He kept running. Down the hill. Down.

He was moving too slow. Time was running out. But he was almost there.

When he finally got to the marina all the boats were gone. No—wait. There was one boat—a rowboat. He clawed his way along the dock to try and move faster, then he was over the edge and into the boat. He sped across the glassy surface, no waves in sight. Wait, no. He wasn't moving at all. The boat was still with no sight of land, the sky a brilliant blue. It turned, spinning on its axis around the earth, and then half of it was night. There were so many brilliant stars it was unreal.

Caleb lay down in the bottom of the boat and looked up, tried to count the stars and lost track. Back to one. The waves lapped softly against the hull. It was so calm, so perfect.

A gull landed on the stern, watching him. Its head cocked to one side, its mouth opened and screamed, *I thought you were dead!*

Caleb opened his eyes, and instinct or self-preservation had his body automatically curling in on itself mere moments before Phil hurled herself onto his bed.

When she was full of emotion—anxiety, excitement, worry—she forgot that she was all sharp edges. Twenty-two years of her finding any excuse to jump on him, had him rolling over to protect George—

The sheets beside him were empty.

"You didn't wake me when you got home!" Phil punctuated this with a whack to his back, her mouth too close to his ear for any time of day, but especially early in the morning.

"Fuck! Get off me. It's too early for this shit."

Caleb strained to hear bathroom sounds, but there were none. Had George heard Phil coming and hid? Rolled over and slithered under the bed? Slipped out to the door to the patio? Was she stealthily seated inside the closet?

"My worry for you is on Eastern Standard Time!"

Phil was sitting on his hip now, making no move to get off. How often had she burst into his room without knocking, jumping on him without any consideration? He loved her, but sometimes she could be completely ignorant of the fact that he might need a moment of privacy.

He reached out an arm from under the covers, grabbed her around the stomach, and flipped her onto the spot George had vacated. Phil rolled over, hands tucked between pillow and cheek, like she hadn't just burst rudely into his room.

"There's this thing called knocking. I know I've mentioned it before," Caleb said, his voice thick with sleep.

Phil just rolled her eyes.

"Can you maybe give me a minute to wake up?"

Phil reached out and booped him. "Morning wood, huh? Make it quick. Mom says you need to come have breakfast with us."

She scooted off the bed, and Caleb heard her stop at the door. He rolled over to make sure she was actually leaving.

When they were little, they didn't have a secret language. They hadn't needed one. Caleb and Phil could look at each other and read everything on the other's face. Their mother loved to bring this up at parties, how they'd been quiet for so long that she'd worried they might both be *developmentally slow*. She always whispered those words, like if she spoke it loud enough time might reverse itself and deal her a shittier hand.

She had brought them to the pediatrician insisting they be tested for all manner of ailments, disabilities. *They gave me my first gray hair,* she loved to say. She was always keeping score.

Now, as Caleb searched Phil's face, he read, *It's fine. But if it's not, I'll take care of it.* Because that's what Phil did—protected him always. It didn't matter that Caleb was twice her size. She liked to say that she'd insisted on entering the world first to make sure the coast was clear.

Phil turned, her steps receded down the hall and Caleb forced himself awake. Bursting in without knocking wasn't okay. What if he and George had been in the middle of something?

He sat up. *Where was George?*

On the bench at the foot of the bed was a neat little pile—his shirt and pajama pants carefully folded. He threw off the covers. In the bathroom everything was in its place, the two towels folded on the rack. The closet held his things, but no beautiful woman. Had last night happened? Or had it all been a whiskey dream?

He walked back into the bedroom and picked up his shirt, held it against his face and inhaled. There was his deodorant, but there was also George. He could swear it.

Over at the bedside table—no note. No, of course there wouldn't be a note. Why would she leave him a note? He'd fallen asleep on her. Hadn't managed to do much else besides kiss her before passing out. He didn't deserve a note. She'd come home with him, got into his bed, took off her clothes, practically served herself on a platter. And he couldn't follow through.

Failing yet again, the voice in his head chided.

Caleb ran his hands through his hair, pulling at the ends until they stood. It was there, embedded in the sensory memory of his scalp—George's fingers lapping like waves, forward and back. It was no wonder he'd fallen asleep.

Giving her an orgasm would have driven him wild, would have made his entire life if she'd screamed his name. But the sensation of her fingers just *there*—he touched the place at the base of his scalp where she'd drawn circles—that was almost better.

How was he supposed to walk into breakfast with his family like last night hadn't altered something in him on a cellular level? And what would he tell Phil when she asked how his night went?

Caleb never kept anything from Phil. But Caleb wanted to keep this—whatever *this* was—to himself. Maybe it was a blip in his timeline, something that would seem inconsequential the farther he traveled from it. Maybe it was a crush that would fuel masturbation fantasies for the rest of his life. Maybe he was overthinking it. Hell, George hadn't even said goodbye.

Whatever this was or wasn't, Caleb didn't want to share it. Not yet. Maybe on the plane home he'd whisper across the aisle to Phil, *Hey, so, that first night you left me alone in town...* Maybe it was okay to allow something that had been promising, but hadn't quite come to fruition, to be everything to him just for a moment.

* * *

In the kitchen, Dara stood at the island stirring a mug of tea. She did that, rattling the spoon around, until someone either said something or got up and walked away. Phil wasn't the type to tiptoe around a subject and the first time she'd asked what their mother was stirring—because there was never milk or sugar in there, just the water and the tea bag—she'd been told, *It soothes my nerves.* Which begged the question—what nerves could a woman worth twenty million possibly have?

She can feel the Botox starting to shift, Phil said once in the privacy of their shared bathroom.

It's all the snails massacred in the name of glowing skin, Caleb insisted. *They're haunting her.*

Phil had choked on her mouthwash, because Dara Browning most certainly did not care about massacred snails or any other creature.

"Did you go out drinking last night?" She asked, her spoon quiet for the duration of the question.

Caleb helped himself to the spread: pastries, breakfast meats, scrambled eggs, fruit, yogurt—it was obscene and mostly untouched. He paused across from his mother and stuck a piece of bacon in his mouth.

"I did," he spoke around the bite, waiting for her reaction.

Her eyes narrowed, a lioness with prey in her sights. He didn't usually talk with food in his mouth. Good manners had been bred into him. Hold the door for others. Don't talk over someone. Defer to elders. Please and thank you. But something about being summoned to breakfast when everything about this trip felt like a farce, had him pushing buttons he knew he shouldn't.

"Caleb Theodore," she began, her voice measured and low.

It was an interesting thing, to come into adulthood and realize that your parents shouldn't have procreated. Being born to a person but cared for by another had done a number on them. Especially because the woman who raised them had been so full of love, while the one they called mother was decidedly… not.

Caleb finished chewing and swallowed. Properly chastised, he joined Phil at the breakfast nook. She tsked him and sipped her coffee like a good daughter.

"I need you two to be good," Dara began. She'd stopped stirring, but made no move to drink the tea.

Phil and Caleb's eyes met. *Generational wealth,* was one of Phil's favorite excuses for their mother's awful behavior. She loved throwing it out in the same way others tacked on *That's what she said.* It served its purpose, getting a chuckle or shake of the head to lighten the mood between them.

"When have we ever not been—" Phil was cut off with a look.

"Philippa Elsbeth, so help me God."

So help me God, Caleb mouthed at Phil. She closed her eyes and inhaled for three counts—one of her therapist's recommendations for diffusing her explosive reactions.

"You will not cause trouble. You will not mouth off to me or your father. I know you think you're adults now—"

Phil's eyebrows practically moved into her hairline at the word *think.* Caleb stuffed a forkful of eggs in his mouth to smother his smirk.

"—But until you're paying for the vacation, you will do as I say. If there's a dinner planned you will be there. On time. You will not get drunk. You will not embarrass me. Am I understood?"

The silence dragged on as Caleb chewed and it occurred to him that she was actually waiting for a response.

"Oh, you're letting us speak—" Phil began, and Caleb pinched her shin with his toes. "Ow!"

"We will behave," he responded for them both.

"Good." The stirring stopped and the spoon was placed in the sink. "I have an appointment and need to leave in ten minutes. One of you will drive me."

Phil smiled pleasantly while Dara took her tea and left the room.

"I want to see this barn that's in all the Jackson Hole tourist pictures. So, let's drop her at the spa and go check it out."

"A barn? Couldn't we do something fun like ziplining or ATVs?" Caleb got up in search of orange juice and returned to the table with two glasses because he was not interested in sharing.

"Caleb Theodore," Phil adopted their mother's voice.

"Philippa Elsbeth," he returned.

"Fine. Barn first and then we'll do something you want to do."

"Fine."

"Fine."

And then from down the hall came Dara's stern, "Ten minutes!"

They both scrambled to make it out of the kitchen first, shoving each other to get back to their bedrooms to change. God help the person who kept their mother waiting.

8. GEORGE

Kathleen and George sat in the alley behind the bar sharing a plate of chili cheese fries and chocolate shakes. It had been Kathleen's treat, having seen the glint in George's eye the moment she walked into work that afternoon. George was not one to say no to a free meal, so she'd handled prep while Kathleen ran across the street, and then they'd snuck out to savor the early evening light.

"I hate that I miss sunset almost every night." George stuffed a forkful of cheesy-potato goodness in her mouth.

"Are you really talking about the weather right now?" Kathleen shook her head. "Quit stalling!"

George pointed innocently at her busy mouth. Kathleen should've known better than to start interrogating while they were eating.

"Oh, for goodness' sake!" Kathleen pulled the food out of George's reach. "You can still nod or shake your head."

George tried not to laugh. She didn't want to choke on her mouthful of potato, but she enjoyed seeing her friend all worked up like this. She was the type of friend who wanted to know *everything* so she could chew on it like cud all night long. It helped pass long shifts behind the bar.

"Was it that guy—the one whose eyeballs were surgically attached to your ass all night?"

George blinked innocently and Kathleen made like she was going to chuck her shake at her.

"Was it?"

George pointed aggressively at her face while she finished chewing.

"Oh girl, he was absolutely watching your booty. Make no mistake."

George sipped her shake instead of responding.

"Agree to very much disagree." Kathleen barreled through the silence. "I saw him leave, but did I miss him come back in?"

George shook her head.

"Okay, so…"

George swallowed and wiped her mouth. It wasn't a healthy dinner, but man, was it *good.*

"He waited for me outside."

"That fucker!" Kathleen stood up so fast that George nearly toppled backwards.

"Not in a creepy way." She reached for Kathleen's arm to pull her back down. Kathleen balled both fists, but eventually sat.

"I'm not joking about this. It's not okay for a guy to stalk you, even if he's cute."

The fire in Kathleen's eyes made George's heart swell and her eyes burn. No one had ever offered to defend her honor before.

"He wasn't a threat, I swear. He was actually really sweet and I think I made him nervous, which was something new and also kind of a turn on? And then I went home with him and we got partially naked, and that was fun, but then he fell asleep before anything really happened."

Kathleen's head tipped sideways, like it had been knocked askew from too much information.

"I'm sorry, can you please repeat that, but this time go slower and enunciate."

George bit down on her smile. The thing was, she almost didn't believe last night had happened. Halfway through her first trail ride that morning she'd bent her nose to her armpit and sniffed, convinced she'd imagined it all. The house, the bedroom, his deliciously warm mouth on her skin. But his deodorant was still there, clinging to her. It had been real. The weight of him wrapped around her, the warmth of his breath tickling her neck. It surprised her, how much her body had wanted his after that first kiss. She hadn't wanted someone like that. Like her body was starving for only what he could give.

And oddly, she hadn't made her escape when he'd fallen asleep. He was bigger than her, sure, but she'd shoved over many a horse when they crowded her space. Instead, she'd run her fingers through his hair long after his eyes closed. And it wasn't like he'd drifted off. More like he dropped head-first into the depths of sleep. He hadn't twitched or moved for a long time after his eyes closed, and George had held on, feeling like she needed to keep him safe.

Or maybe, and this was probably the truth of it, she hadn't wanted to leave that bed. George had never known a bed could be *that* heavenly. Her twin bed over the garage was little more than a straw-filled sack by comparison.

"You little tart!" Kathleen squealed, pointing a fry at George. "You've never gone home with someone from the bar the entire time I've known you. And the guy who ended up convincing you was all finger guns and random words strung together! How on earth did he not spontaneously combust when you got naked?"

Kathleen couldn't eat this story—or the fries—up fast enough. But George had shared enough. She wanted to keep the details of those moments in his bedroom to herself. If she spoke about it, it might all drift away on the wind. Tucked safely in her head it could remain untouched, pristine, perfectly intact.

"You're the worst, you know that?" Kathleen's head swung back and forth, her mouth pinched in fake annoyance.

The nice thing about Kathleen was that as much as she wanted all the juicy bits, she did know when to stop pushing. She slurped up the remainder of her shake and leaned back on her hands.

"Anyways, well enough about you. My news is that I'm considering a change."

This piqued George's interest. In their three summers working together they'd never talked about life plans. It was just understood that working at the bar was their time together and one day that might end. They didn't talk from October to May, and George always hoped that Kathleen would be here when she drove back into Jackson each spring. But what would summer look like if she wasn't here?

"Okay." George watched the clouds coast across the sliver of sky between buildings.

"I think I want to be a chef."

This caught George by surprise. The look on Kathleen's face was so nervous and hopeful that George couldn't help but smile.

"Kathleen, that's amazing! Is there an opening that you have your eye on?"

George watched Kathleen scrunch in on herself, like all the courage to hope and dream was small and fragile. Naturally, George wanted to help her protect that.

"There is, for a line cook over in Wilson, and I already applied."

"Oh my god, congrats!" George couldn't help but be excited for her.

"It's not a done deal. They called today to set up a time to talk, but I feel hopeful." She shook her head and the excitement washed away leaving something that George knew was dressed in self-preservation. "And you know, if it doesn't pan out, I can stay at the bar."

"Of course you can, because you're a damn hard worker and anyplace would be lucky to have you." She gave Kathleen's arm a squeeze.

George had never allowed herself to dream. She'd gotten the job at Tucker's ranch because her boss back in Texas had some long-winded connection to him. She'd never considered leaving Texas until the offer of summers in Wyoming landed in her lap. Then once she'd gotten up here, she'd realized she could fit more into a day than just the ranch. So, she'd asked around until she'd landed the bar back gig, which eventually turned into bartending.

Back home in Texas George didn't dream. She worked herself to the bone and was thankful for whatever that afforded her—a roof over her head, maybe two meals a day. Here in Jackson, surrounded by such extreme wealth, it sometimes creeped into George's head that more might be possible. But still, she didn't allow herself to think on it too much. Because that could only lead to disappointment.

"Well, here's hoping," Kathleen whispered.

"Here's hoping." George held up her now empty cup so they could clink.

Off in the distance a crack of thunder rumbled and moments later the wind picked up.

"I guess that's our sign to head back in," Kathleen mused.

9. CALEB

"I can't tell if dinner being normal is a sign that we're overreacting or that we should be more worried."

Phil was in the passenger seat searching her tiny bag for something. She'd been searching for so long that Caleb was convinced the item in question was molecular in size.

"I shouldn't have made a big deal about the plane. Whether they're getting divorced or not, I am grateful to be here."

Phil stopped digging in her purse and patted Caleb's arm.

"Baby brother, are you growing an itty-bitty conscience?"

Caleb pinned her against the window with one hand.

"Ten and two!" She screamed and Caleb relented. "Just because Dad kissed Mom when he came in doesn't mean everything's good. I think it's worth just taking casual note of things. Yes, Dad golfing is par for the course—"

"No." Caleb took a hand off the wheel to pin her again, but she swatted it away.

"I had to be punny!" She resumed digging in her bag. "Dad golfing and Mom spending a day at the spa is normal. If they weren't doing those things I'd be worried. Or, maybe something is going on and they're covering their tracks by keeping up with normal activities. Shit, maybe I'm looking at this all wrong!"

Phil worked herself up to the point of giving up the search and tossing the bag at her feet.

"Phil," Caleb turned to face her at the next stop sign. "Take a breath. It's going to be okay."

When Phil just stared at him, he took a deep breath, holding it until she mirrored him. When they both exhaled, he started driving again.

"But what if—"

Caleb clamped a hand over Phil's mouth. This was his fault. He'd put the idea in her head. Before, she'd been her usual happy-go-lucky self, ready to enjoy vacation. Now, she was oscillating between panic and calm and back again.

"It's going to be okay. You and me." He held out a pinky as he turned toward town.

When Phil hadn't made the soccer team freshman year, when their mother had told them casually that they made her legs itch, when either of them had befallen heartbreak, they always came together, pinkies first. Forever linked.

Phil gave him her pinky.

*   *   *

Caleb apprehensively followed Phil into Million Dollar Cowboy Bar. She'd compiled a list of things they had to do this week and insisted that his going to the bar alone hadn't counted.

We're going to that bar tonight, Phil stated on their way home from Jenny Lake, and he'd nodded. Caleb still couldn't bring himself to tell Phil. He wanted to. He did. Because he knew she'd find some semblance of a silver lining.

But now, as he followed Phil to the saddles and took a seat beside her, he worried about whether George was working. When you saw someone again after having passed out on them, what was the right course of action? Apologize, obviously, but how was he going to convince her to give him a second chance?

Last night's band had been swapped out for an older, folksy, duo. Phil babbled as Caleb meticulously scanned the bar, but he wasn't listening. He felt like such a creep, but he had to know if George was here.

"Ouch! What?"

Phil pinched his knee with her talons, just like their grandfather had done when they were kids. Except, that had been to tickle them. Phil had adopted a painful version to get his attention in settings where it wasn't acceptable to outright hit him.

"Down the other end of the bar—ohmygod! Don't be obvious and look!"

"You told me to look!" He winced as she punched his thigh.

"Caleb, so help me God!"

He kept his focus on Phil, pushed imaginary glasses up his nose, rested his chin in his hand. The only way to handle Phil when she was amped up was to be silly.

"Why are you the most annoying person ever?"

"Me?" He mused. "I'm just following your orders. I'm not looking at whatever is down the bar that you want me to see, but refuse to let me look at."

Phil had finished off two glasses of wine at dinner. Not that he'd been counting, but he'd taken note when she refilled. Considering the talk their mother had given them that morning, Phil had done it out of spite. Now, she leaned in until her nose was nearly pressed to Caleb's. He could smell the wine on her breath.

"Can't you just be cool? I beg of you. I'm not trying to change you, because I love you, I do. But right now, in this moment, can you please be cool? Just try. For me."

"Me?" Caleb daintily clutched a handful of imaginary pearls.

"I'm seriously about to punch you."

Caleb bit back a laugh when her face scrunched in anger. She swatted him away and adjusted herself as casually as one can in a western saddle.

"There is a woman down the other end of the bar." Phil's voice settled into an eerie copy of their mother's when she was biting down on her temper. "Totally gorgeous and checking me out, and you being annoying right now is ruining the vibe, so I am going to the bathroom to freshen up and you need to get your shit together and order me a drink."

Caleb leaned back, mock-offended. "Philippa, I am the epitome of cool."

"He says while sitting side-saddle." Phil gave him a pointed look and headed for the bathroom.

Caleb looked down at his long legs strewn to one side. Okay, so maybe Phil had a point. He stood, straddled the saddle-stool, and sat.

"What can I get you?"

George stood across the bar from him, hair pulled back in a ponytail, and—*what was that look?* Her features were granite, no emotion whatsoever, hip cocked like he was an inconvenience. She looked away down the bar, like she was too busy to spare him a second look.

Fuck, he'd really messed up.

"Hi." He hated how nervous he sounded, but he was already on unsteady footing and he didn't want to make it worse.

She looked at him and he lost all sense of how to be. He could see her in there, buried under the hours of working on her feet, the sweat, the stink, trying so hard not to let emotion show.

"What do you want to drink?" She asked again, the words sticky with annoyance.

"Wyoming whiskey, neat." Even after last night, he still didn't like it much, but he wanted a redo of the previous twenty-four hours. Except this time, he'd get it right.

Caleb watched her pour his drink, her back stiff, her eyes anywhere but on him. He'd been snubbed by girls before, been made to feel like a loser, but this felt worse. He'd stolen the smile from her perfect mouth and he had to return it.

"You left without saying goodbye."

He handed his card to George as she placed the drink in front of him.

"And your date? What does she want to drink?" She asked, all business.

He took a sip of his whiskey and tried to make the words make sense. And then it clicked. He wanted to laugh, but the look on George's face let him know she wouldn't react well to that. So, he bit down on his smile as he reexamined the way she held her body tonight, all sharp angles and annoyance.

Was George *jealous*? Did this mean Caleb might still have a shot?

He started to lean back, remembering almost too late that he was in a saddle. He righted himself and couldn't figure out what to do with his hands. He held onto the saddle horn to keep them still.

"You mean my sister?"

He watched the words land between them, like a slow-denotating bomb. George looked away to grab a clean glass, but then she seemed to forget what she was meant to be doing. If she wanted to pretend that she hadn't just been upset with him he'd happily allow it. As long as she stayed here talking to him.

"Your sister." She finally looked up at him, eyes clear, and Caleb *knew* he was still in this.

"Philippa will have a vodka-tonic with two slices of orange. Please."

George held his gaze and shivers trailed up his spine, lodging at the base of his neck. A smile finally tickled across her lips and he wanted to gobble it up.

"You left without saying goodbye," Caleb tried again. Maybe they could just go back to that moment in his bedroom and rewrite a better ending.

"I had horses to wrangle."

Caleb could have sworn the way she said it sounded a lot like regret. But maybe he was imagining what he wanted to hear over the noise of the crowded bar.

"I take people on trail rides during the day, then I'm here at night."

"Come home with me," he blurted. From the look on George's face that had been the last thing she'd expected him to say. He took a breath, tried again. "Last night—"

He could sense Phil nearby, heading their way. It was a twin thing. If she entered a room, he knew she was there without turning around. He needed to apologize to George before she sauntered up and forced him to explain everything.

"I shouldn't have fallen asleep. It's not a reflection of you. I swear. I was just really tired and I'm sorry."

He felt frantic, his pulse increasing with each step Phil took in his direction.

"Are you working tomorrow morning?"

George shook her head.

"Come to the house when your shift ends. Please. Give me another chance." Caleb would've got on his knees and begged if he thought it would help, but he didn't think George was the type of girl to appreciate showy displays in front of drunk bar patrons.

And Phil was getting closer.

"This isn't going to become a thing," George said, breaking the spell. "You're on vacation and I go back to Texas in October."

"Is that a yes or no?"

George's face went serious, her eyes locked on Caleb's to make sure he was listening.

"This stays here, in Wyoming."

This was definitely teetering towards a yes. The rest of what she was saying he'd dissect later.

Phil climbed onto the saddle next to him and Caleb realized the conversation was over. And worse, he wasn't even sure of George's answer.

"Hi." George set Phil's drink on the bar.

"Oh my god, two slices! Is this kismet?"

George winked at Phil and walked away to add the drinks to their tab. Caleb scrubbed a hand down his face, because she might as well have poured lighter fluid all over Phil's crush. He could feel Phil's eyes on him, asking him in blinks if he'd been a good wingman, but he couldn't tear his eyes from George as she walked away.

"Okay, so?" Phil picked up her drink and took a tentative sip. "Oh wow, this is perfection."

Down the bar George turned. She nodded and Caleb had to tuck his chin, pretend he was picking lint off his shirt, to hide how immensely happy that one small movement made him.

"Hello! What's the deal? Did you ask for two orange slices or is she my future wife?" Phil probed.

"Unfortunately, she's into guys." That statement tasted so sweet on his tongue, knowing it was one guy she was into and that guy was him.

"So, you're saying you only managed to give her our drinks order and then got flustered and didn't talk me up?"

"Something like that." Caleb hid his smile behind his glass.

Driving up to the house was like returning to a hallucination. George still couldn't believe that homes like this existed and that she was going to spend another night inside.

Sitting in her truck, the engine off, she laughed to herself, because this week had ventured into the absurd. First, getting to sing with The Billings Boys. That had been a dream and something she'd never even imagined. And then, of course, there was the guy holding open the front door of this monstrous house.

Caleb was the opposite of everything George had ever run toward. She'd walked into the arms of overly-confident guys who'd looked at her like she was something they deserved to have, like she wasn't a whole person. And now, she was inclined to run into Caleb's arms simply because he was kind.

There was something about him that disarmed her. Maybe his super power was putting her so at ease that her forcefield never had time to go up. And now, walking up to the front door, being greeted with the sweetest smile, she found herself overcome with need for him. It was like he'd given her a morsel of something—*the absolute best thing she'd ever tasted*—and she was ravenous for more.

"You came."

"You asked," George countered.

Because truly, if he hadn't said something earlier, she wouldn't be here. She'd been irrationally mad at him for bringing a date to her place of employment. She'd have served him, stewed in her misguided annoyance, and been done with him once and for all.

So, thank God he'd cleared that up and asked her to come over.

Still, she felt off-balance walking into the house, and certainly didn't feel like she had two hands on the wheel. He had her head spinning just from being in his presence.

"Can I get you anything to eat or drink? We have a lot of food. I can make you—"

"I'm good. Are you good?"

George wasn't one to interrupt. Grandma Jeane was a stickler for manners no matter the circumstance. But food was the last thing on George's mind. She'd had a long day. Her muscles were achy and she wanted to get out of her dirty clothes and into Caleb's bed.

"Never better." Caleb rocked onto the balls of his feet.

"You sure? You seem a little nervous." George took a step closer to test her theory.

Caleb shoved his hands in his pockets but took a step toward her. She was reeling him in.

"Nope, not nervous at all. Totally chill about you being here. And sober to boot. And wide awake. Not tired at all. Going to be up for *hours*." His brows jumped in meaning.

Every time Caleb's eyes met hers, she felt a zing up her spine. It was like they could see beyond the clothes, the dirt, the bravado and see the real her. It made her feel tethered to the ground in a way she hadn't felt with a guy before. She closed the distance between them and took the hem of his shirt in both hands.

"Then why are we still standing here?"

One moment he was staring down at her, eyelashes fluttering, lips parting around a thought. The next, he was bending down, throwing her over his shoulder with surprising ease, and marching them to his room.

The shock of being upended knocked the air out of George's chest in a whooshing honk of laughter.

As they made their way through the monstrous home, George forgot to breathe, she was so focused on the feel of Caleb's hand splayed across the back of her thighs. It wasn't a caress, shouldn't have aroused her at all. He was simply holding her in place so she wouldn't fall. And maybe too, it was the surprise of being tossed over his shoulder with such unexpected ease that gave flight to the kind of thoughts that flooded her body with liquid heat.

Her head began to spin as he set her gently on the floor next to his bed and went to close the door.

"If that was too much," he started to apologize.

But before he could finish, she was rushing to him, pulling him around so she could frame his face with her hands and bring his lips down to hers. When he apologized, when he was gentle or cautious with her, it made her want to devour him. The truth was, no one had even been gentlemanly towards George.

The night before had been something worth tucking away to savor the sweetness. But now, with her fingers on his stubbled cheeks, George wanted everything. She wanted Caleb's mouth on her. She wanted the weight of him pinning her to the bed. She wanted to know what would've happened if he hadn't fallen asleep.

Caleb shuffled her backwards, his arms wrapped protectively around her so she wouldn't fall when her legs hit the bed, and that act alone had heat pooling between her legs. They broke apart only so they could remove shirts, and Caleb took a step back. George's cheeks burned under his gaze, realizing *she* was making him look like *that*, his chest rising and falling fitfully, his eyes wild with want.

The way he looked at her was like she had given him ice cream for the first time. Like he couldn't believe something this good existed. He reached for her and reeled her in, his mouth coming to hover over her messy hair, and she bit down on her smile when he inhaled, long and deep. She couldn't imagine she smelled all that good, but when he leaned back to look at her his face told a different story.

"You're sure this is okay?" He asked, his warm fingers slipping the straps of her bra off her shoulders and down her arms.

George wanted to be annoyed that his lips weren't already warming her skin, but there was something sweet about him checking in, making sure with each acceleration that she still wanted to be here with him. She reached behind her and popped the clasp, her bra falling to the floor.

"Caleb, I have never been more sure of anything."

She reached for his belt and felt him watching as she tugged it open a bit aggressively. She couldn't help herself and wanted her needs to be just as clear as his, which was apparent by his sharp inhale as her fingers skimmed his waist and in the telltale swelling of his pants.

"Is this okay?" She asked him, teasing her fingers across the elastic of his briefs, and watched him swallow.

George was pretty sure that whatever she asked for Caleb would give. Knowing that made her want to protect him all the more. This man who showed no bravado, who didn't play games, who was genuinely happy to be with her would be so easy to use and hurt, and the idea of that happening knocked something loose in her chest.

George knew she was considered less-than to so many people she interacted with each day. The people she led on horseback. Patrons at the bar. She was a third-tier side character in their lives. And yet, here was a man who clearly had everything available to him. And he was acting like she was *more-than* he'd ever had, like she was the star.

She undid the button on her shorts and shimmied out of them. Caleb's desire flooded his features and George stood a little taller. His fingers trailed up her arms, over her shoulders to cup her neck and she tilted back to look up at him.

The girls back home, did they adore him the way he deserved? Did they appreciate his generosity, his kindness, or mistake it for naivete and abuse it? She wanted to be present, to be only in this singular moment with him, but she couldn't help but think of the Caleb he was outside of this vacation.

She hooked a finger at him and crawled backwards up the bed until she lay against the pillows. Her heart was pounding, but she wasn't nervous. How could she be with him taking such care.

Caleb stepped out of his pants and crawled up the bed to meet her. He stopped to kiss the inside of her knee, trailing kisses up her thigh. When he hovered over her underwear, his breath teasing her through the thin fabric, she wasn't cognizant enough to be embarrassed of the noises she was making. Otherwise, she'd have been mortified that someone was seeing a hem so threadbare the elastic band was peeking through. But this was not the kind of moment that made space for rational thought.

In one tender movement, he slipped her underwear off, locked eyes with her one more time, asking permission yet again, and then his mouth was on her, his tongue doing things she'd never had done to her. Lots of thoughts bloomed in the recesses of George's brain, but all she could do was say his name as he caressed and teased, and brought on waves that started in her belly and rolled outward to her toes.

What had she been doing with all the wrong guys before this? Seriously, what had any of that been? An absolute waste of time, that's what. My god, they'd never made her feel like *this*. The waves kept building and it was getting to be too much, like if he breathed on her she'd spin apart. But she didn't want it to stop. She felt greedy for wanting more. But she wanted him to have something too.

"Caleb, please," was all she had to say. And then he was crawling the length of her, reminding her stomach, her breasts, the valley between her collar bone and neck, that his mouth could be both sweet and savage.

Finally.

It unnerved George how much she wanted him. Her whole life she'd refused to allow herself to be tied to another person. But there was something about Caleb's weight pushing her into the bed that had her rethinking things.

He brushed a strand of hair from her face and she wondered what she must look like, completely unraveled. Wild, for sure. Because that's how she felt, like he had unspooled her on the bed like a tangled skein of yarn.

"How was that?" His brow furrowed like he was afraid of the answer.

"I'm never going to be okay ever again," she whispered, unable to lie to him, and the smile that split his face made her heart leap.

"Well then." Caleb started to descend her body but she stopped him, her legs wrapping around his hips.

"Do you have a condom?" She was almost afraid to ask. At this point, she was willing to give him as many strikes as he needed, but if the night ended right now, she might cry.

George shouldn't have worried. She may as well have yelled *Go!* for how quickly Caleb was off the bed and searching through his things. She laughed when he popped back up with a wrapper in hand.

Within moments his briefs were off, the condom was rolled on, and then he languidly crawled back up the length of her. This unexpected calm, unhurried nature, caught George completely by surprise. Every time she thought she understood what to expect, Caleb brought her up short.

The anticipation was almost too much. Where she expected him to be excited and rushing, he moved slowly, pausing to nip at her breast, then the other, before settling his mouth on her neck. He hovered over her, their breath mingling.

"Just checking in again."

She was going to scream if he took any longer, but true to form, he waited. She almost didn't want to speak, because doing so meant this would all be over soon, and she wanted this moment to stretch into a thousand more.

George pinned Caleb's hips between her knees and threw her body weight up and over until Caleb was the one beneath her, his eyes wide with surprise and a hefty helping of lust. She straddled him, hovering just out of reach.

"Just checking in." She smirked, and felt Caleb's laughter reverberate up through her legs.

"George, I've never been better."

Caleb's hands found George hips and he guided her onto him. She waited for that cocky grin so many guys had when in this position, but it never materialized. Instead, his eyes never left hers. Not when her breath hitched from the initial shock as her body stretched to accommodate him. Not when she started moving, her hands finding purchase behind her on his thighs. Only then did his eyes wander to the place where their bodies joined, blowing wide in wonder. But then just as quickly they were back on her face, his bottom lip caught between his teeth.

Caleb's hands hooked around her thighs, like he was watching a masterpiece take shape and didn't want to disturb the artist. Part of George wanted his hands on her hips, gripping her hard. Or his mouth at her breast, teasing her orgasm along. But she'd never had a moment like this, where the guy let her take control and decided what felt good.

George rocked faster.

It was only a moment later that Caleb took control, jerking upright and wrapping his arms around her like a vice. She wasn't sure what had happened to spark his take-charge attitude, but this position wasn't bad. Not at all. In fact, it was an even better angle. She tried to circle her hips—

Caleb's arms tightened, one hand coming up to cage her head in the crook of his neck as—*a voice.* She stilled and held her breath.

"Okay, so I found this river cruise thing on a blow-up raft, but we don't have to paddle or anything so it would be totally relaxing and—"

Footsteps neared the bed. Stopped. A sharp intake of breath and a screech.

George tried to imagine what was behind her, the look of surprise or horror. Part of her wanted to look, but Caleb's arms were like pythons, slowly squeezing the air out of her.

"SHIT! OHMYGOD-GROSS-GROSS-GROSS!"

The voice sprinted away and the door slammed shut. Then, from out in the hall, "I'll be in the kitchen when you're done! Can't wait to chat!"

The silence filled the room like a weighted blanket and they let out a collective, shaky sigh. George started to laugh. Well, as much as she could laugh in Caleb's tight hold. The absurdity continued from one moment to the next with him. Was it her? Was she attracting this type of energy? Or was it Caleb?

"I'm so sorry," he groaned as he let go of her head.

His arms remained wrapped around her, like he couldn't bear to let her go even after the most ridiculous turn of events, and though they were slicked with a sheen of sweat, it was heavenly.

"I'm guessing that was your sister?" George pressed her lips to Caleb's collarbone and tasted salt. She wished she could bottle up everything about him and take it home to Texas. Especially the feeling of his body wrapped protectively around her.

"I really don't want to talk about her while I'm still inside you."

Caleb's heart pounded against her breast and she leaned back to look at him. His eyes were closed, his brow furrowed, and she felt a tightness under her breastbone looking at him.

She trailed her thumb across Caleb's jaw. He seemed naive in some ways, but there were small moments he'd shown he was sure of himself. Like when he'd carried her into this room. George wanted more of those and less of him worrying about whether he was performing up to standards.

"Caleb," George said, and when he still didn't open his eyes, she moved to see what would happen.

Caleb inhaled sharply, his fingers clamping tightly to her hips to keep her still.

"I'm really trying to last here." His eyes opened and he wasn't unsure at all. He didn't seem afraid of leaving her wanting, of coming up short. His measured breaths spoke of a man who'd signed up for a marathon and had no intention of quitting early.

"You don't need to last. We've got all night." She responded by moving against him.

His arms loosened, relinquishing control, but his hands slid to her hips and held, helping her find the pace that worked for them both.

The thing was, the moment George had stepped over the threshold of Caleb's bedroom she'd surrendered to him. She hadn't even known she was doing it, but she felt it now as he handed the power back to her.

How was she going to walk away from this? She knew next to nothing about him and she'd already told him it wasn't going to become something. But still, she felt herself mourning the thing that never would be between them. Because whatever this was, it would never have a chance to root and grow.

They moved together, slowly at first, building back to the heat and urgency of moments earlier. As George came, she tipped her head back and let all the thoughts of the future fall out of her head.

Caleb's mouth fell to the hollow at the base of her neck, his breath pooling against her skin, his tongue swirling over a tender spot that only added to the pressure building inside her. It was the most vulnerable she'd ever allowed herself to be. This was everything she could give a person and she was giving it to someone she didn't even know. And as she tumbled over into her orgasm, her body tightening around him so that he came moments later, she was only vaguely aware of a ripple of fear coursing through her. Because there was so much about him she didn't know.

Then again, what did it matter when this wasn't going to go beyond the week.

"Fuck. I think I love you." Caleb groaned as he flopped back against the pillow.

And with those words, every molecule of air hightailed it out of George's lungs.

Caleb's love for Phil was something he understood. It had been written into his DNA while they grew side by side. But that was familial. Caleb had only told one other person he loved them. With the clarity of hindsight and three years of therapy, he could confidently say that relationship had not been love, but a twisted, unhealthy cocktail of manipulation poured over his low self-worth. Phil still couldn't utter Maddie's name without spitting.

But this feeling, whatever was happening inside his chest as George's wonderfully naked body lay tangled with his, was unknown to him. So, he'd called it the thing he assumed it must be, even though he knew it wasn't quite right.

Surely, George knew he didn't mean it. He'd just been caught up in the moment, his body flooded with an exhaustive surge of dopamine. And he couldn't be held accountable for what was said during orgasm.

But when she crawled away from him like he was contagious, sweat glistening along the valley of her spine, tiny fireworks of white exploded in Caleb's vision. He closed his eyes and focused on the warm sheets beneath his palms. When he reopened them, George was reclasping her bra. Panic shot through him and he jumped off the bed in search of his own underwear.

"I didn't mean it."

It felt like a good place to start, but George didn't look at him as she searched for her shirt. He tugged on his discarded briefs and barreled on, needing to fix this.

"I mean, I guess I did mean it, but figuratively speaking."

This made George pause, her shirt halted on her forearms. He couldn't not look at her perfect breasts. Moments ago, he'd had them in his mouth and now she was tucking them away, saying goodbye. It took an enormous amount of effort to tear his gaze away and look her in the eyes.

"George, that—what we just did… I mean, look at you. You're gorgeous."

He desperately wanted her to stay. But more than that, he didn't want to have ruined two nights in a row by doing the wrong thing.

"I…"

What he was about to say was probably going to ruin the moment, make her look at him with pity, and he hated the idea of that. But he wanted to be honest with her. How could something be built on a foundation other than truth?

"A couple years ago, I was in a relationship where sex was used as a weapon to make me feel bad about myself, and it's taken a long time to understand that isn't how it's supposed to be between two people."

George pulled her shirt over her head but gave Caleb her full attention, her face open and free of judgement. He took that as a hopeful sign she'd stay to at least hear him out.

"But, I never knew it could be like *this*. What we just did… Did you know it could be like that?"

He was afraid of the answer, but asked anyway. He didn't want to think about anyone else having the privilege of touching her, kissing her, making her eyes roll back like *he* had. Caleb braced for George's pity to flood the space between them, devouring whatever they'd started, but it never materialized.

She looked at Caleb for a long moment, unblinking, and he let her work it out in the silence between them. Then she blinked away and shook her head.

"That was new for me."

Caleb crossed to George and pulled her close. He'd never been on even ground with a woman before. When her arms reluctantly came around his waist, he let out a sigh.

"I don't know what's appropriate in this moment, but I felt like we could both use a hug."

Even though he didn't owe her the truth, Caleb felt better for having shared a small part of his. When he told Phil about this later, how he'd obliterated the best moment of his life by saying—

"Shit. My sister."

He let go of George and went in search of more clothes.

"Yeah, I should probably go."

Caleb found a pair of grey sweatpants just as George buttoned her shorts and scrounged for her keys. He tugged up the pants and pulled on a discarded t-shirt.

"I know this was weird. Phil busting in…" Caleb swallowed at the image of George riding him. "But please don't go. Let's go back to before I said what I said. Remember that amazing feeling? You said you're not working tomorrow. So, we can have that feeling again. And again. And again…"

George closed her eyes and shook her head, but the smile that snuck out had Caleb mirroring it. He knew that she was thinking the same thing he was. That she had a pretty good reason to stay.

"Okay, here's what we're going to do. We go let Phil grill us for fifteen minutes. I'll chug some coffee, we come back in here, and I make you come so hard you say you love me and we call it even. How 'bout that?"

The laugh that burst out of George was so unexpectedly loud that they were still smirking at each other when they entered the kitchen a minute later.

Phil was at the stove with her back to them, so Caleb took a seat on the other side of the island and pulled George between his legs. When she leaned into him, he wondered if she felt how fast his heart was beating. He felt wildly out of control.

If this thing wasn't love, it couldn't just be lust. Was there a name for the way his blood was pumping so hard he felt dizzy? For the way his skin was stretched tight while his bones turned to jelly. Maybe it was unnamable, this in-between thing. And anyway, he needed to focus on the task at hand.

Phil could be a lot, especially to new, unsuspecting people like George. He also figured Phil was probably furious with him, but she was the biggest love once you were welcomed into her space. He had absolutely no way of preparing for whatever was about to happen.

"I've got eggs over easy coming up."

When Phil finally turned, Caleb had his puppy dog eyes at their fullest, a pout waiting on standby. But apparently, she was too mad to be wooed with charms. She took one look at him, then at George, and spun back around to the fridge.

"What do you want on your toast?"

Caleb heard the catch in her voice, noticed the hand wipe at her eye while her back was still turned, and he wanted to reach out and hug her, apologize for lying. But George situated between his legs made that impossible.

"Butter and jam, please." He ping-ponged George's hips with his legs as the panic grew in his stomach.

"That sounds good," George added, holding onto his knees to still him. "Do you always have breakfast after midnight?" She whispered so only he could hear. He nuzzled a *no* into the soft part of her shoulder and felt her shiver.

Phil set the condiments on the island along with a plate stacked with toast.

"I want to apologize for before," she began, not meeting their eyes.

She was constant motion, turning back to the stove and retrieving two plates of eggs before they had a chance to react. She set the first plate in front of Caleb and George to share. The second she kept on her side of the island.

Caleb imagined her clasping her hands in front of her. *I'm sure you know why I asked you here,* she'd say, like they'd been called to the principal's office. Instead, throwing Caleb completely off-kilter, she faced George head-on, her eyes glassy.

"I didn't properly introduce myself, the circumstances being what they were. Again, I'm very sorry for that and it won't happen again. I'm Philippa, Caleb's sister. Obviously."

Caleb waited for the *you're in so much trouble* look, but she never even looked at him. She remained solely focused on George.

"I'm George."

"Nice to meet you, George. You know, it's funny. I could swear you look so familiar."

At this, Phil gave Caleb the pointed look he'd been expecting.

"I served you drinks at the Cowboy Bar," George replied, clearly oblivious to the morse code blinking between the twins.

"Oh, right! How funny."

Phil turned away from Caleb, finally giving him the chance to reach for a piece of toast.

"The bar." Phil turned on the charm for George, but Caleb could sense she very much wanted to smack him. It was fortunate he happened to be out of reach.

"I actually met Caleb last night. He was at the bar alone and very charming." George squeezed his knee.

"My brother, charming?" Phil looked like she'd swallowed a lemon while being told it was candy. She wasn't believing an ounce of this, but was too polite to correct a stranger.

"Yes, me. Charming."

Phil swallowed the figurative lemon and poked at her egg. "So, like I was saying before—"

"You mean when you barged into my room without knocking?"

Phil's front teeth clacked together. She hated when Caleb pointed out a gaffe because she liked to believe she was impervious to such things. She took a deep breath, forcing it out between her teeth and Caleb loved her for how she responded next.

"Again, I apologize."

He knew it was killing her to admit her wrongdoing. It made her shiver like her skin didn't quite fit, like it had shrunk a size in the dryer.

"Apology accepted." He'd let her wriggle on the hook long enough. He didn't get off on seeing people suffer, like other members of their family.

"So, as I started to say, I found a river raft thing, where we don't have to paddle or anything strenuous. We just sit back and relax and hopefully see a moose or something, or even just enjoy the view of the Tetons, and while you guys were—" Phil waved as if swatting a fly, "you know, I took the liberty of booking us tickets for tomorrow morning."

"That'll be so fun for you guys. I've heard it's beautiful."

George settled completely against Caleb, her body softening as the initial interrogation passed. She fit in his arms like she belonged there and it made something take flight in his stomach, like butterflies but bigger. She held a piece of toast over her shoulder for him to bite.

"For stamina," she whispered, and Caleb nearly choked, his body revving up at the idea.

"Oh, you're coming, George." Phil slathered her toast in butter and moved on to the jar of huckleberry jam. "Inclusivity is my middle name. And I've already seen you naked, so what's left to say?"

George stopped chewing and Caleb gave her a reassuring squeeze. He couldn't blame her. She didn't understand Phil yet. This was her essentially giving approval.

"I promise I didn't see anything," she hurried to assure George. "Just Caleb's mortified face, which will probably fuel my therapy sessions for the rest of the year. And I mean, if I had seen a boob—*which I didn't*—I'm sure yours are great, probably stunning." She teetered off dreamily for a second before recovering. "But I've got two of my own! And what's a boob between friends anyway?"

"Philippa."

Caleb was trying not to laugh at her bumbling embarrassment. He was kind of enjoying it for the rare occurrence that it was, but he needed to wrap this up before Phil had a total meltdown from whatever was going on in her head.

"Sorry. We leave at nine sharp and you should wear comfortable clothes and layers, the website said." The always prepared, always in charge Phil had returned.

"I didn't bring anything else." George looked down at her work clothes.

"Those shorts should be fine, but you can borrow one of my shirts."

"Are we good?" Caleb stood, wanting to get George back to his bedroom before she attempted to flee out the front door.

"Nine o'clock. Don't be late."

"Aye aye, Captain."

Caleb shuffled backwards, hands on Geroge's waist, but she reached for their dirty plate.

"We should clean up since Philippa cooked for us." She argued.

Caleb sent a silent plea to his sister which blissfully was received. She owed him.

"No, you guys go. I've got it. I'll leave the shirt outside the door and see you kids in the morning."

Thank you, Caleb mouthed and he could swear Phil's eyes took on a watery sheen. He needed to talk to her alone, explain why he'd kept this from her, and apologize. But she quickly turned away, plates in hand, at the same time George looked down at Caleb's pants and realized why he was trying to rush them out of the room.

"Come on, *big guy*," she said low, so only he could hear. "You've got some promises to deliver on."

She took his hand and led him back to bed.

12. GEORGE

George awoke slick with sweat. Summer in Jackson could get warm, especially in a poorly-ventilated over-the-garage apartment, but this wasn't that kind of hot. She knew she wasn't in her apartment because of how gently the mattress cradled her, supporting every pressure point. The reason she was overheating was the fiery man-body glued to her back, arm wrapped around her, hand cupping her breast in sleep.

At some point, Caleb must've pulled her over to his side of the bed, because an expanse of cool sheets lay before her. She rubbed her fingers over them, trying to absorb as much chill as possible to balance out his heat. But as hot as she was, she didn't dare move. There was something so lovely about waking wrapped in his safe arms.

It would be so easy to give in to this feeling. To convince Caleb to figure out a way for them to be together outside of his vacation bubble. She could be taken care of for the rest of her life. He would do it, she was sure. But that wasn't the way she wanted to live her life.

If she was going to love someone and spend her life with them, they'd have to meet on equal ground, so she wouldn't feel bound to that person. She didn't want to owe him. So, this feeling—of Caleb's broad chest pressed to her back, of this expensively-soft bed, of a full fridge waiting down the hall—it was all pretend. That's all it could be.

George's throat started to close, emotion tightening its grip. The backs of her eyes burned and Caleb's hold on her became too much. She was drowning in it, in him. She needed out. She clawed her way across the sheets until she was surrounded by cool linen and sucked in heaping gulps of air until her panicked heart slowed.

It was stupid to mourn something she'd never had in the first place. She was the one who'd said it couldn't become anything. And yet, here she was on the verge of tears. Because the truth was, she'd never dreamed about this kind of feeling between a man and woman, and now she knew it existed but it wasn't hers to keep.

She choked down emotion as Caleb melted against her once more, like a child snuggling his favorite stuffy, and his hand coming around to cover her heart—where it hurt the most right now. This precious man was going to go back home, fall in love with someone else, wake up each morning with them in his arms. George couldn't bear it. She was jealous of a person she'd never meet because they'd get to keep this sweet man.

Gently, she brought his hand to her lips and kissed his knuckles. How could two people share something as intimate as they had and then say goodbye? Life wasn't fair. George knew that all too well. If life was fair, her mother would still be alive and she wouldn't have to piecemeal work to get by.

Caleb exhaled dreamily behind her. It nearly broke her heart how much she wanted him. So, she stopped thinking. Thinking only made things more complicated and what she needed was for the rest of their time together to be easy and fun. She could deal with reality when their time was up.

George took Caleb's hand and trailed his fingers down the length of her sternum. She felt him stir, his breath tickling the back of her neck as he slowly crept towards consciousness. When his fingers came up against the hem of her underwear his breathing hitched and she knew he was fully awake, but he continued to let her lead.

His lips pressed gently to the back of her neck as she slid his hand beneath the hem, showing him how she wanted him to touch her. His heart beat its steady rhythm against her back, keeping pace with hers.

In the vacuum-like silence of the dark, his fingers followed her cues, and it hardly took any time at all, just the delicious come-hither flick of his finger inside her, his groan hot against her ear. The heel of his hand was almost too much when he held her firmly in place, and she pressed her face to the pillow to stifled her moan, embarrassed by how she'd used him. Because she had. And he'd let her.

She kept her face to the pillow even after her breathing had returned to normal. When he kissed her shoulder, she almost lost it. What was she doing to him? To herself? This wasn't fair to either of them.

"If that's the way you want me to say good morning, note taken." He whispered, the words tickling the hair at the base of her neck.

She could see him in her mind's eye, eyes still closed, that beautiful smile on his lips. She felt a tear slip out, wiped it away on the pillow. She needed to pull herself together.

"George, are you okay?"

How was it that even now he was more concerned about her?

She shook her head, not trusting her voice. If she opened her mouth, she didn't know what truths might slip out with Caleb's gentle coaxing.

She turned around in his arms and his hair was standing on end, that much she could make out in the dark. But she couldn't see whether he was smiling as she slid down beneath the covers. She could hear, however, the low groan he made as she took him in her hands and then into her mouth, and for a moment it made her forget that this was going to ruin them both.

"I got us a tee time tomorrow," John said from the other end of the family room sectional.

It was after dinner, the second they'd eaten altogether as a family, and the two of them were watching the Red Sox play back home at Fenway. Dara had retreated to another part of the house *in search of quiet*, and Phil was scrounging for dessert in the kitchen.

"You and me?"

Caleb checked his phone. He wasn't sure what he was expecting to find. It wasn't like George could text him since they hadn't exchanged numbers. Still, he wished one would magically come through to say she was on her way over, even though her shift wasn't supposed to end for another hour.

The air in the room took on a charge, like there was a thunderstorm on the horizon, and Caleb looked up from his phone to meet his father's hard stare. Caleb shrank into the plush cushions.

"God, you're obtuse."

John turned back to the game, scowl transferring from Caleb to the players on the tv screen.

Caleb couldn't pinpoint when he'd most disappointed his father. Was it three years ago when he started seeing his therapist? That had been at Phil's insistence, and in hindsight Caleb understood that it was necessary and helpful, but from his father's perspective he was admitting weakness. Why did he need someone else to help him work out his problems? You dealt with it yourself. Like a man.

No, it was probably four years ago, when he chose to pursue a minor in English instead of the favored pairing of Management with his

Business degree. Caleb's trust fund had paid for school, and that was set up by his maternal grandparents. So, he'd wrongly assumed that since it was his money he was allowed to choose instead of following his father's more-than-a-suggestion plan.

Or, going back further, maybe it was the summer before senior year of high school, when he'd told his parents he didn't want to play baseball anymore. Somewhere between Sophomore and Junior year it had taken a serious turn. Everyone started going to the gym after practice, stats became currency, and the promise of college ball and scouting seemed to take over every conversation. Caleb loved to play because he had natural skill and it was fun. But when it morphed into this suffocating cloud over everything it lost its shine and he started to dread it.

When he brought up the subject of leaving baseball, his father wouldn't hear it. Caleb would be squandering his ability and that just wasn't done. But in Caleb's mind, if he didn't love it anymore shouldn't he step back and let someone else who was more passionate, more in need of what a position on the team could mean for their future, take his spot?

His father couldn't let it go. Richards did not quit. Baseball became a major point of contention between them. Any slip, a bad grade, a microscopic crack in the façade, was somehow all related to Caleb wanting to quit baseball. Which was why Caleb was now halfway through his MBA when he'd been secretly dreaming of an MFA. Because he'd already failed at so many of his father's measures for being the perfect son and he was tired of the looks across the dinner table, of the way the air turned stormy any time he entered his childhood home.

Which made it all the more ironic that his father was telling him he'd secured a tee time for them while they were watching baseball. Especially considering Phil was the better golfer.

106

Caleb often wished that his father would just hand him notecards with his wishes explicitly drawn out. That way he'd know what to do, what to say, how to be the son his father wished him to be. He knew what his therapist would say. That there were two people in this relationship and he was putting all the blame on himself. But even knowing that, why couldn't he accept it as truth? Why did he continue to blame himself for his father's behavior?

The game cut to commercial and John groaned as he stood. Caleb knew he was dealing with chronic back pain, some old sports injury he never remembered the story of. Maybe playing another round of golf tomorrow wasn't the smartest move, but he didn't dare voice an opinion. It felt like things were better between them when Caleb didn't speak at all.

"Be ready at seven."

John didn't look at him, but put a hand on Phil's head as she entered.

"Goodnight."

She had two bowls of ice cream in her hands, one strawberry, one chocolate. She handed the chocolate to Caleb.

"Golfing tomorrow?"

Caleb nodded, keeping his eyes on the tv as the game resumed. The Sox weren't having a great season, and truth be told he wasn't really paying attention, but he didn't want Phil to get a good read on his thought.

When they'd each eaten half of their bowls of ice cream they swapped bowls. Their mother complained every time she saw them do this. They weren't children anymore. It wasn't hygienic to share food when the proper thing to do would be to have a scoop of chocolate and a scoop of strawberry in each bowl. But Caleb and Phil didn't mind sharing and they also didn't like their flavors melting together.

Caleb could feel Phil's nervous energy pulsing beside him. It wasn't like her to not say whatever was on her mind, and if she kept it in much longer, she'd explode. He finished his ice cream before turning to face her.

"On a scale of you-adore-me to you're-dead-to-me, how mad are you?" Caleb asked.

"Why would I be mad at you?"

Phil looked genuinely perplexed, which had Caleb second-guessing himself. If she wasn't mad, what was that last night in the kitchen? She'd been holding back tears and avoided looking at him.

"Because I didn't tell you about George. At the bar I let you think we didn't know each other, and I'm sorry. I just—I wasn't sure if it was a one-time thing or if it could maybe turn into something and if it was going to turn into something I didn't want to jinx it by getting ahead of myself. If I kept it in here—" he said, pointing to his chest, "then it could be real, even if it wasn't. Does that make any sense?"

They'd had a myriad of fights over the years, as siblings do. From Caleb breaking Phil's Barbie Dream Home (accidental) to Phil getting in the middle of Caleb's relationship with Maddie (purposeful). Some things they had easily mended themselves, others took therapy and time. But they always forgave each other (mostly, though the Barbie incident was still a point of contention two decades later even though Caleb had been trying to fix the elevator, not break it).

Phil might only be minutes older, but she fell naturally into the protector role. Which was why, when his previous relationship became toxic, she'd inserted herself. In truth, she'd already been in the middle since Maddie had been her friend to begin with. Caleb had ruined her friendship by getting involved with Maddie and in the end everyone lost. Phil had tried to hide how much she cried back then, but he knew her too well. And now, she was hiding it again and he hated himself for hurting her.

"You're an idiot." Phil buried her cold toes underneath his leg and rolled her eyes.

It was funny how the same sentiment could be directed at him twice in one night, but while the first utterance had made him shrink, this time he didn't because he knew Phil was saying it in jest.

"Phil, I know you were crying in the kitchen last night." He pulled her feet out from under his leg and held onto her ankles while she squirmed.

She threw a pillow to distract him from seeing her tears and he let go. Her face scrunched, fighting to tamp down the emotion, and Caleb sat very still letting her react how she needed to, even if it hurt to watch.

"I'm not mad," Phil began, wiping her face. "You really are an idiot sometimes."

Caleb threw the pillow back at her, with half the force. He just wanted her to stop crying.

"Do you know how hard everything with—" she closed her eyes and took a breath, "*Maddie* was for me?"

It had been years since Phil had said her former best friend's name, so Caleb didn't dare make a confirmation or denial.

"I brought her into our lives. It's my fault you guys even got together in the first place. And if I had known how she was treating you, I swear to God—"

Caleb squeezed her ankle. He was here, he was okay, better than ever, maybe. It was all in the past.

"None of that was your fault. And I'm good."

Phil bit her lip and nodded, the outburst held at bay.

"Last night… You were so happy, Cay. It was really nice to see. And that's why I got—I mean, I wouldn't say emotional, per se."

"Pretty sure you were crying. Just a little."

"Witness statements can be so unreliable though."

Now, Caleb tickled her until she squealed and kicked.

"I'm glad you're not mad at me."

"Am I mad that you let me go on and on about how George was ogling me and meanwhile your smug ass knew she'd be in your bed later. Dick move, brother."

Phil stretched her legs out to pinch Caleb with her claw-like toes and Caleb swatted her away. They really needed to talk about the past, because it was not Phil's fault, what had happened between him and Maddie, and she needed to know that. But right now didn't feel like the right time to open old wounds.

"So, George is great."

Caleb thought about that morning on the river. Phil and George had spent most of the float side by side on the bow of the raft in each other's confidence. Caleb hadn't minded. Watching them point out wildlife, clutching each other's arms when a young moose came to the river's edge with its mother and stomped around to let them know he was in charge. It made him happy to see them become friends. It also gave him time to think about what had happened earlier that morning.

He knew something was wrong when he woke up. Not at first, because what George was doing with his fingers was incredibly distracting. And he couldn't see anything with the curtains pulled across the sliders, but he could feel it in the air that something was off. It was one distraction followed by another incredible distraction, and by the time they were both spent and the curtains were drawn to the morning light, she seemed fine. Tired and tousled, sure. So maybe what he'd thought was crying was just another product of pleasure.

He'd seen nothing over the hours floating on the river. She'd been all smiles beside Phil. He knew it was a gross misuse of a vacation to spend it staring at a person when there were the Tetons and wildlife just off the port side, but he'd see them another time. Wyoming wasn't going anywhere. But George, would he ever see her again?

"She really is."

"Is she coming tonight?"

"At least once if I do my job right."

Caleb laughed when Phil gave him a look of utter disgust and stood, collecting her bowl and spoon.

"You going to bed?"

Caleb hadn't realized the game had ended. He turned off the television and stood, following Phil to the kitchen with his bowl.

"Nah, I think I'm going to email my therapist and see if I can schedule an appointment to unpack the traumatic events of the last twenty-four hours and work out a game plan for scrubbing my brain clean of the memory of *that*." She waved her hand in a circle meaning him.

Caleb turned on the hot water. There were dishes in the sink and he had a while before George would be done at the bar. Sitting in his bedroom wouldn't help the time pass any quicker.

"Goodnight."

"Night."

Caleb washed his family's dirty dishes, found a towel in a drawer and dried everything, and put it all away. He didn't know where everything belonged so it wasted a good chunk of time going through each cabinet to find each item's place. The kitchen was huge, meant for a team of chefs or a family of ten.

He wiped down the sink, the counter, the island, the breakfast table, and straightened the chairs.

He checked his phone.

George should have clocked out by now. It took twenty minutes to drive from the bar to the house, unless there was traffic in the form of an animal crossing.

He went to the front door, checked that it was unlocked. He went out and stood on the stoop, searching for headlights in the dark. The moon was out, along with a chorus of crickets. But there was no sign of George.

He sat on the top step and waited. It was surprisingly cold at night and he'd come out in jeans and a tee shirt. The stone beneath him bled its chill into the backs of his thighs and he kept shifting to stave off shivers. When an hour had passed, he stood.

She should have been here by now. Something had happened to George. And he had no way of knowing what.

Tucker's office was a small, converted cabin a short walk from the barn. It was the kind of cabin that looked a lot like the Lincoln Logs George had played with in kindergarten. Inside, the space was divided into two rooms plus a small bathroom. The bigger room was a super-organized storage room with helmets, blankets, coats for riders if there was inclement weather, saddle bags, bug spray, anything they could possibly need. The smaller room housed a typical office setup, a table with chairs, and a small fridge. It smelled like old leather and printer paper.

Tucker and George were enjoying a moment of peace before the afternoon rides. The rest of the crew had headed off the ranch for lunch. Tucker might have joined them, but he opted to eat in the office if George was there. She had a sneaky feeling he understood her financial situation, even if they'd never discussed it, because he always offered her half of whatever he had. She almost always declined. She could stretch a loaf of white bread, a jar of peanut butter, and a bag of apples beyond a week.

When she went grocery shopping, she'd watch the carts pass on the way to checkout, and she'd try to estimate that person's bill. Then she'd stand in line behind them and see how far off she was. The problem was that she only ever looked at the prices of items she knew were beneath her threshold. She had no idea what a wedge of Manchego cost, a pound of honey ham, or a bag of artichokes. But it was a fun game of distraction.

"Have you thought about next summer?"

Tucker was working on a fancy-bread sandwich stuffed with all the fixings. His wife worked at one of the restaurants in town and made even the simplest meal look gourmet. He had tiny pickles in one

Tupperware and a sliced peach with hot honey and basil in the other. If he offered a taste of that, George might be inclined to accept.

"Just trying to make it through this one."

Tucker nodded like he understood, but George figured he didn't, not really. The ranch made decent money. Even accounting for all the money spent maintaining the property and the horses, the ranch hosted weddings, family and company gatherings, hikes and outdoor excursions, and had a handful of rental properties on site. They were doing okay, of this George was sure. But she appreciated that he wanted her to feel like he was on her side and could relate to her struggle.

"You ever think about staying in Wyoming full-time?"

Tucker didn't look at her when he asked this. As someone who worked with horses, he was well-versed in how to approach an animal that might spook. He sat back, studying his lunch like it was the most fascinating thing, and it almost made her smile, knowing what he was doing.

"I've got my grandma to take care of. I don't think she'd handle the cold *and* ten feet of snow very well. And besides, it's not like I'd be able to afford anything even remotely close to town and you know my truck. If I had to drive over the pass in bad weather?"

Tucker nodded, mulling this over. She watched him swallow and set the second half of his sandwich down. He made a point of meeting her eyes and holding them for this next bit.

"Isla said there's a position opening up soon at the restaurant. I know you don't have kitchen experience, but if you wanted to try something like that, she knows how hard you work and said she'd be happy to put in a good word."

Tucker wasn't a particularly big man. He was soft-spoken and gentle with the horses, but he could smell an ounce of bullshit on a person and didn't suffer fools. He ran the riding side of the ranch with a kind, no-nonsense attitude and everyone who came through liked him. He and Isla didn't have kids of their own, but sometimes George imagined being their adopted daughter. She hated herself after having these thoughts because she'd had a mother who'd apparently loved her very much. She just didn't remember that.

At the end of every summer season, Tucker and Isla hosted a cookout for all the employees. The food was always outstanding, someone would bring a guitar around the fire, and there'd be whiskey, laughter, and sing-alongs late into the night. These were always George's favorite nights because she'd fall asleep with a stuffed-to-the-gills belly and her cheeks would hurt from smiling so much.

Grandma Jeane was her home, but sometimes Jackson felt like the place her heart was the fullest. Like she belonged here. So, part of her understood the weird, romanticized nostalgia many tourists had about the area, because on some level she had it too. Wyoming was so very special.

"Can I think on it?" George asked, to appease Tucker, because she hated the idea of disappointing him when he and Isla were sticking their necks out offering her a great opportunity. They cared about her and it made her cheeks warm, because she cared deeply for them. But she knew she couldn't uproot her grandmother from the place she'd lived her whole life and move her to a tiny valley in the shadow of the Tetons. She'd never agree to that and they wouldn't be able to afford it anyway.

George loved Jackson, but she couldn't see a day when it was actually her home. Not unless she won the lottery.

The first five holes had gone as expected. John had started off calm but serious, managing to hit a bogey on all but one hole. He belonged to a club in Brewster during the summer and another in Brookline for Fall and Spring. Some might consider him a serious golfer, which was why Caleb only ever played when he had no choice.

Golf, Caleb realized sometime during high school, was a mental game. And playing with his father was an additional game on top of that. There was no way Caleb could perform under that amount of pressure.

You've no one to blame but yourself, was John's famous saying. Because it was true, in golf you really were your own worst enemy. Maybe if Caleb had played on a foursome that didn't include his father, he'd come to enjoy it. As it was, he usually only agreed to join Phil at the driving range and very rarely play a round with her, so long as their father was absent.

When they teed off on the first hole it was chilly, hovering around fifty degrees. By the sixth hole it had warmed into the low seventies and Caleb had shrugged out of his zip-up. It felt nice to have the sun on him, though he was glad he was wearing a hat because there were no clouds.

The view of the Tetons from the sixth hole especially, though they had been a prominent backdrop for most of the course, kept drawing Caleb's attention. The size of the range made him feel miniscule. Staring up at the imposing peaks, everything down here on the valley floor seemed insignificant.

His mind had been on George since the moment he first saw her, but her unexplained absence last night was like a festering wound he couldn't stop poking. Because everything made him think of her. His sheets, his bathroom, sitting at the kitchen island. He swore he kept catching whiffs of her, like she'd just walked by. Away from the house felt like a safe place to not obsess, but here he was, tracing the jagged peaks with his eyes and *still* she was in his head.

John's ball careened off the grass, disappeared into a bunker, and he muttered a string of profanity. This hole was named Cutthroat for a reason. Normally, he would have made an underhand comment as Caleb teed off. And maybe he had, but Caleb was busy scrolling through all the potential reasons for George's absence last night, and didn't hear anything beyond the thoughts in his head.

The thing was, if Caleb didn't try to kill the ball he could play a decent game. And because Caleb was obsessing over George, he wasn't stressing over form and velocity, and in turn began hitting better than ever. Not that he even cared when his focus was elsewhere.

When he got back to the house, he was going to ask Phil for help. She was good at taking something and smoothing out the wrinkles to see a clear picture.

On the seventh hole, John grumbled over his clubs before finally teeing off. Caleb wondered how the perfectionist gene had completely bypassed him. Maybe it had gone straight to Phil in the womb, wrapping itself around her egg leaving none for him. Caleb didn't mind. It had to be exhausting hyper-fixating on every little aspect of every action.

It was on this hole that Caleb finally started paying attention, because in John's backswing something happened. His whole body seized like he'd stepped on a live wire, and the strangled noise he made sent goosebumps up Caleb's back.

"Are you okay?"

Caleb dropped his driver and crossed to his father, laying a hand on his shoulder. He knew better than to crowd his father's space, but surely if he was hurt the unspoken rules of play were void.

"I'm fucking fine." John shrugged him off and headed for the golf cart. It was clear from his stiff gait, some invisible string stretched too tight between hip and shoulder, that he wasn't fine. But what could Caleb do when his help wasn't wanted?

Caleb set up his shot and took a step back, pretending to rethink the line. Out of the corner of his eye he watched his father toss back pills, chasing them with the remnants of his Bloody Mary. It had to be that old injury he was always complaining about, the specifics of which Caleb had never concerned himself.

Caleb knew his relationship with his father wasn't normal. He'd watched his friend Toby interact with his father for years—a pal-like quality between them—and jealousy would slip under Caleb's skin like a hair-thin splinter. He knew better than to suggest going to urgent care, because the last voice his father ever wanted to hear was Caleb's.

So, Caleb went back to worrying about George and played the best game of his life. Until John called it after the ninth hole. No excuses or explanation given and none needed. Caleb was thrilled to have survived a round with his father and now he could deal with the real issue at hand.

There was a moment, as they pulled into the driveway, John no longer twisted in pain, that Caleb allowed worry about his father to seep in. He knew it was pointless, because he wasn't going to open up about what was going on. God forbid John Richards admit to anything less than perfection. But thankfully, the pain pills had kicked in and John slid out of the passenger seat leaving Caleb in one piece.

Maybe one day they'd be so distant from one another that he wouldn't give his father's well-being a second thought. But for now, he still worried about his parents' happiness and their health. Even if sometimes it felt like they never spared a moment to worry about him.

Maybe that was Caleb's greatest weakness. Caring even when he wasn't cared for. Or maybe it was his greatest strength.

Some days George had to admit that the Tetons were magical and today was one of those days. Sky so blue it looked fake. The craggy-sharp edges of the Tetons might've been painted. The wildflowers and tall grasses along the trail were straight out of a nature photographer's dream.

It was hot on the trail and she was thankful for the hat Tucker gifted her the first summer she'd worked here. It was old, the brown felt faded from weather and wear, but the form still mostly held. It kept her neck and face shaded, which was really all she could ask for.

It was too hot for long sleeves, her shirt glued down the length of her spine with sweat. But she wasn't about to go out on a ride without protection from the sun and the dust. So, nearing the end of the day, she unbuttoned this spent button-down and pulled a clean one on—white with little blue flowers. Hopefully it would mask how bad she smelled.

George was stepping out of the barn, fussing with whether to button all the way up or leave the top undone and pray for a breeze out on the trail, when Tucker approached from the direction of the office.

"Hey, I gave Allie that next group."

George felt herself sag. She needed that money. She'd treated Caleb and Phil to lunch at Nora's after the river float, in thanks since they'd paid for her ticket. She knew it was the right thing to do, but it had eaten up a chunk of her savings and she could make that back with a group ride.

Tucker must've seen her face fall because he held up a hand to hold her disappointment at bay.

"You have a private."

George had done plenty of private rides. Usually, it was a couple or a family who wanted to feel like the only people out on the trail. She found that most people came to Wyoming because of this romanticized imagining of the wilderness. It was like they longed for something they thought they understood, this shined-to-a-polish perception of country life, hearty farm-to-table meals, a comfortable home with an unbelievable view. It of course ignored the harsh realities of the exhausting labor and cost of life to create that fantasy.

Her first summer, one couple brought up the Oregon Trail while out on their ride. Apparently, it was a computer game back in the nineties that gave kids a pixelated sense of pioneering. They'd spent part of their ride cracking jokes about fording a river and dying from dysentery. George pretended to laugh along not getting the joke.

Last summer, she'd had a private with a man in his forties who was an author. He spent the entire two hours asking questions about the weather, the horses, if she'd ever come across a bear while out on the trail. He'd recorded the entire thing with her permission. She couldn't remember his name, but she wondered if he'd completed his book, if the words from her mouth had made it onto a page.

This afternoon, George hoped it was a couple vacationing here for the first time. That usually meant they'd keep the conversation to themselves. But then she spotted her charges and every thought high-tailed it out of her head.

Behind Tucker, Phil stepped into view donning a creamy wide-brim hat, bright blue feather tucked into the flashy leather band.

"Ahoy, friend!" She enveloped George in a hug. "Do you know how hard it was to figure out which ranch you work at? Worth it though. I mean, this view!"

George was so stunned she couldn't bring her arms up to return the hug. Phil let go and stepped back and there was Caleb. He was in sneakers, loose jeans that fit so perfectly George had a hard time swallowing, and a tee shirt that fit him like a gentle hug. And he was studying her so intently she had to look away.

George caught Tucker watching her in that way a person who only knows one side of you does when they're confronted with a piece of your life they weren't aware of. She felt like a bug pinned under glass and she brushed at her jeans so her hands had something to do.

"Twins," Phil said, pinching the brim of George's hat. "I had to, right? That and the boots. When in Wyoming!"

Phil kicked one foot up to show off shiny-new cowgirl boots. They were beautiful in the flashiest way, red hearts on white leather, embroidered from top to toe. In a week they would probably disappear into the shadows of a walk-in closet, to appear as if by magic in a decade, like a footnote from the past.

After the river float, after their wonderful morning together followed by lunch, George had headed off to work leaving Caleb with the impression they'd see each other later. But she'd intended it to be their goodbye. It was why she'd kissed him for as long as she had, his back pressed against the driver's side door. It wasn't until Phil coughed that she'd relented and let go of him.

He couldn't be here. Not with whatever was happening in her chest. Not when he consumed her every waking thought. It could only end with her feeling lonelier than before. She'd stood him up knowing he had no way of finding her. It was a clean break and they could both move on. But here he was, looking at her like she'd said no to playing with him while holding his favorite ball.

This was bad. Really, really bad.

Her stomach dipped, and for a second, she entertained the idea of feigning sickness. It wouldn't take much, she already felt like she might throw up if she had to spend the next two hours with him.

Unfortunately, she needed the money.

"I guess you know each other?" Tucker asked George, but Phil was the one to answer.

"We sure do. No one else could get my brother on a horse. But George is pretty special."

George felt herself shrink under Phil's praise. He mustn't have told her the truth of what she'd done. She imagined Phil turning feral on anyone who hurt her brother, but right now there was nothing but happiness on her face.

George had already disappointed one sibling and now she was about to disappoint the other? No, she couldn't do it.

"Why don't you take Sugar and Nez."

Tucker was looking for silent confirmation that George was okay. She wasn't, not by a longshot, but she nodded anyway.

Phil followed George to the post to pull the horses, but Caleb hung back. Was she sweating from the sun or the intensity of Caleb's gaze. *There's still time to back out*, the voice in her head offered, but Phil was already climbing atop Nez, her natural comfort in the saddle apparent.

"Which one is this?" Phil asked while adjusting her own stirrups. George should have known. Horses and money seemed to go hand in hand.

"That's Nez. She's a sweetheart but she will try and eat anything she can along the way, so just watch her."

George turned to adjust Sugar's stirrups to accommodate Caleb's long legs. She could feel him hovering closer now. If he got close enough that she could smell him, she'd be transported back to the safety of his arms, and then she'd be done for. She prayed for a strong breeze and got nothing more than a limp whisper of warm air across her face.

"Aww, Caleb, you have Sugar. That's so sweet." Phil laughed at her own joke, turned her horse's head, and walked a few steps away.

George silently cursed her for not staying put.

"I was worried something happened to you."

Caleb's breath brushed across George's neck and she shivered. Or maybe that was just what her body craved, because when she turned, he was steps away giving her the appropriate amount of space.

"Nope, I'm good."

She led Sugar over to the mounting block and held the horse still while Caleb stepped into one stirrup. She didn't trust herself to say anything more, couldn't even figure out how to explain without laying her jumbled feelings bare. She couldn't do that, wouldn't allow it.

"Yeah, I see that." Caleb hoisted himself into the saddle, reached out of her view to adjust his shoe in the far stirrup.

"I think they're too short," George said, giving Sugar a quick scratch.

"It's fine," he said, his voice dripping with hurt.

"It's not," George said, looking at him until he met her gaze. What she saw there made her eyes burn and she focused on the task in front of her.

Gently sliding Caleb's calf forward, she had enough room to adjust his stirrup. Instead of acknowledging how good he smelled, or how attractive he looked in the saddle, she focused on getting the stirrup length correct so she could put some distance between them.

She gripped the heel of his shoe and placed it back in the stirrup, and simultaneously they exhaled. Without looking him in the eye, she rounded to the other side and adjusted the other stirrup, inhaling through her mouth and keeping her eyes on the horse.

George could handle anger. That was easy to brush off. But Caleb wasn't angry, he was hurt. And that she couldn't stomach. She turned toward her own horse, face on fire. Hopefully they'd run into a moose and could cut the ride short so she had time to dig a hole and bury herself. But George knew she wasn't that lucky.

All summer she'd been riding Buttercup, whose name was deceiving. He was average in size among the herd, but always had to be leader of the pack. He could spook at the most absurd thing, a shrub minding its own business or the shadow of a hawk overhead. This was going to be a horrible combination—this horse, her nerves, Caleb's eyes on her for the next two hours. She could already feel Buttercup picking up on her energy beneath her.

The first hour passed slowly. George led and Phil followed close behind, peppering her with questions about her summers in Jackson, her horse experience, what wildlife she had spotted on the trail. When she ran out of questions, she moved on to telling stories of their previous family travel. George knew what she was doing, filling the void since Caleb was silent.

He sat at the back of their line, a few paces slower, in no rush to catch up. At first, George had been glad for it. For the first time in her life, she was uncomfortable in the saddle. She could feel his eyes boring holes into her back, but whenever she'd chance a look at a curve in the trail, he was staring across the valley or up at the mountains, his worn Red Sox hat shielding his eyes.

As sweat slipped down her back, George realized she was definitely losing her mind. She needed him to disappear from her life, and yet the fact that his eyes weren't glued to her felt like a punch to the gut.

The second hour, Phil sprinkled the silence with mundane commentary that received only grunts of affirmation from the back. When George couldn't stand it any longer, she threw out every bit of knowledge she could scrounge from her brain. Did they know the history of native tribes in the area? Did they know you could feed elk off the back of a sleigh in winter months? Had they soaked in the hot springs?

Meanwhile, she couldn't figure out why Caleb's silence bothered her so much. This was what she'd wanted, so why did it make the pain so acute?

George thought she heard the click of a camera and turned in the saddle to get a better look behind. It was late afternoon and the sun was moving towards the Tetons, on its slow surrender to the horizon. Phil was adjusting her hat and Caleb was looking off in the distance, expressionless. Sugar continued along underneath him on autopilot.

She'd officially lost her mind and was now hearing things.

When they arrived back at the ranch, George kept herself busy. She hated that she was on the verge of tears. Afterall, this was her doing. She rubbed her eye with the back of her hand and felt the gritty transference of dirt. At least now she could blame the tears on something actually being in her eye.

Phil had already dismounted by the time George tied Buttercup and came over to help.

"This feels complicated because you're sleeping with my brother," Phil said gently, stuffing a folded wad of cash into George's back pocket. Her smile was tight but her eyes held so much kindness it made George's throat tight. "This money is in no way related to that, because that would be gross and not representative of his feelings for you. This is simply in thanks for a wonderful afternoon under your guidance and expertise."

George didn't dare check how much was now in her pocket.

Phil said something to Caleb in passing—he was still in the saddle—and they watched her go. She was already in the car, engine rumbling to life, by the time Caleb had dismounted.

Phil put the car in reverse and George felt all her resolve jump in the back of that SUV and escape with her. She'd purposefully left Caleb behind. *Fuck.* There was no avoiding him now.

George took Sugar's reins from Caleb and led the horses to the fence. She wasn't sure what she was hoping for. That by the time she untacked and let them out in the pasture he'd give up and find another way home? Maybe. But she knew one thing for certain. Caleb wasn't a quitter.

He was seated on a hay bale when she returned from the tack room. The sun had slunk closer to the Tetons in that time and he worked the bill of his hat into an anxious fold. She hadn't seen this side of him. It wasn't just nervousness—she'd seen that the first time they undressed. This was something else.

"I keep going over it in my head and I—I don't know what I did wrong."

He stood, and the way he looked at her was too much. Like he was terrified of her answer, equally afraid of never knowing, and also a helping of ashamed at having done something wrong.

George turned away from him and tried to wrangle her emotions. If she'd known what was going to happen when he sat down at the bar, would she have made Kathleen serve him instead? If given the chance, would she erase the past few days?

"Please, George. Just tell me what I did so I can fix it."

His voice was surprisingly strong, like he knew he could fix the problem if given the chance. His hair stuck to his forehead in sweaty clumps and she desperately wanted to brush it back, frame his face with her hands. Two nights together and she was having to fight all her instincts.

"Why didn't you come over last night? Just tell me."

All George could do was shake her head.

"So, I did do something wrong." Caleb nodded once, her silence confirmation.

"Caleb," she started, but forced herself to take a breath instead of choking on the next words. If ever there was a moment to have nerves of steel, this was it. She straightened, tamped down all of her emotions with a branding iron until they melted down in her heels. "Remember a couple nights ago, when I said this can't be anything?"

The look on Caleb's face mirrored her own thoughts—if that was only two nights ago, why did it feel like a lifetime had passed in the span of a week?

"Sure."

"It started to feel like this was getting too big, like it was maybe becoming something."

"Yeah."

"But it can't. You know it can't."

"Okay."

"Stop it with the one-word answers!"

George hadn't meant to yell, but his calm was infuriating. She felt like she was about to jump out of her skin and he was just standing there, hat in his hands, giving her no pushback. She wanted him to get mad, to yell, to be as out of control as she felt.

Maybe she had it all wrong. Maybe he didn't feel the things she felt. Maybe she was making a big deal out of nothing and he was just upset at not getting laid. Except, what little she knew, Caleb wasn't that guy. Not at all.

"George, I'm afraid to say the wrong thing and you just get up and leave again."

So much for having control. The backs of her eyes were hot and screaming at her, so she slammed them shut and focused on breathing.

"Can we go somewhere and talk?" He asked, and the gentleness there felt like a thousand papercuts across her skin.

Where could they talk? There was her truck, but it was too hot to sit in, even with the windows down. There was her apartment, but it was cramped and stifling, and really all there was to sit on was the bed. They couldn't stay here with Tucker probably watching all of this play out from the office window.

"Come back to the house with me. We can sit on the patio. No one will bother us. Please. I just want you to talk to me."

George wondered. If she took off running for her truck, would he catch up to her before she got away? Probably, with legs as long as his.

"Fine," she heard herself saying. Her body was betraying her left and right.

"Do you have more to do or…?"

George looked around, remembering where she was. Her horses were out to pasture munching on grass.

"No, I'm done."

Caleb waited for George to lead the way, keeping a few paces behind. She knew he was giving her space, afraid of crowding her and pushing his luck, but the distance made everything feel off-kilter. She wanted his hand at the small of her back, reminding her he was there. She wanted him cupping her chin, tilting her head back as he crowded her vision and everything else disappeared.

She wanted him, there was no question. But as they got in the truck and pulled onto the road, she reminded herself that no matter what happened next, she could not have him. Talking wouldn't change anything. Their time together was up.

The night before, Caleb sat well past midnight in the kitchen, waiting. For a while, he convinced himself that George was just running late. Really, really late. But she'd still come. When it turned into a new day and she still hadn't pulled into the driveway, Caleb's mind traveled to dark places.

A bear was blocking the road.

She'd slipped on a spilled drink at the bar, fallen, and was now concussed.

She'd fallen asleep behind the wheel and was in a ditch. Maybe she'd made it to the hospital, but he wasn't in her phone so she couldn't call him.

Someone had hurt her as she left the bar.

That thought tore up his stomach and forced him outside to gulp the cool night air until the feeling passed. What if someone hurt George?

At some point, he considered getting in the car and driving around to see if he could find her, but it was so dark and was there even a hospital in Jackson? What would he say if he found it? He didn't know George's last name.

Eventually, he retreated to his room. He didn't have her number. There were millions of Georges on social media, though they all seemed to be men. He could have called the bar and asked what time she'd left, but he'd waited too long and they were closed.

It hadn't even occurred to him that she might be blowing him off. It wasn't until he stepped out of the office at the ranch after signing the waiver and saw her standing there that the answer slapped him in the face.

It had been Phil's idea to find where George worked, when she found Caleb staring off at nothing after golf. She'd called ranch after ranch until she found the right one and then they were out the door and on their way. But his internal turmoil was still too close to the surface, so she'd detoured for food, which led to her buying boots and a hat, and him crawling further inside himself with every passing minute.

But he shouldn't have wasted time worrying because George was fine. All extremities intact, no visible bruising. But the way she'd looked at him and then *wouldn't* look at him, told him everything. She'd ghosted him. He just didn't know what he'd done to deserve it.

Caleb hadn't actually wanted to go on a ride. It wasn't that he was scared of horses because he wasn't. He'd always been jealous that Phil got lessons growing up and he'd been told it wasn't what boys did. But what he'd really wanted was to talk to George. To find out what he'd done wrong and fix it. Instead, he'd been taken on a two-hour forced march with George's back to him the entire way.

Phil, perfect sister that she was, picked up the slack. She'd filled the silence with her usual bouts of positivity, but she was carrying the conversation for three, and it was more than even she could handle. By the end, she'd surrendered to the silence like George and Caleb had done from the start.

Caleb was apprehensive when Phil told him to find his own way home. It forced George to face him and that's all he wanted, but what if she still wouldn't talk to him? Then what?

When she agreed to come back to the house, Caleb felt immediate relief. They spent the entire car ride in silence, the windows down and the wind rushing in. Caleb was so focused on George being there with him that it never even crossed his mind they might run into his family. He was so absorbed in the mission to get her to his room that he jumped when Dara called out as they passed the kitchen.

"Dinner reservations at seven, so be ready at six-thirty. A dress shirt and slacks, please."

George, who had been following, took the hem of his shirt in her hands. He knew it was instinctual, keeping herself hidden in his shadow, but he didn't care. Her being that close was the push he needed to keep going.

"I can't tonight."

Caleb had never said no before. It wasn't that he was a dutiful child, behaving perfectly. He hadn't ever been perfect in his parents' eyes. But once in his life he was allowed to miss a dinner, of that he was sure. For all the times his father missed a meal because of a work-something. For all the times their nanny had eaten with them in place of their parents. He was allowed to miss this one dinner.

"I beg your pardon?" Dara stepped out of the kitchen to get a better look at him, and usually, that would snap him back in line, but not tonight.

Caleb knew the exact moment she realized he wasn't alone, even though George was hidden behind him.

"I have other plans tonight." He wasn't going to explain himself and give his mother time to build an argument. He turned, shielding George from her line of sight, and nudged her into motion.

Dara's silence followed them down the hall and he knew he'd pay for this dereliction of familial duty at some point, but that was a problem for future-Caleb. Right now, there was only George.

In his room, Caleb didn't even glance at the bed as they passed. He couldn't allow himself to think about her between his sheets, or he'd forget why she was here. For him, it wasn't just about the sex and he needed her to know that. So, it was straight to the slider and onto the patio.

Outside, it was a gorgeous evening, the sun inching over and behind the mountains. Every day here had been perfect. Then again, it could have been raining the entire trip and Caleb wouldn't have noticed. This woman was all that had mattered the past four days. She'd shaped his entire vacation.

George took a seat on one of the loungers, tucking her legs under her. Even though it was warm out, Caleb turned on the firepit in front of them. He took the other lounger, hating but accepting the distance between them. Maybe it was for the best that they were too far apart to touch—it was one less distraction.

Caleb was acutely aware of how musky he smelled post-horseback ride. If only he could have showered and had something to drink so his mouth wasn't dry, but he was afraid to leave her alone, considering she'd looked ready to run only a short while ago.

"I just realized the ranch's name," George mused, her face set towards the mountains.

"What?" Caleb couldn't take his eyes off her. He knew the view was outstanding, but given the choice he would rather watch her. Especially after the threat of never seeing her again.

"Golden Hour…"

Her eyes flitted away from him.

He had so much he wanted to ask, wanted to say, but he felt like the best thing to do would be to listen. George was quiet for a long time and it took every ounce of his self-control not to break the silence as it stretched and settled between them.

"I live with my Grandma Jeane in the top hat part of Texas." George started, drawing an imaginary hat on her head. "I come up here to work from May to October every year and this summer I've been renting this room above a garage that's… it's not great. Which was why I was so desperate to use your shower the first night."

Caleb leaned back against the lounger, never taking his eyes off her. It felt like story hour when he was little and he was hypnotized by the idea of Texas George. What did she look like in her day to day back home? What was Grandma Jeane like? Was she a good cook?

"I don't know my dad. My mom got pregnant right out of high school and then a few years later she died in a car accident. So, it's just been my grandma and me. And it's fine. It's good. She's worked really hard to take care of me, but now I kind of take care of her, and she has to have hip surgery in a couple months so I'll help out when that happens. But mostly, I work on our friend's ranch doing whatever needs doing with the cattle, with the horses, anything. And the weird part is, when I'm here in the summer, even though I'm working two jobs, it almost feels like a vacation. Not that I've ever been on one. Definitely not like this."

She looked around the patio and back at the house with wide eyes, and Caleb felt himself shrink under the realization of how grotesque this all must seem. Like his family was content to piss away money while she dreamed of a decent shower.

For a while George focused on the view and Caleb turned to see what was so captivating. The Tetons, sharp as ever, were lit behind by the sun, so that the eastern face was a shadowy blue with golden fingers reaching out from behind its peaks. Caleb didn't believe in God, but he could almost be convinced that there was something out there beyond the science of water particles and light creating the sheer beauty before them.

"I don't think my parents like me very much," he admitted. He could feel George's eyes on him, but he kept his gaze on the glowing sky, burning from pink down to orange. "My father… every decision I make is the wrong one. And my mother would probably tell you, after two or three Cabs, that Phil and I ruined her body and have been nothing but headache after headache for all twenty-two years we've been alive."

"I'm sure that's not true."

He turned away from the mountains so George could see in his eyes that he wasn't being flippant and wasn't trying to one-up her. In this soft evening light, they were sharing honest pieces of themselves and he wanted her to know who he was. Or at least how he saw himself.

"What do you dream of? For the future." Caleb looked back at the sky. Each honest piece of themselves needed gentle handling, not the spotlight of direct eye contact, and he desperately wanted to know everything there was to know about George.

"Nothing."

Caleb blinked over at her, but she was focused on the trees just beyond the edges of the manicured yard. The shadows beneath their boughs had started to deepen and it was no longer a hot day, but transitioning towards a cool night.

"But you want to be onstage with a band, right? Have a song on the radio?"

George laughed, but it wasn't the kind of laughter that reached her eyes. It was an empty, knee-jerk reaction that veered awfully close to a sob.

"Caleb, if I start dreaming, if I let myself *think* about a life outside of my daily reality, then I will never be okay with the life I have. I'll lose my mind thinking about everything I'll never get to experience. I get up before the sun and am dead-tired by the time I crawl into bed long after dark. Daydreaming is a luxury I simply cannot afford."

Caleb sat up. He'd hit a sore spot, the kind that might bruise if he pushed any further. But he couldn't seem to stop.

"But your voice, George. What you did on the stage the other night? That was amazing. I've never heard anything like that. You had me under your spell."

He watched a tear slip down her cheek and his stomach dropped. She grimaced, trying to turn it into a smile, but failed. So, he backed off, facing the Tetons to give her space to feel her feelings.

"I don't have the means or connections to make that happen. But it's really nice to hear."

Caleb didn't want to let this go, because he was certain something would happen for her if she tried. She had undeniable talent, and granted, he didn't know shit about the music industry, but a voice like hers had to count for something. She had to try. But watching her wipe the tears away, he knew he should let it go.

"If there's anything I can do…"

She turned and smiled at him, and though her eyes were still glassy with more unshed tears, this smile had warmth behind it. *Thank you*, she mouthed.

"You know, I've never been to Texas." He knew he should tread lightly, but he couldn't seem to stop. He wanted to tell her every single thought in his head, even the silly ones. No one—well, besides Phil and Toby—had ever really cared what he had to say. But George did.

"No?"

He could feel her watching him as he traced the Tetons with his finger.

"Have you ever been to Boston?" All he wanted was to keep this conversation going. But more than that, he was hoping there was a way through. To extend whatever this was beyond the week.

"To get back to Texas, I go through Colorado, then either a tiny bit of New Mexico or Oklahoma, and then I'm home," George said, drawing a map in the sky with her fingers. "But those are the only states I've ever been to."

Caleb wondered what that drive was like. Were the highways treacherous? How did she stay awake when the landscape stretched infinitely? Did she feel safe when she stopped for gas? He'd never worried about another person like this. Well, Phil, of course. But that was because she was an extension of himself.

His worry snowballed into an idea.

"Did you know that the term "sitting shotgun" comes from the days of covered wagons traveling great distances alone and how one person handled the reins and the other sat with a shotgun at the ready beside—"

George shook her head, understanding where he was heading with this, but begging him to stop. The words dried up on Caleb's tongue and they watched the sky in silence. It was like the painter had added water, red bleeding to pink. Pale blue-purples started creeping up one side of the sky as the sun's rays disappeared beyond the other.

"George, I really like you."

Caleb didn't dare look at her to see how the words landed. He was probably scaring her, but he needed her to know, even if she took them and ran.

"I really like you, too."

He turned and she was watching him, a small smile peeking out. He wanted to reach for her, get up and pull her inside, draw the curtains, and show her just how much he liked her. But for now, this was enough.

"But this isn't going to become something, Caleb."

"Why not?" He needed to hear her reasoning so he could figure out every way to pull it apart, unravel it so they could find a way to build this into something strong enough to last beyond tomorrow.

"We live drastically different lives." She scoffed, waving around them to encompass everything—the house, the multi-million-dollar view, him. "And in different time zones."

George held his gaze to make sure he understood what she was saying, and it hurt, that she felt their differences were too much to overcome. Long distance would be hard, sure, but wasn't it worth trying? He thought it was.

"I can't change where I come from just as much as you can't change where you come from. And we shouldn't care about that anyway, because the important thing is that you like me, George."

She blinked at him, but there was no give in her expression. If he was going to get her to see this from his perspective, he'd have to go about it a different way.

"What if," Caleb started and quirked an eyebrow when George rolled her eyes, "we play pretend."

"You've lost me."

The way she was looking at him though, Caleb was pretty sure he hadn't.

"If this is our last night together, let's pretend…" He was pushing it, for sure. But the curve of her shoulders had softened while sitting here, and the light had returned to her eyes. He had a feeling that as absurd as this next part was going to sound, she just might play along. "…it's our wedding night."

George blinked, and then started laughing. "What? Caleb, that's…"

Caleb tucked his hands behind his head and looked up at the sky like he didn't have a care in the world. The heat from the firepit warmed him as the shadows grew and he studied the flames.

Surprisingly, George hadn't turned and run. That was something. He could feel her watching him, though. Waiting to see what he'd do next.

"It's a few years down the road. We're in our early thirties now."

"Right, sure," she scoffed, disbelief shading around her words.

Caleb bit down on his smile so she wouldn't see how much her faux agreement thrilled him.

"It's early fall and we're at a seaside resort."

"Absolutely not."

Caleb's head snapped in her direction, but he held his tongue.

"We meet here, beside those mountains, and you want to go one-eighty on what brought us together?" George scoffed.

"My sincerest apologies. We're at a… barn… in the woods somewhere." He paused at each word waiting for approval. He didn't get it, but she didn't disagree, either.

George turned on her side so she could keep her eyes on this story and Caleb tried not to laugh. He couldn't believe she hadn't run. So, he kept going.

"I'm in a navy suit, white shirt, matching navy tie, handsome as ever—"

"So handsome," she chimed in and Caleb's heart swelled.

"And you're wearing…"

George rolled onto her back. She took a deep breath and Caleb wondered if he'd finally gone too far. He'd caught Phil looking through a bridal magazine a few years back. When he'd asked her about it, she'd admitted she wanted to be prepared for when the time came. So, he knew that some girls took the whole wedding planning seriously. But he couldn't tell if George was that type, considering she'd just insisted she didn't daydream.

"I scour second-hand stores and find a simple dress, off-white, mid-length, capped sleeves, lace trim. Phil lets me wear the cowboy boots she wore today, as my something borrowed."

The clarity of the image she painted sucked the air out of Caleb's lungs and he thought about running to grab Phil's boots. Because she didn't need them as much as George did. But he didn't want to break the spell by leaving the patio.

"I can't wait to see it."

Caleb's arms were going numb behind his head, so he shook them out and clasped his hands on his stomach. He could see future-George so perfectly, her hair pulled back with little bits coming loose in the evening breeze. He'd make sure to tuck them behind her ear before kissing her.

"Vows would have to be our own. None of that recite after me, generic stuff." She watched him as she said this and Caleb had the sudden realization that she might be seeing how far she could push *him*. Well, if that was the case, she was in for it.

"I'll go first," he kept his hands clasped on his stomach to hide how nervous he'd suddenly become. *This is just pretend*, he reminded himself. But it somehow felt important he get it right. "I, Caleb Theodore Browning Richards—"

"Of course you have four names." George laughed, and Caleb pretended to be hurt.

"I, *Caleb Theodore Browning Richards*," he said again, this time loud enough to drown out her laughter, "promise to learn to cook for you so you'll never go hungry."

George stilled and he watched her swallow like there was something stuck in her throat.

"I promise to never be the cause of your tears. But if you do get hurt, I promise to be by your side through it all." He didn't ever want to make her cry. This was starting to feel serious and he hadn't meant to do that, so he changed tactics. "I promise to never let a day go by without bestowing upon you a mind-blowing, earth-shattering orgasm. The stuff of legend."

She started to interject and he pinned her with a sharp look.

"These are my vows, George. Wait until it's your turn."

She shook her head, but the smile she gave him was all he could want in this moment. It gave him the room to continue.

"I promise to support you on your path to becoming a celebrated musician. I will drive the tour bus and work the merch table, and I will always be your biggest fan."

He watched her eyes go glassy. He kept steering down the serious path and he hadn't meant to, but he couldn't seem to stop.

"I promise to share in the scooping of the litter box—"

"Wait-wait, when did we get a cat?" She asked incredulously, sitting up. She untucked her legs and leaned towards him.

"*And* a dog. If you would stop being so impatient and let me finish, I was going to say I will also share in the walking of our dog because it will be an equal partnership. There, I've said it all."

Caleb sat up and faced her, his feet on the ground, and leaned back on his hands. He didn't want to crowd her. He'd said a lot, only partly joking, and at any time she could call it, tell him he'd gone too far, get up and leave.

George looked back at the sliders and his palms started to sweat. She was definitely planning her getaway. He couldn't just leave it at them opening up to each other. He had to push it into the land of unrealistic expectation, pour a foundation, and build the house. He wouldn't blame her if she fled.

"I need a minute." George stood and walked inside.

Caleb slunk back against the lounger. He had no one to blame but himself. He had to go all in and ruin it. Maybe his father was right about him.

Caleb watched the flames at his feet dance brighter and zoned out. Tomorrow he'd get on a plane and head east, back to his shared condo with Phil, his mind-numbing MBA classes, his empty bed. He didn't expect any of that to change, but he also wasn't sure how to step back in those shoes after this.

How did people meet a stranger on vacation, start to feel things, and then reinsert themselves back into their old life? He didn't feel like the same Caleb from five days ago. He couldn't say how, but he knew he had changed, and he wasn't sure what he wanted, just that he wanted something to be different when he got home.

He didn't realize George was back on the patio until she was standing beside him. He startled, sat up, and swung his legs over to look up at her. She was wrapped in a blanket. Actually, no, it was the top sheet from his bed. It was wrapped around her like a dress and tucked beneath her armpits, leaving her shoulders bare.

"Pretend it's the dress I described."

Her voice was quiet against the oncoming chill of evening, but she wasn't tentative or nervous. She was sure of herself, even as she asked him to imagine this fantasy a little longer, and it drew a gigantic shiver up his spine.

"Okay, yeah. I see it."

George studied him. Her voice was soft when she started again, as if these next words needed to be handled with care.

"I, George Rose Townsend, promise to eat anything you make, no matter how bad it may be, because I appreciate the thought and time put into it."

She swallowed with some effort and Caleb realized his own hands were shaking. He wanted to reach out and take her hand, rub his thumb across the back of it to reassure them both, but he stayed where he was and nodded her on, afraid to break the spell.

"I promise to graciously and humbly accept all orgasms given—"

Caleb started to interject, but she held up a finger.

"You already had your turn."

She cleared her throat and continued.

"I promise to support you in whatever dream you have, no matter how late in life. If you decide at fifty that your passion is knitting, I will buy you all the yarn you could possibly want and proudly wear your mittens even if they are missing thumbs. I promise to share in your joy and your sorrow, because it will also be mine. I'd like to also make an amendment to your vows and say I will need to sleep on the idea of a cat and a dog. That feels like a lot of work right now and I'm not sure we're ready for that."

"This is seven to ten years down the road, remember." He added helpfully, resting his elbows on his knees. Her pull on him was getting to be too much. He just wanted to touch her, brush her hair away from her neck, kiss her forehead in thanks for playing along in this ridiculous game of pretend.

"We can revisit it then." Her face changed, like she'd forgotten this wasn't real and was mentally marking the calendar. "Till death do us part," she said softly as an afterthought.

"Well, dear wife. I believe this is the part where we kiss to make it official."

George stepped between his legs and Caleb's heart banged against his ribs. She swept the sheet out and his legs disappeared beneath the mountain of linen as she climbed onto his lap. She sat back on his knees and pinned him with a very serious look.

"You may now kiss the bride," she whispered.

Just breathe.

He worked his hands under the edge of the sheet until he found her knees. Her eyes took on a mischievous glint as his hands slid up bare legs. They paused at her hips and realization dawned.

"George, are you naked under this?"

He'd already seen her body, had tasted every inch of her skin, and yet he felt himself blushing at the thought of her sitting atop him in nothing but a sheet.

She opened it to welcome him into the cocoon, and he wanted to hold her arms wide and devour every inch of her with his eyes, but he let the circle close with him inside. He had a duty to perform first, an important one, so he hooked his thumbs on her hips while his hands cupped her bottom and pulled her closer.

"You're missing the sunset."

"This view is better."

He didn't dare blink for fear of missing something. The smell of cut grass, of sweat, of *George*. The weight of her warm body in his hands. The crinkles at the corners of her eyes made darker by smudges of dirt. He considered wiping them but he didn't want to alter the memory. George was perfect as is.

"This is all pretend," she whispered, her breath minty and sweet.

"If you say so," he whispered back, and brushed his nose against hers.

Her face went out of focus and when their lips met it was with restraint, Caleb trying to hold back from saying the words that weren't quite right but were all he had. He'd already said them once by accident, so he knew she wouldn't believe him this time. But they almost felt right, like putting on a piece of clothing a size too big but knowing you will grow into it.

George's arms wrapped around his neck like she was trying to tattoo his body onto hers, and the sheet started to fall. It pooled around their waists and Caleb pulled it back up over her shoulders so she wouldn't get cold.

He still couldn't believe it, even with the weight of her in his lap, that this person was here, making absurd promises, with him. He kissed her shoulder, her chin, the dip at the base of her neck. He tasted the salt of her sweat and remembered how dirty they both were. He'd grown so quickly accustomed to her scent that he no longer noticed the horse smell intertwined. It was simply her.

George's lips parted, waiting to see where he'd taste next, but Caleb had another idea.

"Thoughts on shower versus bath?" He nipped at her chin to carry home his meaning.

"Which will last longer?" George shifted in his lap pressing her bare skin against him.

This was single-handedly the most important and sexiest moment of his life. God, he wanted it to last forever.

She kissed his cheek, his nose, the furrowed ridges between his brows, while her hands wound their way into his hair at the base of his neck. She held him in place so that he was forced to look directly in her eyes.

"Do you have any idea what you do to me?" She asked him.

He knew he smelled awful, probably had a thin layer of dirt everywhere, but George didn't seem to notice. He shifted and George climbed off his lap, gathering the sheet around her and making space for him to stand.

He looked down at her, hands clutching the sheet closed at her heart, and realized he hadn't ever felt this much at peace. Standing beside George made all the noise go away. His thoughts stilled, his heart beat a regular beat. He inhaled cool, clean air and felt whole. That voice in his head that so often mirrored his father was silent for once and Caleb felt strong. So strong in fact, that he scooped George into his arms and carried her over the threshold into his room saying, "It's the same thing you do to me, *wife*."

18. GEORGE

George woke well before six. They hadn't thought to close the curtains and the sky was already blushing. The mountains were alive with color but the grass beyond the sliders was bathed in shadow still. She had a little time.

Caleb's body was draped over her in place of the comforter, which was on the floor at the foot of the bed. His hand cupped her breast and she wondered for a fleeting moment what he'd hold onto tomorrow when he went back to sleeping alone.

She needed to leave, to grab clean clothes back at her place before heading to the ranch, but she couldn't get her body to move. Everything about last night had been weird but also dreamily wonderful. Leaving without saying goodbye felt like the shittiest possible conclusion to this week, but there was no other way to do it.

If she woke Caleb to say goodbye, he'd beg her to stay, ask for her number, distract her with his perfect mouth. She couldn't afford to let that happen. For the sake of her job, but also her sanity.

After what had unfolded on the patio, then in the shower, they'd finally made it onto the bed exhausted and completely spent. *I don't want to say goodbye,* Caleb had whispered sleepily, his mouth muffled against her neck. George hadn't responded, pretending she was already asleep. But she'd lain there, her mind spinning as she listened to him fall asleep.

She shouldn't have agreed to come back to the house. She shouldn't have even agreed to talk. But when he looked at her with those eyes of his, she couldn't say no. She'd rebuilt her walls overnight and in one look he'd blown them to bits. And then she'd let him talk her into pretending to get married!

She'd lost her damn mind. That was the only explanation. Caleb was the Kool-Aid and she'd drunk all of it.

Now, she lifted his hand from her breast, resting it against her stomach so she could scoot onto her back and slide slowly towards the edge of the bed. Removing him from her body would be a slow process if she didn't want to wake him. Beyond the physical, it would probably take years to remove the memory of his touch. And then there was his voice whispering promises into the early morning hours.

Caleb crumpled slowly onto his stomach without her body to wrap around, but he didn't wake and she was thankful for that. She gently let go of his hand and stood, looking down at him.

She'd been wrong about him that first night. He wasn't awkward and newly minted and unsure of himself. He'd shown her he thought everything through, weighing all the outcomes before acting. He was kind and stronger than he realized. And most surprising of all, and what made her reach back down and brush a lock of hair away from his beautiful face, he believed in little old her.

The things he had promised her—she would tuck those away and pull them out anytime she felt low. How had he known exactly what to say to unspool every bad thought, every worry she had? My God, for a moment there, right before they'd sealed it with a kiss, she'd almost said something she shouldn't. The kind of thing you couldn't take back. Words that were paper thin for some, but for her, were kept locked away for someday.

She'd never said those words, except to her grandmother. She'd never even thought them in the presence of a man before. And yet, bare-ass naked, wrapped in a sheet on Caleb's lap, she'd felt the words crawl up her chest and hover on her tongue. It had taken everything in her to swallow them back down.

And now here she was, attempting yet another quiet escape.

She was not going to leave her number. She couldn't. Caleb was a distraction when he was in front of her, but with distance he would only grow in size until he blocked out the sun. She'd lose focus on her responsibilities if she was constantly hoping for a text or a call. But she also realized, with a sharp tightness in her chest, that she couldn't allow herself to sneak out without leaving behind something. This went against everything she thought she needed, but the idea of never hearing from Caleb made her feel dizzy, like the earth was caving in.

George tiptoed around the bed until she found Caleb's phone on the floor by his pants. She opened a new contact and saved her email. She'd leave it up to chance. If he didn't find it then she'd be heartbroken, but maybe that was the way it was supposed to go.

She dressed quietly in the clothes from the day before. It felt sacrilege, covering her body in dirty clothes when Caleb had spent so much time scrubbing her clean. As she buttoned her jeans, she had a wicked thought, suddenly desperate for a physical reminder of him. If only to look back and know this hadn't been a fever dream. It had actually happened to her.

She slowly pulled the closet open, begging the doors not to squeak. She grabbed the closest item off the shelf, balled it up, and tiptoed to the door. She looked back, committing the outline of his long limbs, his broad shoulders, that wild mane of hair to memory. She wanted to drop her things, race back to bed, crawl under him, and tattoo a million kisses on his skin.

But it was time to go.

Maybe they'd see each other again. Probably not.

She'd never allowed herself to dream before last night. But now that she'd opened the door, she found she wanted a couple of things. And maybe… she might even try her darndest to get them.

PRE-CHORUS.

date: Oct 20, 2016, 9:04 PM
from: calebtbrowningrichards@snailmail.com
to: g.rosetownsend@snailmail.com
subject: Hi

My Dearest George,
ALL THIS TIME YOU'VE BEEN IN MY PHONE??? PLEASE TELL
ME YOU HAVEN'T MET SOMEONE.
How is your grandmother? Has she had her surgery?
Phil is hovering like a creep in the doorway and says: "Tell her hi
and if she comes to visit I'll give her my boots since I don't wear
them and she'd look good in them." You should come to Boston. If
only for the boots. Since they'll complete *the outfit*.
I miss you. I think about you all the time. I wonder what you're
doing, if it's raining or sunny where you are, if you're daydreaming
about all the orgasms I gave you…
I know we didn't discuss this, but considering your aversion to my
two last names it seems like the obvious choice…
Yours,
Caleb Townsend

date: Oct 27, 2016, 6:19 PM
from: g.rosetownsend@snailmail.com
to: calebtbrowningrichards@snailmail.com
subject: Re: Hi

Caleb,
So, bad news. I met this guy awhile back and I didn't want to admit
it, but he's pretty special. But then he waited three months to
contact me, so I don't know if it's going to work out.
Grandma Jeane is really good. Her hip surgery went well and she
starts back at work in a couple weeks.
Phil's offer is very tempting, but it's hard to take time off when you
work on a ranch. And I've never been on a plane.

These orgasms you mentioned… can't quite remember them. Are you sure that was with me?
Potentially still yours unless you wait another three months to respond,
George

date: Oct 27, 2016, 8:30 PM
from: calebtbrowningrichards@snailmail.com
to: g.rosetownsend@snailmail.com
subject: Re: Hi

I'm really glad Grandma Jeane is doing well. I know she means the world to you.
Now, let's get down to brass tacks. You haven't forgotten the orgasms and you think about me every night when you're in bed. I know this because you're my last thought before falling asleep.
If the promise of orgasms and boots aren't enough to get you on a plane, tell me what is.
If you ever want to talk or text, my number is 617.555.0109. Forget about time zones. If you have a free moment and it's 4am, I will answer.
Yours,
C

date: Nov 19, 2016, 10:29 AM
from: calebtbrowningrichards@snailmail.com
to: g.rosetownsend@snailmail.com
subject: Re: Hi

I know you said back in WY this couldn't become anything and I want to respect your boundaries, but you put your info in my phone. You didn't respond to my last email or call or text, so I'm wondering if I should stop or if you're just busy. Please just be busy.
Yours,
C

date: Dec 25, 2016, 12:27 PM
from: g.rosetownsend@snailmail.com

to: calebtbrowningrichards@snailmail.com
subject: Re: Hi

Caleb,
Merry Christmas.
I just got home from work. Cows don't feed themselves, no matter what day it is. But I have the rest of today off and my grandma is making her buffalo chicken casserole.
I told you, I don't have space in my day to think about you. And yet here I am, thinking about you. I'll be in the middle of something and wonder how I got there, because I was too busy thinking about how good you smell or the way you look at me. I'm pretty sure I fed one pasture twice yesterday because I was thinking about your hands. I don't know how to BE anymore.
I want to tell you it's over and not to contact me. The idea of hearing your voice is too much. But then I think about never hearing from you again and can't stand that either. So I don't know what to do.
George
PS. I'm sorry this is the worst email ever. I really wish you the most magical Christmas. Tell Phil I hope Santa brought her everything she asked for. And you too.

date: Dec 25, 2016, 4:35 PM
from: calebtbrowningrichards@snailmail.com
to: g.rosetownsend@snailmail.com
subject: Re: Hi

I want you to be happy. I don't care about any of the gifts under the tree. I just need to know you're smiling wherever you are. If thinking about me upsets you, that's the last thing I want. Just tell me what you want to do and I'll follow your lead.
Wishing you and Grandma Jeane a very merry Christmas.
Yours,
C

date: Dec 26, 2016, 6:02 PM
from: g.rosetownsend@snailmail.com
to: calebtbrowningrichards@snailmail.com
subject: Re: Hi

This is so stupid! We spent three days together five months ago.
What we think we're feeling isn't even real.

date: Dec 26, 2016, 9:09 PM
from: calebtbrowningrichards@snailmail.com
to: g.rosetownsend@snailmail.com
subject: Re: Hi

George, what I feel for you IS real. Please come visit so I can prove
it to you.
Yours,
C

CHORUS

January 2017

19. GEORGE

When George agreed to visit Caleb, she'd had no idea what that would actually entail. She'd never booked a flight before, didn't know what was required to do so, or even how much flights cost. She told herself she could back out if it was unreasonable. She knew if she told him she couldn't afford it he'd pay for it himself. But her pride wouldn't allow that, no matter how desperate she was to see him.

Luckily, flights weren't as expensive as she'd imagined. But that money could have gone to so many other things—gas, groceries, rent, electricity. It felt wasteful taking a three-day trip when the alternative was to pay necessary bills. When she asked for advice, Grandma Jeane sat her down at the kitchen table and disappeared down the hall. She returned with a shoebox full of old photos—photos of family she'd never met, her mother as a young girl, and a few from her own childhood. She watched Grandma Jeane shift the photos to the side exposing a tidy pile of cash.

"What on earth!" George whispered, afraid to give voice to what she saw, should some robber choose this exact moment to burst through the front door.

"This is for emergencies," Grandma Jeane explained. "And you going to visit your beau is by all accounts an emergency. 'Specially with the way you been moping, lately."

George was horrified to realize the daydreaming hadn't been contained within the inner sanctum of her brain.

"I haven't been moping," she huffed.

"Don't you be giving me the business, Georgie girl. You been out of sorts since you came home. The way I figure it, one of us ought to see the ocean before we die."

George had been at a loss for words. It was beyond generous. She'd hugged her grandma fiercely, knowing she'd never be able to accurately convey how much this meant. But now, she was questioning if it had all been worth it. Getting up at three in the morning to drive to the airport. Middle seats on both flights with a three-hour layover in between. Feeling the bone-chilling wind through the gap in the jet bridge once they deplaned in Boston. And it was pitch-black out so it wasn't like she'd been able to see much of anything as they landed. But as she got on the escalator down to baggage claim, she spotted that familiar head of hair and felt that knot in her stomach unravel.

Caleb's attention was on his phone, his other hand stuffed in his pocket, and George was transported back to that first night on the town square in Jackson, a reminder that this thing she was feeling was real. She hadn't imagined it, hadn't blown it up to unrealistic proportions in her head while distance separated them.

She hiked her duffel up her shoulder and stepped off the escalator, pausing for a second to take him in. He was in jeans, two-tone brown boots, and a dark peacoat, the neck of a creamy fisherman sweater peeking out. Caleb had never not looked good, but this was like a whole new level of attractive that George couldn't wrap her head around. Boston looked good on him.

Her heart sped and she wasn't sure whether she should tackle him or play it cool.

"Hi," she said, praying he didn't hear the quiver in her voice.

He did a double-take, like he'd forgotten why he was at the airport. He shoved his phone in his pocket and crossed the space between them so quickly that she had no time to prepare. And then she was in his arms, her feet lifted off the ground.

"God, I missed you," He sighed, his voice deeper than she remembered.

George laughed as he swung her legs back and forth, her fingers tangling in the hair at the base of his neck. He smelled better than in her memory. Like the first drops of rain, bedsheets fresh out of the dryer, and a tiny splash of spice.

He set her back on her feet but held onto her hips.

"You grew a beard," she realized. If a handful of hairs on his jaw and over his top lip could be considered that. He was also wearing glasses and it suited him.

"Your hair got longer." He twisted the end of a strand around his finger. "And you got even more beautiful. Didn't think that was even possible."

Her whole body shivered at the compliment, coming back to life in his presence.

"Let's get you to the car and crank the seat warmers."

She let him take her bag, even though it wasn't heavy. She'd only be staying for two days. He squeezed her hand and pulled her out into the frigid January cold, but she hardly felt it.

"How was your first time flying?"

He wrapped an arm around her as they made their way through the garage. Her warmest jacket was what she wore to work every day, so Grandma Jeane had sent her off with her own quilted jacket, which really didn't cut it up here in the frozen north. And George realized she had never truly known cold before. Not like this. It seeped in around the edges of her clothes and burrowed in her skin.

"It was good. Long, but I'm happy to be here." And she meant it. It had taken many months to come to terms with the way she felt about Caleb, accepting that it was okay to be vulnerable. If only with him.

"I'm happy you're happy." He brought her knuckles to his mouth and nibbled on them while looking for his car. "Are you hungry?"

He pulled her down the next aisle and unlocked an SUV, setting her bag in the backseat.

"Famished." She'd eaten the sandwich Grandma Jeane had packed her so long ago that it felt like a day had passed since leaving their house.

"I was thinking ramen because it'll warm you up."

Caleb opened the passenger door and waited for George to climb in, before rounding to the driver's side.

"I've never had ramen," she admitted as he turned the key, blessed heat blasting from all the vents. He pushed a button and George's butt almost immediately began to warm.

"This is the second-best day of my life. Prepare to fall in love."

George's stomach bottomed out. There was so much she wanted to say to him. But as much as being around Caleb felt a bit like coming home, it also felt brand new. It wasn't like they were picking up where they'd left off, because whatever they'd started back in Jackson hadn't been held in stasis all these months. Now, they were in a different place where everything was new to George, so it was as if they had stepped off the original path they'd been on and sidestepped onto an entirely new one.

In a way, Wyoming had been simple. It had been low-stakes with an end date. Until it wasn't and feelings had started to grow. But now, here in Boston, it was something else entirely. They'd jumped out of the vacation bubble and into the real world—Caleb's world.

She settled on what felt like a safe response. "That's a lot of hype. What if I don't like it?"

"Do you trust me?"

The way Caleb looked at her then, made her question whether he was even talking about food. She nodded. Because the truth was, even though she still didn't really know much about him, she did trust him. He hadn't given her any reason not to.

Caleb rolled down his window to insert the ticket into the machine. The cold rushed in and George was grateful that at least her butt was warm. He paid and rolled the window back up, turning to her as they waited for the gate to raise.

"What was the first-best day of your life?" She asked, hoping that she already knew his answer. Maybe she just wanted to hear him say it.

"The night I became Caleb Theodore Townsend, obviously."

It took everything in George not to unbuckle and launch herself across the center console, kiss that smirk right off his face. Instead, she snuggled back in her seat, warm with the knowledge it had all been real.

* * *

"George, I'm going to need your side of the story here, because I'm fairly certain I got a grossly-embellished version of events."

George, Caleb, and Toby were seated in a wooden booth in a bar somewhere in Boston. She was so full of noodles, a delicious tomato broth, corn, egg, and she was afraid to admit this—even a piece of *seaweed*. She couldn't wait to tell her grandma about maybe the best thing she'd ever eaten. Ramen, it turned out, was outstanding.

George was happy. Maybe it was the belly full of food. Maybe it was being warm while outside was a frozen tundra. Maybe it was the man beside her with his puppy dog eyes and the smile that refused to dim.

"You wound me." Caleb feigned being hurt, but they were all laughing.

"I know you too well. And you texted me from the bar!"

Caleb's friend Toby was seated across from them because the idea of not being able to touch after months apart had been too much for Caleb and George. They'd sat across from each other at the tiny ramen place, but that had been enough separation. Since leaving there, they hadn't let go of each other.

Now, Caleb's hand was tucked between George's knees, his thumb making lazy strokes back and forth over her jeans. George was turned slightly into him, so she could rest her head on his shoulder between sips of her drink.

"Okay, you may proceed." Toby sat back waiting for an honest account of that first night.

The problem was, this many months later, George couldn't quite remember. She'd replayed that night so many times. Had the crowd roared after she finished singing Miranda Lambert's "Vice" or had they ignored her performance entirely? She couldn't remember because she'd been so high on nerves and adrenaline and there'd been ringing in her ears after the last notes ended.

Maybe what she remembered of Caleb wasn't actually what had happened either. Maybe what she thought she remembered about those days was lacquered with a post-coital shine. She decided to stick with the basics.

"So, this guy decided it was the night to try whiskey for the first time—"

"Didn't like it," Caleb interjected and they all laughed.

"And yet you had multiple glasses." George leaned into him.

"Liquid courage." He squeezed her knee and she felt her cheeks grow hot.

"Well, a lot of good it did you. I had to basically beg you to invite me back to your house."

Caleb's fingers climbed the inside of her thigh and she held his gaze to see what he'd do. His smile deepened as his fingers slid higher and George bit her lip to keep from reacting. But sure enough, he stopped before he went all the way, like a teaser of what was to come later.

"And there it is!" Toby exclaimed. "I knew I wasn't getting the real story."

"Okay, okay. To my credit, she'd just blown the entire place away with her singing and she could've talked to anyone in the bar. So, I had a right to be nervous."

"But I wanted to talk to *you*."

"And I still can't believe it." Caleb leaned over and kissed her forehead.

The bar suddenly felt stuffy. Or maybe it was her stomach full of soup? George's cheeks and ears were hot and she considered dragging ice from her drink down her neck to cool off.

"That's disgustingly adorable." Toby said. "I want to fall in love like you two."

To have someone call out the way she was maybe-possibly feeling, to put the actual words she'd never dared think on the table between them so that she couldn't look away, was a lot to process.

Caleb reached across the table and tried to grab Toby, but alone on that side of the booth Toby had ample room to slide out of reach.

"You're an idiot." Caleb laughed, but he didn't confirm or deny what Toby had said, and that made George's heart beat a little faster.

It also gave her pause. What was the point of having these feelings if she couldn't afford to fly to Boston again. So, what then? Caleb would fly to Texas a couple times? It wasn't feasible in the long-term. Eventually it would have to end. She really hadn't thought this through.

"I'll be right back." Caleb slid out of the booth and immediately George felt cooler, maybe even a little calmer. She wondered what that meant.

"Don't believe anything this guy says." He clapped Toby's shoulder as he headed towards the bathroom.

George took a big gulp of water, appreciating when it coated her throat in momentary cool.

"I hope it's not overstepping, but you make him really happy." Toby nodded in thanks and George squirmed.

"I didn't do anything."

Toby leaned forward conspiratorially, looked over his shoulder to make sure the coast was clear, and lowered his voice.

"George, I know we don't know each other, but don't let this flashy theater major exterior deceive you." He waved to encompass his perfectly coifed hair, his Mr. Rogers sweater. "I say this sincerely with over a decade of friendship with that fool under my belt. Caleb is the best guy I know. Best person, actually. I mean, Phil's great too, but I have loyalty, if nothing else."

George felt her body leaning towards his, wanting to gobble up the next words.

"He came home from that vacation destroyed thinking he'd never find you again, and now—I just want you to know, whatever happens, that you're not going to find a better person than him. So, I hope you'll stick around."

George sucked in a lungful of air so deep that they both laughed. But she desperately needed it after holding her breath, waiting to see what Toby was going to say. This wasn't what she'd expected, considering the way he puffed himself up to hide the drastic height difference between he and Caleb. But now, knowing he was an actor, the false bravado made more sense. She was glad to see he felt comfortable enough around her to be himself.

"I know, right? Way too serious for a Friday night." He downed his drink to hide the emotion that had surfaced, but George saw it before he turned away.

"Thank you. For saying that."

Toby shrugged like it was no big deal. Except, George understood that it was.

"So, a theatre major, huh?" George wasn't sure what the go-to questions were. Was Broadway the only path or was that a touchy subject? She had absolutely no idea.

"Yeah, I'm practical like that. Hard to come by work and meager income? Sign me up!" He laughed, but it didn't reach his eyes.

"That sounds stressful." George took another sip of her drink. She was starting to feel a chill without Caleb beside her.

"Yeah. I like the excitement of the unknown, but to a degree. Too much of it just makes me anxious. Actually, since we're well on our way to becoming friends, I was hoping to use you as a distraction tonight to break the news to Caleb."

Without meaning to, she'd closed the distance between them so their voices could stay just above a whisper.

"Why does this feel like the bad sort of news?" George cupped her glass with both hands, chin resting on the rim.

"Is going to L.A. to audition bad news? I mean, potato, potahto, right? Am I the potahto or the potato? Not important. It's my dream, so I have to try."

Toby chewed his lip and George realized with a sinking feeling that he was asking permission to ruin the night.

"When you say *going* do you actually mean *moving*?"

George wondered if this had been Toby's plan all along. It hardly felt fair to drop something this big onto the table the night she arrived. But she could feel Toby's nervous energy and she knew this was going to be hard for him. If she could help soften the blow then she would try.

When Toby nodded, George steeled herself. Maybe this was why she was here, to help Caleb accept a big change.

"I mean, you get it. You're a singer. It's not like you chose it, it's just who you are."

George felt her mouth open and close like a fish out of water. She wasn't a singer. Not really. She wasn't like Toby, who'd been in every high school theatre production, who'd gone to school for theatre—as Caleb had explained on the drive to the bar, sounding like his biggest fan. She'd only been onstage once for fun. It hardly counted.

"Oh, I'm not—I just sang one time. Caleb was drunk and he's clearly biased. It probably wasn't even that good." She brushed it off and focused on her drink.

"George. I say this as someone who has sat through his fair share of auditions full of over-indulged theatre kids attempting songs they have no business even singing in their shower. I saw the video. You have *the* voice."

George's head went a bit fuzzy. "What video?"

Toby blinked, realizing George had no idea what he was talking about, and quickly began scrolling through his phone. George held her breath as she waited. It had never even occurred to her that someone might have filmed it.

Toby handed his phone to her, volume up so she could hear over the noisy bar, just barely. But there she was, small and a little blurry until the camera focused. She could hardly hear her voice over the drumming of her heart, so she pressed the phone to her ear to hear better above the din. She held her breath and listened.

That was her. That was *her* voice, singing clear and high over the notes of the band. George pulled the phone away and watched, not needing to hear the music because she could hear it in her head. She studied herself, eyes closed as she sang her heart out, the band playing around her like it was an actual thing, not just some girl called up on stage on a lark. She felt it, that moment coming alive again in the pulse of her blood, in the goofy grin that found its way to her lips.

"See, you get it."

She looked away from the screen and met Toby's gaze. He shrugged, like they were both in some members-only group.

"Can I send this to myself?" She asked, already opening a text to send the link to her own phone.

"Yeah, of course."

George's fingers were shaking as she typed in her number. She couldn't wait to rewatch in a quiet place later and dissect everything.

"I didn't know anyone recorded it."

"Are you kidding? Caleb's made me watch that like ten times. He probably jerks off to it."

As if remembering who he was talking to, Toby had the decency to look embarrassed.

"Apologies. But, you know, he probably does."

George tried not to think about what he'd said so her cheeks wouldn't flame further. But this video was like a kernel of unpolished gold placed in her outstretched hand. It was real, what she'd felt on that stage. It hadn't been blown out of proportion, distorted over the distance of time. The audience had actually loved her. They'd *cheered*. Caleb might be her biggest fan, but he wasn't the only one.

"So, you're moving to Los Angeles," she said, returning the conversation to the matter at hand.

Toby nodded, his eyes silently pleading for her to join his team. A team where people pursued the things that made them come alive. A team that might mean leaving loved ones behind in order to take a giant leap. A team that might lead to heartbreak, but also might lead to greatness. And if George was being honest, while joining that team sounded incredibly scary, it also sounded kind of thrilling.

"Okay, fine. Do what you must."

Toby looked up and it was like the weight of it had slid off his shoulders. He clinked his glass with hers and downed what was left of his drink.

"You're the best, George. Honestly, I think Caleb could handle anything as long as you're in his bed at the end of the night."

It was then that Caleb returned from the bathroom, having caught some piece of that last statement. He looked between Toby and George, his head tilted under the weight of some image conjured from those words.

George raised her eyebrows to give Toby the floor.

"Buddy, amigo, friend-of-my-life," Toby began as Caleb slid back into the booth beside George.

Caleb's brow furrowed, picking up on the mounting tension and George placed her hand on Caleb's thigh to distract him from the incoming blow.

"Shit." Caleb put his palms on the table, giving his friend his complete attention. "It's bad, isn't it." It wasn't a question. He knew him too well.

Toby shifted uncomfortably, opened his mouth to speak, but nothing came out. George pitied him, having to break his best friend's heart. Having done that once herself she decided to throw him a bone.

"Whatever he says, just remember," George pressed her body against Caleb's side. She felt him still as she brought her lips to the shell of his ear, making sure only he could hear. "You promised me earth-shattering orgasms and I've come to collect."

Caleb blinked once, twice, like his mind had spun out. He cleared his throat and straightened, giving Toby his full attention. Beneath the table, however, his right leg began bouncing like he was holding back from taking George's hand and racing out of the bar.

"Lay it on me, friend."

Caleb woke to a whisper-soft finger tracing paths along his forearm. He smelled George without opening his eyes, his face tucked beneath her curtain of hair. It smelled like wildflowers and the ocean, surprising him that only a few hours in Boston had been enough to imprint its briny smell on her. He inhaled deeply.

"Good morning," he exhaled and pulled her back flush to his chest. They were yin and yang—him, shirtless and in pajama bottoms, her in his tee shirt and no pants.

"It is a good morning."

Her voice was a song he'd been longing to hear. For the past few months, he'd tried to conjure it from memory each night as he lay in bed. But just when he thought he could remember it clearly time stole it from his grasp. It was never quite right.

"I dreamed of waking up like this again."

She lifted his hand to kiss his knuckles then slid it under her shirt and placed his palm over her breast.

"I like waking up like this, too," he murmured into her hair and inhaled again. He needed to covertly ask what shampoo she used so he could buy a bottle to sniff like a creep when the nights alone grew too long.

"What time is it?" He asked, not daring to move from this perfect position. He knew it was early because the light was muted. This deep into winter it could also mean the edges of a storm.

"It's my fault. I'm on ranch time. It's probably not eight yet, considering the time difference."

"I don't care what time it is. You're here." Caleb gave her breast a gentle squeeze and she bucked against him in response. "Aaaand now I'm awake."

He wanted to roll on top of her, pin her to the bed and kiss her silly. But this hazy, warm place beneath the covers, somewhere between sleep and fully awake, was where Caleb wanted to live. Just for a little while longer. Everything else could wait.

"How are you feeling?" George's nails tickled along his arm like the beginning of a rain storm. "About Toby leaving."

Right. Toby was moving across the country.

"I don't know. I just assumed he'd always be here. But I know he has to go—maybe I've been waiting for this. He deserves the chance to try to make his dream happen. But then I think about not being a part of his life and... We'll always be friends, but it won't be the same being that far apart, him out there, me here. And then I feel shitty for having those thoughts because I shouldn't be thinking about me. I should just be supporting him, being happy for him."

Caleb hadn't meant to pour every thought out between them, but something about being wrapped around George felt safe enough to unburden his mind. Her fingers stilled on his arm and he wondered if he'd said too much.

"I think," she started, gently, "that if you want to be in each other's lives, no matter the time zones and thousands of miles, you'll find a way to make it work. It might not be easy, but if he's important to you..."

Fuck. He'd walked himself right into that one, hadn't he. Now he needed to backtrack so she didn't think he also felt that way about the physical distance between Boston and Texas.

"No, of course. You're absolutely right. I don't want our *friendship* to end regardless of the distance. He's too important to me."

Had George changed her mind about trying to make this work? She'd flown here, after all so that should tell him everything he needed to know. He'd have to broach the subject later, when he was more awake. Maybe after breakfast.

"I have a confession," Caleb admitted.

George squirmed around to face him. Her fingers traced down his ribs like she was playing piano keys, walked over his hip, and splayed like a starfish to cup his ass through his pants. For a second his mind went hazy. He very nearly rolled on top of her, but first he should finish his thought.

"You're very distracting, you know that?"

"Am I?"

He wanted to lick that smile right off her face.

"I promised I'd learn to cook for you and I haven't yet. But—"

She squeezed his ass and he was very close to losing his resolve, but he really wanted to follow through on this one thing.

"I'm pretty capable when it comes to eggs and toast. So, we can either stay here." Caleb reached down and cupped George's ass. Two could play that game. "Or, I can get up and make you breakfast."

He was pretty sure which way this was headed, from the hitch in George's breath, the way her fingers let go of him and traveled back up to press against his heart. She tilted back so she could look at him and the need for him was plain, but different. Like it had been filtered through a new light in which she wasn't afraid to show him how she truly felt.

"That is the sexiest thing anyone's ever said to me. I will eat whatever you cook for breakfast."

She nibbled on his chin, up to his ear, down the length of his neck as his pulse hammered in response.

"I think there's a lesson to be learned here, because if you hadn't snuck out of bed back in Jackson I could've cooked for you—"

Caleb might've finished the sentence, if not for George's lips tracing a line down his stomach, her destination obvious. Eh, breakfast could wait.

* * *

In the end, Caleb did make breakfast, but it was an hour later. Phil was skiing in Vermont with friends, but she'd stocked the fridge in preparation for George's visit as an apology for missing her. Most of the items Caleb didn't plan on using, unless he wanted to showcase how much he still had to learn.

The look George gave him after she took her first—albeit hesitant—bite very nearly sent them back to his bedroom. If that was her reaction to eggs, what would happen when he mastered a soufflé?

"I had an idea," Caleb said over his toast. He'd been thinking about how to spend their time together since the moment she'd agreed to come. "Do you want to see the ocean?"

George had just taken a bite, blissfully chewing until she finished. "I think I caught a glimpse of it when the plane landed."

Caleb's scoff was a gut reaction, but he instantly chided himself for being such a snob. "Yes, that is technically the ocean, but I was thinking we could go to the Cape. My family has a house—" He stuffed a piece of toast in his mouth then. The words came back to him and he saw it on George's face.

173

He'd never really thought about it before. Why should he? When you were raised into something you didn't know any different, didn't understand that from the outside it might look absurdly out of touch. He didn't know the details of George's life in Texas, but he had an idea. And it was so far removed from private jets and second homes.

He'd seen it on George's face when they'd come home from the bar last night, the way she paused inside the front door of the building as if asking permission to enter. And then when they'd reached his floor and he'd ushered her inside, he'd chosen to ignore the way her eyes widened in favor of pulling her straight to his bedroom.

He had no intention of explaining the details of his trust or admitting how much he and Phil had paid for this condo—it had garage parking and a view of the Charles. He knew it was ridiculous, to own this kind of home at twenty-three. But he'd never really thought about it from an outside perspective, until George had crossed the threshold. Suddenly, he was embarrassed about the blasé way he thought about money. Or rather, *didn't* think about it. It wasn't like he'd earned any of it. He'd simply been born a Browning.

"It was a stupid idea."

They'd been having a perfect morning and he had to go and point out the vast differences between them.

"Actually, I promised my grandma I'd see the ocean, so if you think there's a better view of it then I'm all in. Whatever you have planned, I'm game."

He didn't deserve her, the way she trusted him. There was so much light in George's eyes whenever she looked at him and he'd never been on the receiving end of that before. It was like he drew happiness out of her. Or maybe it was his own happiness reflected back at him.

Caleb packed a bag and two hours later they were pulling into the driveway of the Chatham house. It being the end of January, they'd hit traffic only around Quincy—*because there was always traffic in Quincy*—and then it was smooth sailing the rest of the way.

Caleb couldn't remember the last time he'd been to the house outside of the summer season. Main Street was usually swarmed like bees to commercial honey in those months, but in January it was blissfully quiet. He pointed out the place they sometimes went for ice cream, the bar they got into with fake I.D.s at nineteen, the corner where Phil had an embarrassingly public breakup at seventeen.

He could tell that George was taking it all in, but wondered what she really thought. Was she picturing her own wild youth alongside his? Was she imagining herself here next summer beside him? He was too afraid to ask. If she still didn't see them together beyond this weekend he'd be completely destroyed.

"Is someone here?" George asked as she pulled into the driveway.

Sure enough, his father's car was parked in front of the garage. But that didn't make sense. His father never came to the Cape after Labor Day. He called it The Summer Home. His mother, however, sometimes liked to have a week alone down here.

This would ruin everything if she was here. They couldn't stay overnight now. He and his father had barely spoken since the Wyoming trip. At the holidays they were cordial, tolerating each other in the slimmest sense. But if either of Caleb's parents were here, they weren't staying. Caleb would show George the waterfront, let her take pictures to show Grandma Jeane, then eat a meal at whatever restaurant was open in town, and head back to the city.

When Caleb opened the front door, they were hit with a wall of dry heat. He went to check the nearest thermostat—eighty.

"Mom?" He called out, not even bothering to take off his jacket as he moved further into the house. There was no response, but there was a takeout container on the counter, remnants of a burger and fries inside. His mother didn't eat carbs or red meat. Or takeout, for that matter.

George followed a few steps behind as Caleb moved down the hall, then up the stairs to his and Phil's bedrooms. The office, the two guest bedrooms—all empty and made up to perfection. In his parents' bedroom, however, the comforter and sheets were piled to one side, the pillows all over the place, including on the floor. Even though he was starting to sweat, Caleb felt a chill run up his spine.

He pulled out his phone and called his mother while George hovered just beyond the doorway.

"Yes, Caleb," Dara answered on the third ring.

"Are you here? In Chatham?"

"What are you doing in Chatham?" He could hear papers rustling and knew their conversation was secondary to whatever she was in the middle of.

"I came down for the weekend. Are you here? I saw Dad's car."

Caleb took George's proffered hand and led her back down the hall toward the stairs. Her being here added a degree of surrealness, and maybe that's why the house felt off, because his two worlds were merging. Maybe everything was fine and he was overreacting. It wouldn't be the first time.

"Caleb, what are you saying?"

The shuffling ceased on his mother's end as they reached the bottom of the stairs. He let go of George's hand to look out the window and make sure that the car was in fact his father's.

"Dad's car is here."

"Your father is in New York for work."

The edge to her voice made the hair on Caleb's arms prickle. Dara Browning did not get flustered.

"Then why is his car here?" He couldn't make sense of it. Chatham was not on the way to New York.

"Caleb, you're not making any sense." Now she sounded annoyed.

He leaned against the kitchen counter trying to figure an explanation that fit all the parts. The unmade bed. The thermostat turned up. The leftovers. Was he... *Fuck*. He was having an affair. And now Caleb was exposing it to his mother. Yet another thing his father would hold against him.

"Caleb?" George called from the living room. She was standing in front of the window that looked out on the marshy sound.

"Caleb?" Dara mirrored, and he realized he was still holding the phone to his ear. He ended the call without saying goodbye.

"I think I see something down by the water." George pointed out the window at something beyond his view.

The way George looked at him made Caleb's stomach hurt. Because there wasn't any doubt in her voice. She *did* see something down by the water and Caleb had an awful feeling, like he was standing on the edge of something with nothing to grab onto to keep him from falling.

She wasn't sure what had drawn her to the window. Maybe it was the beauty of the Atlantic dancing in her winter whites that caught George's attention. But something pulled her eyes to the strip of sandy shore down beyond the lip of the lawn.

She had been so distracted by the grandeur of the house and Caleb's mounting nerves as they moved from room to room, that George hadn't realized she was overheating. It snuck up on her, only hitting when she stopped to look out the window. They'd never taken their coats off.

She pressed a finger to the cool window glass and just there, beyond her finger, a tangle of grey came into focus. Driftwood first, and then, something else. Even from this distance she was sure of what it was, though her brain was lagging, struggling to make sense of it.

Her heart jumped into a sprint, and not like the kind of racing caused by proximity to Caleb. In her bones she felt that something was wrong, even if she couldn't quite put her finger on it.

Then Caleb was beside her and it was like that moment when a rollercoaster crests the first hill and you know everything is seconds from dropping out from under you. George almost reached for him, but she was suddenly afraid of what his stillness meant. Her brain kept shuffling the pieces around until they finally slotted into place.

Legs and shoes. A person down in the sand.

Caleb pressed a button on his phone and there was a near-immediate echo ringing. He followed the sound, his hip bumping the table, chair almost falling except for his fingers catching it at the last moment. He found the phone between two cushions of the couch and when he lifted it George watched his eyes pinball trying to make sense of it. He turned to look at her, his eyes glazed, like he was looking through her at something else entirely. And maybe he was, because the answer seemed to be beyond her out the window.

Caleb took off like a shot, banging out the door before George could ask what was happening. On some base, instinctual level she knew what was happening, but her brain was incapable of translating.

The wind on this side of the house blasted George's cheeks as she took off down the slope after him and she was glad that in the confusion upon arriving they'd never taken off their coats or shoes. Where the lawn ended the ground turned rocky and a set of weather-worn stairs was tucked sneakily in-between boulders. When she reached Caleb's side and finally looked at the driftwood, those words she'd been searching for slammed against her tongue and she almost vomited.

Brown moccasin slippers. A pair of navy dress pants hitched up to reveal pale white-blue ankles. A whole person. One who looked unmistakably like an older, weather-worn version of Caleb.

"Is that your dad?" George whispered, truly afraid of the answer.

Maybe, hopefully, she was dreaming and she was going to wake up soon. Even if it meant waking up alone in Texas. Anything was better than this.

Caleb either didn't hear her over the wind or he was too shocked to respond. But George knew they couldn't wait. It was so cold. She reached into her pocket, unable to find her phone, and then turned to Caleb.

"Where's your phone?"

He didn't respond, even after she asked a second time. She pilfered his pockets, racing against her own quickening heartbeat. It was like Caleb wasn't there, his body in stasis while his brain stepped away to process, and that terrified her the most.

George had always assumed that in an emergency she'd have a flight response, only because she'd never handled the sight of blood particularly well. But she managed to sound relatively calm as she dialed 911, and maybe that was because she didn't know Caleb's father. Or maybe it was because she wanted to protect Caleb more than anything.

The dispatcher picked up so quickly George almost dropped the phone.

"Ma'am, my name is George Townsend and I'm calling about a person—"

George tried to get Caleb's attention. Knowing his father's name felt important, but Caleb stared with unseeing eyes. She wanted to shake him, but she was more afraid of how he'd react when he did snap out of it, and she could only handle one thing at a time.

"He's um, he's unconscious or…" She didn't finish that thought.

"George, can you tell me your location?" The operator's calm voice helped George's panic ebb.

"Um, well, we're behind the house down by the water, but, uh, actually—" she remembered turning onto the street because it made her think of Wyoming, "—Aspen, the end of Aspen Lane."

"Thank you, George. Can you hang on one second while I talk to dispatch?"

The operator was gone when George responded in the affirmative. She pressed the phone harder against her ear, thinking maybe the call had been disconnected. The wind was so loud. But a few seconds later the operator was thankfully back.

"George, can you tell me if the person is breathing?"

Until that point, he'd just been a sleeping person outside in the middle of January, down by the water in slippers. Like that was normal. But when she looked at him, *really looked*, and leaned down to check if he was breathing, she choked on the reality of it.

"I don't think so." Her voice hitched and she tried to regain control. She had to be strong for Caleb.

She wondered what Grandma Jeane would do, because she was the type of woman to be stellar in a sticky situation.

"George, stay on the phone with me. We've got emergency services on their way to you right now. Can you tell me, does it look like he's fallen? Is he bleeding? Is there any sort of head wound?"

George moved closer, inspecting Caleb's father a little more closely. Knowing that an ambulance was on its way was a huge relief.

"No, ma'am, I don't see any wound or blood. He looks like he just laid down."

The operator was talking, but not to George, her words muffled so that all George could make out was a calm tone. She knew she needed to let the professionals handle it. But still, she felt like she should be doing *something*.

"George," the operator came back on the line. "Can you stand at the end of the driveway so emergency services knows which house to go to?"

"Yes, ma'am, I can do that!"

She turned to see if Caleb had heard anything she'd said, but he was almost as pale as his father. If she'd had a second to think, she might have burst into tears, but she didn't have time for that right now.

George took off running, the phone pressed to her ear. Up the lawn, around the side of the house, and down the driveway to the mailbox.

She was breathing so hard she thought she might collapse, but she stood up straight, hand raised as the far-off call of a siren reached her ears. Then she saw the lights.

"They're here!"

"George, you did great. You can hang up now, okay?"

George waved her arms wildly even though she knew they had seen her. A firetruck and an ambulance pulled into the driveway and stopped just behind Caleb's car.

"They're down by the water!" She yelled against the wind as three firefighters and two EMTs jumped out.

Caleb was sitting in the sand when George returned, arms resting on his knees like he was waiting for the tide to come in. She stood next to him and watched the emergency workers.

"Do you know if he's taken anything?" The first firefighter to reach Caleb's father asked.

"I don't know. He was like this when we got here."

She watched one of the EMTs pat down Caleb's father's clothes.

Caleb stood and brushed off his pants, like he was tired of waiting, and stuffed his hands deep in his pockets. His jaw clenched and his gaze darkened and George looped her arm in his because it felt urgent that she grab onto him, like the wind might carry him away. Together they watched one EMT stick something in Caleb's father's nose.

"What's his name?" Another firefighter asked and George couldn't answer. She looked to Caleb but it was like he didn't hear.

"Is he dead?" Caleb asked the thing George had been dreading.

"I've got a pulse," the first firefighter said.

The relief was so immediate that she had to swallow down the bile lapping at the back of her tongue.

"Can you tell me what happened? How long has he been out here?" The second firefighter asked.

"No idea." Caleb's voice was gravely and low, the wind collecting the words so fast it was like they'd never been spoken.

"Hypothermia?" One of the firefighters said to the other, and George's eyes went to the blue-white skin exposed to the wind.

Caleb finally turned to George and he looked numb. She'd have given everything to erase this moment for him. She squeezed his frozen fingers. It was all she could think to do.

The phone in her hand vibrated. *The Mothership* filled the screen and she handed it to Caleb.

"Mom?"

Caleb's voice was so small that George felt tears burn at the back of her eyes. This was all wrong—her being here, Caleb's father. She was sweating and freezing at the same time. This was her fault. She shouldn't have come. Then again, if she hadn't come to Boston who knows when Caleb's father might have been found.

She held onto Caleb's hand hoping that by anchoring herself to him they'd both wake up from this nightmare. But as the cold slipped in around the edges of her coat and tiptoed along her skin, George grew increasingly sure that this moment had already changed everything.

When Caleb was seven, John took him to Fenway Park for the first time. He remembered it much like a dream, flashes that were hazy and distorted. A huge hot dog in his tiny hand. A too-big hat on his head, the brim slipping down to obscure his view. A hit that had everyone around him jumping to their feet, making him feel like a tiny squirrel on the forest floor, the sun blocked out while he sat in shadow.

It was hard to get his father's attention with so much noise. The announcer, the hum of the game, all of it was overwhelming. He tried, he really did, to tell his father how badly he needed to go to the bathroom. He told him at the bottom of the sixth, again in the seventh, but by the top of the eighth he couldn't stop squirming. It hurt so bad.

John kept telling Caleb to hold it, the game would be over soon. But he'd waited too long. As the opening chords of "Sweet Caroline" began to play, his shame spread heavy and hot, along with the dark river down his pants. Fat, silent tears slipped down his cheeks.

John's nose wrinkled as the smell hit him, and he looked around until finally landing sharply on Caleb's lap. He shook with disgust and turned back to the game without saying a word.

Caleb didn't move or make a sound for the rest of the game. He sat quietly in his humiliation while his pants cooled and the Sox won. Later at home, he didn't tell Phil what happened, though she could tell something was wrong. She knew his moods like they were her own.

John didn't speak to him for ten days. And it would be another ten years before they'd attend a game together. At that game, Caleb's father's company hosted clients in one of the suites. He'd made the mistake of thinking that since it was a work-related event his father would simply ignore him. Instead, John brought up the story as soon as the last notes of "Sweet Caroline" played, pulling attention from half the suite, reforming Caleb's shame into something laughable. Caleb had drowned himself in free booze and caught a cab home early.

Now, heading north back to Boston, Caleb thought about that day. And about the many ways he had disappointed his father since. And in thinking about it, a new feeling caught and spread like fire to parched kindling.

For a moment there, before the ambulance arrived, he'd thought his father was dead, and the relief of that had warmed him through. He'd barely felt the cold. Then the EMT found a pulse and the relief receded with the tide. Left behind like bits of seashells in the sand was twenty-three years' worth of anger.

Caleb was so angry, in fact, he had to pull over at the next rest stop, parking far from the only other car in the lot.

"Caleb?" George asked from the passenger seat as he tore out of the car.

He wanted to punch something. *No*—he wanted to punch his father. Fuck him for holding Caleb to unbearably high standards, where his only option was to come up short! He should've never gone to the Chatham house. Then his father would've… and he could stop caring. Why, after everything, did he still care?

Caleb screamed at the trees until he was empty and heaving. He'd believed his father's view of himself for so long. He'd let him dictate the way Caleb thought about himself, for what? Why couldn't his father love him for the person he was, flawed and imperfect but still good? Caleb had value. It just wasn't what his father valued.

George's arms came around Caleb's waist and he collapsed against her. He was so tired. Tired of always failing. The weariness hit him straight on, turning the waves of frustration into sobs. George's hand cupped the back of his head and he let all of it go. He didn't want to hold on to so much anger when she was this close to him.

"You're okay," she said, and he believed her. "I've got you."

When Caleb was with George, he felt like everything would be okay. Her smile, the song in her voice, the caress of her fingers. He wished he could breathe her in and keep her close to him always.

He felt it then, attaching a name to it in his mind. There was zero doubt. But he couldn't tell her now. You didn't tell someone you loved them in the midst of the worst day of your life.

He wrapped his arms around her middle, crushing her to him, and inhaled the ocean brine as her fly-aways ticked his nose. He was so thankful to whoever or whatever—God, karma, the universe—had put him on this path that intersected with hers.

"Do you want me to drive?" She asked as he straightened to look at her, smoothing the worry lines etched between her brow with his thumb.

He nodded and let her lead him to the passenger seat.

* * *

Dara had insisted the ambulance bring John to Boston. It made sense, to bring him to one of the world's best hospitals. Though Caleb wasn't sure his father deserved it, the more he thought about it. His feelings confused him. Worried one moment, angry the next. He didn't have the energy to figure it out.

As soon as they parked, he was out of the car and heading for the elevators. He pushed the button once, twice, before realizing he was alone. He spun around, dizziness washing over him on a two-second delay. But George was there, swimming in his vision as he tried to focus, carrying his jacket in one arm as she locked the car and slipped the keys into her pocket.

Caleb reached out a hand for her, a lifeline to grab onto before he lost himself completely to the sludge in his head. George reeled him in, wrapping her arms around his waist until he felt the solid ground beneath his shoes, the weight of her against him, the sting of the outside air on his cheeks.

"Take a breath," she said as wheels screeched on another floor of the garage.

Caleb let George lead the way—finding the right floor, the right wing. If pressed, Caleb could not have said what hospital they were even in.

They stopped at an open door, Caleb slamming into George's back, and his father was there, in a bed, under blankets, eyes closed. He looked fine, just asleep, except for the tubes taped to his skin, the monitor just off to the side. *Maybe he'll walk away from this like nothing happened*, Caleb thought. But Caleb was out of his depth. He had no idea if overdosing and being hypothermic, had lasting side effects.

Caleb liked to think he knew some things about how the world worked. But as he watched the hills and valleys on the monitor, he realized he knew so little. Especially where his father was concerned.

Why had his father taken so many pills? Had he planned to end his own life? Or, was he just another addict who hadn't meant for it to go this far? For a man who ruled over his life and family with military precision and control, none of it made sense.

"Darlings, you didn't need to come."

Caleb hadn't even realized his mother was in the room. But there she was, fussing over flowers in the corner.

"Mom."

Caleb skirted around George and moved to hug his mother. He knew it was expected of him, to comfort her even though she'd never been particularly comforting towards him. She let him hold her for a beat, the cloud of Chanel No.5 that followed her everywhere forcing him to hold his breath until she let go.

"Philippa, you didn't need to cut your ski weekend short," Dara began, stepping back. But when she saw George she blanched, her mouth and eyes pinching together in stifled fury. "Who are you?"

"Mom, this is—"

She didn't let him finish, her glare cutting him off.

"This is a *family* matter."

The good will he'd brokered with his arrival evaporated as she lifted her chin towards the door and moved to the bedside, blocking his father from view.

"I'm sorry," Caleb whispered, turning to George. "She's—"

George took Caleb's hands and squeezed. "It's fine. I'll be out in the hall."

He wanted to thank her for being so understanding, but exposing any vulnerability to his mother was like inviting a storm inside. He let go of George's hand and listened to her footsteps retreating down the hall.

There was no steeling yourself before facing Dara Browning. You just took her wrath and dealt with your feelings later. Caleb didn't have the energy to put on a good face for her. He felt his shoulders slump with exhaustion as he walked to the bed.

"Mom," Caleb began, his voice nearly a whisper.

"Why would you bring a stranger in here?" She said, barely masking the razor-sharp edge. "He needs to rest. Having people who aren't family disturbing him is not good."

She shook her head and tried to smooth her husband's hair. The wind had whipped it from its usual pomade-plaster. A huff escaped before she could edit herself and it made Caleb realize that she was actually struggling with all this, façade or no.

"Mom, George was the one who found him on the beach—"

"No." She shook her head, and normally Caleb would have stopped, deferring to the established hierarchy. But everything was different now. The curtain had been pulled back.

"George isn't from here. She doesn't care how it *looks* that he ODed—"

The slap was so unexpected that if not for the lingering sting across his cheek, Caleb wouldn't have believed it happened. He forced himself to breathe. It would be months before Caleb's therapist helped him realize the anger wasn't directed at him. That the person his mother was mad at couldn't fight back and he was the next closest target. But it stung all the same, radiating out in small waves until he was just numb.

Caleb probed the inside of his cheek with his tongue. *This fucking family*, he thought. If not for Phil, he'd have left already.

"When is Philippa getting here?" He asked.

A normal person would have taken steps back or walked away, at the very least putting more than an arm's length between himself and the person who'd just hit him. But Caleb knew his mother wouldn't do it again. One outburst was rash enough, and *with an open door*. She'd slipped, and it wouldn't happen again.

"How should I know that? You're the one who called her."

Of course.

Caleb expelled a lungful of air that bordered on laughter. He was tired of performing and didn't care if it made his mother's eyebrows nearly disappear into her hairline. Of course it was on him to handle. Why wouldn't it be, since he and Phil were one entity in her eyes.

"Unbelievable," he muttered, turning towards the door. His phone wasn't in any of his pockets.

"I beg your pardon?"

"Nothing." Caleb didn't have the energy to fight. Right now, he didn't care enough about the people in this room to argue.

"Tell your sister she doesn't need to bring flowers. But the duck breast from Deuxave would be much appreciated. And maybe the Tagliatelle for when your father wakes up."

For the first time in his life, Caleb was embarrassed to be a Browning Richards. He knew that everyone handled trauma differently, but what was his mother's excuse?

Caleb needed to get out of this hospital. He had to call Phil because no one else had, and it would ruin her weekend, but she needed to know. And then after that was taken care of, he needed to go home. His home, away from his parents, away from all this shit that was so convoluted and gross. He needed the warm cocoon of his bedroom. But mostly, he just needed George.

George knew there were people who left home and never went back. She wasn't one of them. She loved her summers in Wyoming, but there was something about that drive back down to Texas that settled warm and comforting in her belly. Like putting on your favorite sweater on the first cold morning and remembering how perfectly it fits.

She didn't expect to feel that as she followed Caleb back over the threshold of his home. But she did. Not because it felt like her home. It certainly did not, with the cream sectional, the marble mantel, the gauzy curtains. This was the complete opposite of what she knew home to be. But it was Caleb's, and surprisingly, or maybe not surprising at all, he felt like home.

The realization settled like warm honey on her tongue as she hung their coats in the front closet. Caleb turned the lights on as he trudged through the apartment to his bedroom.

"You'll feel better if you shower," she heard herself say, and then wondered when she'd turned into someone's mother. But honestly, a hot shower would do him good, to wash away the day's grime and ease his muscles.

George set her bag just inside Caleb's room and took a look around. She'd been too distracted last night (and this morning) to notice the many photos framed above his desk. Caleb and Phil as children sandwiching a woman with a complexion too dark to be related to them. And yet, the adoration on everyone's face made George think there was something deeply shared between them, something more familial than Caleb's relationship with his own mother.

There was a single photo of Caleb in a baseball uniform, bat in one hand, body corkscrewed, head tipped back to follow what must have been a perfect hit. The intensity on his face brought George's finger up to trace the lines of him, try to reconcile the kind and gentle man she knew with this intense, hardened one.

There was a photo of Caleb standing beside a small Phantom of the Opera—Toby done up in makeup and costume—bouquet in hand, both of them wearing proud grins.

Naturally, she wondered what it would have been like if they'd met in high school. She'd have been a grade above Caleb, not that it would have mattered since she'd lived in another time zone. But imagining if they had been at the same school, what would they have thought about each other?

George had worked at her town's small grocery store in high school. Grandma Jeane was friends with the manager and got her hired at fourteen to bag groceries and restock shelves. Eventually, she'd been promoted to cashier. She'd worked there until graduation, every day after school and weekends. She didn't have time to do the school play or be on a team, and maybe she'd missed out, but there hadn't been another option. Their high school experiences had been very different.

"Hey," Caleb stepped out of his bathroom in sweatpants, his wet hair dripping across his bare shoulders.

"Hey," George exhaled, drinking in the sight of him. It felt wrong to want him so badly after the day they'd had, but here she was undressing him with her eyes. That is, until she noticed the way his shoulders curved in under the weight of everything.

"Toby played the Phantom?"

She figured if she could just distract him for little bits here and there maybe he'd be okay, at least for a little while.

"Yeah." Caleb came to stand beside her, staring at the photo. "He was so good. I mean I knew he was a good singer before that, but he was fucking unbelievable onstage. Everyone said so."

"I hope I get to see him in something someday," George said, and meant it. "He speaks very highly of you, you know."

Caleb sat on the edge of the bed, his eyes on the photo. George wanted to crawl into his lap and stay there for a week. But she could feel he needed a moment to just breathe.

"He comes by the drama honestly." Caleb shrugged off the compliment.

"He said, and I quote, *Caleb is the best guy I know.* You must be an exceptional friend for him to say that." She leaned against the desk, watching him.

Caleb closed his eyes and let out a breath that was wrapped so tightly in grief.

"High school kids can be pretty awful."

He looked up at her with so much sadness that she had to hold onto the edge of the desk to keep from going to him.

"Sophomore year he was dating this Junior, Sarah. She was popular, pretty, played Varsity field hockey—everything a fifteen-year-old guy could want. I don't remember what the musical was that year but Toby was in it, and about halfway into production he realized he liked the lead."

"Okay." George understood so far. Or thought she did, until Caleb grimaced. Like he felt sorry for her for not understanding what was coming next.

"The *male* lead, Archer McPherson. Sarah's older brother."

"Oh." George could sense what was coming, like a storm rumbling in the distance.

"If you ask Toby, he'd tell you he always admired guys in theatre and thought that's all it was—admiration. But being around Archer, it was different. He realized he was attracted to him. So, he went to Sarah and told her, thinking she'd be on his side and would help him work through what he was starting to understand about himself.

"So, he pours his heart out and she listens, acts like she understands, plays the perfect, open-minded girlfriend. I didn't know any of this, by the way. Toby planned to tell me after school the next day, but it never happened."

Caleb turned to his open bedroom door, like he was watching the scene play out in the hall.

"You're just so naïve at that age, you know? Just dumb."

The hairs on George's arms stood and her stomach rolled over, threatening to be sick. Wherever this story was going, she didn't want to go there. She wanted to go back in time and stop it from happening.

"So, Toby walks into school the next day thinking everything's good. He asks me to get dinner with him after baseball, says he has something he wants to tell me. I'm like, sounds good, just any other day, you know? He goes one way, I go the other. Phil finds me after lunch, pulls me out of class to tell me she heard he was taken to the hospital, that it's bad but she doesn't know the details. So, stupid me, I go looking for Sarah, thinking maybe she knows what happened."

Caleb laughed then, but in doing so a tear broke free, racing down the side of his nose. He didn't wipe it away, just kept wringing his hands.

George had to remind herself that she'd seen Toby just last night. He was fine. He was happy and healthy. This was all in the past.

"Sarah apparently told Archer that Toby had slept with her all to get to him. None of it was true, but she was upset and a stupid teenage girl. And Archer, fucking douchecanoe that he was—probably still is—beat the shit out of Toby in the boys' bathroom. Jason Belden found him and got the nurse, and then she drove him down the street to the hospital."

"Was he okay?" George asked, stupidly. Of course, he wasn't okay if he had been taken to the hospital.

"He had a broken nose, bruised ribs, stitches under his eye, a concussion."

Each additional injury was like a punch to the gut. The picture George conjured in her head of Toby crumpled on the floor of a bathroom stall hurt deep in her chest, like seeing a car crash happen in your rearview mirror. She wished she'd known last night so she could have hugged him tighter when they said their goodbyes.

"He's lying in the hospital bed, bloody and bandaged, and he says to me, *Do you think makeup will cover this?*" Caleb laughed, his hands unclasped and braced his knees.

"Did he press charges?" George wasn't sure how justice was dealt here, but surely it was meted out accordingly. At the minimum, Archer had to have been expelled. At best, he now had a record.

Caleb looked down at his hands and color crept into his cheeks.

"So, um, I was dealing with a lot back then. And I didn't have a therapist yet so I, um…"

Caleb held George's gaze, his fists pinned between his knees, eyebrows raised like he still couldn't believe what he was about to say.

"I smashed all the windows of his Beemer."

George bit her bottom lip to keep from reacting. Because the longer she thought about it, the easier it was to picture Caleb destroying a car to get back at a person for hurting someone he loved.

"Archer knew it was me. Even on Toby's best day he'd never be able to wield a bat like that. So, he knew. His parents threatened the school to find out who'd done it, but Archer knew if he accused me, he'd end up facing charges for what he'd done to Toby. So, he kept his mouth shut."

George felt like she was missing something. Caleb came out looking like the hero of the story, getting revenge on the school bully for hurting his best friend. So why did he look absolutely devastated admitting this?

"I fucked it up for Toby. He couldn't say who'd hurt him or else I'd get in trouble. He said he hadn't seen who beat him up because they'd come from behind. Archer's windows got replaced and Sarah just continued on like she hadn't almost got my best friend killed."

He angrily brushed the tears away, like he was disgusted with himself.

"Caleb, none of that was your fault."

George crossed to the bed, tucking herself next to him so she could thread her arm in his and pull him close. There was nothing she could say to make it better, she knew that.

"If I'd just taken a breath and thought it through."

George leaned her head against Caleb's shoulder and looked up at the picture of him and Toby, a year or two after the incident. They both looked fine, happy. But the more she thought about it, pieces of Caleb clicked into place. He carried so much weight on his shoulders, guilt about things he shouldn't have to carry. More than anything, she wanted to take that weight from him and see the person he could be when there was nothing bearing down on him.

"Come on, slugger. Let me make you dinner." She stood and held out her hands.

* * *

Their bellies full, George tucked herself into the corner of the sectional. She had a view of MIT over one shoulder while a nature documentary played on the tv. Caleb melted into the couch, his feet tucked against the far arm, his head cushioned in George's lap. Within moments of him laying down, her fingers combing through his hair, he was asleep. It had been her goal. Get him cleaned up, fed, and rested. The crescent moons under his eyes assured her he needed sleep, but she worried about his dreams. Would they be a replay of today?

Caleb hadn't divulged what happened in the hospital after she'd left him with his mother. But she'd noticed his red cheek when he found her in the hall, the barely muted anger that splintered into heartbreak the moment Phil answered his call. He wasn't okay and George worried about what would happen after she left tomorrow.

George had zero interest in infantilizing Caleb. He was a grown man and had done just fine before she'd walked into his life and would continue on after she left. But who was going to take care of him? Because he needed help.

George knew Caleb's relationship with his parents wasn't great. She could tell things were very different from her relationship with Grandma Jeane. But thank God for Phil. At least he had her.

197

The clink of keys and the clatter of shoes being kicked off down the hall brought George back to present. A moment later Phil stood at the edge of the room, her cheeks splotchy, eyes bloodshot.

"Caleb." George gently shook him and he stirred, coming from somewhere far away. She hated to wake him, but Phil's bottom lip was already trembling, the tears were falling, and under the weight of Caleb's head George could do nothing to comfort her. And anyway, she wasn't who Phil needed.

"Hey," Caleb blinked up at George, the hint of a smile surfacing. But then his head jerked in the other direction, and he was up and moving, and Phil disappeared within the protection of his arms.

George quietly slipped down the hall to Caleb's room. She'd never know the intricacies of having a sibling, especially what it was to have a twin. As she was closing the bedroom door she heard Phil break, the sob clawing its way out of her throat, followed by Caleb's murmuring that it would be okay. But would it?

From what George had seen of their relationship, Phil was the one who assumed the role of caregiver. But now, seeing the roles reversed, it was like it had always been that way. Caleb had all the qualities to take care of others and maybe this would be the way through for him.

George curled up on Caleb's bed, savoring the softness of it. She rubbed her hands across the duvet, wondering what it had cost, how long it would take her to save for a blanket like this. She wasn't tired, but she also didn't want to intrude when it wasn't her place. As much as she hated to admit it, Caleb's mother had been right. It was a family matter and George wasn't family.

She leaned back against the headboard and looked around the room. A leather-bound notebook on the bedside table beckoned to her. It was not meant for her eyes, she knew, but the temptation was too strong. What was the harm in peeking?

She traced Caleb's handwriting with her fingers. His letters were surprisingly small and neat, painstakingly practiced. She pictured him as a child, tracing letters over and over, molding them like clay until they were perfect. She couldn't explain why, but it made her chest tight.

There were short, succinct poems. Paragraphs of scenes on a city street. A garden with ducklings all in a row. Boats that looked like swans. There were small moments, things that were unextraordinary. Scenes you saw on a Tuesday and didn't think twice about. And yet, in Caleb's writing they became heartbreakingly beautiful glimpses of people she'd never meet and he'd never see again. It stole her breath away, knowing he was capable of this kind of writing.

She read page after page—short stories that ended far too soon and poems that made her laugh. She only forced herself to stop when her eyelids grew too heavy.

She awoke sometime later in the dark. Caleb's arm was wrapped around her side, his hand over her heart. She sighed at the sheer relief of him. If she was brave, she'd tell him how he made her feel. But when was the right time—after you'd shared a traumatic event or on a Sunday afternoon before disappearing into the clouds?

"Hi." She rolled onto her back. She hadn't heard him come in and had no idea what time it was. But she supposed that didn't matter. It could be eleven or three and she'd still want to be awake beside him.

The city lights out the window illuminated the planes of his face, his hair slinking into darkness. His eyes were open, but even in the fractured light she could read the exhaustion there. She wanted to wipe it all away and put that smile she coveted back in place.

Holding his hand over her heart, she reached up with the other to push the hair out of his eyes. She traced the sticky path of an old tear along the ridge of his nose, stopping when she lost track of it at the crest of his lip. He smiled, finally.

"Do you know how beautiful you are?" She asked, but he shook his head.

Her hands followed the speckled light down the line of his throat, along the shadow beneath his collar bone, pausing at the curve of his shoulder. She then let gravity bring her hand to his heart and discovered that his frantic beat matched her own.

"Please don't go," she thought she heard him say as he rolled onto her, pinning her hips to the bed with his own. But at the weight of him between her legs, silence flooded her ears and she couldn't be sure if she'd imagined it. Because that was exactly what she wanted to hear, even if she couldn't stay. She might be leaving tomorrow but she was here now. That much she could give him.

On top of her, Caleb's face was like the Phantom, half in shadow. She could see him beginning to crack under the weight of so much sadness, and it stole her breath away.

"Are you okay?" She whispered, afraid to hear the answer.

But Caleb's response was to kiss her, heartbreakingly gentle, like everything about this moment hurt. When she opened her mouth to him and met his tongue with her own, she might as well have broken the dam. His need for her was everywhere—his hands tangled in her hair, his tongue at that ticklish spot just under her jaw. His leg tangled with hers so she could hardly move. Not that she would—there was no place she'd rather be than under him.

"I need you."

His mouth flamed along her neck and up over her chin and then claimed her lips in a way that had her pushing with all the strength she had to get his sweatpants down. He needed her and she would do everything in her power to meet his fire with her own. But she could only reach so far as she had barely any room to move beneath him.

"I know, but I can't—"

Caleb pushed up off her and sat back on his heels to do the rest himself giving George the chance to pull her shirt up and over her head. She settled back against the pillows watching him, committing every inch of his shadowy body to memory.

They hadn't talked about what the plan was after tomorrow. Emails? Calls and texts? And then what? George couldn't afford to take time off or pay for another flight. And it wasn't fair to put everything on Caleb just because he had the means.

She shook these questions loose as he tugged off her underwear, drinking in the way his eyes caressed every inch of her, like he still couldn't believe she was his. She mourned the day this might end, when he'd no longer look at her body with wonder, with so much gratitude, and instead allow undressing her to become mundane. Or worse, wait for her to do it herself. Because at some point, surely, he'd no longer be this enamored.

She didn't want to think about that right now when he was kneeling between her legs like he had come to pray at the alter of her. She grabbed his shoulders and pulled him down so she could kiss him, savoring the taste of him. Her name was a strangled noise as he buried his arms beneath her, and rubbed himself against her, snuffing out her tenuous thoughts.

You are my home, she thought. And then, the words almost left her mouth, if not for the fact that his tongue was in the way.

She got lost in the dance of his mouth on hers, the push and pull and swirling perfection of it all, that she somehow missed him rolling on the condom. She was lost in a way she'd come back to on lonely nights and wonder if it had all been in her head. How a lungful of his musk made her feel dizzy and she couldn't get enough of it.

"Is this okay?" He hovered over her, his body heat just out of reach. She arched up off the bed in search of it, of him.

George nodded, because she didn't trust her voice to stay clean when she felt this frenzied beneath him. She refused to sully the moment with what she really wanted to tell him to do to her.

And even though it was clear they equally wanted to devour the other, fire consuming fire, he waited, the anticipation nearly killing her. And she thought for half a second, *This is it. I should tell him.*

A horn honked outside and George startled, looking towards the window, even though they were too high up to be seen. When she looked back at Caleb the moment was gone, having slipped off into the shadows, and she wasn't sure how to coax those three words back into the light.

Caleb nudged her leg up with his knee and she hooked it around him, holding her breath as he entered her. She might not have said the words, but she'd thought them. She imagined those eight letters washing over them both like a salve.

But for now, his gaze hooked on her mouth as he watched her lips part around a gasp, the air in his bedroom growing thick and heady as she clung to him, it was enough to have thought them.

With each torturously slow thrust, his eyes glued to hers, she thought them. Again, when she bit his bottom lip and he picked up the pace. When he clamped his hand over her mouth to keep her from screaming his name, she thought them. And no, it wasn't the same as saying them out loud, but on some level, George imagined he must know that this had moved into that territory. That her heart had jumped out of her body and attached itself to him.

That she was forever changed.

24. CALEB

Caleb woke to watery morning light and cursed himself for forgetting to close the curtains, but he'd been too distracted by how badly he'd wanted to bury himself inside George to think of anything else.

Was it possible she was still asleep? He desperately wanted to curl himself around her, wake her the way she claimed to adore, but she was on her stomach, so he slid a hand under the duvet and molded it perfectly to her butt. Her eyes remained closed, but a smile snuck across her lips, and Caleb looked up at the ceiling pleased with himself.

He had the perfect Sunday planned. First: naked time. Then: shower together. After: brunch and a bookstore in Beacon Hill. They'd walk home along the Charles taking so many pictures together that she'd be sick of him by the time they returned to pack her things.

"I can hear you thinking," George said, opening one eye and slipping a hand out from under her pillow. She curled it around Caleb's bicep and snuggled closer, her breath tickling this skin. He gave her a squeeze in response.

"I have big plans."

He pulled her leg across him like a blanket. She ran cold, even under the duvet, and he had more than enough heat to spare.

"Big plans indeed." Her leg nudged him and she smirked.

Caleb pinched that spot right above her hip that he knew was ticklish, and George squirmed and squealed as he continued to tickle up her side. The moment they paused to catch their breath she straddled him so she could kiss every inch of his face. She was the most beautiful first thing in the morning, with sleep still in the corner of her eye and her tangled tresses sticking out like a lopsided halo. He wanted to savor it.

This was how the weekend was supposed to go before everything bad happened. It was supposed to be fun, a reminder of the things that had brought them together in Jackson.

Even after all these months, could Caleb say he really knew George? They'd spent a total of five nights together and half as many days. And yet the things they'd been through, the gamut of emotions they'd experienced in that time, it felt like he knew all the important parts of her, the stuff that truly mattered in knowing a person.

The knock at the door brought reality crashing back down around them.

"Caleb?"

This was all too familiar. But at least Phil knocked this time.

George slid off Caleb as he pulled the blanket up around her.

"What?"

Phil opened the door a crack, but kept her eyes shut.

"Everyone decent?"

Caleb checked once more to make sure George was covered before responding.

"Yeah, you can come in."

Phil opened the door, but remained on the threshold. She had a pair of cowboy boots in hand—the ones she'd promised George if she ever came to Boston. When she straightened, Caleb realized she was dressed, hair pulled back, ready for the day.

"Hi George, sorry for intruding yet again. Just wanted to see if you were ready to go?"

The emotions of the previous day rushed into the room like a gust of blisteringly cold air. That was the thing about being in George's presence—Caleb didn't care about anything beyond her. He could forget the outside world, the emotions, the exhaustion of what had happened, and give all of himself to her.

But as the memories of the day before rushed back in, with them came a sliver of guilt. His father was across the city in a hospital bed and here Caleb was in the comfort of his home not giving him a single thought. If the roles were reversed, would his father be worrying about him?

"To the hospital," Phil added when the silence stretched too long.

"It's George's last day. I'll swing by after I drop her at the airport."

Phil knew how important this weekend was to him. How hard he had wished for it. She'd even offered to buy George's plane ticket on top of offering the boots just to get him to stop moping.

"Caleb." The look she gave him was pitying but stern.

"I'll go later." He sat forward, keeping an arm low so the duvet wouldn't shift off of George.

"Mom is expecting us there in an hour."

The mirroring of their mother's tone sent a zing up Caleb's spine. Phil never sounded like her, unless it was mocking behind her back. But this wasn't mocking and it made Caleb's skin itch. One mother was plenty. Phil was supposed to be on his side.

"Philippa, I said I will stop by later."

Neither of them blinked as their eyes narrowed. Why didn't Phil understand how important these last few hours with George were?

"I'm sorry," Phil smiled apologetically at George before turning. "I'll give you thirty minutes and then we're leaving."

The door closed and the perfect bubble they had awoken in only a minute ago burst, the moment soured.

George's nose crinkled, like she was trying to keep in a sneeze, as Caleb fell back against the pillows.

Phil knew how much pressure he'd put on himself to make this weekend perfect and how he needed today to rectify how badly it had been knocked off course. He turned to George, wondering how quickly he could get them back to where they'd been just a few minutes ago, but she was staring at the boots beside her bag.

"She's right. You should go be with your family."

"Hey," he said, reaching up to tuck her wayward hair behind an ear so he could see her whole face. "I'll go this evening after I drop you at Logan."

She shook her head and forced a smile.

"Caleb, he's your father. What if something happened overnight. You need to be there. He needs your support and *Phil* needs you."

It felt like she'd stollen the air right out of his lungs.

"But it's your last day."

She nodded and hugged her knees. She was right though. He needed to be there for Phil, as annoyed as he was with her.

"Fine. I'll go for an hour and get back here in time to take you to brunch. We still have—" he looked at his phone, "—plenty of time to do almost everything. We just might need to rain check all the orgasms I had planned for you."

The laugh he got out of her was halfhearted at best.

"She said you have thirty minutes."

It took Caleb a second to recalibrate. The plan for the day might have been knocked off course, but they could still make the best of it.

"I do my best work under pressure." He winked, throwing the duvet off the bed so there was nothing to get in the way of what he had planned.

"The mouth on you!" George gasped, clutching imaginary pearls. It quickly turned to giggles as he prowled up to place a kiss on her mouth. But when he hovered over her, his eyes on the valley between her hips, his intentions very clear, the smile was replaced with shallow breaths, her lips parted in expectation.

"Twenty-nine minutes," she whispered, daring him.

I love you, he wanted to say, but his mouth was already on her and he didn't dare stop when she was making noises like that.

Some people lived life preparing for things to go wrong. *Just in case* prefacing their every move. Bring the umbrella—*just in case.* I packed us snacks—*just in case.* George didn't live like that because for her every day was structured: wake at four thirty, work till five, bed at ten.

So naturally, when Caleb left, she didn't think to hug and kiss him goodbye in case he didn't come back. She was pulling her clothes out of her bag when he called from the front hall that he was heading out. He'd be back in an hour.

She took her time in his bathroom, at the last minute deciding that since she wasn't in a rush she might as well make use of the tub. She never had time for a bath at home, because she was always bone-tired, and a tubful of water was so wasteful when you lived in such a water-dependent state. She added a pour of Caleb's body wash and lounged in the dizzying smell until the water grew cold. It was almost perfect. If only Caleb had been there.

When she got out, she checked her phone on the bedside table.

He's awake, Caleb had texted half an hour earlier while she was soaking.

That's great! She texted back.

She dressed, repacked her bag, and finished the nature documentary she'd been watching the night before when Phil arrived home. Outside, the Charles River sparkled in the January sun. It was deceptive, knowing it must be freezing out there while being toasty-warm inside.

She checked her phone. Two hours had passed since Caleb walked out the door. She waited, even as her empty stomach churned.

At 11:05, Caleb texted again. *He's getting discharged. Go ahead and eat without me. The nurse says it might be another hour.*

George would have been lying if she'd said her heart hadn't dropped at those words. Deep down she knew he'd rather be spending the day with her, but he didn't have a choice. So, she made herself eggs and toast and ate it while looking out at the river.

By noon she started to feel like a princess trapped in a tower. Caleb had taken his keys, assuming he'd be racing right back, so George had no way of returning once she left the building. If she wanted to go explore and make up for the time they'd lost, she'd have to take her things with her.

So, she continued to wait.

George watched the cars rush along the street below until it made her dizzy. The day was slipping away. They'd had a handful of ridiculously good minutes in bed together, but she'd have forgone all of that just to take a walk with him and get to experience his neighborhood. She needed to see if she could imagine herself here with him. Because— crazy as it was, considering she'd never let herself dream before meeting Caleb—if she couldn't picture herself here, then what was all of this for?

She started pacing and forced herself to stop before she wore a path into the rug. But what could she do to distract herself from being trapped here without him?

In his bathroom she sniffed all the things. She took pictures so she could look them up when she got home on the off-chance the pharmacy sold them. Not likely, but it was worth a try.

In his closet she touched all his dress shirts, picturing him in a suit. Would she ever get to see that? She was sure if she did it would turn her knees to jelly. She'd already taken a sweatshirt, which she still hadn't

210

told him about. Did he even realize it was missing? It was tucked neatly in her closet back home. She only wore it in the privacy of her bedroom because she was petrified of getting it dirty and having to wash it, even though it had lost all trace of him.

For one embarrassing moment she considered leaving a pair of her underwear for Caleb to find at some point in the future. But something about that felt cheap and dirty. If she was going to leave anything for him to find it needed to be a piece of her heart.

Then, it came to her. She propped the pillows up on the bed and settled with his notebook on her lap. Flipping to the very last page, she put pen to paper.

Out there beyond the window pane
Above the valley, three girls, never tame
And snow may stay even while grass runs dry
Hooves or feet, they all stop by
Along the river, always and never the same
Ebbing, flowing, moods subject to the rain

Rain or sun, rise or set
Catch me in the meadow, that'll be your best bet
Tug my hand once, of course I'll follow you
Back home, blinds drawn closed, let's pretend to be blue

When she was done, she couldn't explain it, but she felt heartbroken. Another hour had slipped by and the apartment was still empty. Maybe it was the thick quiet around her, but George couldn't shake the feeling that this was somehow the end.

She tucked Caleb's notebook back in its place, making sure it was as it had been before she'd touched it. It was funny, putting together the many intricacies that made him whole. The boy who went to bat for his best friend. The man who strung together beautiful words but kept them secret. A closet full of expensive suits, when he looked the most comfortable in jeans and a tee. The man who set her body completely on fire.

Her phone rang. *Caleb.*

"Hello?" She leaned back against the pillows, her hand absentmindedly reaching for Caleb's side of the bed, finding nothing but soft linen.

"George, I'm sorry." Caleb's voice hung low, like he was trying not to be heard. "I…"

Caleb must've covered the phone then, voices muffled to almost nothing. George strained to hear but couldn't make out words. From his tone he was barely keeping his anger in check and she wished she could reach through the phone and sooth him, tell him it would be okay.

She just wanted to hug him. It was stupid, but it felt like everything would be okay if they could just hold each other for a moment. Touching him was like a reset for George, bringing everything back to level.

"My father got discharged and now we're heading to my parents' house. The only reason they need me is because I can shoulder his weight up the stairs." The breath he let out was enormous, like he was holding in enough to smother a person.

"Are you okay?"

If he said he wasn't, she would find some way to get to him, no matter the cost or how far she'd have to travel across the city.

"I wanted to spend the day with *you*. This is so fucked."

"It's okay." But it wasn't, and they both knew that.

"I'll be quick and then I can at least drive you to the airport."

The tension between George's shoulders eased just knowing Caleb would be here soon. Even though they'd lost out on spending the day together, she could still hold his hand on the drive to the airport, hug him for a solid five minutes just committing his smell and the weight of his arms around her to memory before getting on that plane.

"Okay. I'll see you soon."

They hung up and George rechecked the zipper on her bag. She walked around the apartment one last time to make sure she hadn't forgotten anything. Then she pulled on Phil's gorgeous cowboy boots— *now hers*—and looked around at this beautiful home. She was saying goodbye, but she hoped she'd be back. She wanted to come back.

An hour later and she was still waiting. And now, she was afraid of missing her flight. She dialed Caleb's number but it rang to voicemail. She started to sweat. Should she wait? What happened if you missed your flight? She mapped how long it would take to get to the airport and the worry spread like a stain.

George put on her coat, shouldered her bag, and walked out Caleb's door closing it softly behind her. It hurt to do so, but what choice did she have?

She assumed you just hailed a cab on any street corner like they did in the movies, but it took twenty minutes to find one. As she climbed in, sweat pooling under her bra despite the chill, she was nearly in tears.

It wasn't Caleb's fault. She wasn't upset with him. She was upset with the situation and that she hadn't planned for *just in case*.

Her phone vibrated somewhere in her bag, but she didn't go searching for it. George was worried about getting to the airport on time without losing anything. And how much was this going to cost? If it was Caleb calling, which it most likely was, hearing his voice would crack her open. She was not about to trudge through a crowded airport bawling her eyes out.

At Logan, she exited the cab and stood looking down the line of cars at the curb depositing people. Every person was Caleb for a split second until her eyes focused. She wished she hadn't let him leave this morning. No, that was selfish. She would never have stopped him from going. Family was the most important thing. But she should have told him she loved him.

It occurred to her that this was probably how he'd felt that final morning in Wyoming when he opened his eyes and she was gone. She owed him an apology because that was an awful thing to do to a person— sneak out under the pretense of making things easier for everyone by skipping the goodbye. It wasn't easier. It felt like a knife was cleaving her chest in two.

She sucked in one last lungful of salty ocean air, wiped her eyes, and headed into the airport knowing that everything had changed. Caleb had unraveled her, and now held pieces of her that she'd never get back. And yet, he didn't even know her heart was in his hands, because she hadn't told him. She'd waited and waited for it to be *the right time* and in the process of waiting she may have missed it. Or worse—she had the horrifying thought as she handed her license over to the TSA agent for review—maybe there was no right time. There was just time, plain and simple, and it became the right time in hindsight after the telling.

Either way, they hadn't talked about their feelings or plans for the future. And as she plopped her things on the conveyor belt to be screened, tears once again threatening to make a mockery of her, she choked down the idea of never seeing him again. It was entirely possible that they wouldn't be able to make it work across time zones. And if that was the case, she'd regret not telling him she loved him for the rest of her life.

26. CALEB

from: g.rosetownsend@snailmail.com
to: calebtbrowningrichards@snailmail.com
date: Feb 27, 2017, 6:13 PM
subject: Hi

Caleb,
Since we both have crazy schedules (and the time difference doesn't help), I thought emailing might yield better results than us continually missing each other's call.
How are you? That last call sounded like you might be getting sick? I'll attach Grandma Jeane's chicken soup recipe. It always makes me feel better and I know she'd be thrilled if it made you feel better. She thinks your "a handsome fella" by the way. I showed her the picture Toby took of us. She said you have kind eyes.
How is your dad doing? I still can't believe he has no lingering issues. He's a lucky man, especially to have you as his son.
I know you said you wanted to come visit, but I only get Sundays off and I can't really ask for more time off for a while. So, I was thinking, I know it's a ways off, but I could head to Jackson a week early and you could meet me there and that way we'd get some time together without any distractions.
Please tell Phil I say hi and a very belated thank you for the boots. I'm keeping them tucked away for a special occasion.
Yours,
George

Caleb read the email three times before closing out of it without responding. Calls with George, when they even managed to connect beyond leaving a voicemail, were stiff, neither of them quite knowing what to say, so they filled the time with meandering talk about their day. Caleb couldn't figure out how to take everything out of his head and put it into words. There was just too much.

For starters, he'd ruined their last day together and he was so fucking sorry, but apologizing wouldn't fix it. It was already done.

Actually, he'd ruined the whole weekend by suggesting they go to the Chatham house in the first place. And then to cap it all off, he hadn't been able to say goodbye because his family was ruinous.

No. That wasn't exactly fair. Phil was going through something Caleb didn't understand, and it wasn't fair to let her recent words and actions color their entire relationship. Even if he and Phil weren't exactly talking right now, Caleb knew they'd eventually patch things up.

Phil and Caleb had grown up having very different experiences with their father. Phil was naturally talented and took criticism in stride, so she fared well in the lifelong game of pleasing their parents. Caleb couldn't say the same. He had natural talents, but he had never taken criticism well. It always compounded into larger wrongs until he couldn't breathe, couldn't move forward under the weight of it.

When Caleb had entered his father's hospital room that Sunday at the end of January, it was like the room was split in two. On one side, in technicolor, Dara and Phil fussed over John like he was a man who'd been dealt a shitty hand. On the other side, in a twisted sort of parallel universe doused in shades of grey, Caleb stood by the window returning his father's scowl.

John Richards was not the man Caleb believed him to be. As it turned out, Caleb had been right to worry back in Jackson. He had scrapped the private plane fees months earlier in favor of feeding his addiction because he'd secretly been unemployed (*fired* from his job of twenty-five years) for nearly a year by the time they got on the commercial flight to Wyoming.

The craziest part was that Caleb actually felt bad for him, pitied him even. His father was so afraid of being seen as less than perfect that he'd nearly died rather than raise a hand for help. It was sad to realize the truth about him. And worse, to think about all the time he'd wasted trying to meet his father's impossible standards.

But, while Caleb was having an existential crisis about all this in the hospital room, John stared at him with deceptively watery eyes. Phil and Dara probably mistook it for exhaustion. And why wouldn't they when his body had just fought its way back from death? But Caleb knew that look intimately. It was emotion burning so hot behind the marble façade that steam had to escape somehow. And when Caleb recognized the look, he instinctively started sweating, goosebumps prickling his skin.

Except, what right did his father have to be mad at him? For showing up unexpectedly and saving his life?

Caleb's own fury began to build as these thoughts churned and tangled in his head. All the while, Phil fussed over the hospital's lack of urgency and attention, her fuse growing shorter with each article of offense. Dara, meanwhile, was making calls, arranging for an in-home nurse to come by after they got him discharged.

And all the while, Caleb thought about George. How he'd have chewed off his own arm to get out of the room. He'd promised her brunch. Then he missed the morning entirely. He'd promised her a tour of his favorite spots around the city. He wasn't able to follow through on that. And when his father was finally discharged and they caravanned back to Beacon Hill, Caleb kept thinking he was closer to escaping their clutches and returning to George.

Helping his father out of the car and up the stairs had been like entering the first level of Hell. Phil and their mother went ahead to unlock the door and get things figured out—would it be better to turn the living room into a temporary bedroom since it was on the first floor, or get him situated in his room on the second floor even if it meant he might be stuck up there for a few days until he got his legs back under him?

No one was around to hear the words saved for only Caleb's ears on this special occasion. There were no thanks, no gratitude. John Richards had not been changed by his brush with death. If anything, it only made him sharper around the edges, like a honed weapon. And with Caleb in reach, he began to slash and cut as if making up for lost time.

Caleb's skin crawled as he shouldered John's weight up the eight steps from the sidewalk to the front door. Words steeped in self-loathing were turned around and dumped on Caleb en masse. And Caleb, though he felt changed by the previous day's events, like he finally had a clear lens on his life, didn't have enough time to shield himself. It took everything in him, every ounce of self-restraint from the ends of his hair down to his toes, not to nudge his father backward down the stairs.

Huh. Maybe he had changed after all. To be able to push through a moment of pure rage and not commit a felony was something fifteen-year-old Caleb hadn't been able to do.

John seethed and Caleb kept his mouth shut. Phil could be mad at him all she wanted after this, but he would not be coming back to their childhood home again. He'd shouldered more than a child should ever have to and he was done. This was his breaking point.

The moment his father was settled in his bedroom on the second floor, Caleb ran. He didn't say goodbye, not even to Phil. She could find her own way home. He nearly rolled his ankle on the way down the steps, trying to make short work of them and misjudging his athletic ability. He drove like a maniac back to his condo, double-parking out front so he could race upstairs only to find George gone. And then he drove like a masshole trying to make it to Logan in time for what—a tearful apology at the curb? A quick kiss goodbye?

George deserved so much more. He wanted to give her clam chowder in the seaport and skating on the Frog Pond, and instead he'd shown her the absolute worst side of himself, screaming his throat hoarse at a rest stop and falling asleep on her.

In the end, he did manage to make it to Logan in time to see her off. But she didn't know he was there. He watched her walk through the metal detector to collect her things and stood like a lunatic, hands in his hair trying so hard not to pull it all out, as she slipped out of sight. He wanted to scream but his mouth just gaped in horror at how badly he had fucked everything up.

He called her once he knew she was already in the air. Because he was a coward.

"George, I'm sorry. I'm so sorry. I had these grand imaginings of how this weekend was going to go. You were going to come here and fall in love with... Boston. And then it all went to shit. I... I hope you have a safe flight and just call or text when you get home so I know you got there. Okay, I... Bye."

Minutes later, he'd looked down at his bed, at the indent George left behind on the duvet, and wondered what he'd said in the voicemail. He had no memory of it, just prayed he conveyed how sorry he was and knowing he probably hadn't. He was so fucking sorry.

She'd texted when she landed. He didn't blame her for not calling. He wouldn't want to hear his pathetic voice either. But he didn't have much time to overthink it, because Phil arrived home and they had a fight. The kind of fight that alters sibling DNA, a catastrophic crash that some relationships never recover from with scars that wide and deep.

It wasn't like Phil to walk through the door guns blazing. She could certainly be over the top when she got worked up about something. She was passionate about what she believed in and those she cared for. It was one of Caleb's favorite things about her, the thing he hoped she never lost. But she'd never outright attacked him before her shoes were off. And they always said sorry within the first twenty-four hours post-argument. But this time…

"I know you're sad about George leaving," she began, her voice already frosty as she barreled down the hall. She stopped when she found Caleb in the kitchen, blocking his path so he was forced to face her.

"But you were so cold today. To all of us. Dad almost *died*, Caleb!"

"And it's a real shame he didn't follow through."

The words were out of his mouth before he even realized he was thinking them. A day spent under his father's glare, taking hit after hit while Phil and his mother were out of earshot—Caleb had tried. He really had. He'd taken it all without volleying anything back, because you didn't kick a person when they were down and his father was so far down. But Caleb realized he was alone in this. Phil was on a different planet where their father was concerned, and their mother only acknowledged Caleb when it suited her needs. He had no doubt she'd choose her husband every time over the son she treated with contempt.

Phil jolted like she'd been slapped. Her jaw dropped and she blinked once, twice, tears threatening to spill over.

"What the fuck, Caleb!"

Caleb almost apologized. Not because he was sorry for what he'd said. He wasn't. His father had said worse a million times over. But Caleb was sorry for upsetting Phil. She was the last person he ever wanted to hurt. They were supposed to be on each other's side no matter what. It was built into their genetic code, to be each other's strongest support.

"You have no clue, Phil. You think he's the greatest dad on the planet because he buys you horses and praises everything you do."

Caleb had never seen Phil this mad, her face going pale before flushing splotchy-red, like she was holding her breath, saving it up so she could roast him alive.

"We have two very different dads. You have no fucking idea."

"Bullshit!" She screeched. "And regardless of whatever it is you think he's done to you—"

Caleb fell back a step at that, the floor dropping out beneath him at the implication that she didn't believe there had ever been a solid reason for him to be upset. That it was all in his head.

"—you should still behave like a respectable person in public. I mean, Jesus, Caleb! Was it too much to ask to get some ice? I wasn't asking for your kidney! And when Mom asked you to help get Dad inside—you're twenty-three! Act like an adult already! Stop being a whiny bitch when your day doesn't go as planned!"

Phil took two steps into the kitchen, her finger raised like a weapon, and Caleb stepped back until he hit the counter. He would not retaliate. She could be upset and he'd take it. Phil hated not being in control, and worse, she hated to cry. So instead, she got irrationally mad.

"George isn't going to sit around waiting for you to step up and be a man, Caleb. You think she wants to be with someone who turns into a petulant child when something doesn't go his way?"

Phil stopped, her finger hovering just out of reach, testing him. The last time he'd hit her was when they were sixteen. She'd laughed at him for getting a boner while they were watching Aquamarine. It was his fault for letting Phil pick the movie. He lifted a hand to push her into the couch pillows right as she turned toward him and the heel of his hand connected with her nose. Their mother screamed at him for an hour. Not because Phil was hurt, but because they'd gotten blood on her Hermès pillow.

"You're an embarrassment," she spat, and walked away from him. "Grow the fuck up."

Caleb waited until he heard Phil's door slam before allowing a tear to spill. It was too much to keep in. Angry with his father, hurt by Phil, and then there was the ample self-loathing. He bit his lip until he tasted blood and the tears ceased.

There was no point trying to get Phil on his side. She'd never believe him. Her father wasn't his, and she'd probably never choose to see things his way. He understood now that he should have told her everything from the beginning. But he was too late.

Caleb didn't tell George any of this. Not over the phone, not via text, certainly not in a long-winded email. He didn't want to prove Phil right by being a whiny bitch. He wasn't about to bog George down with his sad, privileged life. Not when she worked her ass off just to get by.

But deciding not to tell her about what was going on meant that Caleb had nothing to talk about when they finally connected on the phone. He filled his side of the conversation with superfluous nonsense and then hated himself afterwards for wasting her precious time. So, he stopped calling. It was just easier that way.

At the same time, he desperately wanted to know everything happening in her world. It was like oxygen, inhaling the pictures she painted of daily work on the ranch, of living with a grandmother who adored her. He'd draft an email and reread it, feeling stupid when it looked annoyingly like interview questions. So, it would go unsent.

Phil stopped talking to him. She went from work to their parents' house, or so Caleb assumed. Some nights she didn't come home at all and Caleb would pretend he wasn't worried until her girlfriend sent the *Hey, she's spending the night here* text. The relief would nearly drown him.

He'd never imagined something would tear them apart. They were a pair, two of a kind. Until suddenly they weren't. It was like losing a limb, a part of himself there one day and ripped away the next. He felt unbalanced and wondered what that said about him, that he was twenty-three and on his own for the first time. Maybe he'd depended on Phil for too long. This separation was overdue.

Caleb kept his usual therapy appointment the first week after his father's overdose. But two weeks later he canceled, not even bothering with a flimsy excuse, and then it just became something he couldn't face. He didn't want to sit in his feelings, sift through them, work on coping mechanisms. He didn't want his father to occupy more of his mental space when he'd already taken up too much.

But that line in George's email was like a worm wriggling on a hook. *I know it's a ways off, but I could head to Jackson a week early and you could meet me there.* It was something for Caleb to grab onto and hoist himself up out of the shadowy depths he'd descended into.

The more Caleb thought about it, he realized that Wyoming was the answer. It had always been the answer. If they could just get back there—not the same physical house necessarily, but the mental space they'd both occupied while there—maybe everything would be okay.

If Caleb had shared any of this with his therapist, he might have been forced to realize that piling so much hope on one incredibly expensive gamble was a recipe for disaster. Instead, he didn't tell anyone as he contacted a realtor and started his search.

Phil still wasn't talking to him. She would have worked up a pros and cons list to make him see reason, and if he still wanted to go through with it, she would have offered to fly out with him and look in person. Because making a purchase from two time zones away was crazy. But his voice of reason wasn't talking to him so he bulldozed ahead.

Caleb still had half of the initial amount that had been made available from his trust when he turned twenty-one. Him and Phil going halfsies on a Back Bay condo, while an exorbitant price for anyone else his age, had made complete financial sense. Boston real estate would always increase tenfold, so it was a solid investment. He didn't squander his inheritance on a closet full of shoes he'd never wear or weekends in Vegas. He'd been smart. So Caleb wasn't at all concerned about using up what remained.

Jackson Hole was an expensive place to buy property, sure. But it was where the wealthy loved to play and that wouldn't change, so again, he was investing in a sure thing. And in a year and a half, when he turned twenty-five, Caleb would have access to the remaining amount in his trust. It wasn't like he was spending everything he had because there was still more to come.

He didn't tell George any of this because he knew she'd be horrified if she knew how much money he had and what he was spending it on. He didn't know the specifics of her home in Texas, but he knew they were at different places along the financial spectrum. She'd probably be horrified if she knew how much he'd spent on takeout since Phil stopped cooking for him.

The whole thing was rife with disaster, this plan to recoup their feelings. But all Caleb could see was golden hour on that patio, the weight of George in his lap and the feelings behind their words. They needed to get back there, to that moment in time when nothing mattered outside of themselves.

He had his sights set.

BRIDGE

2017

date: Apr 5, 2017, 2:37 PM
from: calebtbrowningrichards@snailmail.com
to: g.rosetownsend@snailmail.com
subject: RE: Hi

George,
I have a place waiting for us for May. The view of the Tetons is supposed to be the best in all of Jackson Hole. I'll send you the address and details. I can't wait to see you.
It might be worth it to pack those boots…
Yours,
C

date: Apr 6, 2017, 6:17 AM
from: g.rosetownsend@snailmail.com
to: calebtbrowningrichards@snailmail.com
subject: RE: Hi

Prepare to be climbed like a tree.
George

date: Apr 7, 2017, 11:01 AM
from: calebtbrowningrichards@snailmail.com
to: g.rosetownsend@snailmail.com
subject: RE: Hi

I don't know what that means but it sounds fun.
I still can't believe you agreed to come home with me that night at the bar, but I'm so thankful you did.
Yours,
C

date: Apr 1, 2017, 6:29 PM
from: g.rosetownsend@snailmail.com
to: calebtbrowningrichards@snailmail.com
subject: RE: Hi

You clearly don't remember how I smelled like spilled drinks and
cheap perfume or how greasy my hair was. I was just going to use
you for your shampoo and bodywash and make a run for it, but
then you were being *you* and I was done for.
Can we plan to do nothing that whole week? I just want to sit on
the porch and have nowhere to go. I don't need anything else. Just
you and me.
Yours,
George

date: Apr 2, 2017, 5:49 AM
from: calebtbrowningrichards@snailmail.com
to: g.rosetownsend@snailmail.com
subject: RE: Hi

Even if you had ducked out after using me for my toiletries, I'd have
still said it was the best night. But I'm forever grateful that you
stayed.
I've spent the last month learning how to make carbonara, salmon
with smashed rosemary potatoes, gnocchi with brown butter and
sage, and chocolate chip cookies. If nothing else, prepare to have
ALL your appetites sated.
C

date: Apr 5, 2017, 7:42 PM
from: g.rosetownsend@snailmail.com
to: calebtbrowningrichards@snailmail.com
subject: RE: Hi

Caleb, I'm going to need you to stop talking dirty until we're in the
same time zone. I don't even know what some of those foods are.
You could have just led with the cookies and I'd have got down on
my knees.
Yours,
George

date: Apr 6, 2017, 7:16 AM
from: calebtbrowningrichards@snailmail.com
to: g.rosetownsend@snailmail.com
subject: RE: Hi

I'M THE ONE TALKING DIRTY???!!!!!!
C

In May, a week before Caleb was set to get on the plane to Wyoming, he was making dinner when Phil arrived home. He hadn't seen her in three days, though he'd heard her come in and grab things from her bedroom before heading back out. This time, however, she stopped in the kitchen.

Caleb was making carbonara for the second time in a week because he kept scrambling the egg and he was determined to impress the hell out of George. Their upcoming week together was going to be perfect.

He pushed the chopped bits of pancetta around the pan while the spaghetti cooked. Last time, he'd nearly burned the pancetta, so this attempt he refused to take his eyes off it.

"Smells good," Phil said behind him and he jumped. He'd heard the front door open and assumed she'd gone straight to her room. They hadn't really spoken in three months, if you didn't count the monthly, *I need your half of the electric bill.*

The kindness in those words—*smells good*—made his eyes water and his stomach twist.

"Onions," he explained the tears away. He could see her watching him out of the corner of his eye but he couldn't think of anything else to say. In all his imaginings of how their first conversation would go, this had never been the opening line.

"What are you making?" Phil wasn't a cautious person in any sense of the word. She barreled headfirst into everything without weighing the pros and cons. But here she was, her voice traveling across uncertain ground. It immediately softened the muscles in Caleb's back.

"Carbonara. I can't seem to get it right."

If ever there was a way to pull her back in, it would be in needing her help. Phil's natural state of being was taking charge of any situation. She was quiet a moment and Caleb could hear her brain working.

"With *onions*?" Her voice curdled with judgement and he could feel her taking a step closer to peer into the pan. Caleb knew he'd been found out.

Phil *hmm*'ed at the lack of onions then disappeared into her bedroom, but she didn't shut the door behind her and that was huge.

The following nights she slept at home and each evening they shared a few more words. Whoever got home first *accidentally* made too much food for one person. The fridge returned to being overly full. Fresh flowers appeared in a vase on the entry table, another on the dining table the following evening. The condo started to feel like home again, no more thick silences balled up in each corner like dust.

Two nights before Caleb was set to leave for Wyoming, he came home with takeout from Phil's favorite Pho place. He thought telling her about the upcoming trip would be a good ice breaker and they could exchange more than a couple sentences based solely on the food they were sharing.

But when he opened the front door, something was off. Phil's shoes were strewn across the entryway. There were two duffels dropped and forgotten in the hall. Phil was the epitome of a clean freak, so the sight of carelessness sent a shiver up Caleb's spine.

"Philippa?"

He dropped his keys on the table and made his way down the hall. She wasn't in the kitchen or the dining room, though there was a discarded jacket, arms bunched as if she'd torn it off in a hurry. It suddenly occurred to Caleb that there was an obvious answer for why there would be discarded things leading towards her bedroom. Having been on the receiving end of a similar disturbance, he backpedaled.

He poured Tom Yum into one of the gigantic bowls Phil bought specifically for soup and made his way to the living room. He turned on the news and tucked into his meal. But after a while he still hadn't heard a sound—*not that he wanted to*—so he muted the TV. The silence stretched while he slurped and chewed.

Figuring that maybe she'd dropped things off and left in a hurry, Caleb made his way down the hall to Phil's door to check. He hesitated before knocking, straining to make out any sign of life on the other side, but there was only silence.

"Phil?"

And then, a muffled whimper—the sound of pain. Caleb burst into the room without another thought.

"Phil?"

She was curled up on her bed, Beary-Bear tucked protectively under her chin, arms wrapped tight. Caleb hadn't even known she still had the stuffed animal.

"What's wrong?"

Phil tried to speak, but she couldn't seem to get the words out. Air went in and in, as she worked herself into a frenzy, and then it exploded out in a keening sob.

Caleb eased onto the bed and lay a hand on her ankle to ground her. It had to be their father. That was the only thing he could think of. Maybe he'd finally shown Phil his true colors and broken her heart. Caleb didn't wish for that because Phil hurting was like a hot poker to his own chest. But the idea of no longer being alone in his feelings towards their father brought a sense of relief.

"I'm here." He'd never really gone anywhere, but now was not the time to get into semantics.

"She. Broke. Up. With. Me!" Phil struggled to get each word out and punctuated the effort with a hiccup.

Of all the things Caleb had expected to hear, this hadn't even been on the list.

"Amelia broke up with you?"

Phil and Amelia had been together for two years. They'd met at a bookstore in the South End, both circling the "Suggested Reads" table. Amelia was inspecting the cover of *The Fault in Our Stars* and Phil, obsessed with YA books, admitted she'd blazed through it in a weekend. She suggested stocking up on tissues if Amelia was going to purchase it.

They'd exchanged numbers under the pretense of Amelia letting Phil know what she thought about the book, but then they'd continued on to a bar down the street, and then later back to Phil's dorm room. They'd been together ever since.

Phil nodded through her tears, sucking in air like she was drowning. With each lungful she could only expel one word at a time.

"She. Said. I. Changed."

Caleb crawled onto the bed and held Phil as she cried. He'd forgotten how small she was. Or had she gotten smaller over the last few months?

There was nothing Caleb could say that would fix her heartbreak, so he held her tightly until her breathing slowed to normal. His shirt was damp between them, but he didn't dare move. And then, spent of emotion, she slowly drifted off to sleep, her head against his shoulder.

It had been so long since he'd been in her room. Where Caleb had stuck to mostly navy and white in his room, Phil designed hers with all colors of the rainbow. Throw pillows in vibrant patterns and an unnecessary number of blankets in shades of yellow, pink, and blue. Gauzy white curtains for too-sunny days and blackout curtains in deep purple for overnight.

An armchair sat by the window, a small pile of books stacked on its seat. It was upholstered with a scratchy green material, small horse and rider duos leaping over fences.

Their childhood rooms had been white and beige, and kept immaculate so they wouldn't have to withstand a lecture about taking pride in one's things. It had been drilled so heavily into them that they both kept their rooms neat even now, but Phil allowed her true colors to shine through.

Phil had stopped showcasing her ribbons and awards after high school, but framed photos were everywhere. Showing her first pony, then her first warmblood, all buttoned up with pigtails and jodhpurs. Action shots of her playing soccer at BB&N, cuddle puddles with her friends, and school dances. But Caleb saturated her shelves the most—them as toddlers attached at the hip, them at the middle school science fair, various graduations, in matching Christmas pajamas year after year.

On her dresser was a photo Caleb hadn't seen before. It was a panoramic shot of mountains. Not any mountains, *the Grand Tetons*. Squinting at it, he remembered they'd stopped at a pull-off after the river float—Phil, George, and him. Phil had stayed in the car while he and George got out to take in the view. Phil had begged them not to take long because she was starving.

The background was the entire mountain range, trailing off at both ends. It was lit from above, the jagged peaks grey, white, gold—the sky overhead clear-blue. In the foreground, Caleb stared ahead, taking in the vista, his back to the camera. He remembered thinking the air smelled better there, and for the first time, he'd enjoyed feeling small in front of those imposing peaks. Beside him, George's head was turned, looking up at him. It felt like a punch to the gut to be seeing this photo so many months later and never having known of its existence. Why did Phil have this and why hadn't she told him? It was easily Caleb's new favorite photo. Well, second favorite photo.

Phil slid down Caleb's side as she fell further into sleep. He extricated his arm from under her and covered her with the closest blanket. There was so much they needed to talk about before he left for Jackson, but right now she needed to rest.

* * *

"Amelia said I've become a different person."

Phil sat on the floor, an open container of leftovers from a recipe Caleb had tried a few nights prior on the coffee table. She hadn't even reheated it, just popped the lid, grabbed a fork, and plopped down. He muted the tv and settled back against the couch.

"I guess I've been cold and closed off. Her words. And when I said I'm going through something, because *duh*, she said it didn't feel like it was solely the stuff about Dad. She said it started then, but that she didn't begrudge me—"

She stopped momentarily to chew.

"She didn't *begrudge me my family drama*. She said that! And of course I've changed! I'm going through some serious shit!"

Phil realized who she was talking to and closed her mouth. They hadn't talked about it yet. She'd only just woken up and this was the first thing on her mind. They had a lot to unpack. Caleb was nursing a glass of wine that Phil had placed in front of him.

"Did you have any idea she felt this way?" He tread lightly.

"None." Phil took a sip of her wine. Her face was puffy from crying, but while Caleb would normally have teased her about it to make her laugh, he didn't dare mention it with their relationship still so fragile.

"And then she tells me she's actually been unhappy for a while, but because Dad OD'ed she didn't think it was appropriate timing, so she just kept waiting for the right time TO BREAK UP WITH ME!" She screeched. "*Three months* of being unhappy because I was too fragile to handle the truth."

Phil started to cry again, but the anger won out and she swatted the tears away.

"It hurts so much. I just want to—what the hell did you put in this?" Phil's mouth opened, the masticated food proffered on her tongue.

"It's supposed to be cumin but I confused it with the curry container. And it clearly didn't bother you that much." Caleb pointed at the nearly empty tupperware.

Phil shrugged and Caleb swallowed a smile.

"I thought maybe she was the one, you know?" Phil's eyes were glassy, more tears threatening to spill.

"Phil, you're only twenty-three. You have plenty of time."

Phil swallowed, her head tilting as she studied him. She blinked twice, dramatically.

"I'm sorry, what is happening here? Why are you giving me advice like an old biddy?" She scoffed, finishing off the rest of her wine and reaching to refill the glass.

"I don't know what that means." Caleb pushed his own glass towards her for a refill.

She held off pouring, instead studying him with such intensity that Caleb gave up and learned back against the couch.

"Are you and George still together?" Phil asked.

Caleb raised his eyebrows. If she wanted an answer, she'd have to refill his glass first. Phil let a few drops fall, then pulled the bottle back, stopping the flow. Caleb rolled his eyes in response.

"I'm flying to Wyoming in two days. We're spending the week together before she starts work for the summer."

Phil clucked her tongue and filled his glass halfway.

"Huh."

"What?"

Phil pushed Caleb's glass towards him and sat back on her hands.

"I don't know. I guess I thought it would peter out, you know? She's way over there and you're here and it would be too big of a hurdle for a lot of people. But I'm glad you're making it work."

"Making it work?" Caleb laughed. "Phil, I'm in love with her."

"I know."

Caleb hadn't expected that response and it brought him up short. A laugh at his naivete, maybe. Or a standard, *how can you possibly love someone you barely know*? But confirmation? He'd never expected that, not even from his sister.

"What do you mean, *you know*?"

When Phil realized Caleb was seriously asking, she leaned forward on the coffee table, resting her chin in her hands.

"My dearest baby brother, I know you better than anyone. Admittedly, I thought it was just infatuation at first. I mean, who wouldn't be obsessed with George saying yes to crawling into their bed. In another life—"

"Philippa Elizabeth." Caleb let his head fall back and closed his eyes. Maybe he hadn't missed this.

"Caleb Theodore."

Silence filled the room until Caleb opened his eyes and met Phil's knowing gaze. There was something else there, in the way she was looking at him. Parental maybe? Almost like she was worried about him.

"I'd be willing to bet my trust that you've been in love with her since that first night. I didn't get to see you two meet, but the next night? When you played me for a fool—which I am planning to hold over you forever, by the way, because that was incredibly rude. But the way you look at her… Caleb."

Caleb wasn't sure he could pinpoint when he started to feel things for George. It was all jumbled with no clear beginning. Like maybe he'd been running towards her forever without a distinct starting line.

"That picture of us in your room. The one of George and me with the Tetons?"

Recognition washed over Phil so quickly that after an *Oh!* she jumped up and ran out of the room, returning with the photo in hand.

"I meant to give this to you as a birthday present, but I kept forgetting to get it printed and framed, and then I was going to do it for Christmas but again, forgot. And then! I was going to give it to you after

George visited as like a *Maybe this will help with the whole missing her thing*. But Dad."

She placed it on the coffee table between them and Caleb knew one thing for certain as he studied the photo. His eyes were on the mountains, but he'd already begun falling—tumbling head-first without a way of stopping.

"I'm happy for you." Phil pushed herself to standing and started collecting the empty container of leftovers. "I am. I just wish you weren't leaving right now."

It hurt to hear that she needed him, that she wanted to be around him after avoiding him for so long.

"It's just a week."

"I'll be fine."

Caleb almost believed her. Except, he heard the hitch in her voice and saw the curve of her spine. He got up and followed her into the kitchen and wrapped his arms around her. For a second she was fine, but then he felt her breath turn jagged.

"It'll be okay," he whispered into her hair. Because Phil always came out on top.

"It doesn't feel that way," she sniffled against him.

"I know. But I promise it will be."

28. GEORGE

The best part of the drive from Texas to Wyoming was the view out the window. It changed so drastically over the course of fourteen hours. The plains in Texas were so different from the snowcapped mountains in Colorado. Maybe one day she'd write a song about it, but right now, George was racing towards the man she loved.

Caleb's plane was supposed to land at noon. Service had been spotty for the past several hours so she hadn't heard from him yet, but even if he was delayed, he'd still make it there long before her.

She'd wanted to leave yesterday after dinner and drive all night to be there at the airport when he landed, waiting on the curb, for the movie reunion. But Grandma Jeane had detested the idea, fretting that she'd fall asleep at the wheel somewhere in no man's land and some long-haul trucker would disappear her, never to be seen again. There was an argument to be made that perhaps Grandma Jeane had watched one too many episodes of Dateline, but George didn't argue. The last thing she'd ever do was worry her unnecessarily. Instead, she'd compromised by leaving Texas just after five, before the sun was up.

Her grandma woke with her and handed off a paper bag packed with a warm egg sandwich for breakfast, a turkey and cheese for lunch, a meatloaf sandwich for dinner (leftovers, repurposed). Also, an apple for when she started to get sleepy and needed to get her sugar up, and five cans of Coke. George wouldn't go through more than two—it would mean too many bathroom breaks. But she appreciated the care with which it was all packed.

"I just have this feeling in my heart, Georgie girl. This summer has something in store for you." Grandma Jeane had hugged her hard and kissed her cheek before letting go. And even if George didn't believe it, the fact that her grandma did made her feel treasured. Because neither of them had ever voiced dreams and hopes like that before Caleb.

Since her return from Boston, Caleb had been distant. She knew he was dealing with incredible things, having nearly lost his father. She'd watched the trauma of it slice him open and crawl inside his skin. But he wouldn't talk about it no matter how hard she tried to get him to open up. Anytime she asked, he'd deflect and turn the conversation back to her. So, this week was important. She'd find out how Caleb was really doing.

This week was going to be George's first real vacation... ever. She wouldn't have to run off early in the morning for work. They could sleep late, go for a hike up Snow King, splurge on coffee and pastries at Persephone, or just sit in the house looking at the view he'd promised her. They would open themselves to each other, letting go of the last ten months, talk about their feelings, and make a game plan. It was going to be perfect.

George knew she'd regained cell service south of town because her phone started dinging—first a voicemail and then a handful of texts, but it was dark now. A rolled trailer north of Boulder had tacked on an additional fifty minutes—and there was always the chance of a moose on the road this time of night, so she didn't dare look away from the road. But those waiting messages were like a fire in her belly doused with kerosene. She knew it was Caleb letting her know he'd landed and probably asking when she'd arrive. He was so close.

On the drive, she'd decided she was going to say the words the moment he opened the door. Before he had a chance to distract her with his hands, his mouth, those disarming eyes. She wasn't going to let him say hello. She would stand just out of reach on the doorstep, all full of hope and promise, and finally speak the words she'd been thinking for too many months. And *then* she would climb all six-foot-something of him as promised.

She pulled into a gas station, grabbed her grocery bag of toiletries, and headed for the restroom. If she was going to say these words for the first time, she couldn't have meatloaf breath and greasy skin. She might not be bright eyed and bushy tailed after fifteen hours on the road, some of which had been with the window open whipping her hair around. She needed to freshen up enough to make the moment as perfect as she could.

Teeth brushed, face washed, and hair wrangled, the woman staring back at her from the cracked mirror was ready to take a leap. If they decided to try to be together, even if that meant uprooting her life and starting over somewhere new, she was ready to say yes to that. She wanted to try. Whatever happened, she was going to find a way forward.

Back at her truck, she remembered to check her phone. She pressed play on the voicemail.

"George, I didn't get on my flight. Please call me as soon as you get this."

According to the timestamp, the voicemail had slipped silently into her inbox while she was crossing the border from Colorado, six hours earlier. He could have gotten on another flight in that time and still be heading her way. Her hope faltered for a moment. Then she looked at the texts.

Hey.

Please call me.

You must be in a dead zone.

Drive safe.

She wondered if he'd drafted other texts in that hours-long span of silence, ultimately deciding to delete before pressing send. Imagining how worried he must have been, she felt herself winding tighter, and called him, praying that each unanswered ring meant he was in the air.

"George. Hi."

It was a good thing she was seated because the sound of his voice after so long made her knees buckle. But then, she registered the dip of resignation and she knew almost certainly that he wasn't here.

"I just pulled into Jackson." Her voice was quiet, hoping that by doing so there was a chance time could catch up and fix whatever had tangled Caleb's path to get here.

"You must be exhausted. I'm glad you made it there safely."

It was quiet, wherever Caleb was. She pictured him nearby, on a dimly lit balcony, searching the darkness for her truck. He was in jeans and a hoodie, and when he lifted a hand to run it through his hair a small stretch of creamy skin peeked out. She ached to lay her eyes on him.

"You're not here."

His response was to inhale for long enough that she had her answer. Tears sprung to the backs of her eyes, hot and stinging.

"My father relapsed." There was sadness in his voice, but something else, too. Annoyance? Resignation? "It's a never-ending loop and—it's not important. He's not important. I wouldn't have missed my flight for him. I just—it's a fucking mess here. There's a lot I haven't told you."

George let her head fall back against the seat. She'd known there was something he wasn't telling her, but this felt like a dam breaking, them on opposites sides as the water began to rise between them.

"Phil and I haven't been… we only just started talking again and she—she's losing it. I need to be here for her. I'm not getting involved with whatever is going on with him, but I need to be here for Phil. I don't know how long it'll take to get him into a treatment program, but once that's done, I'll book a new flight. It may be a couple days."

The last word was a whisper, as if it was stretching all the way from his lips in Boston to reach her ear. A single strand tethering them together for only a second and then gone.

"I should've told you how bad things were. I didn't want to burden you with it and now I've ruined yet another thing that was supposed to be..."

It was weird, that even while tears slipped silently down her cheeks, she wanted to tell him. The perfect moment she'd imagined wasn't going to happen, but maybe giving him those words would be a small gift to buoy him through whatever was unraveling back in Boston. But she shouldn't say them for the first time over the phone, should she? Maybe it was better to wait until he got out here. What was a few days in the grand scheme of things?

"It's okay," she said instead, mulling over letting go of everything she'd imagined happening this week. The lazy mornings, coffee on the deck, watching the sunset every night and reliving that moment back in August. She could still do those things, but doing them alone didn't hold any of the excitement.

"It's not. But it's nice of you to pretend so I don't feel even shittier than I already do."

"Caleb, I—"

"I know."

Except, he didn't know. He didn't know that just thinking about him turned her stomach molten, the memory of his mouth on her skin could make her toes curl. He didn't know that she'd splurged on a bottle of his body wash so that each night when she crawled into bed she imagined for half a second that he was there with her. He didn't know that one night a couple weeks back, over a dinner of hamburger helper and watery bagged salad, she'd broached the subject of moving with Grandma Jeane. She'd asked, cautiously, what she'd think if George decided to leave Texas. She'd left it vague. George could easily find full-time work in Jackson if she tried. But Grandma Jeane had seen straight through her, simply answering, *I just want you to be happy, wherever that may be.* As if happiness was enough to sustain a life and pay all the bills. Like it was just that simple.

But most importantly, above all else, Caleb didn't know that George was in love with him. She was no longer afraid of falling. She'd realized, as her plane sped down the runway toward Boston many months ago, that she'd been falling since that first night she agreed to go home with him and she hadn't ever stopped. And there was no point in being afraid of something when you had no way of crawling up out of it. Especially when you didn't want to.

"The condo is yours for as long as you want to stay there. All summer, all year. Whatever you want."

"What?" She wasn't sure she'd heard correctly.

"I'll come out as soon as I can, but you can stay there as long as you want. I got it for you."

George was speechless. They'd only planned to spend this week together. Presumably, he'd go back east at the end of the week and she'd move into the same crappy rental over the garage until October. They hadn't talked about him flying out a second time, and yet he'd rented a place for longer than a week?

"Caleb, I can't accept that. It's way too much."

"It's done. Just check in at the front desk—a key should be waiting for you. George, you have no idea how badly I want to be there right now. I need you to know that. It's killing me not to be with you. I just—things with Phil—I have to."

"You don't need to explain," George interjected. She couldn't imagine them fighting, their bond was too strong for that. But if things weren't good, they needed to fix it. She couldn't be mad at him for that. Above all else, she just wanted him to be happy.

"George—"

If he said it right now, she'd say it back. It was there, hovering between them, and she knew he could sense it too. But the proactive feeling she'd had while looking at her reflection had begun to waver throughout the call. If she said it now, it wouldn't be any less true, but it would distract Caleb from whatever he needed to take care of at home. His focus needed to be on what was happening there so that when he finally landed in Jackson, she could have all of his attention. George wanted to be the thing that lifted him up, not the thing that weighed him down when he was already carrying so much.

And anyway, he didn't say it.

"Tell Phil I say hi," George said, filling the silence.

"I will."

"Okay."

"Okay."

"Goodnight Caleb."

"Goodnight George."

She ended the call and closed her eyes. She couldn't see through the tears and there was no point driving until she got them all out. Her collar was damp by the time she turned the key in the ignition and pulled back onto the road.

Following the directions, she turned left as though heading to Wilson, and then right into a dark valley. She'd driven by here so many times that even in the starless night she could picture the pasture on her left, the rolling hills beyond, and further still, The Tetons. She passed under the ranch gate and wound her way up the side of a mountain, her ears popping with every switchback. At the top she parked under the light of the Visitor Center and went inside. It took a moment for someone to emerge from a back room, but once she was handed the key it was like pushing the doors to her exhaustion wide open.

She followed the front desk's directions along winding dark roads atop the mountain and made it without incident to Golden Hour II. The carved sign over the garage door was lit from above so she could make out a hand-painted sunset over three peaks.

What are the chances, she asked herself, too tired to really think about how slim they actually were. She grabbed her purse, her toiletry bag, the backpack that held her pajamas. Everything else could wait until morning.

The light illuminating the front door was thankfully on. She wondered if that was standard or if someone had come recently to turn over the bedding and towels from the previous renters and kindly left it on. She unlocked the door and shouldered her way inside.

She flipped a few switches illuminating the living room, walls of windows, the view she could not see. It was all rustic and beautiful, high ceilings and so much wood, but she was too exhausted to appreciate it. She flipped lights on as she went until she landed in a bedroom.

George dropped her things and went to the windows, pulling the blinds closed in the hopes she might trick her body into sleeping past six. The duvet beckoned her into its cloudy-white depths and she almost gave in. Except she could feel the grime submerged in her pores. She couldn't sully those crisp, white sheets.

In the bathroom she set up her things, placing Caleb's body wash on prominent display on the shower shelf. She wanted to see him walk in and realize. She ached for his smile, for his eyes to land on her, like she was their only destination. She turned the water as hot as it would go, until the glass steamed. And then she nearly fell asleep standing under the spray. Thankfully, she'd already brushed her teeth back at the gas station, so after toweling off she crawled between the sheets.

It's such a waste, she thought, exhaustion closing in. *This gigantic bed and no one to share it with.*

She tucked the duvet in tight behind her, pretending it was Caleb's warmth ensconcing her. But there was nothing quite like *him.* She was out before she even remembered to turn off the light, the hours spent alert, eyes glued to the road, finally catching up with her. If she hadn't succumbed to sleep so quickly, she might have noticed the photo, blown up and framed with white matting, hung perfectly center above the headboard. In it, the sun's rays slashed the photo diagonally in two. The bottom half held the horses legs, crispy-dry grass below, the boots of its rider, decidedly female in their design. Above the yellow-white rays, the wide-brimmed hat turned as the rider started to look back, her long ponytail flicking outward to mirror the horse's tail.

If George had been awake and of sound mind, she might have squinted. The boots and hat, even the ponytail looking suspiciously familiar. Maybe she'd have noticed the speckled fetlocks and marveled at yet another familiarity. Too many to be a coincidence, especially in this town. And then maybe the name on the sign nailed to the front of the condo might've kicked back up in her mind—another tick on the too coincidental to be coincidental list. And maybe she would have realized that the bed she slept in, the house, the view she would wake up to, it was all for her.

The thing with promises, especially grand, all-encompassing promises, is that there really is no way to follow through. If only Caleb had told Phil that her heart would heal, or that she'd find love again. But he'd promised something impossible.

It'll be okay.

The following afternoon, Caleb was packing for Wyoming.

"Hey. I'm thinking of ordering pizza and you can have the leftovers while I'm away."

He'd answered the phone without waiting for Phil to greet him and after he stopped talking there was silence on the other end. His hackles rose.

"Philippa?"

He heard her attempting to suck in air, each breath getting higher pitched until it all came out in a moan. Caleb stood, knowing that he needed to be wherever she was, but he had no idea *where* she was.

"Phil, what's wrong? Are you hurt?" He ran to the front door and stuffed his feet into the closest pair of shoes, grabbed his wallet and keys before she'd managed a single word.

"Can. You. Come. Here?" She was crying so hard, each word punctuated by wheezing.

"Where are you?" Caleb jumped down the stairs and nearly crashed into Mrs. Biederman as she opened the door to the garage.

"Oh!" Her shopping bags rose to shield her, eyes the only part of her face registering any surprise. Phil had explained to him after they'd first introduced themselves, that Mrs. Biederman was obviously addicted to fillers.

"Sorry Mrs. Biederman!" Caleb took off through the door. It wasn't until he was buckled in the driver's seat that he finally got the location out of Phil.

Of course she was at their parents' house.

Twenty minutes later, Caleb found Phil in the kitchen, her eyes on the ceiling. When he stepped into the room she startled, his name coming out in a squeak. She clung to him like he was a life vest in a raging sea, and started sobbing all over again.

"Are you okay?" He'd asked this question a dozen times on the phone and still not received an answer. She shook in his arms and he had to pry her off him to do a once-over. There were no obvious signs of injury—no cuts, no bruises, just a splotchy face, and a trail of tears.

Phil shook her head, but let go of Caleb long enough for him to fill a glass of water from the sink. She took a sip, then another, then set it on the counter.

"Phil, are you're okay?"

He watched her eyes flit around the room, unable to focus or settle.

"Yeah," she finally managed, though it was clearly a lie.

Caleb hadn't stepped foot in their parents' house in over three months. It looked the same, impeccably clean and expensively curated. But it was eerily quiet. There was no whisper of music two floors up, no groan of century-old floorboards down the hall.

"I stopped by on my way home since it was so nice out, you know? Mom was out back and we were talking about how Tilly Anderson is engaged and having her wedding at the Museum of Science. Mom got an invite, naturally. She goes, *How gauche. Will Leonard Nimoy be officiating their wedding in the planetarium?* Which, honestly? I'm impressed she even knows that reference. But I said *No Mom, he narrates the Omni theatre, not the planetarium.* Probably could have let it go, but I couldn't help myself. And you know how much Tilly loves that place. It's a perfect venue for her. I mean she worked there every summer—"

"Phil." Caleb hated interjecting, but it felt like they were skirting the real story.

"Sorry. Sorry."

The water sloshed around in the glass as Phil's hands trembled, so Caleb took it from her before she dropped it.

"I guess we were out there for a while, or I don't know. Then I came inside to look for Dad, just to say hi before walking home."

Phil looked back up at the ceiling. But in the quiet, Caleb couldn't tell what she was listening for. Out on the street, a car horn honked three times in urgent succession and then quiet resumed. It was only then that Caleb remembered where they were and who should be there. He'd been so focused on Phil.

"The water was running, so I figured I'd just wait until Dad's shower was done, and I went up to our rooms and was poking around— you should really go through the boxes up there in your closet before Mom decides to just throw everything out."

The sudden mothering gave Caleb whiplash, but he didn't comment on it. He waited for Phil to continue with the story.

"I'm up there going through things and realize he's been in the bathroom for a really long time and I'm like, maybe I should check and make sure he hasn't fallen or something. Because, you know."

She hiccupped and tears started slipping down both cheeks.

"I knocked on the door but he didn't answer so I started to freak out and I went in with my eyes covered and the water was—I guess it'd

252

been running for so long that it was overflowing and was all over the floor and I called his name and I heard something—"

She looked at Caleb as she spoke, but with a glaze over her eyes like she was watching the replay. She shook her head to clear it of the images.

"He was on the floor in Mom's closet. Like he'd fallen, because all the clothes on one side were on the floor like he'd grabbed them on the way down. And he was just sitting there babbling, but his words were slurred and he wasn't making sense. And I thought he was having a stroke so I screamed for Mom and she called an ambulance and they came and took him back to the hospital. I don't know if I can go back there, Caleb. What if—"

Caleb put his hands on her shoulders, holding her still. Her eyes ping-ponged between his, but her frenetic energy started to slow. When they were little and one of them was upset, the only thing that calmed them was being touched by the other, knowing they weren't alone.

Their mother had joked about it to friends and family, anywhere she had a captive audience. She made them out to be strange children who didn't want their parents' touch, who only craved each other's attention. But it was because they didn't ever get that kind of comfort from their parents, especially not when they really needed it. The twins' parents would have rather let Phil and Caleb cry themselves hoarse than sit in discomfort and take the time to work through emotions.

"Do you want me to go with you?"

Caleb hated offering this. He needed to do laundry and pack for Wyoming, and most importantly, he didn't want to see his father, regardless of what was happening. But Caleb wanted to be there for Phil like he should've the first time. They'd made so much progress repairing their relationship, and he never wanted to go months without speaking. So even if it made his skin crawl thinking about facing his father again, he'd do it for Phil.

Phil looked away—at her feet, at the spotless corner of the kitchen, then finally at Caleb's chest. But she would not meet his gaze.

"One of the EMTs asked if there was a chance he was on something."

Caleb stilled. He hated that a part of him actually cared what Phil was saying. As much as he'd thought he'd erased his father from his life, it turned out a tiny piece of him still cared.

"She said it didn't look like a stroke, that he was presenting with signs of use."

She blinked and looked up at Caleb and he felt a chill trickle down his spine. He watched her nose scrunch as she fought off more tears, hurt giving way to anger.

"Apparently, the drug the doctor put him on to wean him off the Oxy is just as addictive and he's basically been high this entire time. I thought he was getting better and basically nothing has changed except that I've been essentially feeding his addiction every time I gave him pills!"

Phil started to bounce under the weight of Caleb's hands, her heels rocketing up and down at lightning speed like there was a live wire connecting every time they touched the ground.

"It's my fault! He's in the hospital right now because of me."

Caleb had thought he'd seen her at her lowest. But this was a different kind of heartbreak. It was like adding water and watching something dissolve, slowly at first and then suddenly gone. The rate at which she was unraveling, Caleb worried that if he didn't contain it soon, he'd never be able to put her back together.

* * *

Caleb hardly slept that night. He spent two hours at the hospital supporting Phil, shouldering her exhausted weight back to the car at the end. He made dinner when they got home and let Phil babble on for another hour until she passed out on the couch. He'd thought about carrying her to her bed, but in the end covered her with a blanket and let her be. But as he turned the lights off, he knew what he had to do.

He fought with himself over the decision, because he hated having to make it. Maybe it wasn't that he was fighting with himself, but with the universe. Asking why every time he and George tried to be together something always came crashing in, Kool-Aid Man style, to destroy their plans.

He knew he had to call George but he was a coward. He waited until she was already in Wyoming, justifying his decision by telling himself it wasn't safe for her to drive that far alone while upset. And, he wanted to know she was safe before he delivered the news. At least there was this tiny shred of comfort in knowing that when he wasn't there to greet her, he'd still be providing a safe place to sleep.

To be fair, Phil hadn't asked him to stay home and he didn't tell her he'd canceled his flight. He knew she'd tell him to go. Giving up a week of no distractions, a straight seven days of George, initially felt insurmountable. But, like he'd said to Phil, it would be okay. He was just going to be delayed a few days. He would fly out after things settled and Phil was on solid ground again. Then, Caleb could spend his nights at the

255

bar while George worked, they'd still fall asleep together, and maybe he'd go riding with her again. It would still be more than they'd been able to have before.

But then he'd made the call, and hearing George's tears on the other end gutted him. He knew she was trying to make it seem like she was okay, but she was sniffling too much to be convincing. The plan had changed, but he wasn't about to let it be ruined like last time. He had to show George that no matter the obstacles thrown in their path, he'd find a way to her. He'd prove that he was steadfast when it came to her, that he could be counted on. He just needed a few days and he'd be there.

But a few days ended up stretching into a week before Dara was able to find a rehab that suited her requirements. According to Phil, John was insistent that he didn't have a problem, and behind closed doors their mother was coming undone. Phil assured Caleb after that first night, that she didn't need him to go with her to the hospital, their parents' house, or later, the rehab facility. She knew their mother was prone to taking her anger out on him. Mostly, Caleb was there to take care of Phil when she came home. She was hardly eating, except when he forced food on her. She wasn't sleeping, if the shadows under her eyes were any indication. But she urged Caleb to rebook his flight out, insisting that she'd be fine. He didn't believe her, but he stocked the freezer with all her favorites. And while Phil acted like he was being dramatic and overbearing, he could tell that it meant a lot to her to be taken care of for once.

"George is a lucky girl," Phil said from the kitchen as Caleb double-checked his things at the front door. His ride was still five minutes away so he headed back to the kitchen and wrapped Phil in a bear hug.

"I'm going to be fine," she insisted, laughing a little when he only hugged harder.

"I'm happy to hear that."

"Okay, okay." She squirmed out of his grasp and pushed him towards the door.

"It's only a week," Caleb reminded her.

"God, stop mothering me and go have your romantic getaway already."

With one last wave, Caleb was out the door.

He hadn't told George he'd rebooked his flight out. There were so few opportunities in life to truly surprise someone and he spent the first flight daydreaming of arriving at the condo. She might be reading on the couch or making food. He could picture the shocked scream morphing into the kind of smile that he'd tuck away for every future rainy day. Maybe he'd catch her napping and curl around her so she'd wake in his arms. Somewhere around Ohio, Caleb realized she might actually be working when he landed and his imaginings were edited for public spaces.

The Jackson Hole airport was as quaint as he remembered it—one big room for all gates and the most scenic view imaginable across the tarmac. He was in his rental car within ten minutes and entering town shortly after that. He was going to pass Million Dollar Cowboy bar on his way to the condo so decided that would be his first stop.

He paused out on the sidewalk, taking a deep breath of mountain air to calm his nerves. He felt so much better already, just being here. Was it the lack of pollution? The ratio of acres to people? What was it that made Wyoming so special? Maybe it was simply that George was here somewhere.

Caleb wished he was wearing something more impressive than his travel-creased jeans and pilly fisherman sweater, but George had never seemed to care what he wore. He stepped through the door of the bar and was transported back to nearly a year earlier. Pool balls clacked, the air was warm and thick, and the ceiling was lower than he remembered. The saddle stools were still there—he hadn't imagined them. But George was not behind either bar. It was relatively empty compared to that first night, so Caleb was able to get a bartender's attention easily.

"Is George working?" He tried so hard to come off sounding nonchalant, but his knuckles white on the bar betrayed him.

"Let me check." The bartender turned to his colleague down the other end mixing a drink. "Is George working tonight?"

The second bartender looked up and blinked, thinking hard. He turned off the tap.

"I don't think she's on the schedule."

"Sorry," the first bartender apologized. But he couldn't know that Caleb was secretly thrilled at this news. Sure, she might not be at the condo. She could be shopping or meeting a friend for dinner, but eventually she'd come home. And that's where Caleb would be waiting.

For Caleb's first time driving to the condo, it actually felt like coming home. Every turn was one moment closer to George. Her truck wasn't in the driveway which meant he had time. Time to bring in his things, to see the place for the first time before he was insanely distracted by the woman who filled it, to think about how he wanted to greet her.

He stepped inside the door and set down his bags. The place was everything the listing photos had promised and more. It wasn't as huge as George had made it out to be in her texts the morning after he was supposed to arrive. Three bedrooms, three baths, a decent kitchen, and a wall of windows in the living room that framed the Tetons. Outside, a porch with two knotted-pine chairs that were waiting for coffee or cocktails to be served.

George had been living here for a little over a week and already he could feel her in every room. The kitchen was clean and yet he could sense her having made meals here, probably sipped her coffee on the couch while staring out the window.

He wandered from room to room marveling at everything. This place was his. Not his and Phil's. His alone. He found the bedroom he'd fallen in love with through the listing photos, and there it was, the photo of George he'd had blown up, framed, and shipped here so the management company could hang it in advance of their arrival. Caleb could look at this photo of her for a hundred years and never tired of it. On its own it was a surprisingly professional-looking photo, despite the fact he'd taken it sneakily with his phone. But beyond that, it held so much meaning for what had transpired that day. And how it had ended with them pretending to wed.

Caleb could smell George in this room especially, and like a creep he pressed his nose to the pillow. There was no hint of horses like the summer before, but he knew she wouldn't start working at the ranch until later in the month. But she was there, smelling of sunshine and a splash of vanilla.

As Caleb looked around, he realized how neat she'd kept it. Where was her things? He opened the closet and all the hangers were empty. The dresser drawers were clean. The bathroom was void of toiletries, no shampoo in the shower, no products on the edge of the sink.

Caleb retraced his steps, searching for anything, some item that told him George had been here. But in every room, he came up empty. The fridge held a half-eaten bag of grapes, a pizza box with two remaining slices, and a small carton of milk. None of it had spoiled so that had to mean she was still here. But where were her things?

Caleb thought about the George he knew, whose life was so regimented. She carried so much on her plate, working a long day then a long night, and maybe it made the most sense to keep a change of clothes on hand at all times. And maybe she'd been afraid to unpack and dirty what she thought was a rental.

Was the condo too much? Probably. But Caleb hadn't told her the specifics yet. Once he explained that it wasn't a rental, that it was his and hers—if she wanted to stay—maybe then she'd feel comfortable unpacking her things.

Caleb heated up the leftover pizza and settled on the couch to pass however long it would be until George came home. It was dark when the worry started to slither in and settle beside him on the sectional. He wanted the grandeur of a surprise, but more than that he just wanted to see her. So maybe calling her and finding out when she'd be back wouldn't hurt. He could play it off like he was just checking in and then when she got home, he'd be waiting.

"Hey!" George answered over background noise so loud it nearly washed her out.

Caleb switched the call to speaker.

"Hi! Where are you?" He pictured her in a bar downtown and was ready to run out to the car. He'd walk through the door and sweep her off her feet in the next ten minutes.

"Denver! Did you get my email?"

Caleb closed his eyes, as if that would shut out the extraneous noise and help him hear better. Because he could've sworn she'd said—

"Denver?"

"Sorry, it's so loud here! I can barely hear you. It's so crazy, right? I mean, I'm doing it! Or I'm doing some version of it. I wish you could be here to see. Never mind, I think that would make me more nervous. Oh—yeah, I'm here!" She yelled to someone lost in the background noise and Caleb worried for a second that the call had cut out.

"George? Are you there?" He stood, wondering if cell reception was bad on this hill. He hadn't thought to ask those kinds of questions before the closing.

"Hi, sorry. I have to go! But I'll call you soon and let you know how it all turns out. Okay? Thanks for believing in me, Caleb. I miss you."

"I miss you too," Caleb said, but the call had already ended. And then, because his brain slowly began to catch up, his fingers clicked over to his email app because that's what she'd asked him at the start of the call. *Did you get my email?*

It was the tenth email down after a slew of spam and it sucked the air out of his chest.

date: May 11, 2017, 1:27 AM
from: g.rosetownsend@snailmail.com
to: calebtbrowningrichards@snailmail.com
subject: RE: Hi

This should really be a call, but it's so late and there's the time difference and I don't want to wake you. I could wait until tomorrow, but I'm worried I'll burst into tears the moment I hear your voice. Part of me only thinks this is happening because of how much you believe in me.
Remember the band I sang with last summer? The Billings Boys came to Jackson last week to perform. I took some shifts at the bar to keep myself distracted from how empty this huge condo is. Seriously, why did you think we'd need *three* bedrooms?
Quick aside: I should've started by saying I know you have to be home with Phil. If the roles were reversed and something happened with my grandma, I know you'd be understanding about it. That being said, I miss you a whole lot. I need you to know that. Like A LOT.

Okay, so last week I'm working the bar and The Billings Boys were there and we got to chatting and they asked me to sing with them again and it went really well. I didn't know it, but their manager was there and he was really impressed with me. So then tonight I get a call that the band wants me to play a couple shows with them. Can you believe it?? I'm leaving in the morning for Colorado and then maybe Arizona after that, depending on how I do I guess? I don't want to jinx it, but there's a part of me that can't help but think, is this really happening?? I wish you'd been there to make sure I heard it all because I feel like I blacked out for a bit. Grandma Jeane said she felt like something was going to happen this summer and I guess she was right!
Anyway. I'll let you know when I'm back in Jackson so we can find another time for you to come out. I don't know if you can get your money back, but you should try to cancel the rental since no one will be there to use it.
 I truly can't believe this is happening.
Yours,
George

VERSE II

2021

THE COUNTRY CROONER & THE ONE TO WATCH

By Sylvie Sanders, Globe Staff, October 2, 2021

Ripley Carlson is exactly as charismatic and ruggedly handsome as you think he is. He walks into the restaurant thirty minutes late with the swagger of someone who knows you'll be waiting.

"Charmed," he says as he takes my hand, and it's true. I am charmed. The country singer, 32 has risen gradually over the last two years, as one would expect with his good looks, devil-may-care attitude, and the kind of voice that makes panties drop. I don't say that glibly. If you've attended one of his shows you know that the panties fly up onto that stage.

"Did you have any idea when writing "Lace and Love" that women would react the way they do?"

Honestly, I'm embarrassed to even ask the question, but it's a natural thing to wonder, considering.

"Did I think every time I sang it I'd get underwear thrown at me? No." But he smirks all the same.

We're interrupted then by a pair of teen girls wringing their hands as they ask with the merest hint of calm for a photo. Carlson obliges and asks if they're attending the show tonight. When they squeal *Of course*—he tells them they just made his day. I watch them cling to each other for support as they skitter away, the thick musk of excitement and desire lingering long after they've gone.

"Hoped, maybe," Carlson continues as if we hadn't been interrupted, his attention focused on me in a way that makes me forget it ever wavered.

I understand now why in mentioning to several colleagues that I'd be interviewing him, the adjective that came up the most was *swoony.*

Hailing from Alabama, Carlson went the traditional route. Moving to Nashville at twenty and singing anywhere that would have him until he was in the right place at the right time.

"Timing is everything," Carlson intones over a shared basket of onion rings, of which he will have exactly three and I will happily finish off. "It doesn't matter how good you are or how hard you work, unless the right person sees you at the right time."

That person was Mark Lingrell, who happened to stop in the bar that Carlson had a regular Tuesday-night gig at. "It was just a feeling," Lingrell told me over the phone before my lunch with Carlson. "I was meeting a friend for dinner next door and I was early. I'm never early. But that night something cosmic must have been at play because I went in for a drink and I left with a new client."

Lingrell set Carlson up with a writing partner. "It's strange how well we work together. Lace & Love took an hour and it was just..." The dreamy, far-off look in his eyes as he retells stories of creating what has just crested double platinum is enough to pull me under the spell. It's enough to make a country music fan out of me—a self-certified pop girl through and through.

"How did the duet with Georgia Rose Townsend come about?" It has to be asked.

Prior to this tour, on which Townsend, 29, is opening for Carlson, she was relatively unknown. With an undersold EP under her belt, Townsend was making ends meet with writing credits around Nashville.

"My writing partner knew of her and said I had to meet her, thought maybe we'd write a hit together. But the moment I heard that girl sing—" Carlson's whistle draws looks from the tables around us, but if he notices, he makes no show of it.

"She's got quite the voice," I add.

Townsend's EP is bright and airy, if a bit generic. In showcasing her voice, it does fine, but it lacks heart. And so, I kept digging. Because if this unseasoned singer was brought onboard to open for Carlson's headline-making tour there had to be a reason.

And then, I found it. Back in the summer of 2016.

The Billings Boys, a band out of Montana who seem overly fond of head to toe denim, played at The Million Dollar Cowboy Bar in Jackson, Wyoming. They're still around and definitely worth a listen if you're into that wistful sort of lonesome cowboy music. Truth be told, I may be a convert.

One night in August, and the only reason I know this is because there is video proof if you search the interwebs hard enough, they brought a bartender up on stage to sing with them. The song she picked? "Vice" by Miranda Lambert. Townsend, clad in denim shorts and a branded bar tee, drew near silence from what is usually a rowdy crowd for the acapella opening to the song.

Townsend's social media is sparse, starting only a few months prior to this tour, likely insisted upon by management to sustain what they hope will become a healthy following. Her debut album, which was released to coincide with the start of this tour, has a more polished feel than her EP, and I am willing to bet she gets radio play by Thanksgiving.

But back to Carlson. Because he's the reason I'm here.

"That she does," he agrees and I might be imagining it, but I sense something more behind Carlson's smile. Or maybe it's that I've seen the pictures of them strolling through the Public Garden a day earlier, Townsend posing beside the Make Way for Ducklings statues while Carlson played the role of photog.

In those pictures, there is hand-holding, the kind of looks that are basted with lust and secrets. And I know I should try to get confirmation on whether they are or they aren't, but what intrigues me the most is how a girl from Texas with no known ties to New England has come to be in possession of a Buckingham, Brown & Nichols sweatshirt. Specifically, and I'm not proud of how much digging it took for me to deduce this, one that appears to be circa 2008.

"I saw pictures yesterday," I hedge, as Carlson nurses his beer. For those wondering, he did choose a Harpoon IPA *to see what the locals are into*. If he knows what I'm after, he doesn't let on.

"The sweatshirt Georgia was wearing, does she know someone who went to BB&N?"

This will be the first and only time Carlson frowns in our entire time together, mostly because it's the only question he doesn't have an answer to. I genuinely believe him. Which begs the question, how did Townsend come into possession of the local hoodie?

A quick call to BB&N's school store confirmed Townsend did not stop in and buy the sweatshirt herself, though if she did back in 2008 they were unable to say. It seems unlikely that a local Goodwill would be reselling private high school goods, but you can't count it out.

Perhaps a question for another day. Because right then, Carlson asks if I have any interest in splitting a slice of Boston Cream pie. "Sweets are one of my many weaknesses," he tells me conspiratorially, and I'll be damned if I'm going to say no to him.

Autumn is when Boston truly shines. Cool mornings, warm afternoons. Leaves washing through yellow, orange, and red. In the early morning hours, crew teams practice along the Charles like an opening scene in a movie, the coxswain's voice punctuating the quiet.

As Caleb clipped on Rosie's leash this morning, it seemed especially true that Boston was beautiful. In the summer months, when sticky heat settled in every crevice of the city, Caleb would take Rosie out for their run before the sun was up. That was the only way to survive. Neither of them was made for the heat. But in October, they could sleep a little later, heading out at seven.

It had been almost three years since Caleb adopted Rosie (né Cheesy Mac) from a local rescue. She'd come up from Texas on a transport at one year old, having been found as a stray. She was microchipped, but her previous owners hadn't been interested in claiming her, the bastards. Caleb hated them for throwing her out like trash. At the same time, if not for their callousness, he'd never have been able to adopt her and fall in love. And in love with her he very much was.

She wasn't perfect. She'd been scared of the stairs at first. The silver lining of that being his legs and abs had never looked so defined after carrying her in and out three times a day. It took a month to figure out how to communicate with each other so he'd know when she needed to go out. Phil hadn't even batted an eye at all the puddles around the house. That had surprised Caleb the most. He'd expected the constant admonishment that it was his dog so it was his mess. But Phil had taken to Rosie like the favorite aunt she was always meant to be—sneaking treats when Rosie didn't need them, spoiling her with toys when the basket in the corner was already full, buying her clothes for every occasion.

Caleb couldn't remember what life was like before Rosie. What had been in that corner of the living room where her memory foam bed lay? The condo must've been so quiet before the click of nails coming down the hall like fanfare announcing her royal entrance. For whatever she had survived before entering Caleb's life, he would forever spoil her with all she could ever want.

On this particular morning it was cloudy and cool. Caleb put on Rosie's fall coat—a Phil purchase of plaid pastels. The building was quiet as they made their way down the stairs and out onto the street, headed towards the traffic already thick on Storrow. Then, up and over the walkway to the paths along the river. This was why he and Phil had settled on this particular condo—the proximity to the Charles. First, views out the living room window, but also the miles of paths along it. He kept telling himself that he should run the entire loop, down to Mount Auburn and back towards the city on the Cambridge side, but it hadn't happened yet.

They set out at a slow pace, warming up. Not that they ever ran hard. They were both lazy lopers.

When you ran at the same time you clocked regulars—the guy who ran in short shorts and no shirt until November, the two girls with high ponytails and matching spandex sets, the old man and his chihuahua who liked to sit on the same bench and watch the rowers. No one ever said *Good morning* in passing, but there were nods and blinks of acknowledgement, all rituals of this early morning crew.

On mornings like this Caleb missed living with Phil. He'd kick off his sneakers at the door and tell her about the things he noticed so eventually she'd asked for updates on the riverside regulars. He'd known they wouldn't live together forever, but he hadn't expected their separation to happen so soon. When it was time for him to buy her out of her share of the condo, it felt like the end of something that he would never be allowed to return to. It felt a little like heartbreak.

Home again, Caleb let go of Rosie's leash once they were inside the building so she could trot ahead up the stairs. She liked to remind him, waiting in a perfect sit at their front door and not the least bit breathless, that he was getting older. He unlocked the front door and pulled off her jacket. She trotted ahead of him down the hall to get water while he kicked off his sneakers. If Phil were here, she'd be yelling at him from her room, completely ignoring the fact that others in the building might like a quiet morning. In place of her now, there was the soft hum of the dishwasher and the clack of heels from his bedroom.

Caleb peeled off his sticky shirt and pushed open the bedroom door. He was hit with a wave of sharp and sweet perfume, and then as he moved toward the bathroom, a second wave of lingering bodywash—strawberry scent.

"Hey babe," Kenzie popped out of the closet. "Can you zip me before you get in the shower? I have to leave in five."

Mackenzie Donaldson was the kind of woman every guy dreamt of marrying—equally happy to watch the game at a bar with friends or stay home and cook together. She drew attention everywhere she went—her voice preceding her and drawing eyes, her looks holding them there. They'd met on a dating app, which Phil had insisted on setting up for Caleb. Their first date had been drinks in the Financial District. Their second was apple picking out Route 2, followed by baking their spoils together at Caleb's, which led to their first night together.

Caleb knew he was a lucky man. He'd somehow managed to attract this beautiful woman who adored him. He still wasn't quite sure how. Six months in, she'd instigated the *move in together* conversation, which had prompted his buying Phil out of her share of the condo. It was the adult thing to do. Caleb knew that. But it still didn't sit right with him and he couldn't explain why.

Phil hadn't put up a fight. She was happy for him—successful in his professional life as a real estate agent and now as half of a new partnership. She moved to Watertown, buying a condo with a different view of the Charles and less traffic out the window. And though they'd only separated themselves by two miles, sometimes it felt like they were time zones apart. Where they used to be able to yell to each other down the hall, sometimes hours would pass between text responses.

Caleb crossed to the closet where Kenzie was already turned, her back to him and hair pulled out of the way. She was a former ballet dancer turned Marketing Exec, who couldn't seem to put on weight no matter what Caleb cooked. Not that he was trying, but he wondered if at forty, fifty, sixty her spine would still be as prominent as now.

"Did you have a good run?" She asked over her shoulder as Caleb zipped the dress.

"Yeah. Carl and Dug were on their usually bench."

Kenzie *hmmed* as if listening, but Caleb knew she didn't care about the riverside regulars the way Phil did. She was a practical person and thought his stories silly. It was why he still hadn't told her about his writing.

"Dinner tonight at Chickadee. Please don't be late." She kissed him, picked up the jacket strewn on the bed, and disappeared through the open door.

271

As someone who had always followed the protocol of the woman in charge—first his mother and then Phil—Caleb couldn't understand why it bothered him that every week was planned for him. He used to love dinners out, and yet now, he found himself longing for spontaneity, the thrill of canceled plans and an excuse to stay in. His feelings about it had gotten worse since their engagement.

Toby said it was normal to be stressed leading up to a wedding. Not that Toby had any first-hand experience in the matter. But the thing was, Caleb hadn't told Toby the truth of it. Technically, he hadn't proposed to Kenzie. It had all been an accident, a miscommunication.

Engagement was something he'd imagined far off in the distance, something he could worry about later. But then one afternoon in July, he and Kenzie were out on the back patio at the Chatham house. Dara was on vacation elsewhere, maybe the Berkshires this time, and Phil was back in Boston. They'd been drinking since noon and it was early evening at this point. Caleb was thinking about work, worrying about his clients refusing a really good offer just because it wasn't cash, when Kenzie asked, seemingly out of nowhere, "Do you want to get married?"

Thinking back on it, he imagined Phil rewatching this scene play out and whacking him across the back of his head for not paying closer attention. The signs had all been there—a weekend alone, they'd been living together for months by then. Kenzie was so focused on her upcoming birthday and how thirty was *so old.*

"Yeah, I want to get married. Do you?"

Caleb was on autopilot, his response regurgitated from some reptilian corner of his brain while the rest of him mentally wrote and edited an email to his clients. Yes, cash was wonderful, but an over-asking offer with no contingencies was nothing to scoff at. In fact, his professional opinion was that it was the better option.

Kenzie squealed then and Caleb realized he'd missed something important. But he was too afraid to ask for clarification knowing she'd be annoyed that he hadn't been listening to her. It registered that she'd said yes, though to what he had no idea. And then she was wrapping her arms around his neck and kissing him all over and he assumed that whatever he'd agree to he could probably afford, within reason. It wasn't until later that night—when she'd insisted they go out for dinner to celebrate (clue #1) and then over oysters she asked if he'd already bought a ring (clue #2)—that Caleb's brain started to catch up, piecing the clues together into a slightly terrifying equation.

He'd proposed? How had that happened? And then, realizing there was no way to rewind himself out of this situation without major consequences, started to panic sweat. This wasn't the type of thing you walked back. And anyway, wasn't this the natural progression of things—date, move in together, marry? It was happening to him instead of him being an active participant, but shouldn't he be happy that it was happening at all?

"Chickadee at seven," he parroted back and walked into the bathroom.

"Phil's calling you!" Kenzie yelled from down the hall, the front door clicking shut.

Caleb headed back to the kitchen to catch Phil before the call dropped.

"Hey, hang on one sec while I feed the princess." He scooped Rosie's food into her bowl, her eyes on him while he kept her waiting in a sit. "Okay," he told her and she sprang forward, nearly inhaling her kibble in one go. He really needed to get her a slow feeder.

"What's new?"

At this hour, Phil would be in the car on her way to pick up coffee.

"It must be Head of the Charles coming up with how many rowers were out this morning."

Caleb walked back to his room, passing Phil's old bedroom, which was now full of Kenzie's things—furniture she couldn't part with and racks of clothes that wouldn't fit in the closet in his bedroom.

"Yeah, it's this weekend," she said. There was a moment of silence so heavy with concentration that Caleb figured Phil must be parking. "That's not what I meant though."

Caleb opened his closet. Normally, he wore a button-down, but he didn't have any appointments today so he could get away with jeans and a light sweater. It would be fine for dinner, too. They were meeting Kenzie's friends, people he'd already met and didn't need to impress.

"Hmm?" He laid the clothes out on the bed.

"What are you doing?" There was an edge to Phil's voice, something that made him stop rifling through his sock drawer so he could give her his full attention.

"Picking out my clothes for the day, why?"

"Are you and Kenzie good?"

He heard Phil's car door close and pictured her walking into Intelligentsia. Personally, Caleb didn't love coffee enough to have a place, but he understood her need for regularity.

"Yeah, why?"

274

"Because I was perusing the usual clickbait this morning when I stumbled upon an interesting article about a certain someone."

Caleb wandered into the bathroom and turned on the shower. In this old building it usually took a minute for the water to warm.

"Whatever you're trying to say, just say it. I need to jump in the shower."

The glass started to steam and Caleb put the call on speaker so he could undress.

"George was in town, Caleb. For a concert with Ripley Carlson. Did you know that?"

Caleb turned off the shower, water pooling beneath the open glass door. This wasn't going to be a quick call after all.

He hadn't spoken her name aloud in years, not since their emails grew farther apart as George got swallowed up by the music industry. He thought about her all the time, though. When he was running with Rosie, when he had ramen, alone in the shower. He knew it wasn't okay to think about her now that he was engaged, but he couldn't help it no matter how hard he tried.

But Phil didn't know any of this. She'd stopped asking about George a month after their failed meet-up in Jackson when Caleb was so consumed with heartache that he stopped answering her barrage of questions. He'd been miserable to be around, hating himself for being so upset when he should've been happy for her success.

Caleb waited for two weeks in Jackson, but George never came back. She continued on to the next gig and the one after that, and he hated himself for wishing more than once that she'd return to him.

He'd discussed with his therapist how it was a feeling of being left behind. First, by Toby. Then by George. At least with Toby their friendship had remained intact regardless of the distance. Because they'd both worked hard to meet each other halfway. With George though, both of them had let go of the other and never tried to work their way back.

Caleb had refused to answer his therapist's question about that—*why do you think that might be?* But his silence hadn't meant a lack of knowledge. Caleb knew why he'd let George go without a fight. Because he wasn't good enough for her. Because she was going to go be somebody and he'd never amount to anything. Because at the end of the day he wasn't sure love was worth fighting for. At least not his love.

"George was here, Cay. She opened for Ripley Carlson. And apparently, they might be together, which I mean, she can definitely do better. But that's all background noise, because what caught my attention, and that of the Globe writer, *by the way*, is that she was wearing your sweatshirt. So, I ask again, are you and Kenzie good, or is there something you want to share with the class?"

Standing there naked, Caleb felt himself start to sweat. Surely Phil didn't know about the google alert he'd set up years ago or the fact that he'd been following George's Instagram account since its inception. Which was how he'd known to buy a ticket for the concert when it went on sale. He'd bought a ticket on the floor and seriously considered making a #1 FAN tee for the show. But that morning as he lay in bed beside Kenzie preparing to lie about where he'd be that night, he couldn't go through with it. He hadn't spoken to George in years and though he was insanely proud of how far she'd come, what did he hope to gain from standing there beneath the stage in that shirt? He was engaged to a beautiful woman and George was touring the country. And, as Phil was astutely pointing out, she'd moved on with a successful singer. How could he ever compete with that?

Full of shame, he'd sold the ticket the day of and pretended like it never happened.

"How do you know it's *my* sweatshirt?"

Caleb rewound to a different time. Had he given George any of his clothes? He had no memory of it, but if she'd asked, he'd have given her anything, so maybe he had.

"Well, *I* didn't give her one of mine and it looked big on her so deductive reasoning says eenie, meenie, miny, you."

Now he couldn't seem to catch his breath. Had he made a mistake not going to the concert?

"Can you send me the link?"

This couldn't be right. Why would George be wearing his sweatshirt?

"My friend, it's like we didn't share a womb. I already sent it."

The silence around Phil morphed into a low hum of conversations and orders being called and he put the call on speaker again so he could click on the link. It took a moment to load and when it did tears inexplicably burned at the back of Caleb's eyes.

There she was. Maybe more gorgeous than in his memory, and that was saying something. She'd always seemed comfortable in her skin, like she understood the power she had in hand. But now it was like she'd settled into a place of not needing to announce it with a lifted chin or elevated posture.

George was in the Public Garden by the ducklings, head tipped down like she was tucking away a smile. And yes, wearing a BB&N sweatshirt. Possibly *his* BB&N sweatshirt?

"What does this mean?"

He wanted to reach through the image and ask her if she'd thought of him as she zipped it. Had she hoped he'd see this photo? Or was it completely accidental, her grabbing a sweatshirt worn thin over time and having lost the connection to its original owner. Did she remember where she'd gotten it or was it simply just a garment now?

"That's why I asked how you and Kenzie are. And *still* you haven't answered me!"

"We're fine, Phil. I haven't heard from George in years. It's probably just a weird coincidence."

Phil laughed and Caleb had to admit how absurd that sounded, that George just happened to wear *that* sweatshirt while in Boston.

"Maybe you should reach out," Phil offered, the background noise receding and going completely silent as she got back in her car.

"Why? What good would that do when she's clearly in a relationship and I'm…"

Caleb still wasn't comfortable saying what was on the looming horizon.

"Getting married?" Phil finished, unhelpfully.

"Yeah." That.

"I guess I just thought since you're both mature adults who've clearly moved on and don't harbor long-held feelings towards the other, you could maybe be friendly and ask how she is, see if she wants to offer up free tickets the next time she's in town or something. That sort of thing. What could it possibly hurt to just say hi?"

Like it was that easy composing an email to the person that Caleb had held in his heart for so long that at times he wasn't sure he'd ever be able to move beyond the feelings of sorrow, of being left behind. What would he even say? *Hi George, not sure you remember me. I'm the guy who promised to spend my life with you and then couldn't follow through. Remember me? Nearly fell off a stationary saddle at the sight of you. Yeah, that guy.*

What could it hurt? Famous last words.

Sometimes your performance was so euphoric that you forgot what day it was, what city you were in. That was how much of the tour had been for George. After the third stop, she lost track. It was one city after another, quick glimpses of skyline as they entered the outskirts. Unload, soundcheck, scarf down a quick meal, perform, crash into bed, get up and do it all again. Everything started to bleed together, combined with the exhausting hours, and George lost track of where they were.

Maybe the fourth night—Albuquerque, she remembered that much—Ripley brought her onstage like usual for their duet towards the end of his set. Audiences had been loving it, whether it was the actual song the loved or just Ripley in his jeans and tight tee, she couldn't be sure. Maybe they loved her a little bit too. Whatever it was, their duet always set off deafening screams.

On that night, when Ripley let go of the final note, he'd pulled her into a kiss, surprising the hell out of her. George had been standing beside him, taking in the crowd's reception. She wanted to remember this feeling forever—the way people looked up at her with wide, expectant eyes like she was something to behold. When he pulled her into him, pressing his perfect lips to hers, it was so unexpected that she'd been unable to reciprocate as the crowd screamed themselves silly.

George had chalked it up to a stunt and a good one at that. Their duet was about heat building into wildfire, so selling that tension mounting between them was a reasonable thing to do. George knew Ripley appreciated how hyped the crowd was after her set. He'd said so on many occasions, how she got them warmed up for him. It felt like the greatest compliment, considering this was her first time touring.

But that kiss…

Ripley flirted with everyone. Fans, journalists, bartenders, the people working their merch tables, *everyone*. It was his currency, showing you how important you were to him. She just hadn't realized that his flirting with her was something more.

She saw him later on the bus, but he didn't say anything, just gave her his gorgeous smile as he closed the door to his bedroom at the back. She wondered if she'd imagined the whole thing—the heat she'd felt when his mouth met hers. *It was just part of the performance*, she thought to herself and lay awake for hours as the bus rolled along towards the next city. Did he plan to do that every night to get the crowd (and her) riled up? She didn't think she could handle another ten cities of that.

Two nights later in Houston, Ripley found her in her dressing room wiping off the heavy makeup her manager insisted she wear. She understood the stage lights made her look washed out without it, but it still felt weird when she was used to only lashing on mascara and going. This, along with the wardrobe they'd picked out for her, all took some getting used to.

Ripley knocked once and opened the door without waiting, and George would later wonder what it meant that her first instinct was to think she'd done something wrong—sung offkey or missed a cue. He crossed the room in lazy strides, not in any hurry. That was the thing about Ripley. His confidence was endless. She wondered if she'd ever have that kind of confidence, whether you grew up with it or if success in the music industry shot it into your veins.

He stopped behind her and spun her chair around so he was boxing her in. He smelled like whiskey and musk and she felt high off him. He leaned down to tilt her chip up and hovered an inch from her face, watching her. He smirked, like he knew what he was doing to her, how heat had begun pooling low in her belly. Honestly, it was the unexpectedness of it all that took her breath away. Never in a million year would she have thought this was where things were headed.

When they met a year earlier, it was so she could write a song for him. Ripley didn't write his own songs, though everyone believed he did. George had worked with his writing partner, Carole and was privy to this secret, so she'd been prepared to do all the work. She'd brought her notebook filled with songs she hadn't yet recorded and an open mind.

Carole had said that Ripley would come in, explain the story he wanted to convey in the song, and then leave her to it. So, when Ripley introduced himself and asked her to sing something she'd written, she never expected him to sit and stay. But that's what happened after she finished the first chorus of a song she was hoping to record soon. He sat at her feet, back against the scratchy couch, cowboy boots crossed at the ankles, and asked her to keep going. The bill of his Rangers ball cap had blocked her from seeing his reaction as she sang so she'd had no inkling he was into it.

"I want to write a song with you." Ripley said, finally turning around to look up at her with piercing green eyes, and George had felt the tightness in her stomach unwind. "It'll be a duet."

She'd had some crush-like feelings while writing the song. How could she not when Ripley sang the words she'd written, and especially when he insisted on using words that made her blush. But she'd never imagined it would all lead to this moment in her dressing room with him hovering over her.

Ripley kissed her then, stealing the air from her mouth as he sucked her bottom lip between his teeth. He liked to have a drink after walking offstage and she could taste whiskey on his tongue, warm and sweet. Sometimes had a drink before the show, too. He claimed it, *turns all the lights on in the house*, and no one could find reason to disagree when he had everyone on their feet night after night.

George could only handle hot water with honey beforehand. She worried about her voice cracking in front of so many people. But Ripley could split his pants on stage, forget his lyrics, sing offkey—it would just be greedily consumed like the kisses he blew to the audience.

"Oh," she said, when he pulled away. "I thought…" She didn't know what she thought.

"What did you think, Georgia?" Ripley watched her lips as he talked, like he couldn't wait to taste them again, and her insides clenched with the knowing of where he wanted this to go.

"You can call me George."

When she'd arrived in Nashville, naïve and so incredibly hungry for any scraps that came her way, she hadn't argued when her manager said they needed to change her name. Professionally, she was now Georgia, but she made sure that the people around her knew her real name.

"I like Georgia. It's prettier."

A memory tried to surface then, of another lifetime when a man had told her that her name was beautiful, but she shoved it back down. She would not think of him now, with another man licking the taste of her off his lips. The man who had plucked her from relative obscurity and brought her on his cross-country tour, changing her life completely.

She grabbing Ripley's shirt and pulled him in so she could lick into his open mouth with her tongue. The whiskey, the smell of his sweat and cologne, it all overwhelmed her senses and smothered the thoughts that kept fighting to surface. She wanted to be here, present in this moment only, not in the past.

"I thought the kiss was for show," she admitted when they came up for air. She was pretty sure she had beard burn all over her face.

"It is."

Ripley scooped her up and carried her to the couch, pulling her onto his lap. She was a little bit dazed, a lot confused, but didn't protest because *My God,* was this really happening?

He pushed the hair away from her face, his thumb resting over her pulse, his other fingers wrapped around the back of her neck. A devilish smile slid across his mouth and she felt it land heavily between her legs. He could feel her blood racing beneath the pad of his thumb, she was sure of it.

It felt dangerous. Anyone could walk in and see them and what would they think? That she'd slept her way onto the tour. Which she most certainly had not. She'd worked her ass off to get here. For the first time, she wondered if people already thought that.

"I don't know if we should..." George whispered.

"If we should what?" Ripley asked, his fingers moving into the hair at the nape of her neck, applying hardly any pressure at all, so that she wasn't sure if she was leaning towards him of her own doing.

"What will people think?"

She was still so new to Nashville. Well, she wasn't that new. She'd been working hard for years behind the scenes. But she was new to the spotlight and worried about mis-stepping and ruining it all. Everything that had happened, it could all disappear in an instant.

"We don't have to tell anyone." Ripley leaned back and looked her up and down, his eyes stopping where their bodies met.

The idea of not telling anyone confused George. On the one hand, keeping this thing quiet meant they could figure out their feelings without external interference. Building a relationship while on tour would be hard enough, but if they kept it between them, they could nurture it without outside variables.

On the other hand, the idea of sneaking around made her uncomfortable. They could share stolen moments in shadowy backstage areas? How could a relationship possibly grow under stifled conditions?

"Georgia, don't get all up in your head about it. Don't you want to come back to my room?"

He pouted then, his full bottom lip jutting out dramatically as his brow furrowed under his sweaty mop of hair, and George couldn't help but laugh. How did anyone ever say no to this man when he pulled something like this? He could have anyone, she reminded herself, and he was choosing her. How could she say no?

"Yeah."

Ripley whooped in response and George bit into her smile. This man was trouble.

* * *

A week later, they were in Baltimore for a night before heading up to Philly for two shows. By then, George had been sleeping in Ripley's room every night, to the point where the tour manager canceled her hotel rooms for the rest of the tour. George didn't care. She was drowning in lust-filled bliss, and though Ripley had said they'd keep it quiet, the band and everyone involved in the tour seemed to be well aware of what was going on.

Each night they sang their hearts out, playing up their duet even more now that they could consummate it later. They didn't always kiss at the end of the song. Sometimes they'd tease the audience with it, breathing each other's air like they were going to, but at the last second breaking out in shit-eating grins and pulling apart. That drove the crowds insane. George liked the thrill of not knowing which way each performance would go, but also knowing that at the end of the night they'd fall into bed together.

On this night, she stood at the bathroom sink washing her face. Ripley had wanted to have drinks with the band after the show, but George was exhausted after weeks on the road, so she'd gone back to the hotel. It was thrilling, the whole experience, but it was also draining giving her all onstage each night and then not getting a good night's sleep because Ripley couldn't keep his hands off her. She tried not to let the weary feeling in her bones get to her. She was so incredibly grateful. She'd happily run on empty as long as she could keep singing.

She heard the door open and close, followed by Ripley's heavy footsteps past the bathroom door.

"Hey," she called out as she rubbed moisturizer all over her face and neck. It was the one piece of advice Grandma Jeane had given her before she got on the bus—if nothing else, to take care of her skin at the end of each night. That, and stay hydrated.

She did one more swipe of deodorant, combed her fingers through her hair, and looked at her pajama-clad reflection, wondering what it was that had attracted Ripley. They didn't talk about it. Actually, they didn't talk about anything outside of the tour. He'd slap her butt in passing during soundcheck, tell her she looked sexy under his breath, but that was kind of the extent of it. They were both running on fumes, she chided herself. There'd be time for getting to know each other after the tour.

She walked into the bedroom and stopped at the foot of the bed, biting back a smile. Ripley was propped against the pillows, arms tucked behind his head, wearing nothing but his signature smirk. His eyes roamed her oversize tee and ratty pajama pants like he could see the skin beneath them, and he settled deeper into the pillows, letting out a sigh as she made her way to the edge of the bed.

"Why aren't you naked already?"

There was something about these nights in hotel rooms across various cities that simmered beneath the surface of her consciousness. Something that kept wanting to call attention to itself, but George wouldn't give it air. Because if she did, it would shade all these nights with Ripley in a color that she wouldn't like.

At first, she was so consumed by the lust between them that she didn't pay small details any mind. But what seemed to be happening more and more was this—Ripley lying in wait and George having to undress herself.

There wasn't anything wrong with it, per se. She loved the way he watched her pull off each item of clothing like a predator devouring her bit by bit. It made her feel powerful watching that desire deepen in the corners of his eyes as each item hit the floor. *She* did that. *She* was the one he made eyes at onstage. *She* was the one he fell into bed with each night.

But there wasn't any care or tenderness in what they were doing. It was completely carnal without any heart.

Finally naked, George crawled up the bed, slowly lowering herself onto Ripley while he watched her, his eyes growing hazy as he entered her, his hands finding their usual place at her breasts. He was a creature of habit and knowing what he wanted made each night easy.

They both woke each morning with their individual needs satisfied, but there was never any romance to it. George couldn't help wondering, if she didn't put in the work to get herself off, would he make sure she got there? Because usually, as soon as he came, Ripley was spent. That was the one positive of him always being a few whiskeys deep when they crawled into bed. It took him a while to come, which gave George time to meet him there.

George hadn't slept with anyone else since Boston. It wasn't that she'd purposefully abstained, it was that she couldn't seem to open her heart to the idea of being with another man. She'd fallen in love and then been unable to find a way to make that love work. If she was honest, she hated herself a little bit for not trying harder. Then again, he hadn't tried either, his emails and calls dissipating when she hit the road.

So maybe Caleb was always a little bit in the back of her mind, her subconscious casually making comparisons between the love that had been and the lack of it in her current relationship. And maybe that was why, when they pulled into Boston for two shows and a free afternoon in between, George pulled on the hoodie she'd stolen from a closet in Wyoming a lifetime ago.

date: Oct 4, 2021, 11:23 PM
from: calebtbrowningrichards@snailmail.com
to: g.rosetownsend@snailmail.com
subject: Did you steal my sweatshirt?

George,
It's been a while. I hope this is still your email now that you're a famous singer on a world tour.
I hope you're doing well and a huge congrats on the music! If you feel like writing back great, but if you're too busy I understand.
Also, please tell Grandma Jeane I make her chicken soup all the time. It really is the only cure when you're sick.
Your biggest fan,
Caleb

date: Dec 19, 2021, 10:07 PM
from: g.rosetownsend@snailmail.com
to: calebtbrowningrichards@snailmail.com
subject: Re: Did you steal my sweatshirt?

Hi!
I was so surprised to see your name in my inbox! I'm sorry it's taken me months to respond but I just got home from the tour. I didn't check email the entire time we were on the road. And to be clear, it wasn't a world tour. Just a handful of US cities.
Grandma Jeane says hi. She's thrilled to hear her recipe lives on beyond our kitchen. We live in Tennessee now. She moved with me about six months after The Billings Boys took me on tour. She said she'd seen enough of Texas and it was time she had some new scenery. Our home is nothing fancy, but she's got a little garden out back that she takes a lot of pride in.
How's Phil? How are YOU? I've wanted to write, to tell you everything, but I didn't know where to start. Those first weeks were crazy and I kept rolling with it and it worked out the way it was meant to, I suppose, but I'm sorry I didn't work harder to keep in touch.

Did Toby tell you he came to the show in LA? I forget when this was—November maybe? My brain is mush when it comes to dates. He seemed really happy and the girl he was with was adorable. Do you see him much? I have some time off now so maybe I'll be able to watch one of his movies.
I have so many questions, but I mostly want to know how you are. Are you still in Boston?
Okay yes, I did steal your sweatshirt the last morning in Jackson. It was the only time in my life I've ever stolen anything. I should have come clean and I'm sorry. I can mail it back to you, maybe with an album and some merch for my biggest fan?
Yours,
George

Caleb stared at George's sign-off for what felt like days. He kept coming back to it.

Yours.

He'd reread all of their old emails, every emotion bubbling up to the forefront like he'd stepped through a doorway into 2017. He remembered every moment with her and how her absence afterwards had felt like a weighted blanket holding him down. It had taken him a long time to shake off that feeling, mostly because he'd held onto it so tightly. Letting go of that had meant she was truly gone and he couldn't seem to say goodbye to what had been.

Yours.

Caleb hadn't asked her about Ripley Carlson because he didn't want to know, but also, he hadn't needed to. A week after the tour ended, Ripley was spotted at a restaurant in L.A. cozying up to some actress Caleb had never heard of. Then Phil sent him a link to an article confirming that things were over between Ripley and George. Caleb had almost fist-pumped when he read it, his excitement bubbling up like a shaken bottle of soda. But immediately he knew that was the wrong reaction. She was probably heartbroken and he was in a relationship. So why was his gut reaction to do a happy dance?

Outside of her romantic endeavors, Caleb was torturously curious about George's life. He tried to imagine the house she shared with Grandma Jeane, her neighborhood, did she have a coffee spot? What was her day like when she was working on music? Were any of her songs about him? He had so many questions that he was sure she'd be happy to answer. But Caleb was too chickenshit to ask. And he really didn't want to tell her his life updates.

He told himself it would be rubbing salt in a wound to tell George he was engaged when her most recent relationship had just ended. But that wasn't the whole truth. He just didn't want to think about what the truth might actually be.

Now, with Toby visiting for the holidays, he knew he could get some answers if he was stealthy about it.

"I'm heading to North Carolina after I leave here," Toby said from his seat across the dining table. He'd managed to fit in time to see Caleb while he was home, and to finally meet Kenzie.

"You're really doing it," Caleb mused. Not that he'd ever doubted Toby's talent.

"I really am." Toby held out his glass across the table to clink with Caleb's.

"So, who have you met that I would know?"

Kenzie didn't watch a lot of movies. Mostly just Bravo shows and the kind of reality faux-love that made Caleb uncomfortable. Anytime she started watching her shows, he'd excuse himself and take Rosie out. Or, he'd sit at his desk and write. What had started out as annoying had turned into something he now looked forward to because it meant time alone to work on this silly thing that made him happy.

"Hmm," Toby took a drink and swallowed, thinking. "I had a small part in a Jen Garner movie. She's just as wonderful as you'd imagine."

"I don't think I know who that is," Kenzie frowned. "What about someone from Real Housewives or Love is Blind?"

Toby snuck a quick look at Caleb who scratched his stubbled jaw in answer. How could he convey the seriousness of her question without embarrassing her? Kenzie would be mortified if she knew they were sending each other morse code signals regarding their mutual distaste for reality tv.

"Um, no, I don't think I have. I've been thankfully working a lot, so I usually just crash when I'm back in L.A."

That seemed to mollify Kenzie and she stood to clear their plates. Once she was out of earshot Caleb lowered his voice.

"I heard you saw George."

"Dude."

Toby leaned in over his wine glass. It brought Caleb back to their high school library, the two of them arguing about the best Manga while trying not to get shushed by the librarian.

"Vanna's a Ripley Carlson fan so she already had tickets, and I said I'd go without knowing anything and then when we got there and I saw the marquee and was like, huh, well this is interesting."

Caleb hadn't told Toby about buying his own concert ticket. If he'd asked himself why he kept it from those closest to him he might have been forced to admit that it made him feel like a piece of shit. He should have told Kenzie about George from the beginning and asked if she wanted to go with him, instead of sneaking around.

"We were waiting for her to go on so I texted to say I was there and was excited to see her perform. Truly never expected her to respond, but she did during Ripley's set, so we hung around and got to see her after the show."

It was like Caleb hadn't had anything to drink in days and Toby's words were cold spring water. He wanted every detail, all of it, until he was drunk on it.

"How was she? How did she look? Did she seem happy?"

"She was amazing on stage. Everyone loved her. I think people were expecting just a whatever-opener, someone unremarkable filling the time. But between their sets her merch table was packed. She asked about you."

"Who asked about him?"

Both Caleb and Toby startled, not hearing Kenzie reenter the room with a plate of brownies and a fresh bottle of wine. Toby's eyebrows lifted as if to say, *how do you want to play this?*

Caleb's neck warmed as if the thermostat had suddenly been turned up high. He wasn't someone who lied. So why was he doing it now? This wasn't the kind of person—the kind of future husband—he wanted to be.

"Toby went to a concert a couple months ago in L.A. and the opening act—"

"George Townsend," Toby added helpfully, then took a drink of wine before he said more.

"She—um—I know her from—Phil and I know her from Wyoming."

Kenzie's brown pinched, like she was waiting for something more from him to help place the name. He couldn't explain or justify it, but he didn't want to share George with Kenzie.

"Wait, do you know someone famous, babe? Who is he?"

"She," Toby and Caleb said in unison, and then Toby took a bite of brownie.

"A woman named *George*?" Kenzie wrinkled her nose as this and Caleb had to bite his tongue to keep from making a comment about glass houses. It would benefit no one and the whole point of this was to fix a wrong he had made.

"George is a musician—"

"An insanely talented one," Toby added before finishing off his brownie.

Caleb blinked at his friend, pleading with him to stop helping. Or whatever Toby thought he was doing.

"Okay, wait. How famous is this George person? Would I know one of her songs?"

Kenzie leaned forward in her chair, suddenly interested. Meanwhile, Caleb leaned away. He'd done it. He'd told her about George. He didn't need to go into detail about how well he knew her because that was in the past.

"Do you know Ripley Carlson?" Maybe it was the wine or maybe it was the chocolate, but Toby was going all in on the unhelpfulness.

"Wait," Kenzie closed her eyes to think. A second later her eyes flew open. "Ohmygod, yes! Country singer? Something about lace… am I right?"

Caleb refilled his wine glass while Toby and Kenzie fed off each other's excitement.

"Yes! He has a song, Burn For You. It's a duet."

"Wait! Ohmygod, I know it. It's in some movie…"

Kenzie looked at Caleb for help but he played dumb and continued sipping wine.

"You're useless! Wait, do you know Ripley?" She pinballed back and forth between Toby and Caleb, eyes wide. And though Caleb shook his head, she continued staring at Toby, clearly hoping for a different answer.

"The girl he sings the duet with, that's George."

Toby turned and smiled at Caleb like a dog returning the ball to his owner's hand, and Caleb had to forcefully swallow the groan that threatened to spill out of him. But, he had no one to blame for his discomfort but himself.

"Ohmygod, so you do know someone famous!" For the first time since Toby had walked through the door, Kenzie looked awfully charmed. She turned that same gaze on Caleb and he felt himself shrivel, because he still wasn't telling her the whole truth and now he realized he couldn't.

"These are really good, by the way," Toby held up a second brownie.

"They're from a box. I sadly do not have any skills in the kitchen, but that's why I have him." Kenzie squeezed Caleb's arm and he tried to muster a smile.

"Since when do you cook?" Toby laughed, his voice flirting with disbelief.

Since he'd vowed to cook for George. But Caleb couldn't say that.

"When my father overdosed and Phil and I stopped speaking, I had a lot of time, so I learned to cook so I wouldn't starve."

"I didn't know that, babe." Kenzie took his hand in hers and set it in her lap. She ran hot, just like him, and together their hands started to sweat, but he held on because he was an asshole for keeping things from her.

"The whole package, huh?" Toby shook his head teasingly, and though Caleb was annoyed with his friend—but mostly with himself—he was thankful to have him here. It had been too long since they'd been together.

"He really is. How did I get so lucky?" Kenzie looked at Caleb with such open adoration that he knew. It wasn't even a choice. The decision had been made. He couldn't keep emailing with George. Here was his soon-to-be wife and she deserved all of him. He should never have emailed George in the first place. Reopening that wound had been a mistake. He should have left the past alone.

Toby caught his eye. Even with years spent on opposite coasts he could still read Caleb like a book. So, Caleb pushed every thought and feeling about George down. It was done, buried. He'd focus on what was in front of him and be thankful for it.

Kenzie continued, unaware of Caleb's inner turmoil.

"We're sending out the wedding invites soon so I figure now's a good time to ask. Are you planning to bring Vanna—that's her name, right?"

Toby nodded.

"Our planner is on us to start the seating chart. Apparently, that's the biggest issue when planning a wedding, so I'm just trying to get a jump on it so we give the powers that be, aka our mothers, enough time to make edits."

Caleb was lucky to have her. She had taken on the whole wedding planning thing with gusto.

"As of right now, she's my plus one. But if I'm being completely honest, I don't know where we'll stand by the time the wedding comes around. That's months away—"

"Five months," Kenzie amended.

"Five months. Wow."

Caleb hated that it took effort to make himself smile in response. What he hated more was that Toby could see every pause, every flinch.

"Listen, a lot can change between now and then, so if it's a big deal just put me down as coming alone and I'll RSVP officially when I get home from the next shoot and see where my relationship stands."

That seemed to satisfy Kenzie. She loved this stuff and considering Caleb couldn't tell the difference between ecru and off-white, he was perfectly content to let her make all the decisions. Especially when it made her smile like she was smiling now.

"Have you started planning the bachelor party yet?" Kenzie looked to Toby.

The—*what*?

"Oh, that I have." Toby's smile was mischievous enough to make Caleb nervous. "I'm sorry, did you think I wasn't going to plan the most epic party for my best friend before his wedding day?"

Caleb was oddly humbled by this, that Toby would want to plan something. Their friendship continued to amaze him after all these years.

"Do you want me to ask if we can use the Chatham house?"

Toby scoffed and followed it with an eye roll for good measure.

"Caleb, we're leaving Massachusetts for this. Phil and I have been in cahoots for weeks."

Kenzie giggled beside him and Caleb turned to take in her reaction.

"Did you know about this?"

She shrugged sheepishly. "Only which weekend, because that's when my bachelorette is happening. It's on the calendar in the kitchen. If you ever flipped ahead, you'd see it."

It was then that Caleb realized just how consumed he'd been with thoughts of George and his neck burned with shame. His loved ones had been planning the future while he'd been mooning over the past.

"I don't deserve either of you."

Kenzie leaned in and kissed Caleb, a teaser for later. Toby smirked over the top of his wineglass.

"Honestly, I'm a little offended you thought I wouldn't plan something. It's like you've forgotten how much I love a theme party and any excuse for costumes."

That brought Caleb up short, his eyebrows rising as he looked across the table at his friend.

"I'm sorry, what?"

date: Jan 1, 2022, 11:02 PM
from: g.rosetownsend@snailmail.com
to: calebtbrowningrichards@snailmail.com
subject: Happy New Year!

Caleb,
Did you and Phil do anything fun to celebrate NYE? A friend of mine had a dinner party and it was lovely, but what I've found is that everyone is a musician here. After dessert someone pulled out a guitar, then another, a harmonica, a ukelele, and it was a full sing-a-long until midnight. But it was a good time.
Now that my new album is officially out (!!!), I have sixteen dates starting later this month. I have my own opener and everything. The other tour was unreal. There were some things I wish I could have done differently, but you know me, I never had a dream to begin with. And maybe that ended up being the best way to approach it because everything that happened was amazing because I didn't have expectations. There was nowhere to go but up. And now I get my own tour! Is this real life?
I'll be at the Royale in Boston on January 26th. No pressure at all, but if you and Phil want to come I can leave tickets at will-call. It's a tremendously smaller budget this go-round. I'm coming into Boston from Maine that day so it'll be kind of hectic before the show, but maybe we could get coffee the next morning before I leave for Philly? It would be nice to catch up in person.
Tell me everything. Are you still living in the same place with Phil? A ramen place opened in my neighborhood last year and it made me think of you. It's not as good as the place you took me to, but it does the trick on a cold night.
Look at me writing you a novel. I would've called but it being New Years I wasn't sure if you'd be awake, hungover, with someone, etc. Or if your number is even still the same. My number hasn't changed.
Yours,
George

Every day George checked her email obsessively. She refreshed her sent folder, her internet connection, even went so far as to ask a friend to send a test email. Everything was fine on her end, but there was nothing but silence from Caleb.

She reread her last email, over-analyzing every line and wondering if she'd overstepped, but she couldn't figure out what she'd done wrong. And then she came around to the idea that maybe it wasn't her. Maybe something had happened to him.

Spinning out of control with worry did her absolutely no good. She was supposed to be preparing for her first solo tour. Instead, she was writing thoughts and feelings in a notebook and staring off at nothing. A single email—or lack thereof—after so many years of silence, had her unraveling.

She met a friend for coffee the following week. Simone was a songwriter, and though they'd never worked together, they quickly became friends a few months after George moved to Nashville. Simone was a California transplant, with a chic blonde bob and constant cat-eye. To those who didn't know her well, she seemed soft-spoken, a bit standoffish. Those on the inside understood that she was studying, processing, and forming sharp-witted opinions.

"I'm going to need you to start from the beginning," Simone said as she sipped from her steaming mug.

George took her back to 2016 and worked forward, sticking to what was most important to the timeline. She felt herself falling back into it all, emotions resurfacing as she pictured the sunsets, the warm body wrapped around her back, holding back tears as cold wind bit her cheeks.

"You loved him," Simone sighed when George finished.

George returned her dry corn muffin to its plate. She coughed to clear her throat and took a gulp of water to wash it down.

"Oh." Simone's brow furrowed and her smile turned down at the corners into something pitying. "You're still in love with him."

George felt the backs of her eyes burn as the words splattered on the table between them. She'd been in a weird place at the end of the last tour. Things with Ripley had been exciting and fun in the beginning. And then somewhere, without her realizing it, they settled into this weird thing that George wasn't sure how to talk about, but which made her feel tarnished. She hadn't been able to work out how to get out from under a situation that held so much power over her future.

She'd continued playing her part through the end of the tour, scrubbing herself raw under the scalding spray while Ripley snored on the other side of the bathroom door, splayed naked, satisfied and seemingly unaware of George's heart. Or maybe he'd never cared to get to know her at all. Maybe this was what he did and it was never meant to be anything more, anything real.

It didn't matter. When the tour was over, so was their relationship—if you could even call it that—and hopefully their paths would cross as minimally as possible going forward. Not likely, considering Nashville was small, but George continued to hope.

Her second day home after the tour ended, she was a mess. It was like she'd turned a part of herself off in order to get through it all. The exhaustion and excitement that went hand in hand with the tour finally caught up to her and overwhelmed her system. She tried to start a load of laundry and stood there, frozen, unable to complete a simple task. But it wasn't really about the laundry.

Grandma Jeane found here there, crying over a basket of dirty clothes and George couldn't explain herself.

I'm just really tired, she said once she'd calmed down enough to speak actual words.

Grandma Jeane had rubbed her back until George could convincingly say she was fine. Later, she found a pot of chicken soup simmering on the stove. Knowing that Grandma Jeane loved her no matter what was enough to make her cry all over again.

Unimaginable things had happened over the last few years, starting in Wyoming and working across the country to here, now. Her life was steadily gaining upward momentum and sometimes it just felt incredibly overwhelming. She tried to be grateful for it all, but after the tour George felt like a dry, old husk.

And then Caleb's email was waiting in her inbox, like a shot of adrenaline straight to her heart.

She'd devoured it, not realizing how hungry she still was for him, and responded without editing herself. And when he'd replied, her heart beat again and she'd grabbed her notebook.

The words came in dribbles, like a leaky faucet. More of a feeling than a complete thought, the idea not yet fully formed.

> *You could say that I'm naïve*
> *But once I loved a man so good*
> *Kind, smart, flowers on a Sunday sweet*
> *I'd like to know him again if I could*

And later, another song. It pushed and tore its way out of her, like it would suffocate if it stayed in her head a moment longer.

It poured out of her, a song about then and now and all of it about Caleb. It was like his emails had turned on a spigot inside her, memories and emotions and touches she'd long repressed pouring back in and filling her up.

She was a different version of the person he'd known. Older, a little bit wiser, maybe a bit worn around the edges from wear and tear. But her feelings from so long ago were just as strong as they'd once been and she started to wonder. Now, with the financial means to travel, could they try again?

When he didn't respond to her email on New Year's Day she wanted to shrivel up and cry, to pull the drawbridge up and fortify her walls, to swear off men forever. But for some reason, maybe because it was Caleb, she didn't. She held out hope.

"Maybe he's traveling. A lot of people go on vacation around the holidays. He could be out of the country. Give it another week." Simone reassured her now. She might be thirty-four and single, but her advice on everything from who to steer clear of in the industry to where to buy the best produce had always been sound.

"I wrote a couple songs." George sipped her coffee and let that sink in.

"Can I see them?" Simone's chair scraped against the floor as she scooted forward closing ranks.

George had brought her notebook with her, desperately wanting reassurance that she was on the right path. It felt different from the songs she'd kept to herself all these years, hoping for the day she could have complete control over an album.

The new stuff was coming out with a refined sheen. She was looking back at something with the perspective of age and distance while still firmly planted in the emotions of that time. The songs felt really good, and yet she wondered if she was out of her mind with exhaustion and unresolved emotions. Maybe she was looking at a child's watercolor and calling it Monet.

She turned away while Simone scrutinized each page, terrified that she'd lost it and this was all a silly delusion. She sipped her coffee and swallowed down more dry muffin while watching the other patrons.

George didn't ever want to lose her deep appreciation for the things that came her way, but sometimes she felt so alien in this city and missed the monotony of home, of no one giving a shit who you were or what you could do for them. Back in Texas everyone was who they said they were. There were no masks, no pretenses. No one there had time for bullshit.

"George."

She met Simone's gaze and her heart stuttered. If her words really were crap that would be the end of it. She'd have to pack up Grandma Jeane and their things and move out of town. Because writing was her currency here and without it she had nothing.

The look spreading across Simone's features was confusingly similar to annoyance. But why would she be annoyed with George?

"Tell me the truth. The honest to God truth, Simone. How bad is it?"

It had come too easy. Songs didn't just pour out of you like that, no need to edit or reframe. She didn't want to be placated or coddled. There was no place for that in this shark-eat-shark business.

"George," Simone whispered, her head leaning in conspiratorially. "This is so fucking good."

George felt her shoulders drop in heavy relief. She hadn't realized she'd been clenching in preparation for the worst.

"Tell me you've sat down with Bear and recorded something already."

"Nope, only voice notes on my phone. I'm supposed to be prepping for the tour next week."

Simone groaned and let her head fall dramatically on the table, narrowly missing her untouched scone.

"You're killing me. I need to hear it so badly. Like, right now, filling my head with romantic notions and making me weep with jealousy."

Simone lifted her head and rested her chin on her fist, a big, droopy pout making its way across her face. It made George laugh, at the theatrics put on for her benefit, but also with gratitude at having this kind of friendship.

"God," George sighed. "I was really starting to worry I was losing it. I've been so tired since getting back, my emotions have been all over the place, and I was thinking maybe it sounds good in my head but outside of here," she swirled a finger around herself, "it's nonsense."

Simone took one of George's hands in both of her own.

"Ripley did a number on you, huh?"

George could feel her face scrunch in what—disgust? Embarrassment? She'd been so easily dazzled by the sparkle of it all that she hadn't thought it through before jumping. And it wasn't like it was a relationship between two nobodies. There were pictures of them kissing in magazines for prying, judging eyes to dissect. What was the saying? Once something was on the internet it was forever. Well, now she would forever be the girl Ripley Carlson kissed onstage no matter what accomplishments followed after.

"I just feel so gross about it. Like, it was fun and exciting for a minute, then I felt uncomfortable about it, and now anytime I take a meeting with someone I'm wondering, is that the only reason they wanted to meet with me?"

A shiver raced up George's spine at the thought.

"No one's going to take me seriously now. I'll be a punchline or a bar trivia answer forever."

Simone's eyes rolled back in her head like this was the most idiotic thing she'd ever heard.

"Ripley is an over-used copy and paste of so many guys in this town. There's nothing remarkable about him. But you, my dear…" Simone knocked twice on George's notebook. "Am I going to have to beg?"

George blinked, unaware of what Simone was referring to.

"You're going to make me beg. Okay, fine. I'll grovel. Give me a second to stuff down my pride." Simone pretended to shove things underneath her seat on both sides, then surveyed her job, nodding once when she was satisfied.

George laughed, ignoring the heads that turned in their direction.

"I'm just a girl, sitting in front of her best friend who also happens to be a musical genius, asking her to let her—*me*—write an album with her—*you*."

It took George a second to comprehend the convoluted sentence, but when it registered, her face split in two. But within a second the smile was melting at both ends under the heat of the emotions burning their way to the forefront.

"You want to write with me?" She choked out, failing to keep the tears at bay. Simone had a Grammy for songwriting on her mantle. The idea that she was begging to write with George was too much. It felt like her heart was going to explode.

"Yes!" Simone said, while her face emoted *FREAKING DUH*. "Focus on your shows, sing your heart out, collect more fans, and when you get back, we can hole up at my house for a week and see what we come up with. Let's make some magic together."

George could only nod. All the words had been knocked clear out of her mouth. From the start, she'd felt so comfortable around Simone, like they'd grown up together. George had no qualms about laying herself bare before her friend and being completely honest about her feelings. That was the only way she could see to handle these songs that were gurgling up out of her like the hot springs in Yellowstone.

date: Jan 19, 2022, 5:17 PM
from: g.rosetownsend@snailmail.com
to: calebtbrowningrichards@snailmail.com
subject: Re: Hi

Hey,
I'm playing in Boston at the Royale on the 26th. Absolutely no pressure to come, but I'll leave two tickets for you and Phil at will-call in case you're free. It would be really good to see you.
Yours,
George

George had zero delusions about her own tour being anywhere near the same experience as she'd had on Ripley's tour. For one, she didn't have the fanbase he had. Or the budget. Ripley was big crowds, big venues, big money. They'd stayed in hotels—a first for George—and had cushy dressing rooms backstage. This tour was going to be different, not the least reason being she wouldn't have to sleep with anyone to keep her opening spot.

It wasn't going to be a glitzy tour. They'd be sleeping on the bus each night, George and her band. She couldn't get enough of that. *Her* band. It was outrageous that she was here. Sure, the venues were small in comparison to the places she'd opened for Ripley, but this tour was all *her*. That was beyond thrilling. And also a little terrifying.

Her team hadn't offered up any info on tickets sales and she was too afraid to ask. What if she showed up each night and there was a handful of people in the audience? This was why she'd never allowed herself to dream. Because you could be so high one day only to fall flat on your face the next. The music industry was fickle. But man, did she feel lucky to be part of it for however long it last.

George figured she had Caleb to thank for some of it. If he hadn't pushed her to dream, she may never have on her own. She might still be back in Texas not ever seeing a west coast sunset or realizing she'd never known humidity before stepping foot in South Carolina.

Maybe that was giving Caleb too much credit when she'd done all the work herself. But however you looked at it, her life had changed after meeting him. She needed to tell him that, to his face, and thank him. She wanted Caleb in her life, and if all he could give her was friendship that was fine.

If he was open to more, well…

When the bus crossed into Massachusetts, having kicked off the tour to a surprisingly electric crowd in Portland, George felt her blood start to hum. Even though Caleb hadn't responded to her last two emails, which she refused to overthink because she really needed her head to be clear, there was a chance that he would come.

The city spread out before them in dreary winter greys and nothing could dampen George's mood. During sound check she had to concentrate on breathing slowly, her voice threatening to crack from nerves.

It had happened the first night opening for Ripley, because she'd never stood in front of that many people before. She'd never even imagined how it would feel to stand before a crowd that big or the heat of that many eyes on her. But after a few chords, she'd absorbed their excitement and she forgot to be nervous.

But this wasn't singing in front of a crowd. This was potentially singing in front of the only man she'd ever loved.

She wondered if people bought tickets expecting her to sing "Burn For You". What if that was all they knew of her, the girl who dueted with Ripley Carlson? She'd loved writing that song and singing it the first twenty times. But now, she never wanted to sing it again. Maybe she'd feel differently ten years from now when the words didn't conjure memories of sweat and whiskey, but if the audience was expecting that each night of this tour, they'd be leaving disappointed. And she hated to disappoint anyone.

As the opener—a trio that her label had chosen, but who George would have picked anyway—kicked off the show in Boston, George wouldn't allow herself a peek at the crowd. She was too afraid of spotting a familiar face and forgetting everything. Because she knew when she saw Caleb again, she would likely forget how to breathe.

It felt like Caleb was her gravity, as ridiculous as that sounded. Even when he wasn't there, and it had been years now, it was like she was tethered to him. Maybe it was just the memory of him, or maybe it was the confidence he'd instilled in her and which she carried still.

The opener finished, the sets were swapped out, and then George took a deep breath and stepped on stage.

Her first song was a little shaky, her nerves getting so bad at one point that she thought her legs might buckle. But she fought through it, explaining—or rather, apologizing—to the crowd that it was only the second night and her first solo tour. They seemed to appreciate the honesty, cheering her along. By the first chorus in the second song, she felt more assured, more herself.

As she was singing the last words of her fourth song, "Bluebells and Bourbon", George looked down at the people closest to the stage. So many of them were singing along and she took a moment as the band played their remaining notes to make eye contact with each person, acknowledging them and how much their being here meant to her. They surpassed her expectations, already knowing the words to an album that had only been out a handful of months.

Then she landed on a face so familiar that George forgot where she was and what she was doing.

"PHIL—OHMYGOD!" She screeched. Her band paused, startled by this unexpected reaction, and every head turned in the direction of George's words.

Phil reached her hands up, fingers spread wide like her mouth, and George kneeled down at the edge of the stage, thankful that she was wearing pants tonight. She clasped Phil's fingers and felt tears prick the back of her eyes.

It was a second before she realized she was holding up the set, and while everyone's eyes had been on her for the last thirty minutes, this was a confusing interlude for everyone outside of her and Phil. George gave a squeeze and let go, standing back up.

"I'm so sorry about that," George said to the quieting crowd. "Nearly blew your ear drums out there. I just got so excited seeing someone I know!"

The crowd laughed, eyes returning to her as she went back to the mic stand to steady herself. She snapped it into place and looked back at her band to signal that she wasn't quite ready for the next song. Her drummer sat back, his sticks resting on his thighs.

"This may be taking liberties with our relationship since it's early stages. We're only just getting to know each other. But let me tell you a quick story before the next song. I think it'll bring us just a little bit closer. 'Cuz that's what friendship is, right? Sharing stories and experiences with each other, and my goal tonight is to be real good friends by the time you leave.”

George could see heads nodding along, smiles and wide eyes, but she didn’t dare look too closely, for fear of seeing Caleb and forgetting how to speak.

“First impressions are important, right?”

The crowd echoed back—*Right!*

“Have you ever met someone in the most awkward way possible?”

George tapped her nose and pointed at Phil while a few people whistled and cheered in the crowd. It took a second for recognition to dawn, and then Phil was laughing and mouthing *I’m sorry!*

“Okay now, how many of you ever met someone for the first time while in a compromising position?”

George winked and the crowd tittered in response. She could feel them hanging on her every word. She was giving them something private, bringing them into her confidence, and creating a moment they wouldn’t soon forget.

She’d watched other performers do it time and again and wondered how they had the casual ability to weave honest moments through a set without it feeling rehearsed. But here she was doing that very thing.

“I’m talking best night of your life, lose feeling in your toes, forget your middle name kind of night. You understand my meaning?”

“Get it girl!” Someone yelled in the crowd and laughter rose up like the tide.

“May we all be so lucky, right?” George laughed with them.

Her cheeks started heating at the thought that Caleb was out there watching this, hearing her talk about their past in front of hundreds—a thousand?—people. Was he cringing? Or was he remembering those moments with fondness?

"So, picture me—wait, no-no! Ohmygod, don't actually picture me! What am I saying? Is it hot in here or is it just me? Did I just ruin it? Are we no longer friends?"

George peeked under the shadow of her hand to try and gauge the depth of the crowd. She couldn't stop smiling. She had them eating out of her hand. If this was what every night was going to be like this tour would one hundred percent outshine her memory of Ripley's tour.

"No! Still friends!" They replied, a delicious chorus.

"Phew! Okay, so, *friends*, I'm in the midst of this glorious, beautiful thing—picture what you will—and in walks this girl right here—"

George pointed and every head swung in Phil's direction. She hid behind her hands in mock shame but George could tell she was actually loving the attention.

"—and she's babbling on about a river for a solid minute before she even realizes what she's walked in on."

There was laughter and whistles, conversations gurgling up beyond the edge of the stage and it occurred to George suddenly, like a light had been turned on overhead, that she had quite possibly segued herself organically into the next song. If she could just land it, the people in this room might never forget this moment.

"I know! Oh, she apologized, friends. Don't you worry. But what a wonderful first impression, right? And she ruined what was quite possibly one of the best… well." George winked at the crowd. She loved getting to play with them and put on this show of being a flirty, boisterous character, someone so much bolder than she truly was.

Someone whistled from the back of the room and more shouting and laughter followed. George wondered if that whistle was Caleb giving her a sign that he was here. She'd never felt more alive and appreciative than this moment right here.

"You know, back home we have a saying for when someone storms into a situation they have no business being in. I know we're a long way from Texas tonight, but I wonder if maybe you're familiar with that saying. And if not, I'd like to introduce you to it. It's one of my favorites."

George looked over at her lead guitarist and gave him a subtle nod. She felt the band shift around her as they readied for the cue.

"Darlin, bless your heart!"

* * *

After the set ended and the house lights came on, George stood just out of sight waiting for the crowd to thin. She spotted Phil easily as she lingered at the edge of stage, but Caleb wasn't beside her. George pictured him waiting by the bar, an ode to their first meeting, but she couldn't see the bar from this angle. Her heart was racing faster now than it had when she was under the lights.

When the crew began disassembling the setup and the crowd was mostly gone, George slipped by the merch table and made her way through a handful of congratulations, a couple of pictures, and one request for a signed album. Finally, she made it to Phil.

Phil squealed as she enveloped George in a bear hug, swaying together like trees in a storm.

"Oh my god, George! That was beyond! Don't take this the wrong way, but who knew you were such a dynamo!" Phil finally released her. "Like, I knew you could sing because of the video. And because Caleb said so. And then the album. And all the clips of you and he who shall not be named performing together. Regardless of whatever happened, you can do way better, by the way. He's going to burn out so fast and you're going to continue being *everything*."

George had forgotten how Phil babbled when excited and it overwhelmed her, processing this slightly older, even more polished version of Phil. It took a moment to figure out how to respond. But before she could say anything, Phil hugged her again.

"Thanks for the tickets, by the way!"

"Thank you for coming, Phil. It really means the world to me."

George's heart felt so full in Phil's presence. This was only the second show of the tour and already someone she knew had come to support her. She didn't expect that to happen at any other stop, but so many people had come and if this was a sign of how the rest of the tour was going to go, she felt sure it would be a success.

She allowed herself to look then, over Phil's shoulder towards the bar, but she couldn't find him. It had been years. Maybe he'd changed, finally grown that beard he'd been coveting. Whether he'd put on weight or was sporting a man-bun, she didn't care.

"He's not here," Phil said softly, taking both of George's hands in hers.

George felt something shift between them as Phil gripped her tight. It was like George had taken a step into thin air not realizing she'd been standing on a ledge.

"Does he know about Ripley? Because we aren't a thing anymore."

Phil shook her head.

"I tried to get him to come, but he, well…"

George watched Phil's shoulders soften as she stepped closer, blocking everyone else out.

"He's engaged. I'm so sorry to be the one to tell you that. He's an ass for not doing it himself."

George's mind went blank, like the curtain had dropped, the scene fading to black. Maybe this was what it felt like when your heart imploded and a black hole was created inside your chest turning you inside out.

"Oh," she said, or at least meant to say. All she knew was that she didn't cry and that was something. Because bursting into tears in front of strangers who were watching her was the last thing she needed.

"I'm so sorry." Phil squeezed her in another hug, this one delicate, like she could see the decimation on George's face and didn't want to crush her further.

"It's okay," George managed.

Except, it wasn't. A door that she'd thought might still be unlocked had shut before she was ready. Or, more likely, it had closed a long time ago and she just hadn't known.

"I really am sorry."

"No, it's okay. I'm happy for him." George forced a smile but the grimace Phil returned told her just how poorly she was acting. Caleb's happiness was all she'd ever wanted. Of course, she wished it were her that he came home to every night, but their lives had always been too different to work. Why would she think that now, in the midst of a tour, would be the time it might actually happen for them?

She felt someone hovering behind her, probably waiting for a picture, and Phil gave her one last squeeze.

"It was seriously so good to see you, George. Truly. Highlight of my year. Next time you're in town we have to get dinner. I want to hear all the stories."

"Absolutely." The world around George slowed as Phil walked away, and two other women stepped in to have their moment.

So that's that, she thought as she dropped into her bed an hour later. The chapter of her life where Caleb played a starring role was officially over.

She lay back against the pillow and opened Instagram. Caleb's account was easy enough to find, and while she knew it would be hard to accept, she needed closure.

The blue bar below his picture blared *Follow Back* and George realized he was already following her. For how long? Had he scrutinized every one of her pictures? Could he tell how hard it was for her to post something and write a caption that was equal parts lyrical and genuine?

As she scrolled, each photo of Caleb's was another drop in the bucket. The most recent was a dog with expressive eyes donning a plaid jacket and a tongue-lolling smile. *Ready for our morning constitutional,* it read. Then a photo of a beautifully decorated Christmas tree, and George's heart skipped into a sprint at the realization that it was Caleb's home in Boston where she'd stayed with him. He sat in the middle, one arm around the adorable dog from the previous picture, the other around a beautiful woman. All three were wearing matching pajamas and sleepy, morning smiles.

George continued to scroll, stopping to study every photo. The same woman appeared five more times and though she was tagged in each one, George couldn't bring herself to click over to her page and discover more about Kenzie Donaldson. George found herself stalling on the photo of Caleb and Kenzie, a diamond-encrusted ring finger extended to the camera. There was no denying their happiness. But she kept scrolling anyway.

She saw the life that had almost been hers. It wasn't a searing-hot pain. No, it was more like a torn muscle that never quite healed and she just kept reinjuring over and over, the pain lingering just enough to remind her it had never really gone. It could have been her in the engagement photo, her under the Christmas tree, her holding a cocktail in a booth beside Phil. Caleb got younger as the years unraveled, his hair changing as he aged in reverse. And then George felt herself gasping for air as tears trickled down her face.

She checked the date below the image.

August 22, 2016.

Not that she needed confirmation. She would recognize that horse, those boots, the hat, her hair, even in a sun-splashed photo. The trail had been bending left, so Phil was out of the frame. It brought George right back to that afternoon, them ambushing her at work and how annoyed she'd been.

She found herself smiling through tears. God, she had loved that man, even though she hadn't named it at the time. And this photo made her realize he had probably loved her too. He could have deleted it years ago. But here it was, a reminder of what had been between them.

She pulled out her notebook, flipped through what she'd already written, and opened to a clean page. This was the beginning of a new chapter, one in which she remembered with due fondness what had been, what could have been, and what never would be. And with that in mind, and with a swirling tangle of sadness, longing, heartache, and love, she started writing.

> *I'm better when I write things down*
> *Give me time to think things out*
> *Always seems to come right back around to you*
> *I never would have given up*
> *But now I know you're better off*
> *Giving her that wide eyed look you do*
> *It was my favorite part of you.*

It didn't matter that they'd been out drinking until one the night before or that Rosie was back home in Boston with a dog sitter. Caleb was wide awake at seven, his body refusing to take a day off. He pulled on shorts and a tee, tied his sneakers, and slipped out of the rental house while his friends slept off their hangovers. Out on the street, he hit play on a Rolling Stones album and set off.

At home, he gravitated toward the Charles. He had no interest in running along sidewalks where he'd have to pause at each intersection and wait for the light to change. Along the river he could run for miles without interruption and lose himself in music, in thought, in nothing.

Naturally, Caleb found his way to a river here in Nashville. Back home the trees were still bare, the ground muddy, the temperatures yoyoing towards Spring without committing. But here things were well on their way, and as the Caleb's head emptied out and he ran until he no longer was thinking or feeling, his body moving on autopilot.

Toby texted halfway through Caleb's run to say he was heading out in search of sustenance and dropped a pin. So now, Caleb stood on the sidewalk outside of said coffee shop catching his breath and watched a couple walk out hand in hand. Was their relationship new and thrilling, he wondered. Would they grow old together, continuing to frequent this coffee shop because it reminded them of being young?

Sometimes Caleb thought about his life, job, home, his fiancée. And he wondered, what if he'd moved away after college? What if he'd gone to California with Toby? How different would his life be in another place with different people? Who would he be today?

The thought of not being in the right place at the right time to adopt Rosie was enough to stop that train of thought from going any further, and just in time because Toby stepped out the door with two coffees in hand.

"Thanks," Caleb said and guzzled the iced-whatever he'd been gifted.

"How're you feeling?" Toby asked, the two of them falling into step on the sidewalk. It was a half mile back to the rental and knowing how hard the guys had partied last night, they didn't need to rush.

"Fine." Caleb slowed to match Toby's pace. As much as he hadn't needed a bachelor weekend, it was nice getting to spend time with his best friend.

"You seemed pretty subdued last night. Everything okay?"

Caleb could see Toby watching him out of the corner of his eye, but Caleb focused on his coffee.

"Just a long week."

Caleb reached an arm across Toby, saving him from walking into a telephone pole. Toby startled, realizing how close he'd come to slamming face-first into something.

"Shit," Toby sidestepped the pole and clapped Caleb on the shoulder. "Good looking out for my money maker."

"What would you do without me?" Caleb asked with a modest smile.

They walked a block in amicable silence, but Toby just couldn't help himself. And because of their years of friendship Caleb was waiting for it.

"You sure you're okay?"

Caleb inhaled for three counts and let it out slowly. When Toby got hung up on something he didn't let it go easily. Caleb needed to nip it in the bud or be prepared to face questions for the rest of the weekend.

"Toby, I'm fine. I promise. Planning a wedding is just a lot. And on top of it, my mother is constantly harassing me to get a prenup. Not to mention, she's making me invite my father even though he and I have barely spoken in years, and—"

"Hey." Toby held onto Caleb's arm forcing him to stop. "It's okay to not be okay. That's a lot for anyone to take on."

"It is what it is," Caleb responded, because truthfully, he wasn't allowing himself to process his feelings. He worried that if he stopped and did just that, he might never start again. He'd feel so overwhelmed that the only thing to do would be to run away and never look back.

Caleb started walking and Toby jogged to catch up, his coffee held aloft to prevent spilling.

"I see you don't want to talk about it."

"Not right now."

"Well, I'm here. This weekend, next week, a year from now. Whenever you want someone to listen, I'll always be your guy."

Caleb nodded and the two of them continued the rest of the way in silence. It was funny how people changed. In high school, if Toby had sensed this sort of energy in Caleb, he'd have forced him into an empty classroom and poked and prodded until everything was out in the open so they could work together to find a solution. But now, almost two decades of friendship later, Toby knew when to let it go.

Maybe Caleb would call him in a week, overwhelmed and running out of ideas to keep the stress at bay. Or maybe he'd bury it inside and pretend it wasn't an issue. But either way, he didn't want to have that kind of emotional unspooling right now. He just wanted to eat good food, drink until he was numb, and enjoy whatever activities Toby had planned.

* * *

They ate dinner at a Mediterranean restaurant, split a bottle of whiskey, and ended up at the bar Toby had picked as tonight's destination. There would be pool tables, live music, and if it ended up being a bust there were ample options along the street. Toby was meticulous and considerate in his planning.

Late afternoon, they'd stopped at a thrift store—all eight of them—and paired off. Each person sneakily picked out the night's outfit for the other, and then back at the house they'd taken turns gifting each other with the most absurd suits, no takebacks.

Two of the guys ended up in Christmas print suits, one with Santas and the other with decorated trees. There was one bright pink suit with black lapels and trim, one floral (which actually didn't look half bad), two that were tweed and plaid, respectively. Toby was in animal print, and looked fantastic—no surprise there.

Somehow Caleb ended up with the most ridiculous suit of all. It was too small, so the pants landed at his calves. The jacket couldn't be buttoned. If the pattern had just been the universe it might have been okay—black with shades of purple and a tasteful splatter of stars. But there were astronauts, *lots of astronauts*, and when you looked closer you realized they were all cats.

Caleb should have expected this because Toby loved the spotlight. Since leaving their rental, every person they passed gawked.

Their server at dinner had found it amusing while other patrons openly stared.

It was all in good fun, Caleb knew. But he'd never enjoyed being the focus of attention. From years of therapy, he understood it was due to his childhood. It didn't matter that he'd barely spoken to his father over the last five years. That fear of drawing attention, especially his father's, was so ingrained in him he didn't know if he would ever be able to untangle it.

Alcohol had never been a coping mechanism, but Caleb was in a new city. He couldn't sit in a quiet corner, pull out his notebook, and write. He couldn't go for a run with Rosie. He couldn't lose himself in a recipe, focusing solely on measurements, temperature, and time.

So, he drank.

He started with gin before dinner, then whiskey with their meals. After, at the bar, someone ordered a round of shots. Then another.

A bachelorette party merged with them, and there were even more shots as the group found celebratory common ground. Names were shouted and quickly forgotten, and the bride-to-be ended up corralled next to him, presumably what? So they could discuss the merits of renting silverware versus buying or compare honeymoon destinations? Within two minutes they'd both lost interest while their parties flirted.

Caleb wasn't that involved in the planning of the wedding. Or, he was, as much as he thought he needed to be. Kenzie had strong opinions about things that Caleb just couldn't pretend to care about. He let her pick the venue, the date—well, that had been approved first by his mother— the guests, the number of people in their wedding party, the menu. Truthfully, he hadn't acknowledged it until now, but he hadn't made much in the way of contributions. Was he content to let Kenzie make it her dream wedding, or was it something more? And what did it say about him as a partner that he couldn't feign excitement over it?

As Caleb continued to drink, he stared at his groomsmen and wondered how he got here. Not here as in this bar. He remembered the turns they'd taken to arrive here from their rental house. No, here, as in almost twenty-nine and on the cusp of being someone's husband. The word bounced chaotically around his head, like every place it tried to land repelled it.

One moment, Caleb was pleasantly warm and the next he was very, very drunk. Carry-me-home drunk. If he closed his eyes, he might fall over drunk. He could barely hear his friends over the noise and didn't understand what they were saying.

Then suddenly, he was sucked under an immense wave of noise as it rose up and over him.

Music.

There was live music. He only realized it as the tide of people around him washed away from the bar, carrying him with them toward a stage at the other end of the venue.

It was LOUD. Was this a symptom of being almost thirty? Had Caleb entered that phase of life where he wished he had earplugs?

Caleb understood music was an integral part of Nashville, but somehow the connection had not solidified in his mind until this moment. He couldn't understand the words blaring out of the speakers, but everyone around him was cheering. So he turned to see what the fuss was about.

His vision blurred. Then narrowed.

Toby stood between Caleb and the stage, and slowly he looking back over his shoulder towards Caleb. *Just like The Exorcist*, Caleb thought, as Toby's eyes widened, his mouth parting as if to yell a warning. There was a blast of noise—drums, guitar, vocals—and Caleb fell back a step, only to be propped up by the person behind him.

As he righted, his vision swam. When it finally focused—

It was the alcohol.

Or maybe his brain just didn't want to acknowledge reality for fear of how his heart would react. And rightly so, because the moment his eyes processed the red and white boots, snapping him back to a time and place, his stomach started to revolt.

"I didn't know!" Toby shouted at him, and Caleb shook his head.

To absolve Toby of any guilt? To clear the vision and try again in the hopes that his eyes were playing tricks?

But no. The boots were still on stage. Attached to legs. Legs he'd spent hours touching, tasting, tangled up in.

Caleb closes his eyes and begged the universe to let him wake up anywhere else. When he opened them again, he couldn't look away from her. She was everything he remembered.

And more. *So much more.*

In Caleb's memory, George had always been beautiful. But somehow, she was even better. The lines of her longer, curvier, almost otherworldly, in his whiskey-soaked vision. He blinked, rubbing a hand over his face, but it didn't help. He couldn't see straight and couldn't focus on the words she was singing.

Why had he had so much to drink? If he'd known…

If he'd known she was going to be here he wouldn't be wearing a cat-stronaut suit. He'd be sober and able to sing along. He'd get her attention and tell her to meet him at the bar after. So, he could see her. Talk to her. Hug her. Be near her.

But that was wrong, wasn't it? To want anything to do with George when he was here on his *bachelor weekend*. Celebrating the fact that he was getting married. To someone else.

His vision ran, Toby's face splitting into two and wobbling off in opposite directions only to come crashing back together. Caleb sensed Toby's panic and swatted it away, his hand landing on someone's shoulder.

He shouldn't be here. He couldn't let George see him. Not like this.

Something crawled up his throat, bubbling towards his mouth with enough force that his legs started moving on their own. He couldn't speak or he might accidentally vomit on someone.

A hand landed on his shoulder and Caleb shrugged them off, maybe with more force than necessary. But he had to go. He needed air and a quiet street corner to exorcize everything without witnesses.

How he made it back to the rental, Caleb would never know. His feet managed to carry him even though he couldn't see straight enough to read the street signs. At some point along the way he did vomit, because he smelled it on the suit as he stripped in the bathroom later, stuffing it unceremoniously in the trash before realizing his phone and wallet were still in a pocket.

Both retrieved, he slumped down on the cool tile floor in his underwear and called Phil on speaker.

"Hey!"

Caleb winced as she yelled over an onslaught of noise on her end of the line.

"Philippa Elsbeth," he breathed, finding comfort in her name.

"Caleb?" She yelled a second time, and if Caleb hadn't been so completely obliterated, he might've heard the edge to her voice, or Kenzie's voice in the background asking to talk him. He might've also heard Phil's response.

"I think he's drunk. He just used my middle name."

"Tell him he better not be having too much fun!" Kenzie's voice filled the Nashville bathroom, a shrill birdcall echoing off the tile.

Two time zones away in Vegas, Phil excused herself from the chaos of the bridal shower suite and closed the bathroom door.

"Caleb?" Phil's voice strained through the phone, sensing something was wrong. Call it twin-tuition.

"She's here," Caleb whined, his voice little more than a whisper.

"Who's there?" She whispered back, her voice edging towards panic.

"She's wearing the boots, Phil. The boots she's supposed to wear to our wedding. To match that dress—vintner—vinge—edge—*old stuff*."

Caleb punctuated the nonsense statement with sniffles, and on the other end of the call, Phil pressed the phone to her ear wishing she could travel through the soundwaves to his side.

"Caleb, you're not making any sense. Kenzie's here in Vegas."

"No, no, no—the summer—outside on the patio. The mountains—and the sunset—she was the best view. We got married, Phil. Not for real. But it *was* real. Because I love her. I love her, Phil. I do. And I—her..."

Even if Phil had been in the bathroom with Caleb, she wouldn't have been able to make sense of what he was saying. It was like his thoughts had been sifted through a sieve made of alcohol and only a handful making it through, none of which formed a coherent thought.

"And she's heeeeere." He barreled on. "Not here, but there. Tile's nice and coooooool. I'm—"

In Vegas, Phil pressed the heel of her hand to her eyelid until she saw stars. She was so confused.

"Caleb, can I talk to Toby?"

"Mmm, nopers."

Phil put the call on speaker, turning the volume down so Kenzie wouldn't overhear. Because Caleb did not get wasted like this. Not ever.

She opened a text to Toby and typed out: WHAT IS HAPPENING THERE? CALEB IS CRYING ON THE PHONE AND CLEARLY WASTED.

"I love her," Caleb repeated like a mantra, his voice getting smaller with each pronouncement, like he was losing steam.

I LOST HIM. DO YOU KNOW WHERE HE IS??? Toby finally texted back, and Phil's stomach dropped. Why had she agreed to go on this stupid bachelorette weekend when she should've been at the bachelor party to keep them from doing stupid shit like this?

"Caleb, where are you?" Phil interrupted, her voice sounding unhinged even to her ears. If he passed out before someone could find him, she was going to have a heart attack.

"Bathroom," he mumbled.

"At a bar?"

"House," he managed, and Phil was flooded with relief.

HE'S AT THE HOUSE, Phil texted. GET YOUR ASS THERE RIGHT NOW OR I WILL HURT YOU SOOOOO BAD, TOBIAS.

Toby had the balls to send her a saluting gif in response. The cheek on him.

"Caleb, why don't you take your phone and go crawl into bed, okay?"

Phil loved him. With all her heart. But when did taking care of him end? Was this just the deal, to forever be on-call to pick pieces of the other off the floor, or would she pass him off to Kenzie on his wedding day and never have to worry about him again?

Caleb struggled to get up from the bathroom floor, his legs giving out and sending him towards the toilet before he miraculously caught himself, his forearm breaking the fall. It would be bruised in the morning and he'd have no memory of how the purple-yellow streak got there.

His phone made it to the bed with him, Phil's voice filling the silence with a song that registered as familiar to Caleb, but his brain was already shutting down for the night. He tugged the blankets off the bed and faceplanted, the phone landing somewhere amongst the pillows. His eyes were already closed, his breathing deepening as Phil babbled on about her day.

"Caleb, I don't know if you can hear me right now," she said as his open-mouth breathing mingled with her words. "I love you. I really, really do. But I am *not* happy with you right now. I hope your subconscious hears this because I deserve a quiet, spa weekend in the Berkshires after this and I'm cashing in when we get home. Do you know your fiancée waxes her butthole? Please don't answer that because I don't really want to hear your response. But this is the kind of shit I had to listen to at brunch. Eggs benny and buttholes, Caleb! There are lines that were crossed today that I can never recover from. And after this, I am going to go be subjected to male strippers, Caleb! And you know speedos give me the heebie-jeebies! I'm doing this for you and you're not even conscious to hear it! So, you owe me a spa weekend. Also! I've been thinking about repainting my living room and you've got two working arms, so guess what? That's how you're going to pay me back for all of this."

"Did Kenzie happen to say if men are also supposed to be waxing their assholes or is that strictly for female bodily maintenance?" Toby asked on Caleb's end.

"I don't fucking know, Toby!" Phil let out a groan. "How's my baby brother?"

Phil was taken off speaker, Toby's voice clear, the snoring removed from the background.

"He's asleep. I… It's my fault. I could tell something was going on with him all day, and he said he was just stressed about the wedding, but he was drinking hard. And then George was there—"

"*What?*" Phil's voice jumped an octave. Caleb's words earlier started to move around making a bit more sense. Summer. Mountains. *Boots.*

"They brought her onstage as a surprise guest at the bar we were at. It was not planned, I swear."

"Fuck."

"Yeah."

Caleb hadn't been talking about Kenzie at all.

"And I knew he was drunk, but when he saw her, it was like—I thought maybe he'd boot and rally, but he ran. And he's so fucking fast! By the time I made it outside he was gone. Honestly, the fact he made it back here is kind of miraculous."

The image stretched between them on either end of the call. Caleb's bright, smiling face in a neon bar. His cheeks rosy with drink, completely unaware of what was happening around him. A deer trapped in the confines of oncoming headlights.

Apparently, he wasn't over George. He might have gotten engaged, but George had changed him. She'd made him lighter. He'd smiled more. He'd stood taller. And maybe Phil hadn't loved all of it. It had torn their family apart. But she was willing to admit that what was good for her wasn't necessarily what was good for him. And it was clear to her now that Caleb needed separation from their family. She wished she'd seen it clearly back then, but she was so blind to it, so burdened with her own feelings.

"Fuck," was all Phil could manage, having nothing new to add.

"Yeah."

She could tell from that single word that Toby knew what she knew, even though they'd never discussed it before and probably never would. Because it wasn't up to them to reconcile with. Caleb was a grown man.

But it was clear now. It didn't matter if he refused to accept tickets to George's shows, if he claimed he didn't want to know how she was doing, or discuss her music. He could say whatever he wanted, but both Toby and Phil knew it was all bullshit.

Because Caleb was still in love with George.

George hadn't thought she could top the tour with Ripley, simply because she knew she'd never be able to fill gigantic venues. Before going on this tour, she didn't know that people liked her outside of her duet with Ripley. So, she'd been blown away by the number of people who turned up for *her*. The number of people who sang along was staggering. She wasn't the least bit embarrassed to admit that she shed tears each night of the tour from overwhelming gratitude.

The label was so happy with the turnout that they decided to send her out on a second leg. Another ten cities, similarly small venues, but George didn't care if they were rooms in the back of a bar. She was having so much fun and falling even further in love with music because of the fans showing up for her.

She'd left Ripley's tour in such an emotionally rundown state, but when she got home from the first leg of this tour she was energized. It instilled in her that she was doing what she was meant to be doing. And even though people around her had been saying this for a while, she finally agreed with them. It felt like she had "made it" and it didn't matter that she wasn't on the radio, because out there people were downloading singles and even buying the whole album, and that was everything she'd hoped for.

Being as busy as she was meant that George hadn't had time to sit down with Simone yet. But she kept writing in her notebook. Lines, phrases, sometimes a verse, but nothing quite complete. It was bits and pieces, feelings really. She'd send a voice memo to Simone with a couple lines and a melody, and hoped that when she was back in Nashville it would all make sense.

After the Boston show, George had an ugly cry. She locked herself in the bathroom, while her bandmates loaded up the bus, and let it all out in heaving, keening breaths until there was nothing left.

She was happy for Caleb. She only wanted the best for him, and if he had found the woman he wanted to grow old with then good for him. But she was also able to admit that she was devastated. Some small part of her had been holding out hope that one day something would bring them back together when the timing was right.

But life wasn't like the movies. George knew that all too well. You didn't grow up without parents and assume that everything just worked itself out like a rom-com.

A few days after seeing Phil, the darndest thing happened. The hurt was still there. George figured it might never go away and that was okay. Maybe that was just part of knowing you had loved someone. But there was something else beyond the hurt.

Maybe she was tired from the long days, everything taking on a hazy, romantic quality. But somewhere in the mid-Atlantic region of the tour, George was able to look back on the moments she'd shared with Caleb and see them for the perfectly imperfect thing that they were with deep fondness. There was sadness, sure, but that was life. And in looking back at her time with him she was able to draw out of herself the most honest thoughts she'd ever put to paper.

> *I was working out in the summer heat*
> *Didn't want to talk when you came to find me*
> *Dirt, dry grass, the long snaking river*
> *Following behind me on a heart-strung bender*
>
> *Staring up at the mountains sitting feet apart*
> *You were earth, air, fire, I was a lonely heart*

George knew on some level that there was a chance Caleb might one day hear these songs, depending, of course, on whether her label would let her have artistic control over her next album. But that wasn't why she wrote them. And this wasn't a last-ditch effort to win him back.

She wrote these words for herself. An ode to the past versions of George and Caleb who had whispered promises to each other out on that patio and in the warm cocoon of 12 AM, hands splayed over each other's hearts. And even hidden among their silly emails. Each song was a love letter to them. It felt like the only way to say goodbye.

When the second leg of the tour ended, George gave herself one day to do laundry, get reacquainted with her home, and with Grandma Jeane. And then she went off to find Simone and see what they could create together.

Simone was a unicorn. Or a fairy princess, depending on what you wanted her to be. Basically, George looked at Simone and saw a magician. Maybe it was what happened when you grew up with a musician father. When you were born into the land of instrumental experimentation, given a generous helping of encouragement, and accessibility.

Simone played guitar and piano. She knew her way around the drums. And occasionally, usually when alcohol was involved, she was willing to show off her high school flute skills, rusty as they were. Beyond these talents, Simone could hear things that George could not. It was like she was tuned into a different frequency, one in which music played endlessly, songs ready to be plucked out of the air.

While George was touring, Simone had been compiling the piecemeal lyrics George texted, along with muffled voice memos sent in the middle of the night from beneath the blankets in her bus bunk. When George showed up at Simone's house, they were already farther along than she realized. Because Simone had listened to George's memos and heard all the notes that were missing.

She'd tried to explain it to George once. "It's like I can already hear the final version so I just fill in what's missing."

George had stared in equal parts wonder and fear, because that was not at all how she wrote a song. She had to try everything, like a mix and match game, until it fit as best it could. If only she could hear a song like Simone. But thankfully, they were now a team.

It was a rainy day when George pulled into the driveway of the bungalow, notebook in hand and ready to work. Simone poured cups of orange-lavender tea with honey and led the way to her back room. It was part music room, part lounge. Simone liked to be completely comfortable when she worked, so there was a sleek, blue velvet sectional facing a wall of built-ins stacked with books, albums, trinkets of significance. There was art on the walls and framed photos on the side tables. A handful of the softest throw blankets were tucked in a basket under a side table.

They curled up on opposite ends of the couch and George assumed they'd go through each page of her notes and get a general lay of the land before diving in, but Simone was of a different mind.

"I think we need to do this linearly," she began, blowing into her delicate floral teacup.

"How so?" George asked, flipping back to the first page of notes. She looked down at what was written there:

I think I maybe sort of love you
But you don't really know me yet
If we had time, I would tell you
Don't want to be something you regret

"This?" She'd written these lines on the back of a napkin she found in her glove box the day she'd stolen Caleb's hoodie, back in Wyoming. It had been a wild thought, considering where she was in her life at that moment. But she'd written it down anyway and found it months later still in her truck. She'd almost tossed it, but something had kept her from doing that, so she'd tucked it in a drawer, later transferring it into the notebook.

"I think, and you can disagree with me on this because it's your album, so whatever you say goes on this and I'll honor that one hundred percent, but I'm envisioning the story from start to finish, so the album begins when you meet him—" She waited, her hand held up like a platter.

"Caleb."

George felt her heart skip a beat. Not because saying his name was hard to do, but because she had big feelings about the potential of this album. About reliving these memories and appreciating them for the amazing thing they had been, but also sharing them with whoever bought her album. It was a feeling of exposure at the most intimate level.

George wasn't naïve to think that she was the only one on the planet who'd ever felt this way about another person, had this kind of love and then lost it before it had a chance to really grow. Even though she was going to sing about a specific person, place, and time in her life, she hoped that anyone could listen and relate those feelings to their own experience.

"So where do we meet Caleb?"

"At a bar."

"The country music of it all! I should have known. All right then, let's meet him."

The excitement in Simone's eyes drew a smile out of George. In fact, she couldn't stop smiling. Maybe it was sharing these feelings and memories of Caleb. Or maybe it was feeling like this was where George was meant to be. On this couch, in this town, feeling safe and supported by her friend. It sucked that she'd had to lose Caleb in order to arrive here, but what a place to be.

"You got a package," Kenzie called from the front door.

Rosie got up from splooting at Caleb's feet and trotted down the hall to check it out. He could hear her nails clacking on the wood as he doctored his coffee at the kitchen counter.

"I don't remember ordering anything," he said, right as the toaster popped.

Kenzie pushed the large box into the dining room and left it on the floor next to the table. Rosie sniffed it twice, then followed her into the kitchen. She plopped down at Caleb's feet, knowing she was likely going to get some of his breakfast if she was cute. She was always cute.

"Hey." Kenzie came up beside Caleb and leaned into his shoulder.

"Do you want me to make you some breakfast?" Caleb set the toast on a plate, preparing to give it to her if she asked.

"I'm good. I had a latte at the salon."

Kenzie turned back toward the dining room and a cloud of hair products settled in the space between them. It wasn't bad. It was perfume and baby powder and a hint of flowers mixed together. But Caleb preferred morning smells. Coffee grounds, bacon crisping, and a warm breeze through the open window.

He sipped his coffee and dabbed clotted cream on his toast.

"Did you buy something on your bachelor weekend?"

Caleb took a bite before turning. Kenzie was already cutting through the tape.

"I don't think so."

"It's from Nashville." She pulled open the flaps and a few packing peanuts flew out.

Caleb carried his plate and mug to the table and sat. Rosie settled at his feet, sniffing the fallen packing peanuts as if they might be something worth tasting, so he quickly scooped them up and set them on the table.

"Maybe it's from Toby?"

Kenzie reached in and pulled out a round basket in the shape of a small beehive. They stared at it, then at each other, their furrowed brows mirrored in confusion, and laughed. Kenzie set it on the table and went back in, pulling out two white hand towels followed by a book. She inhaled sharply, as her confusion morphed into excitement.

"I think it's a wedding gift—our first one!"

Caleb tore off a piece of his crust and let Rosie take it from his fingers. She dropped it between her paws to lick it to death. He'd been so hungry only a second ago, but lost his appetite watching Kenzie's hands plunge back into the peanuts. She grunted and strained, and out came a blue mixer, which she set on the dining table with a *thunk*.

Caleb reached for the accompanying book—*101 Bread Recipes*.

"I thought both your grandmothers were dead."

Was he imagining an accusatory tone in Kenzie's voice? That seemed to be happening a lot lately. Like she didn't quite believe him when he said he was going for a run. But then he felt stupid because if something was wrong why was she begging him to fuck her every other morning before leaving for work?

"They are."

Caleb sipped his coffee and flipped through the book, excited building as he realized he could become one of those bread-obsessed people he watched on Instagram. He'd been wanting to attempt brioche for a while, but kept talking himself out of it. This gift felt like a sign to start.

"Then who's Grandma Jeane?"

Caleb choked on his coffee, which quickly evolved into a coughing fit. He pushed back from the table and went to get a glass of water from the kitchen. When he could finally breathe again, he returned to the dining table.

The way Kenzie studied him made goosebumps prickle along his forearms. It wasn't so much that she was concerned that he'd been choking. More like, she'd found a loose thread and was deciding whether to pull on it.

Caleb waited for Kenzie to hand him the card, but when she still hadn't, Caleb reached for it with a shaking hand.

"How are you related?"

It was a simple card. White with embossed bells on the front. Inside was typed: *Wishing you happiness. Love, George & Grandma Jeane.*

The coffee in Caleb's stomach threatened to revolt as he read the words over. When had he begun to sweat? His scalp started to tingle and he could feel his body tipping towards panic. He returned to his seat at the table and focused on regaining even breaths.

How did George know? Had Toby told her he was getting married? No, he'd have given Caleb a warning. There was only one possible explanation and he was seeing her later today. They were going to have a serious talk about boundaries because this…

As ridiculous as it sounded, he didn't want George knowing he was getting married. He couldn't explain it, couldn't justify his reasoning beyond it feeling like a betrayal. But maybe that was giving himself too much credit. Maybe George wasn't upset at all by the knowledge he was engaged. She'd clearly moved on with her life and was just being a genuinely good person in congratulating him.

"Hmm?"

Caleb realized that Kenzie was still watching him, like she could read his every thought scrolled across his forehead. What were his options? He could lie, but he had never really been able to do so convincingly.

"I've actually never met Grandma Jeane, but George is… Do you remember when Toby was here at Christmas and we were talking about the country singer Georgia Rose Townsend?"

Caleb continued to sweat under Kenzie's gaze. Her face was void of any emotion, like she was hiding it behind a wall of steel. That, or she really had no idea what he was talking about.

"It sounds familiar."

"She toured with Ripley Carlson." That named burned like acid in his mouth. He'd seen the photos of them kissing, had dissected every inch of each image—where Ripley's hands were on George's body and vice versa, their posture, the emotion on their faces. He didn't blame Ripley. How could any man possibly resist George? But that was the problem. For a moment in time, Ripley had everything with George. And that's what made his name taste like spoiled food. Because in that respect both Ripley and Caleb were the same. They'd both had her and let her go.

"Remind me how you know her?" Kenzie looked down at the gift laid out on the table between them.

"We met a long time ago in Wyoming. I think Phil still talks to her sometimes, so she must've told her about the wedding. The chicken soup I make? That's Grandma Jeane's recipe."

Caleb had meant to add that last bit as a way to make it seem like a homely connection, a friend's grandmother passing along recipes, instead of what it really was. He wished he'd kept it short and simple because now Kenzie seemed to be working something over in her mind, and the hair on Caleb's arms continued to rise.

Kenzie sucked on her front teeth, eyes narrowing in on him like she had something to say. Then, she turned and went into the kitchen leaving it at that—a wedding gift from an old friend.

Caleb knew he'd dodged a bullet. Because Kenzie did not let things go easily. If she knew the extent of his relationship with George it would forever be a contentious footnote she'd circle back to any time she needed leverage. It would always be the thing she held over him. Much like the fact that he hadn't warned her about his non-existent relationship with his father before walking into his parents' house on their first Thanksgiving together. He knew he was in the wrong for that, but more than a year later, she continued to bring it up as a reminder of Caleb's missteps.

Caleb tucked the card inside the bread book. He wanted to use it, but now he wondered if every time he made bread Kenzie would comment on it. *Oh, is this bread from that book a girl from your past gifted us?*

The air grew thick, like in the minutes before a thunder storm breaks across the sky, and Caleb realized he'd missed something. Kenzie was waiting for a response.

"Sorry, what?"

"I said, I forgot I have something this afternoon so please give my apologies to your mother."

They were supposed to be having lunch at his parents' house to discuss final planning for the wedding. It had been on the calendar for weeks.

"But we have to go over everything and I don't—" Caleb closed his mouth. The way Kenzie was staring at him told him he had stepped in it. And rightly so. He hadn't helped with any of the planning for their wedding.

"Then maybe you should have helped out more so you'd know." She said, her lips pursed in annoyance.

He watched her take a deep breath in through her nose and let it out in a sigh so heavy he felt the weight of it on his chest.

"I know, Kenz. I'm sorry." He was failing at being a good partner and he hated himself for it.

He watched her struggle with how to react. Her leg started bouncing like she was considering sprinting out the door, but she shook her head and came back to his chair, bending in close. She brushed his hair out of his eyes. It was getting long and she kept asking him to cut it for the wedding. But that was still a month away.

"You're a pain in my ass, you know that?"

"I know."

"Why do I put up with you?" Her frown was forced, a grin threatening to break through.

"I couldn't even begin to say."

She smiled then, and he knew they were okay. He'd fucked up but he could start putting in the work now. It wasn't too late.

She kissed him, holding his chin between her fingers. And just when it was getting to the point where Caleb was about to stand and drag her into the bedroom, she pulled away.

"It's fine. I'll come. Your mom is expecting us and we need to get this out of the way."

She turned and headed towards their bedroom.

"Are you sure? If you have an appointment…" But Caleb was so relieved at not having to face his mother alone. If she asked him anything about the wedding, he'd be unable to answer. And with his father there, it would end with a list of Caleb's failings.

"It's fine. It's best to face Dara Browning as a united front, right?"

"Right," Caleb wholeheartedly agreed. He handed the last bites of toast to Rosie. She'd sat patiently under the table waiting this whole time and Caleb's appetite was long gone. He was about to spend the afternoon with his parents. But at least he wasn't going alone.

He wasn't sure how long they'd be there. So, preparing for that, he made sure to take Rosie for a long walk at noon just in case it was late when they returned.

He loved their morning runs, but sometimes he enjoyed their slow afternoon walks more. Tourists gravitated further inland, along Newbury Street or the Public Garden, so Caleb's neighborhood was quieter. He could walk a slow couple of blocks, letting Rosie sniff wherever she pleased, with minimal interruption. And it gave him a chance to notice the changes happening, make a mental note of which properties were going up for sale, which ones were new to him, which ones he was already aware of, and think which of his clients might be interested.

Real estate in Boston always seemed to be on the cusp of something, everyone around him moving as fast as possible. Caleb understood that was the business, but it added this insane pressure, like being chased by something with very sharp teeth. If he didn't keep ahead of it, he worried it would eat him alive.

Back in the condo, Caleb unclipped Rosie's leash and watched her trot off towards her water bowl. He had about thirty minutes to get read before they needed to leave.

"Hey babe, I just need to shower and then we can go," Caleb said as he passed through the bedroom on his way to the bathroom.

Kenzie was on the bed with her computer on her lap, so deep in whatever she was reading that she didn't respond.

Caleb undressed and stepped into the shower, shivering when the water started. It took a minute and then it was blissfully hot.

The lunch was probably going take anywhere from one to three hours, and then he wouldn't have to see his father again until the wedding. Caleb just had to get through today.

He lathered up his hair and heard the door hinges squeak as Kenzie entered. He half expected her to be hanging a dress shirt for him on the hook by their towels, but as he rubbed the soap from his face, her blurred outline hovered in the doorway.

Sometimes he'd catch her watching him in the mirror as she applied her makeup, the mascara wand frozen as she stared openly at him. But even though he couldn't make out details through the steam, something about the way she was standing felt different.

"We need to talk."

"Okay, give me a second."

She made a noise in her throat that sent shivers up his spine, even under the scalding spray. He swiped quickly at his hair, standing directly under the spray until it ran clean, then turned the faucet off.

Had something happened while he was out walking Rosie? He'd had his phone with him and never received a text from Phil or his mother about lunch changing. Maybe it was something to do with the wedding, an issue with the caterer or the flowers.

While he wrapped a towel around his hips, he mentally prepared to be the silver linings pro. Any issue could be worked around. Everything was fixable if you just put your thinking cap on. That's what his nanny had instilled in him when he was little.

Caleb stepped into the bedroom, an *I'm here to help* smile in place.

"Okay, whatever the problem is I'm going to fix it." He clapped his hands together like he was ready to get to work, but when he met Kenzie's gaze he faltered. Because something was wrong.

"Are you cheating on me?"

Caleb's mouth opened and closed like a fish starved for air, but nothing came out. In his silence, Kenzie pressed on, her eyes shiny like she was fighting off tears. Caleb's spine went soft.

"I read the emails. Is it over or is it still going on?"

Caleb licked his lips, stalling as he tried to work out what she was saying. Half-naked and still dripping, he started to sweat, his fingers going clammy as his heart beat an erratic pattern.

"What do you think I—"

Kenzie held up a hand and he was immediately back in his mother's kitchen at age six, having been caught sneaking cookies out of the pantry. He closed his mouth, his mind racing.

"Don't. I'm not going to stand here and listen to you lie to me."

"Kenzie." Caleb moved until he was within reach of her, but he kept his hands to himself. She was like a cornered animal, ready to lash out, so he spoke softly as he continued.

"Caleb, I swear to God."

"I am not lying to you. I don't know what you're talking about."

Kenzie pushed past him to the bed, where she turned the open laptop around. From this distance Caleb couldn't read a single word so he started to shrug, but that just threw gasoline on the fire. She picked the laptop up and shoved it in his face.

Caleb read quickly, realizing it was one of George's emails.

"What are you doing in my email?" It was his computer she'd been using.

"Are you fucking kidding me?" Kenzie's cheeks went red like she was burning up, and Caleb's first instinct was to defuse her, to pull her into a hug and rub her back until she calmed. But he was still confused about what she was doing in his email.

"I'm not cheating on you, Kenzie. You know me. I wouldn't do that."

"Do I know you? Because I'm not so sure. Those emails don't read like someone who's *about to get married*, Caleb!"

Rosie's claws skittered on the wood outside the bedroom and he pictured her racing to get as far away from the raised voices as possible. He moved to close the door, knowing that something had traumatized her in her life before him and wanting to protect her from being scared.

"Calm down. The neighbors—"

"Oh, I'm sorry. Am I acting too crazy for you?"

Caleb took a step back to put space between them, but also to think before he next spoke. Because he couldn't organize his thoughts. How was he saying all the wrong things? Usually, he knew how to appease Kenzie, but his footing was so unsteady he hardly understood which way was up.

"She signs her emails *Yours*, Caleb. She was here a couple months ago for a concert and she lives in Nashville *where you went on your Bachelor weekend*, so don't even think about lying to me."

The anger turned so quickly to hurt that Caleb felt it like a knife to his gut. Kenzie's swatted angrily at her cheeks as the tears fell, betraying her true emotion. He'd never wanted to hurt her. That's why he hadn't responded to George's emails, why he hadn't gone to her concert.

"Kenzie, let me explain. Please."

Kenzie shook her head, like he wasn't explaining fast enough, so he barreled on.

"Yes, I did see George in Nashville, but she didn't see me. She was singing at the bar we were at, but the moment I saw her I left. Ask Toby. He'll tell you. And I didn't see her when she was here in Boston, but she may have seen Phil. I don't know. That could be why she sent the gift, but I have not seen her in *years*. Those emails were nothing. They were two old… friends," the word felt wrong, but he forced himself to continue. "We were just catching up. That's all."

He imagined how pathetic he must look in her eyes, but he'd get on his knees and beg, plead for her to believe him if he had to. He couldn't bear the thought of having hurt her with something that wasn't even an issue. Not anymore.

"Friends," Kenzie scoffed.

If Caleb had only been honest from the beginning he wouldn't be standing here, dripping on the floor, trying to diffuse a fire that had no business burning. There was only one option and that was to tell her the truth.

"I met George when I was twenty-two. And we were... I honestly don't know what we were. But it wasn't real. It was just a fantasy. We were playing at being... something. And then when we tried to take it out into the world it didn't work, things kept getting in the way no matter how hard we tried. And when she left it was like she took all the air with her leaving me with nothing and I couldn't breathe. I couldn't breathe! It fucking broke me, Kenzie. Because that's what fantasies do. They make you believe this perfect thing is possible and then they suffocate you with the reality of it."

Kenzie's tears stopped over the course of this declaration, all the anger leeching out of here until she looked like he'd punched her in the gut, her shoulders curling forward, hands hanging limp at her sides. And Caleb was disgusted with himself for causing this. His father was right about him. He ruined everything.

"This was so long ago and I'm sorry for not telling you, but I didn't think it mattered because it's so far in the past it feels like a different life."

Kenzie looked at the floor, then up at the ceiling, and Caleb could see her trying to believe him, though it was a struggle. He took a step towards her, ready to pull her into his arms if she'd let him, but it was a mistake. She retreated a step, her hand rising between them as a barrier.

"I don't think I can marry you." Her voice caught on the last word like she was struggling not to scream. She pressed her lips together and shook her head at him and the tears flew.

"What? No. It's over, Kenz. It's *been* over. For a really long time."

Kenzie kept shaking her head and Caleb wanted to pull her in, hold her so she'd feel the truth of it, but he couldn't seem to make himself take that last step to reach her.

"I'll never be the air you breathe, Caleb."

She swallowed, preparing to go on, and Caleb froze. There was so much he wanted to say, to argue, but something told him to listen. Kenzie deserved to be heard after everything he'd done to upset her.

"When you talk about her—there is—your face, it—you've never looked at me like that. Not once the entire time we've been together. I didn't even know you *could* look like that."

She met his gaze, and even with red eyes, with streaks running through her makeup, she was beautiful. She clutched at her chest, like she was making sure her heart was still beating after the blow he'd just dealt, and Caleb was utterly disgusted with himself. How had he managed to fuck this up so horribly?

"Kenzie, I love you."

Kenzie's mouth turned down at the sides, like she was trying to smile but her mouth simply refused to comply. She stepped to him and exhaled on a hiccup as she brushed the wet hair off his forehead. It was so heartbreakingly familiar.

Caleb was used to explosive reactions when he did something wrong—his mother's palm against his cheek, his father's sneer, Phil's elbows and knuckles. He waited for Kenzie to hit him, but she lifted onto her toes and touched her lips to his. It was a ghost of a kiss, and Caleb knew in his bones that she was saying goodbye. Somehow it felt worse than if she'd sucker-punched him.

"You think you do, but I just saw the way you look when you're really in love with someone. And that someone isn't me."

Kenzie pushed away from him and Caleb didn't fight it. He couldn't move, couldn't process, couldn't react. Fifteen minutes ago, he was mentally preparing to spend the afternoon with his family to talk wedding planning, and now he was standing wet and shivering before a woman who no longer wanted to spend the rest of her life with him.

"Kenzie," he said, because all other words seemed to have abandoned him.

"Fuck you, Caleb."

Trying not to cry, she backed towards the door. She opened it and stood there a moment, like she was waking up from a dream. She looked at him, eyes widening, and Caleb felt the moment to fight for her slipping away.

And he let it.

Caleb watched her turn, tears rushing down her cheeks, and when she was out of view his body finally came alive enough to drop onto the edge of the bed. His hands stretched over his thighs, like they wanted out of his body. His relationship had just imploded and he'd been standing there, arguing while wrapped in only a towel.

He was a horrible person, he told himself, as his body started really shivering. He hadn't fought for their relationship, hadn't even tried to stop Kenzie from leaving. And even now, as he felt the weight of what he'd just done settle heavily across his shoulders, he didn't shed a tear.

Maybe he was numb.

Did he even have the right to be upset when a few weeks ago he'd been crying on the floor in Nashville over George? Yeah, he remembered that. Or at least some of it. Most of the night was a blur. But he'd awoke the next morning with a hazy memory of calling Phil. They hadn't discussed it. Toby never brought it up either. But it was there between them like a sinkhole. All three knew it was there, but no one wanted to be the one to point out the danger.

The front door snapped closed with a bang and Caleb walked out into the hall. Rosie was back on her bed by the couch looking at him with wide eyes and a furrowed brow, asking, *Are we okay?*

He found himself, still in his towel, moving from room to room. Looking for what?

Everything was the same, except in Kenzie's absence an odd sense of relief started to wash back in, replacing the numb feeling in Caleb's limbs. But that wasn't right, because how could the end of a relationship that was supposed to be forever bring him a sense of release?

Caleb took a deep breath and let it out, turning back towards the open bedroom door. This was the same home from an hour ago and yet the light seemed to filter in differently through the windows. Was it brighter in here or was it Caleb that was lighter?

Guilt washed in, but his phone started beeping before he could sit with it.

Are you on your way? Phil texted.

Right. He was supposed to be heading to his parents' house for lunch.

To talk about the wedding.

That was no longer happening.

Be there in twenty, Caleb texted back. This wasn't the type of news you called or texted. No matter how much he hated the idea of facing his parents alone, he had to tell them in person. And he wouldn't really be alone. Phil would be there. Whether she'd hate him for what he'd just done remained to be seen. Maybe she'd be so mad at him that she wouldn't speak to him for a month. He deserved it for breaking Kenzie's heart. For wasting two years of their lives. But he'd survived Phil not speaking to him before and he could do it again.

His parents might yell, they might threaten. Maybe they'd never speak to him again. Or—and where before this would have chilled Caleb to the bone, he was now beyond caring—his father might nod and say the usual, *Of course you couldn't follow through.* And that was okay, because this time it was what Caleb deserved.

Whatever happened, he'd already survived a heartbreak he thought would kill him, and he'd come out the other side. So really, this lunch would be a piece of cake.

* * *

Caleb had a feeling he'd need to walk off whatever happened during this meal with his family, and it was less than a mile from his childhood home back to his condo. The fresh air would be good for him and parking within three blocks of the townhouse was nearly impossible, so he got a Lyft to Beacon Hill.

He steeled himself out on the sidewalk as the car pulled away. In two or three hours he'd be back home, family time would be over, and he could figure out what the hell to do about it all. Maybe he'd take Rosie up to New Hampshire for a few days and hike until his head cleared.

The ownership was all on him, but he was having trouble processing what he'd done.

He'd blown up his life.

He'd hurt someone important to him.

And yet, Caleb felt oddly calm about it all. But that's how shock worked, right? You couldn't process the destruction of a relationship in under an hour. He needed time and he was sure the weight of his actions was about to come crashing down on him any second now.

Caleb took a big breath and decided to rip off the band-aid. There was no point in dragging this out longer than necessary.

"I'm here," Caleb called as he stepped into the entryway.

Phil popped into the hall and they made eye contact, but reading his weird energy, she halted midway to him, her brow pinching.

Caleb shook his head. Whatever she wanted to ask—*Where's Kenzie? Is she running late? What's wrong? Are you okay?*—all the answers were going to be the same. *Don't ask.*

"Is Mom going to have to be committed after this?" Phil whispered, linking her arm with Caleb's and leading him into the dining room.

He only shrugged.

Dara Browning never needed an excuse to host, and even though it was just lunch and just them, she'd done her best. There were shucked oysters, salad niçoise as well as a Greek salad, thinly sliced smoked meats, thickly cut cheese, smoked salmon and capers, brioche rolls and all manner of spreads. It was an absurd amount of food for five people, considering one of them hardly ate.

"Oh good. You're finally here." Dara looked up from placing a second uncorked bottle of wine on the table. "Your father will be down in a moment so we can start."

There were very few times that Caleb could remember his mother smiling at him, like he had actually done something right. It was almost enough to make him stall, just to savor this moment for what it probably was—the last time she'd look at him this way.

Phil rounded to the seat opposite Caleb and sat, pouring herself a healthy glass of white wine. She then decided to fill Caleb's glass, even though reaching across the table received a sharp noise of disapproval. Phil stood to pour an appeasing glass for their mother and then sat.

Caleb remained standing behind his chair, his fingers wrapped around the ornately carved wood. There was no point in sitting, at least not until he said what he'd come here to say. It was a shame, since the food looked delicious and he'd only had one piece of toast this morning.

"Where's Mackenzie?"

Caleb met his mother's inscrutable gaze over the rim of her glass. When he didn't blink and look away, she set her glass back on the table without drinking. She smoothed her hands over the delicate tablecloth like she needed a moment to compose herself, her eyes ping-ponging between her children looking for answers and receiving none.

Phil sipped and sipped, her eyes remaining on Caleb until the glass was empty. As long as he had her on his side, he'd be okay. He didn't need anyone else's support.

"Caleb Theodore, what have you done?"

Dara sucked on her teeth like his name left a film there, and Caleb wished he could rewind two minutes to when she'd smiled sweetly at him. But that moment was over, her approval rescinded.

Phil's eyes sparkled with anticipation as she refilled her wine glass and sat back. If their father didn't arrive soon, she'd be drunk before Caleb had a chance to say his peace.

"Philippa, do you know what this is about?"

"No, I do not."

Phil began serving herself, knowing that the afternoon had already begun unraveling and manners might be overlooked this one time due to Caleb's distraction. Once her plate was full, she began eating, not waiting for the final member of their family to grace them with his presence.

"John!" Dara yelled, trying not to sound shrill and losing the battle.

The floorboards groaned overhead, but there was no urgent movement in the direction of the stairs.

Caleb shifted his feet, keeping his fingers tightly on the chair. He really wanted to stuff salmon in a roll and walk out the door. As if reading his mind, Phil began making that exact sandwich on her plate, adding in a spoonful of dill cream. Caleb's stomach growled, but he didn't move. His mother was a viper waiting to spring if he even breathed wrong and he wanted to get out of this alive.

The stairs began their xylophone of groaning as John slowly descended. Phil paused her eating in deference to him and waited until he'd entered and taken his seat at the other end of the table before settling into the remainder of her wine.

Caleb's eyes remained on his mother as John sat, the chair groaning as he settled. Caleb looked down at his empty plate, readying himself for a fight.

Shortly after his father's second overdose, he'd had a series of strokes. The doctors had caught them in time to save his life, but part of his face was now palsied, the right side of his mouth stuck in a downturn. *Fitting*, Caleb thought, when Phil had tearfully explained the situation.

The slight limp and loss of strength in his hand had ending his golf game. And while another woman might have divorced John Richards after uncovering the pile of lies and how much money he'd squandered, not Dara Browning. Caleb's father was still a well-kept man. Because even after everything he'd put them through, she cared more about outward appearance.

"Your son was just about to tell us what he's done."

She sat with two fingers resting on the base of her wine glass, the other hand on her untouched fork, giving a false impression that she was calm. But Caleb knew better.

Phil set her glass at the top of her place setting, her mouth softening to encourage him on. He couldn't imagine surviving this without her support.

"Kenzie and I aren't getting married."

There was a long moment of silence as the words settled among the decadent spread, and then Dara sighed deeply, like this should have been expected, Caleb fucking up yet another thing. What else was new?

Laughter split the silence, a booming sound that had every eye snapping to the far end of the table where John's usual grimace had morphed into a gruesome sneer. On any other day, Caleb would have been flooded with anxiety for what was to come, but right now he was simply too numb to care.

Phil nodded at Caleb encouragingly and he pushed on.

"I'll pay you back whatever can't be refunded."

Dara kept surprisingly silent while Caleb waited for the barrage of negative comments. He almost welcomed the idea. Maybe it would knock the numbness out of the way so he might actually feel the devastation that must be waiting around the corner.

"I have a question," John slurred out the side of his mouth, leaning back in his chair like he was enjoying this.

Phil turned a wary eye on their father as she continued to drink. Was that her third glass? Caleb didn't have the bandwidth to worry about her too. Instead, he faced his father's watery features.

"What did you do?"

"Dad—" Phil tried, but John waved her off with his good hand.

"I think we deserve to know. He owes us that much."

Phil's gaze spun to their mother at the other end of the table, but Caleb kept his eyes on his father, silently standing his ground.

"Mom—" Phil tried, but received no help.

"You got a little too greedy and she caught you with another woman? Is that it? Or maybe—" John's mouth ticked up at one end, "— she grew bored with you. Is that it? Did Miss Donaldson realize she could do a hell of a lot better?"

On any other day, Caleb would have ground his teeth, forcing his anger down as he was played with like a mouse caught under his father's paw. But three years of limited exposure had allowed Caleb's heart to callous over and cutting words no longer hurt like they used to.

"Cay, don't—" Phil tried to interject, to save him maybe. But he no longer needed saving.

"I don't love her," he said, feeling the weight of that truth along his spine. "Not the way she deserves." It was a hard thing to admit, but Kenzie deserved better than he was able to give. She should be adored.

John scoffed and Caleb turned toward the other end of the table to face how his mother's wrath. She sat ramrod straight, her gaze focused on the surplus of food, and Caleb marveled at how beautiful she was even when she was livid. On some level Caleb figured he'd probably always care about his parents, because that was what children were supposed to do. But right now, with a feeling of lightness growing in his chest, he knew this was goodbye. He was done being his parents' son.

"You don't love her," John parroted back, the last word smothered in sarcasm.

"Dad, come on." Phil tried one last time before giving up and refilling her glass.

"You don't love her. I see. So, you went through all of this, wasted your mother's time and our money planning this ridiculous wedding only to realize *today* that you don't *love* her."

Caleb didn't blink.

"Today," John nodded knowingly. "Mere weeks before the wedding. What a perfect time to grow a heart."

"Please stop." Phil begged halfheartedly, reaching for an oyster. Then another, because why not.

"I realize love might be a foreign concept to everyone in this room."

Caleb rooted himself in place, not wanting to show emotion. But he wasn't going to stand here and take his father's scorn. If this was last time they saw each other, then Caleb was going to stand up for himself. For all the times he hadn't.

John laughed, a broken sound that made both Dara and Phil flinch.

"And you think you know what love is?" John continued. "You're a child! You don't know anything."

Caleb ignored the barbs. He had known love once and he'd been stupid enough to think it wasn't worth—that *he* wasn't worth—fighting for. Could his father say the same?

"I know the only love I've ever received in this family is from Philippa." He looked across at her and his insides twisted. She was crying. *Fuck.* He'd come to say the wedding was off and leave as quickly as possible, and now he'd upset Phil.

John sat up in his chair readying his next attack, but Dara cleared her throat, and every head snapped in her direction.

"I'll let you know what cannot be refunded," she said, sharp eyes pinned on Caleb. But there was something more behind them, something he couldn't translate for lack of never having seen it in her before.

"Thank you." Caleb was relieved beyond measure.

He took a breath to commit his mother to memory, her lips pressed tight in what might have been a smile, hair tucked into a low bun, makeup understated and precise. Her features were beautiful, if a bit severe, and in thirty years Phil might look the same, except that she'd never be able to keep her emptions behind closed doors like their mother.

Caleb smiled at her one last time, a goodbye smile that camouflaged a sadness lodged under his breastbone. He turned and walked out of the room without a parting glance at his father. Whatever was left behind belonged to the past and he didn't feel the least bit of sorrow at leaving it there. All the pain, the hurt, the fear of being a disappointment stayed behind, trapped within the walls of his childhood home.

Outside on the street he took a deep breath, savoring the warm spring air. It smelled sweet, like… freedom.

"Are you fucking kidding me?" Phil screeched, slamming the front door and nearly tumbling down the front steps as she raced to catch up to him. She shoved a salmon-stuffed brioche in his hand and let out a sigh that bordered on musical.

"I know, I'm sorry. I'm an asshole. I already feel like shit and I don't need you yelling at me too. You can go back inside, I'll walk myself home."

Phil hooked her arm through his and fell in step beside him.

"I'm not going back inside. I need all the details. And I'm not letting you have your Braveheart moment and not bending the knee! O Captain, my captain, and all that."

They headed down the hill in silence until they hit Charles Street, then turned towards the river.

"Plus, I'm like three sheets to the wind and I was not about to handle cleanup. Did you see how many oysters Mom got? Who was even going to eat all those?"

Caleb felt the fresh air fill his lungs and warm his skin with each step he took away from his childhood home. With Phil walking beside him.

"You're going to be okay," Phil said, giving his arm a squeeze.

"Yeah, I know." He was sure one day it would be true.

38. GEORGE

"Gram! I'm back," George called as she entered the house. It was late in the day, the sun starting to set, but it being May, the heat had already settled in for summer. The house was quiet as she made her way to the bedroom and dropped her bag inside the door.

Her bed was made and George knew that the sheets had been washed in her absence. It had only been a few days, but Grandma Jeane always said it was better to come home to a clean bed. And, unsurprisingly, she was always right.

George was tired, but the good kind of tired. She and Simone had been working on the new album and the writing was nearly done. But they'd agreed that it was missing something, though they couldn't figure out what. So, they were taking a few days to reset in the hopes of coming back fresh.

George made her way through the small house and stepped through the back door into the yard. Back in Texas their yard had been crispy, brown grass with a small garden bed that held easy things. Herbs that did well when forgotten for a couple days and of course tomatoes. Grandma Jeane loved to can tomatoes—sauce, jam, whole.

Here in Nashville, Grandma Jeane's garden took up half the yard. There was one bed strictly for herbs. When the kitchen window was open, the breeze smelled of lavender, sage, and basil, and it calmed George like nothing else. She loved to sit out here with a cold drink, close her eyes, and listen to the bees.

"You here for the night?" Grandma Jeane asked from her spot kneeling before the marigolds. She plucked a dead bud and continued working.

"A couple nights, probably. We both needed a break. It feels like a song is missing and the problem is I'm fresh out of ideas."

"You'll figure it out." Grandma Jeane's unwavering confidence was fuel to George. It was the one thing she knew she could never live without.

George sat at the little table they'd found on the curb their first month here. It was rusted and probably put out for the trash truck, but with a little sanding and a sheen of new paint it looked like it belonged outside a French café. Not that George would know, having never crossed the ocean, but she'd seen photos. It amazed her what people discarded.

Grandma Jeane stood, wiped her hands on the apron tied at her waist, and walked around the side of the house. The hose turn on and a minute later she was back, the weight of the watering can affecting her gate.

"Here, let me help you with that." George started to stand, but Grandma Jeane waved her off. She was stubborn like that, didn't want any help when she was perfectly capable after two hip surgeries.

George watched her grandmother take care to water each row, repeating the process before she was satisfied. Then she sat heavily in the chair opposite George, a sigh escaping as she leaned back, her work done.

"It looks beautiful."

"It should, considering how much time and energy I've put in."

George could tell her grandma was tired, but the smile that spread as she surveyed her work told a story of the good kind of tired. The kind that George felt right now as well.

"You miss it?" Grandma Jeane asked.

"Miss what?"

"Texas. Wyoming. Everything that came before."

George hadn't really thought about it. She'd been too busy chasing this new life that she'd hardly processed the loss of everything before. Maybe it wasn't a loss, but a new path running parallel to her previous one.

"I guess some parts. I miss the view. And the horses. And the quiet. Different kind of quiet," she added as they listened to a birch chirp just over the fence in their neighbor's yard. "Do you miss it?"

She realized she hadn't ever asked. Grandma Jeane had come along on this adventure, uprooting herself from the only home she'd ever known, and George hadn't questioned it. Of course her grandma wanted to move with her. They'd never lived apart for more than the summer months. But what if she wasn't happy here and she was suffering in silence because George had asked her to come?

"I think I do miss ole Tex. But when I think about it, I think it's your mama I'm really missing," Grandma Jeane said, and George felt her breath catch.

She couldn't remember the last time they'd talked about her. Maybe when George was in high school when she'd asked if her mama had been in any clubs or played any sports. Lillian Townsend, or Lily as everyone called her, had been in the school chorus and played softball every spring. There were blurry photos tucked in an album somewhere. George remembered looking at them when she was little, trying to see if the face was familiar to her. On a cellular level she knew the girl smiling back from the glossy page, but she didn't have any fixed memories of her.

"You never talk about her," George said softly.

This conversation felt so fragile, like a soapy bubble that could burst at the slightest provocation.

"I know, Georgie. It's hard to talk about her and not feel sad. And I don't like sitting in sadness."

George reached across the table and put her hand over her grandmother's. Her skin was warm from working out in the sun, and Grandma Jeane flipped her hand over so she could hold George's back.

"You look so much like her. But sometimes I look at you and wonder, is that what Lily would have looked like at your age? She was so young when she passed."

Grandma Jeane's eyes pinched at the corners, like she was fighting off a wave of emotion and George felt her own eyes start to burn with the effort of keeping her emotions under control.

"What was she like?" She whispered.

A smile worked its way across her grandma's face and it was like sunshine and bluebirds.

"She was a smart girl, your mama. She loved her books. She'd make me take her to the library every week. If you asked her what she was reading she wouldn't tell you about the story. She'd tell you where she was going—Paris, Alaska, an island in the Caribbean. For her, reading was traveling somewhere new and making friends."

George found herself smiling, imagining the mother she hadn't had the chance to know.

"She'd have been in awe of you. Of the person you've become, George."

Tears pooled in Grandma Jeane's eyes, but her smile only grew brighter.

"In fact, she'd probably have begged to go on tour with you. She'd have been your biggest fan. My word, she'd have loved this life you've made for yourself."

George's breath hitched as a tear snuck out the corner or her eye. She'd never wondered about that, how her mother might have fit into her life, because opening herself up to the idea would have hurt, which it did now as she let the idea marinate. But all the same, with her grandma holding her hand, it was nice to imagine.

"She'd have loved this garden. I named her for the flower you know."

"Lily of the Valley? I didn't know that."

"Mm-hmm. She was so small and they put a little hat on her head, and all I could think about was those flowers, how tiny they are, how fragile."

George wiped away the tears with her free hand, not daring to let go of her grandmother.

"She was set on the name George from the moment she knew about you. Didn't matter if you were a boy or a girl, she said. She wanted you to have a strong name."

"Then she'd hate that I changed it for this." George waved her arm around to encompass Nashville, the music industry, the man.

"Well," Grandma Jeane said disapprovingly, her opinion on the matter well-known. "Your middle name though, that was her passing a piece of herself on to you. From one flower to another."

George felt a sob claw its way up her throat. Maybe Grandma Jeane felt it too, because she took George's hand in both of her own and squeezed it tight.

"I may not talk about her, but she's with you. I know it. I feel her in the garden, in my cooking, in the way you sleep like the dead curled up on the couch. She's in me and she's in you, and she'd be so proud of your music and the woman you are."

George let herself cry then, for the mother she couldn't remember, for the life that was lost to her. Grandma Jeane held tight to her and let her feel her feelings, a sad smile hovering on her own lips.

"Shoot," George laughed when the emotions started to settle and she could see clearly again. "I thought I was coming home to rest and here I am falling apart at the seams."

"It's good to have a cry from time to time. It lets all the air out before we get too full of ourselves."

Grandma Jeane patted George's hand and pushed to standing.

"Look at the time getting away from me. It's getting close to dinner and I haven't even thought of what to make."

George watched her grandmother make her way towards the back door, her gate stiff from decades of working herself to the bone.

"How about I order from that place you like down the street," George offered, because she could afford to do that now and it would be a nice treat for them both.

"Oh. Now that's an idea." Grandma Jeane paused in the open door, her tired features brightening with the release of having to cook. "I'll just clean myself up then."

George pulled out her phone and searched for the menu. After entering their order for delivery, she sat staring up at the pink-purple sky as the sun started to set. Their view here was different from the views she'd had before. Trees framed the entirety of it giving them a limited perspective, and something about the sky at this time of day always brought her a sense of calm. She'd made it through another day and she was still here.

It came to her then, as a goldfinch landed with a flutter of wings on the nearest tree. The song that was missing.

"Hey," George said when Simone picked up on the second ring. "I know we said we'd take a couple days, but…"

There was laughter on the other end, as if she had been waiting for this call.

"Tomorrow then?" Simone asked. "At least let me sleep in."

"I'll see you tomorrow."

George hung up and pushed herself to standing. She couldn't write an album and claim it was one hundred percent her without telling the story of the women who made her. She needed to thank all the people who got her here, to this sunset, and all the others that came next.

CHORUS

May 2022

39. CALEB

A week after the breakup, Kenzie was completely moved out. She left her key but took the ring, and that was fine with Caleb.

During a terse phone call days later, Dara claimed that she was able to recoup nearly everything she'd spent on the wedding, and whether that was true or not, Caleb couldn't be sure. But when he asked her how much he owed she said it was all set and Caleb didn't push.

Through the summer, he struggled with a constant cloud of discomfort that had nothing to do with what he'd done and everything to do with where he was. Caleb loved Boston. But somehow it had begun to feel like wearing an outfit that no longer fit, like old wool that had lost its shape, the neck stretched and lopsided, the arms shrunk too tight.

Overwhelmed by the desire to get away, he took Rosie camping in Vermont. Then, a weekend in Maine. He flew out to L.A. for a couple days to be with Toby. It all helped in the moment but when he returned home it was like putting that old sweater back on. Something was off, and Caleb couldn't ignore that maybe it was him.

He talked about it with his therapist and journaled every night. He toyed with the idea of going back to school, but looking at courses online didn't excite him the way he'd hoped.

One Sunday in August, Phil came over. It was sweltering outside, but inside the condo Rosie burrowed under a blanket to hide from the air conditioning. Her head popping out like an overstuffed jelly donut when Phil walked through the door.

"You're not you," Phil began, only a few feet inside. She was never one to sugarcoat things, least of all with Caleb.

He pulled a loaf of cinnamon-raisin bread out of the oven. It was absurd to be using the oven when he could probably bake the dough simply by sticking it out the window, but he'd become addicted. He tried a new recipe from the book every Sunday. It was the way he marked time now.

He flipped it out of the pan and onto a cooling rack, fanning it for a minute. He was supposed to let it cool, but how could he be expected to wait when it smelled this good? He cut two pieces, reveling in the sweet steam that filled the kitchen, and slathered each piece with butter.

"Aren't you supposed to wait?" Phil asked, accepting the slice and practically devouring it.

"Not bad," Caleb said to himself, and made a notation in the book to go heavier on both the cinnamon-sugar and raisins next time.

"If you ever open a bakery, you are welcome to name it after me. I'm sure you can think of something punny. Phil Me Up or… Get Your Phil."

Caleb raised his eyebrows in a way that made it clear he would not be entertaining that idea.

Phil had been stopping by every couple of days since Kenzie left. It was often unexpected, but not unwelcome. Sometimes she went on walks along the river with him and Rosie. Other times she'd bring food and they'd watch a show or sit at the table while she regaled him with her latest dating adventures. Caleb had returned the room that had once been hers to a guest room and sometimes they'd go out to a bar around the corner and she'd stay over even though she lived ten minutes away. It almost felt like old times.

"I've decided that I'm ready to let you go." Phil said as she cut herself another slice.

Caleb stopped chewing and swallowed. The look on Phil's face was like Kenzie's when she'd walked out the door the final time, heavy with sadness, but with unwavering finality and no room for argument.

"Why does it feel like you're breaking up with me? Do I need to remind you that we are stuck with each other for life."

Phil smiled through the beginnings of tears.

"Silly old bear, I know that. But you're not happy here and I'm not selfish enough to make you stay just because I love having you within arm's reach."

"So, you're making me leave?" He laughed at the incredulity of it. "Where am I supposed to go?"

Phil slathered butter on her second piece and shoved it into her mouth. Then she went into the fridge and pulled out the bottle of wine she'd opened two nights earlier. She poured two glasses and set one in front of Caleb while taking a hearty swallow of her own.

"I think we both know you're happiest when you're out there in the wild, with the mountains and the sunsets."

She was telling him to go to Wyoming.

It was true. Every time Caleb flew into that airport, he couldn't help but smile. There was something about landing alongside the Tetons that made his problems feel small and insignificant. It reminded him about perspective and that there was so much more than the trivial bullshit running around in his head. It forced him to pause and take a breath.

"You want me to go on vacation?"

Phil shook her head, her lips pressed tight to strangle a cry.

"You want me to move there."

Phil shrugged, like she loathed the idea but knew there was no other option.

"Rosie hates the cold. Do you know how cold it gets in the winter in Jackson?"

Caleb pointed to the canine in question, still bundled in the blanket on the couch. Phil rolled her eyes and scoffed.

"As I recall, you have a fireplace out there, no? And we both know, now that you're single, the princess is back to sleeping in bed with you, and you, my friend, are a human furnace. It's a moot point. Rosie will be fine. Cay, I don't want you to go, but we both know you need to. It's the only place that makes you undeniably happy and lately you've been really unhappy."

There was no give to Phil's words. Much like their mother, she was telling him what he was expected to do. But Caleb knew Phil was right. He needed a change. He could go to France for a week, travel to Bali and surf for a month, or he could go back to the place that made his heart feel lighter, just him and Rosie.

"You better watch it," Caleb gave Phil a pointed look. "Without me here to keep you in check you might just turn into Mom."

"Take that back!" She screeched while launching herself at him like they were still seven.

* * *

373

In September, Caleb found renters who would move into his condo the following month. He donated all the things he no longer needed and boxed up what he couldn't part with. His car was stuffed to the brim, though many things were shipped on ahead. Up in the passenger seat, Rosie was buckled in and ready to go.

Caleb had decided not to sell the condo because he wasn't ready to say goodbye to Boston. It would always be his home and it would be nice to have some money coming in while he figured out what to do next. That, and Boston real estate continued to climb, so holding onto the condo was the smartest financial move.

Phil didn't want to be there when Caleb drove away, and he understood how hard this was for her, though it hurt a bit to not get that hug goodbye. But she promised to fly out and spend Thanksgiving with him. He was sad to leave, but as he got on the Pike heading west, a warm feeling spread through him.

Was this happiness? The thrill of the unknown? Or just caffeine kicking in?

Their first stop was a dog-friendly hotel in Chicago. Caleb had never thought to take Rosie on a road trip before, and watching her take in everything out the window was enough to kick himself for waiting this long. On the map, he'd planned to attempt the drive in three days, stopping each night in hotels along the relatively straight shot from Boston to Jackson. But that night in Chicago he rethought the route.

Fifteen—almost sixteen—hours driving had been a lot. He was exhausted and the idea of doing it again tomorrow was a lot to stomach. And when would they ever get this chance again? Dogs didn't live forever and he didn't have a job or a person waiting on him, so why not enjoy this trip for the gift it was?

From Chicago, they detoured north to Wisconsin. Why not? They both loved cheese. In Minnesota they spent a night on the edge of a lake, and watching the joy on Rosie's face when Caleb let her off-leash to roam and swim was the happiest he remembered being.

Next, they stopped to bid adieu to the presidents residing in South Dakota. Both of them were underwhelmed and Rosie had a touch of diarrhea, so, point made. Caleb wanted to head to Boseman next. He'd never been and he had a feeling it might be a new favorite place to check out, but with Rosie not feeling well he figured it might be time to wrap the tour up.

They got on the road early, crossing state lines just after nine. Caleb had been back to Wyoming many times since purchasing his condo, and Fall was his favorite time of year there. The aspen trees were turning neon yellow as they drove down through Teton National Park.

It was a warm day, September could either be in the sixties or snowing, so they had the windows down as they passed the airport and continued towards town.

"This is your new home," he said to Rosie, her tongue lolling out the corner of her mouth as she took it all in, and Caleb found himself laughing.

Phil had been right.

It was good to be home.

Caleb stayed in his condo for the first six months and it worked just fine for him and Rosie. If anything, it was more space that they needed. But while the view was undeniably breathtaking, he realized he actually wished they were closer to town. He wanted to be able to walk out the front door and swing by Cowboy Coffee without the necessity of his car.

His condo was located in an area that was mostly short-term rental properties and he craved neighborly relationships. So, he started perusing the local listings hoping for the universe to throw him a bone, but nothing called out to him. Everything was big, sleek, and modern. He wanted cozy and simple.

By some crazy happenstance that some might call fate, he was at the base of Snow King throwing a ball for Rosie one afternoon the following spring, when a couple that looked close to his age descended the trail with their dog, Shirley.

The dogs greeted each other and Caleb started chatted with them. Eventually, the conversation turned to his search for a new home. As luck would have it, they had a friend who was getting ready to sell down the street from them. Caleb was doubly thrilled because if it all worked out, he'd have a new home, cool neighbors, and Rosie would have a friend.

Numbers were exchanged and a week later Caleb was standing in an incredibly outdated twelve-hundred square foot ranch that backed up to Flat Creek. It took all of ten minutes for the homeowner to accept Caleb's offer and a month later he was moved in.

The ironic thing was that Phil had always beat him at Monopoly. But here Caleb was, with a property in Boston bringing in rental income, a small house in downtown Jackson that had no standout qualities except that he loved the location, and another a mile away bringing in premium vacation prices due to the view.

Caleb realized shortly after the closing that he was delusional in thinking he could renovate his new house. He had zero qualifications or experience. The extent of his knowledge of tools ended at hanging art. He asked around and hired contractors to update the house one room at a time, and in the process made friends.

Sean was originally from Arizona. He fell in love with skiing when he was in his teens but was forced to learn a trade (plumbing) by a wise parent. Now, he worked half the year, skied all winter, and loved Jackson Hole immeasurably. He introduced Caleb to MacGyver (not his government name), another ski bum who happened to be a licensed electrician. Then there was Bob, who was not a ski bum but an amateur photographer who had endless opportunity to hone his craft in his backyard. He was a carpenter the rest of the time.

Within six months, Caleb was content with the state of his home. His mother would have fainted if she ever came to visit, because there was zero elegance to it. He'd picked minimalist grey granite countertops, the bathroom tile was matte grey, the walls were white, the floors had a clear stain. It was simple, unfussy, and most importantly, home.

Phil flew in every couple of months. She called it her restful reset, insisting on meals at all her favorite restaurants and one night in a saddle at Million Dollar Cowboy Bar for old time's sake. Luckily, there were cheap, direct flights from L.A., so flying out to see Toby or getting him to fly into Jackson was easy, and so their friendship grew even stronger. It wasn't the same as it had been, when they'd all lived in the same city, but they were happy in their new lives.

Caleb started working part-time at one of the real estate agencies in town. Technically, he didn't need to work and he could go days without speaking to another person and be perfectly happy. But he knew what Phil would say. And anyway, he liked the people he worked with. The best part was that Rosie was able to come to work with him on the days he went into the office, and she became the company mascot, spoiled with treats and attention.

Rosie still hated the cold and would only step outside once bundled in dog pajamas, booties, and a coat during winter months. Caleb felt like the town laughingstock anytime they passed a neighbor. But once she was dressed, she loved being outside. She galivanted around in the snow like a puppy, and her happiness instilled in him that being here was the best decision he'd ever made.

A year in, one of his coworkers insisted on creating a dating profile for him. Caleb fought it for weeks but eventually relented, and the first date he went on ended up being fine. A friend of a friend, actually, since the town was that small. Their second date was great, in that they both realized how awesome it would be to continue hanging out as friends. And so, Kathleen O'Hara became Caleb's first friend that was a girl, since Phil didn't count.

It took three months of hikes, pizza and beer, coffee and breakfast hangouts, and endless texts, for them to discover they had met years prior at Million Dollar Cowboy Bar. When Kathleen discovered that Caleb was *George's* Caleb she lost it, gave herself a cramp from laughing so hard. And then, because Kathleen couldn't help herself, she pushed and pulled until Caleb divulged everything. Not the private moments, obviously. But the parts she hadn't heard about, the things that happened after George left Wyoming that first summer.

When Kathleen and Caleb parted ways that night, she gave him a long hug, the kind that settles in your skin like a memory. She said she couldn't explain, but it felt like maybe George had brought them together when they both really needed a friend. Caleb didn't believe in karma or fate, but if his friendship with Kathleen was the thing that stood the test of time from his meeting George then that was a pretty great outcome.

Once the house was no longer a construction zone, Caleb decided it was time to do something truly for himself. The house, he rationalized, was for Rosie as much as himself. But Caleb had always wanted to write. It was why he dug through his boxes in the guest bedroom until he found the old notebook he'd kept beside his bed back in Boston. He read through each page, conjuring the places he'd been in his life when he'd written each thought. But then he came to the last page and unfamiliar handwriting stopped him, stealing the air from his lungs.

How had he never noticed?

There was only one time that George would have had access to this notebook and it was when she came to Boston. So many years had passed since then, and yet he could still remember every detail of their time together. As he read her words—first, a short poem or maybe a song? Next, a note that apologized for snooping but transitioned into a heap of flowery language telling him just how much she loved reading his words—Caleb's face flamed with pride. He'd never shared his writing with anyone and the one person who'd read it had been bowled over. It was the push he needed to sign up for the writing group at the library.

Caleb knew that another white, cis male perspective was the last thing the literary world needed. He didn't have anything groundbreaking to add to the conversation. But he figured that maybe, if he could learn to write well, to hone his craft, he might also manage to do some serious self-reflection (and maybe even healing) in the process. And anyway, he really enjoyed being with the people in the writing group.

It was a small group, only five other people including the instructor, but everyone always managed to find positive things to say to each other. There were no harsh words, no one trying to tear another down. This room within the library's walls was like a serene, safe space where you could read your innermost thoughts, your ideas in-progress, and at least one person would be able to think of something constructive to help you on your way towards revision.

Caleb mostly shared poems. For a while he played with the idea of compiling a bunch of them and self-publishing, maybe asking around at the local bookstores if they'd carry a copy. But he talked himself out of it. Who was he kidding calling himself a poet?

The day he shared a short reflection of that winter day in Chatham so many years ago, the entire group was silent for a long time after he finished. A chill ran up his spine as the silence stretched around the circle. He immediately wished he could take it all back, erase it from their minds, and read something else. He shouldn't have shared something so bleak. What had he expected, a round of applause for depressing everyone?

But when he looked up at Josie, the woman sitting directly across from him, she was gingerly wiping her eyes with her sleeve. Next to her, Charlie was blinking a lot, eyelashes fluttering like hummingbird wings, his smile stuck somewhere between clownish and grimace.

"Caleb, I..." Lynn started, and then stopped.

"Forget I said anything. I should've stuck with the poetry." Caleb apologized, fidgeting with the papers in front of him. The back of his neck burned with embarrassment.

"Well fuck me." Charlie added, his voice raspy from seventy-plus years of usage. There were gasps and laughter. "That was so damn beautiful I hope you never stop writing, kid."

There were murmurs of agreement around the circle as Caleb coughed to clear his throat. Something hot and sharp had lodged about halfway to his stomach.

"Does anyone have anything constructive to add?" Lynn asked, trying to steer the group back on course.

Caleb blinked back the tears he could feel threatening to surface. Whatever was in his throat had broken free and dropped into his heart causing it to beat sporadically. He couldn't seem to get ahold of himself. His hands had started sweating and his pen slipped into his lap.

"I'm really sorry that happened to you," Maryanne said quietly beside him. "I think that line about the contrast between how wild the water was and how still the body was really packs a punch. But I think the lines after that could maybe use a little tweak because the momentum loses steam."

There were murmurs of agreement and nods around the group, and Caleb wanted to get up and hug each one of them for being so kind to him.

"Charlie, why don't you go next," Lynn suggested.

"I wrote about chopping wood," he grunted. "There's no way I'm following Dickens over here."

That got more laughs from the group, but when everyone settled Maryanne raised her hand.

"I'll go next," she offered. "I wrote about my cat, Fitz. It's nothing award-worthy, but I'd love to get some help on it."

When Caleb called Phil that night to retell the story, he could hear her sniffling on the other end before he'd finished. He apologized, realizing too late that bringing up their father's overdose and the subsequent fallout between them was a sore subject.

"I'm not crying about that," she corrected. "I'm crying because I'm proud of you, and you better email me whatever you wrote so I can read it!"

Caleb wasn't healed by any stretch of the imagination. He might never be after growing up a Browning Richards. Maybe traumatic baggage sat differently with you over time, though, the size of the load shifting as you moved through your daily life. He couldn't erase his past, but he could continue writing about it, and move forward giving his father's words less value.

Maybe distance had provided that. Learning to build a new life alone in a new state had certainly played a part. Or maybe Caleb had just outgrown the person he had been. The boy who'd been terrified of disappointing everyone, too scared to take chances or grow outward. Maybe now was the time to be bold and try new things, see what kind of person he could be when he had nothing to prove.

41. GEORGE

September to October, 2025

As it turned out, having one of your songs used in a movie was a gamechanger. Sure, George's duet with Ripley had gotten radio play, but none of her solo songs had. Maybe that was a conversation regarding Country music's less than equal play of female artists, or maybe George just hadn't gotten big enough. Either way, when "I Do" was woven into a wedding scene in a major movie, downloads skyrocketed. They called in the *wedding song of the season.*

Between sales of her EP and two full albums, she was doing okay. Well, better than okay. Grandma Jeane could retire if she wanted to, but she claimed to love working, even just part-time. She said it gave her purpose and she wasn't ready to retire to the porch. That time would come, she told George, but she wanted to live a little first.

Grandma Jeane's seventy-fifth birthday happened to fall the month before George was scheduled to start her 2025 tour. She knew she had to do something big, something monumental to celebrate the woman who'd raised her. She packed bags for both of them, Grandma Jeane fussing the whole time that George better tell her where they were going so she could pack her own things. But George insisted it be a surprise.

They hopped in George's truck, still kicking after all these years traveling from Texas to Wyoming and back many times, and then all the way east to Nashville. George was going to drive it until the engine fell out, rather than waste her hard-earned money on something new. This industry could move on from her at any moment and her grandmother had taught her to always be prepared.

They drove nine hours heading east. September air blew in the open windows and they sang along to Dolly, Emmylou, and Hank. George could have cried from how happy she was with her grandma in the passenger seat beside her. Look how far they'd come.

Simone had recommended the Wentworth Mansion for its antique charm. It didn't disappoint.

"Georgie girl, what have you done?" Grandma Jeane gasped as they pulled up, her eyes watery and wide. George kept mum as they checked in and were directed to their suite.

She had anticipated her grandmother crying over the sheer opulence of it. The ornate bed. The fireplace mantel. The bathroom. But Grandma Jeane was rendered speechless, her fingers gently tracing lines across every surface.

When she tried to unpack in the sitting room by the couch, George ushered her back into the bedroom.

"I'm taking the couch," she explained, much to her grandmother's horror. "It's *your* birthday, so you get to be treated like the queen you are."

Still, her grandma said nothing. She went into the bathroom for a while, probably to freshen up, but when she came out, she seemed restored to her usual vigor.

"I suppose we better go see her now," she said, and George was struck dumb, wondering who they were meant to be meeting in Charleston, considering her grandmother hadn't known where they were headed in the first place.

"See who, Grandma?"

"The ocean, Georgie. That's why you brought me here, isn't it?"

George laughed, and then laughed again when they kicked off their shoes thirty minutes later and waded ankle deep into the water arm in arm. It had all been worth it. Every exceptional high and every heartbreaking low, to arrive at this moment right here. She'd do it all again, just to see her grandma this blindingly happy.

After their whirlwind weekend came the new tour. George's one stipulation, now that she had some sway with her label, was to be able to bring The Billings Boys on as her opener. They'd been the first people to give her a chance, and after that one summer night a million years ago that could have been the end of it. She might have moved on and never thought about music again. But they'd asked her back. She owed them so much and the least she could do was give them more exposure. They happily agreed to come along.

George hadn't planned the route they took. She just agreed to twenty venues starting in Nashville. Grandma Jeane was able to come to that show, and she dedicated her final song of the night to her, pointing her out in the crowd, much to her grandma's horror. George would never know if her mother would truly be proud of her, but to see the way her grandma looked up at her as she sang the words she'd written, that was all she cared about. She could end the tour right there and know she'd done something good with her life.

But on they went, heading up the coast for four stops, then back south for a bit before heading west. All the days blurred together, and yet each night stood out in her mind, little flashes framed in the scrapbook of her memory.

A mother and daughter just off the stage in Asheville, the daughter holding a handmade sign with lines from a song turned into a callback to George. She waved at them and sang that line directly to the girl and received the toothiest grin in return.

A proposal that stopped the song "I Do" in Tuscaloosa, because my goodness! How could you not let the couple have their moment? It was a yes! Everyone cheered. Some people even dabbed at their eyes. It was so special. George found the couple afterward and took a photo with them.

After the show in Salt Lake, a woman waited in line for an autographed album and a photo. She was bubbly and sweet and divulged that she'd never been interested in Country music before hearing George's album. George was bowled over after the woman walked away, that she had the power to change someone's perspective.

In Seattle, she met a young man who waited around for an hour after the show to catch her as she was about to step onto the bus. He was soft-spoken and she hugged him, thanked him for coming. He was so bird-like in her arms, but his grip was strong, and when they pulled apart his eyes were watery.

"Your music is bringing my mom and I back together," he said, so quietly that George might have missed it for all the street noise around them.

She couldn't explain it, but that statement brought tears to her own eyes, and then she was hugging him again, both of them laughing through tears like old friends.

Their last stop was Bozeman, which the team had put serious thought into. The turnout for The Billings Boys accounted for at least half of the people in attendance. They brought her onstage during their set to sing "Vice" for old time's sake and the crowd went wild. George's cheeks hurt from smiling so much. And then, returning the favor, for her final song she brought them back onstage to play with her.

For the rest of George's life, she would count this night in her top five best nights. It hadn't been perfect. There were some cues missed, a broken guitar string, but the feeling she walked away with after the final photo was more than she had allowed herself to dream of all those years ago when she first sang with them.

As she stepped out into the night, not yet ready to accept that this tour was over, she had a ridiculous thought. It was late, but she made the call anyway. When she asked for the manager, she was put on hold, but then a few minutes later a familiar voice picked up.

"Kathleen?" George couldn't believe her own ears.

"This is her."

"*Kathleen O'Hara*, are you the manager of Million Dollar Cowboy Bar?"

"Wait… Holy shit! GEORGE?!"

Kathleen screeched on the other end, and then must've stepped into the back office because it grew quiet behind her excitement.

"George Townsend, you little shit calling me out of the blue!"

That just made George laugh harder.

"Where are you calling from?"

"That's the thing. I'm in Bozeman—just finished a show. And I was wondering… I know this is probably a long shot considering the late hour, but is there any room for a couple songs tomorrow night? I should've checked the website first, but I literally just called on a whim without thinking this through."

Kathleen's smile could be heard across state lines.

"Well, what a coincidence, my dear. There's no one playing tomorrow so the stage is all yours. Oh man, this is going to be insane! I haven't seen you in…"

"Almost ten years," George finished for her.

"This is—people are going to come out of the woodwork for this. I'm going to post this on social. Oh my god! I've gotta call—you know what, I'll just leave it at *I'll see you tomorrow*. Come by whenever you get in. I'll be here somewhere."

"I can't wait. Seriously, Kathleen. Thank you."

Kathleen scoffed.

"Thank me? You're the one doing me favors here. It's off-season, so this'll bring in way better than usual for the night."

Images of neon yellow Aspen trees filled George's head. It had been too many years since she'd been to Wyoming.

* * *

It felt like going home. That was the only way to describe it.

She let her band sleep in. They deserved it after playing their asses off for nearly two months, and now they'd agreed to do an unscheduled detour when they could be heading home.

Nothing had really changed since the last time she'd been to Jackson and yet it also felt new, like she was seeing it through the viewpoint of a different lens. She met Kathleen at Jackson Drug because how could they not? The air smelled amazing, the food was delicious, and yet somehow it all was better than she remembered. Like time had dulled her memories.

Since there was no band on the schedule, Kathleen said she could perform as long a set as she wanted. So, George decided to play the songs that meant the most to her. The ones that had come from this place.

It was stuffy and overly warm in the bar, just like she remembered, even with the late October chill lingering beyond the open door. The saddles were still there and she couldn't help but picture Caleb on one of them like that night so many years ago. She still thought about him when she sang certain songs, but as the album had come together, she realized each song was less about him and more about her. There was no lingering sadness in having lost him, because loving him had given her this amazing gift—the words, the feelings they evoked, and so many faces singing along because they'd lived similar experiences.

"I see some familiar faces out there," George said between the first two songs, the audience dulling to a murmur to make space for her to speak.

People continued ordering drinks and playing pool in the back, but those up front were focused on her. She spotted Tucker and his wife at a table. Her heart was full to bursting and it was taking every bit of strength to keep from crying happy tears at seeing them. This was the first and only time she'd gotten him to come to the bar, after working together so many summers.

"For those of you who don't know me, my name is George Townsend and I used to spend my summers here. I worked over at Mayfield Ranch with this wonderful gentleman, Tucker Mayfield," she pointed to him and got a whistle from somewhere in the crowd.

God, it was surreal to be standing on this stage again. For all the stadiums she'd played with Ripley, all the small venues she'd played solo, this one right here was by far her favorite spotlight.

"A round of applause for Tucker because he is a really great boss and a wonderful human being. And probably some of y'all's neighbor."

More whistles followed with a hearty dose of clapping.

"I worked nights right here behind the bar. How many of y'all know Kathleen O'Hara?" George pointed to where Kathleen stood behind the bar, hardly changed at all from however many years ago when she'd stood in that same spot and cheered George's first performance.

Lots of hollering and whistling echoed around the bar from bartenders and waitstaff, and Kathleen feigned embarrassment. But George knew she was loving it. She was thrilled to hear Kathleen had bounced around at a bakery in town, then managing another restaurant, before coming back to Million Dollar. She was the right person to be calling the shots here, without a doubt.

"So, the songs I'm singing tonight were all inspired by this place. I fell in love here. With the horses. The Tetons. The sunsets."

Agreement rose up like a chorus throughout the bar.

"I also fell in love with a good man here."

Kathleen whistled sharply from the bar and George had to lean away from the mic to laugh.

"This next song brings me right back to summer nights here. I hope you like it."

When she sang "I Do" in this place, to these familiar faces who had known her back when she was twenty-four and a nobody, it was like coming full circle. No matter what happened next, whether she ever got played on the radio. Whether she made another dime from her music. This was the moment she truly felt she had made it. If not for this place and these people helping her survive her early twenties, who knows where she'd have ended up.

She pictured Caleb in one of the saddle seats, his head turned in her direction, a glass of whiskey in front of him. What if he hadn't come in that night and sat at the bar? If he'd never believed in her? If he'd never loved her? She truly felt lucky to have had it all, even for a short while.

For her last song, she sang the one that almost hadn't made it onto the album, if not for that conversation she'd had in the backyard with her grandma. Usually, she played it with her full band, but on this night, it felt like she was sharing a piece of her heart, leaving it here to burrow along the bank of the Snake River, to bloom again next spring. So, as it was a special night, she asked her guitarist to play acoustic and the rest of the band retreated offstage.

"Before I sing my last song tonight, I just want to thank every one of you for coming out. For those who just stumbled in and stayed, I'm thankful for you as well. You've really made my heart full. This is called *A Song For My Mama*.

She took a sip of water from the bottle at her feet, trying to commit every sense to memory. The heat of the lights. The background noises—the clink of glasses, clack of pool balls, conversations ongoing. The smell of her own sweat and others, of perfume and spilled booze. Individually, each sense was nothing. Together though, it added up to a perfect moment.

She began to sing.

My mama had me on a quiet night in June
Only four years later she was gone much too soon
My grandmama nursed me, turning rust into gold
If I'm even a quarter as brave and as bold

The women who raised me
They're quiet, they're strong

Flowers bloom from the ashes
I carry them along

Just after graduation, ventured off on my own
To the mountains for a cowboy, I was but barely grown
What I found here was precious, gentle, so kind
Standing tall, never small, the most marvelous find

The love that he gave me
It makes my heart strong
Promises left unbroken
I carry him along

I took that belief in me and carried it east
To the man with the money to set my heart free
I will sing for my dinner, I will sing for a dime
Tell my gram I turn homeward, I think it's 'bout time

The women who raised me
They're quiet, they're strong
Flowers bloom from the ashes
I carry them along

To you who are with me
Let's try to be strong
Come, unload your burden
I'll carry you along

George had tears running down her cheeks as the final notes landed, but she wasn't sad. Far from it. She couldn't stop smiling as she stepped down off the stage and embraced Tucker in a fierce hug. Unfamiliar faces stopped her to offer congratulations or get a picture with her. It was half an hour before she made it towards the bar and the heat of the room grew to be too much.

"I'm getting some air!" She called to Kathleen and hooked a thumb in the direction of the door.

Outside was much quieter, one antler arch lit up like Christmas. It was chilly out here with no jacket on, but George just needed a minute, and the air felt too good on her skin, like diving into a lake on a sticky-hot day.

She crossed the street and entered the square. There were people on the sidewalks going to and from restaurants and bars, but within the four sides of town square George was alone. She sat on a bench, the cold metal seeping through her clothes, and smiled up at the stars. There were so many. She'd forgotten how clear the sky was here.

She didn't think. She just tipped her head back and soaked the night sky in, letting the cool air cleanse her. She'd done it, the thing she'd dreamed of. What more could she ask for?

When the cold got to be too much, she stood, wiping at the moisture pooling at the corners of her eyes. But she wasn't sad. She was so far from sad that a new word needed to be created because *happiness* didn't cover it.

Hugging her arms, she headed back under the arch and turned towards the bar. Kathleen had promised her a celebratory drink, and since she was now off the clock, she was going to take her up on that offer.

Someone jogged across the street, stopping just head of George on the wooden sidewalk, and she stopped to prevent imminent collision. A lifetime ago, George had stood before this man and noted the forward curl of his shoulders, the hands shoved deep in the pockets of his jeans to hide his nerves. Now, this man's broad shoulders were back, his head held high, but his hands betrayed him, balled inside his pockets like caged animals trying to break free.

"Hi."

George laughed at the absurdity of it. She was twenty-four again, standing in front of a stranger, not at all scared. When their eyes met, each of them taking in the differences, clocking what was unchanged, George noted the look in his eyes. How was it possible after all this time that she still hung the moon?

"Hi."

"You're here." It was like he'd found a treasured book right where he expected it to be.

"I thought I saw you in there, but I figured it was my mind playing tricks."

Caleb nodded, like he had experienced the same.

"How are you here? I only just made the decision to come last night. Did you fly in just for this? How did you know I was coming?"

Caleb shook his head, amusement bubbling to the surface.

"Kathleen called me this morning, said I should come have a drink, thought I'd like the band."

"Kathleen?" George blinked, not understanding.

Caleb's hands broke free from his pockets and reached ever so slightly in her direction before returning to his thighs.

"You were great up there. That last song…"

His breath came out in spurts, like he had just finished running a race, and George felt her heart kick up in similar fashion.

How was this happening? He'd gotten on a plane that morning to see her? But Kathleen had called him? How did he know Kathleen?

"I'm sorry, I feel like I'm having the weirdest déjà vu. You're really here? Or am I losing my mind?"

George looked up at the starry night, rubbing a hand over her eyes. It probably was smudging her makeup worse than her earlier tears, but she didn't care. When she looked back at him, Caleb was still here, a step closer than before.

"I'm really here, George."

A breathy laugh escaped at his words.

"No one's called me that in forever."

"That's a shame. It's a beautiful name."

Something sharp lodged itself in her throat and without thinking she crossed the space between them, her hands coming up to curl around his biceps and make sure he was real. His arms were firm beneath her fingers and larger than she remembered them being. This was happening, both of them in the same place.

Caleb reached out and tucked a strand of hair behind her ear and George shivered. His fingers were so steady and warm, like they'd done this just yesterday.

"Do you have somewhere you need to be right now?"

She shook her head. Or at least, she didn't think she had somewhere to be. And if she did, none of that mattered anymore. Because Caleb was here.

"Do you want to come home with me?"

George laughed, the absurdity bubbling up out of her mouth to break across the night. This was so familiar and yet completely different, like laying two drafts of the same song over one another.

"I thought you were married."

She didn't want to beg the universe for anything. She'd been given so much already. More than a person could ever want, really. But this one small ask—well, huge ask—would be the last thing she'd ever wish for.

Caleb's head shook once, like he was clearing it, and George was immediately embarrassed by how much hope that gave her.

"I sent a gift."

It was Caleb's turn to laugh.

"I know. I make damn good bread now."

"I'm not surprised. You were always really good with your hands."

Caleb laughed and mortification burned up her neck, over her cheeks, and to the tips of her ears. She hadn't meant to say that out loud. If she was twenty-four again, then they had switched places. She was now the awkward one letting inappropriate things slip past her filter and he was calm and self-assured.

The myriad questions must've played across her face because Caleb filled in the blanks.

"Rosie and I moved out here a couple years ago."

He said this as if it explained everything, but George only found herself asking more questions.

"Rosie's… your daughter?" She pictured him as a father, doting on a small girl that had his eyes. He probably read to her each night, using different voices for each character. And he for sure convinced her that her crayon drawings were worthy of the Louvre, because he was wonderful like that.

"My dog."

"Oh." Not a daughter. And then it dawned on her. "*Rosie?*"

He shrugged, as if it was natural to name his dog after her.

"Okay," she said, questions still whirling around in her head.

There were lines at the corners of Caleb's eyes now. They made him even more handsome, and he'd always been handsome. He was older, more confident, and even in the dim light of the town square George was overcome with feelings she'd thought she'd laid to rest.

"Do you want me to come home with you?"

There was a moment when their eyes locked, trying to ask and answer so many questions without words. But there'd be time for all that later, to fill in the blanks of what each had missed.

"George, it's the only thing I've ever wanted."

George laughed first, the overwhelming feeling of this moment repeating itself—*a do-over*. Caleb laughed too, a deeper, gentle chuckle that reverberated in George's chest as he tucked another strand of hair behind her ear trying to get a better look at her. His gaze turned down, arriving at her mouth, and she licked her lips in response, but he didn't bend to kiss her. Instead, he wrapped her in a hug that felt like crawling into bed under your favorite blanket. The smells the same, the weight just how she remembered it.

"You have no idea how much I missed you," she whispered into his hair.

"Yeah," Caleb whispered against her ear. "I think I do."

OUTRO

Caleb leads George to where his car is parked and it feels as if time has skipped back over itself. They are where their story began. They know each other in some ways, in really important ways, but there is so much more to learn about the other.

He drives them to his home, her hand tucked inside his like he is afraid to let go. Afraid that this moment might not be real. But unlike their first night together nearly a decade ago, they won't head straight to his bedroom.

George will stop inside the front door to be inspected by her namesake. She will fall quickly and irrevocably in love with Rosie and the adoration will be requited, naturally. For how could a dog not love the person who loves her owner as much as she?

The three of them will make it to the couch, where George and Caleb will spend the entire night taking turns petting Rosie. They will split a bottle of wine and talk until their voices are hoarse, sharing the missing pieces of their lives until there is nothing left unsaid.

And then, as the sun begins to lighten the sky outside the window, Caleb will hold George, whispering once again the promises he still fully intends to keep. And George, having thought long and hard about that evening on a patio that inspired an entire album, will amend her previous vows to fit this moment in time. And only after the mountains are lit in vibrant yellow and grey, will Caleb lead George to the bedroom where his favorite image of her taken all those years ago hangs.

She will cry during their first kiss, because how can she not after so years spent missing him. His tongue tangling with hers will be the sweetest taste she's ever had. And when Caleb finally tells her he loves her, that he's always loved her, George will cry harder. But Caleb will kiss those tears away, returning the smile to her face, and make her forget that they were ever apart.

It took them many years, but they are back in the place where it all started. They are older, wiser, weary from how far they have traveled to get here. But their bodies will remember each other intimately, even though the curves and dips have changed a little.

George's hand will find its home in Caleb's hair. Caleb's mouth will stall over George's heart. And just like that first night, they will fall asleep before either of them comes, because sometimes being in the arms of the person you have longed for and loved for a decade is all you need.

It's more than enough, actually. In fact, it's everything.

Author's Note

A handful of years back, I was in the saddle on a ridge overlooking the Snake River, and though I was towards the back of our group, my head firmly in the clouds, I caught snippets of our leader mentioning that she led trail rides during the summer months and helped out on her cousin's cattle ranch in Oklahoma the rest of the year. Later, as I drove away, that tiny kernel of a life burrowed in my brain and started to take root. As I passed the multi-million-dollar houses on my way back to town, the roots spread further until Caleb and George started to take shape. But as life happens, the story got tucked away for another time.

A year later, I was in one of the saddles at Million Dollar Cowboy Bar. I'd been riding on that same ridge again that morning, this time in snow, and as my friend and I defrosted and sipped our drinks, George popped back into my head to say hi and suggest that maybe she was more than just a ranch hand. Maybe she was also a bartender and secretly a singer-songwriter who hadn't figured out that pursuit just yet.

For a while after that, anytime I tried to write Golden Hour I would get stuck after two chapters. See, the thing back then was that Caleb was kind of a dick. He had a severe chip on his shoulder and was full of himself, and in this version of the story George's role was to slam him back down to earth and make him a better human as he fell under her spell. I should also add that at this point it was not going to be a romance and was going to end when Caleb's family vacation ended, him having changed for the better, but their love story not continuing.

It had been years since I'd written a novel and I really wanted Golden Hour to be my next one, but I was not excited to write it. So I kept putting it off. Then I read the first book in a series where the MMC is a walking red flag and got so annoyed that characteristics like that were being romanticized that I decided I wasn't going to write Golden Hour. I couldn't add another little shit to the romance landscape when reality is hard enough.

(Sidebar: I'm not trying to yuck anyone's yum. I've read my fair share of dark romance. I fully support reading what you enjoy. I just realized I didn't want to contribute to that red flag roster, as is my prerogative.)

And then I thought, what if I was looking at this all wrong. What if these characters didn't have to change each other in order to fall in love. What if they were both wonderful, complicated, full characters already and the timing just wasn't right? And what if the story didn't end when the week does, what if we see where life takes them over the next nine years?

Suddenly, I was excited to write this book and here we are.

I guess we're at the part where I thank some people, places, and things that helped me in the process of writing, editing, and publishing this book.

Firstly, back in August 2016, Miranda Lambert asked a packed Gillette Stadium to quiet down so she could attempt the acapella opening to "Vice". I was in that crowd looking down on the stage, and when the instruments crashed in around her my heart leapt into my throat and I knew that one day, one of my stories would need that song and the drama it brings. It's a damn good song and I always play it twice.

Music was obviously instrumental (*badump-tsh!* I'm not apologizing for that) in creating this story. Should this ever reach her hands, I think the biggest thank you truly has to go to Kacey Musgraves. Golden Hour is a perfect album. Period, no notes. Without it I'm not sure where my Golden Hour would be because it influenced so much of the way Caleb and George view the world and each other. It's ridiculous how many times I've listened to the album, but I never tire of it, and it holds a special place in my heart. From one horse girl to another, you're a gem.

Thank you to the wonderful, amazing, supportive women who have read numerous drafts of so many things I've written—I'm talking truly awful first drafts—with gusto. I cherish you all so, so much. Erica, I'm specifically picturing you in the pool in Turks reading a draft of God knows what, instead of sipping a cocktail and reading something *good*. You're a dear. Have you figured out where Wyoming is yet?

To my beta readers Paige and Dianis, who not only love books with as much passion as myself, but who gave thoughtful commentary and are maybe the kindest humans. To Bevin for catching so many spelling mistakes (I'm sorry) and making me laugh with her comments. I hope we get to meet IRL sometime soon! Any errors that slipped through the cracks are my own.

To Jess, thank you for inviting me along on your work trip to Jackson way back when. Thank you for being the place I always know I can 100% be my weirdo self and for the best hugs.

To Maria and Liv, who would probably rather be reading a Fredrick Backman book instead of trying to come up with constructive things to say about my writing—I see you and I'm there with you. I mean, he is the best. But thank you for reading my stuff too.

To Kaitlin and Molly, for saying yes when I asked if they wanted to do a podcast with me where we just blabbed about books. For always being as excited as I am about anything book related, for talking me off ledges, for eating anything I cook, for not judging my love of fantasy and smut, and occasionally reading the things I suggest. I don't know where I'd be without you both. Truly.

To my 95 year old nana, who will undoubtedly read this, I hope it wasn't too saucy for you.

To my mother, who taught me to love books, but who used to cry at *everything,* which meant she'd be unable to finish the sentence she'd been reading aloud. I'd be in bed, snuggled up beside her, frustrated as all get-out because I needed to know what happened next. Well, jokes on me, because now I cry at literally everything.

To my father, who taught me how to use power tools, how to tile a bathroom, and who likes the gross houses as much as I do. When I say I'm going to do something, like publish a book, he always answers with *okay,* like it's just that easy to set your mind to something and do it. Which, I suppose, if you just aren't willing to give up, almost anything is possible. Twenty-two years later and still writing books even after *so many* rejections. Well, my father didn't raise a quitter, so here we are.

To my sister, who has to put up with me constantly saying, *I can't think of the word but it starts with a (blank) and is kind of like (blank).* The likelihood of her reading this book in its entirety and stumbling upon this paragraph right here is slim to none because she's a party pooper when it comes to romance. Marissa, my darling baby sister, if you are reading this sentence AND you read the whole book then congrats! You win a free dinner at the place of your choosing! (Don't anyone dare tell her about this! She has to do the work to win the prize.)

To Scout, who insisted on lots of pets while I wrote a few chapters at his house. Forever a good boy.

To Skylar, my neighborhood bestie, for acting like I've just come ashore after a year at sea every single time we see each other. It doesn't matter if we stumbled upon each other while her mom (Hi Thea!) was walking her yesterday, we are long-lost soul mates running open-armed towards each other every single time. Dogs are the best and I am so thankful for them.

To George (the dog) who sat beside me for the final edit and insisted on mental health breaks down at the beach. You are the very best boy. And no, I did not name George (the girl) after him. Coincidences abound.

To Willie and Mickey, who are the best ponies, and Laura, who took a chance on a stranger responding to her post asking for a volunteer horse handler, who welcomed me into the fold, and who I would muck stalls for any day.

Bethanie, thank you for saying yes when I asked if you'd be interested in creating the cover. You are the coolest person I have ever met and so incredibly talented. When I grow up, I hope to be even a smidge as cool as you… but without having to scale the Tetons or do any of the crazy-cool shit you do on the regular. Next time I see you, drinks are on me.

Just a few more tres important thank yous… honey-lavender lattes, huckleberry bbq sauce, the Caesar salad at Glorietta, Murcell's grizzly bears, National Park rangers, ranch hands, trail horses, cowboys (even though there are none in this book, I love them), LIBRARIANS,

Isshindo ramen, McDonald's Sprite (because it's just *better* and I don't understand why but it just *is*), tapered candles, bookstores, bookstores, bookstores. My local faves: Belmont Books, Porter Square Books, Boujee Bookstore, Lovestruck Books, but also every indie romance-centric bookstore across the planet for creating pockets of happiness. To booksellers everywhere for being the best people on the planet, but specifically Kolby, April, Cat, Cara, Zay, & Ester, who fuel my caffeine addiction, and my favorite booksellers: Carina, Paige, Crystal, Emily, Abby, Dona, Sharyn, Amy, Courtney, Derek, Joe, Kate, Marina, Carrie, and Kathleen—I adore you all. If I forgot anyone, I am sorry.

Lastly, to my floofy dude, Mr. Bingley, who sat on my lap for the entirety of this book. My butt and legs may have gone numb at times, and my arms may have been working extra hard to type with a head resting on them, but you are a stalwart gentleman who refuses to give up when there's a chance of cuddles or kisses, and I thank you for keeping me company on this emotional ride. Adopt, don't shop.

THANK YOU for reading all these silly words I strung together. I hope they made sense and you felt something and maybe love George, Caleb, Phil, Toby, Wyoming, Boston, Rosie, all of it. If you ever find yourself planning a vacation to either Jackson or Boston, message me. I have suggestions. And if you didn't love Golden Hour, I'm sorry. I know I can't please everyone, but as an eldest daughter I have a reeeeeeeally hard time with that. As I'm writing this, I'm a nobody-imposter-syndrome-suffering writer, but if by the time you read this you have liked, shared, or forwarded something of mine, please know how truly grateful I am for your support. Words cannot express what that means to me, so just THANK YOU.

PS. It being Fall 2025 as I write this, it means that Caleb and George just had that night at Million Dollar Cowboy Bar where they reconnected. Right now, they are probably walking hand-in-hand with Rosie to Picnic for coffee. If you're in Jackson and happen spot them, please say hi for me.

About the Author

Stephanie Blackburn is a lifelong New Englander (though she did head to upstate New York for college—*Go Bombers!*), but what is hopefully clear is that her heart resides in Jackson, Wyoming.

She hosts a podcast with her girlfriends—Plans Are Booked—where Kaitlin, Molly, and Stephanie discuss a new book each week in a thinly-veiled attempt to normalize the insane number of books in their TBRs. There are way worse vices.

When not writing, Stephanie renovates absolutely disgusting houses with her father. She's formed a pretty strong love/hate relationship with tiling, and as someone who doesn't allow *outside clothes* on her furniture, she sure made an interesting career choice.

To follow along on Stephanie's writing journey and for updates on future books, please follow: @authorstephblackburn on Instagram.

www.ingramcontent.com/pod-product-compliance
Lightning Source LLC
Chambersburg PA
CBHW031331300726
48830CB00002B/9